D0557013

The Ghost Brush

KATHERINE GOVIER

The Ghost Brush

HARPERCOLLINS PUBLISHERS LTD

Published by HarperCollins Publishers Ltd.

First Edition

HarperCollins Publishers Ltd
2 Bloor Street East, 20th Floor
Toronto, Ontario, Canada
M4W 1A8

www.harpercollins.ca

Library and Archives Canada Cataloguing in Publication

Govier, Katherine, 1948–
The ghost brush / Katherine Govier.

ISBN 978-1-55468-643-8

I. Title.
PS8563.O875G46 2010   C813'.54   C2010-900524-4

Inside cover map: "Oedo ezu" by Izumiya Ichibee.
Reproduced courtesy of the Sir Hugh and Lady Cortazzi Collection,
Sainsbury Institute for the Study of Japanese Arts and Cultures

Printed and bound in the United States
RRD 9 8 7 6 5 4 3 2 1

FOR NICK

Part 1

1

Introduction to the Ghost

"hey, you! You with the big chin! Oei!"

He's calling me.

I don't answer him. Not yet.

I dip the tip of the brush in the ink bowl.

I let it sink. I lift it, turn it, and press it down into the ink again. Then I lift and tap.

I press it against the edge of the bowl, twisting so ink beads at the tip of the bristles and then drops back into the small, still, dark pool. Again I press the hairs of the brush into the ink, flattening the bulb against the bottom of the bowl, rolling it.

"Don't press so hard!" the Old Man barks.

I bare my teeth. "Shut up, Old Man." He laughs. Thinks he's distracted me.

But my hand is zealous. To spite him I press for one full minute. I lift the brush from the bowl. It is not dripping, not full, but fully moist. I hold it over the paper, balanced in my fingers. I raise and lower it, ever so slightly, giving it breath, and then touch the point to paper. I begin the fine, fine lines of the courtesan's nape hair. That which he has no patience to do, and no steady hand.

"Oei!"

I don't answer. I stay inside my head.

I am Oei. Katsushika Oei. Katsushika I take from the place where my father was born. Oei is a pun on how he calls me. It means "Hey, you!" I have other names: Ago-Ago—he gave me that too—meaning "chin-chin," calling attention to my big, stubborn jaw. Then there are the brush names:

Iitsu, meaning "one again"; Tipsy, meaning just what you think; Flourishing Woman, self-evident, you'd think. I've answered to many names. Though in this matter, as in others, I am no match for him.

He named himself for the North Star, and for the Thunder God; he named himself the Old Man Mad about Painting; he has named and new-named himself twenty times. To me he's just the Old Man.

Some people call the Old Man difficult. I don't agree. He is not difficult. He is impossible.

True, I'm not easy myself. I do not comply. I mock, I dissemble, I glower. They say I was never properly trained to be a woman. The more sympathetic blame my father himself for this failure. It is a scandal. "She paints but does not sew," they say. Hah! That could be my epitaph. Perhaps it is. But you would have to find my grave to know.

And that you cannot do.

2

EDO, 1800

I WAS BORN.

Into the red squall of dawn, the teem of city. Into the vast numbers of townsmen with only one name.

The earth was flat.

The Shogun ruled.

It was a Virtuous Regime, a Benevolent Regime, and there was no unexpected event.

I screamed. And why not? After Miyo and Tatsu, I was Ei, the third daughter of a penniless artist. My father's first wife, who produced the first two daughters and also one son, was dead. My mother was the second woman to take on the job.

She looked critically at me, first of her children, fourth of his.

"She has large ears," said my father in a tone of delight. He seized me. "This one is mine!"

My mother was morose. "Large ears are lucky in men. Not in women."

"She looks like a little dog, a Pekinese," he said. "And look at this!" He chucked my peculiar outsize chin. "I will call her Ago-Ago."

Chin-Chin. Another of my flaws was thus pointed out to my mother. She became even more unhappy. I, on the other hand, became defiant and thrust it farther.

"There is self-will in that face," she said. "It must be broken."

But my father laughed in amusement and delight. His laugh was like milk to me. He took me in his arms and I was his forever.

It was as if he'd never seen a baby before. He fed me rice water with the tip of his finger. He tied me in a sling and wore me under his ribs, or on his back if he was working. From that day there were two of us, together. We slid through the clamorous throngs of our burgeoning city like carp in weeds. He said I was his good luck charm. He did not break my self-will but made it.

And my black eyes did not close.

In years to come he did call me Ago-Ago, when he remembered, but most often he just called me.

"Hey, you. Come here!"

I was born in a hard time.

We the townspeople led an unmarked existence. We had rights to nothing, only to witness the grand Shogun's parade: the march of the doomed man to the Punishment Grounds, details of his crime painted on the placard he carried over his shoulder. We fed on brown rice and whispers of love suicides. The mouths of our actors were red gashes. We, the *chonin*, had one name—and no face.

In the years before my birth there was an artist called Sharaku. He made gargantuan faces with vast white, empty centres marked only with deep black lines for eyes and mouths spread in rage or fear or greed. But few people bought these pictures—they came too close to home, I think—and before long Sharaku and his work disappeared. Some people said he was a Noh actor and died of poisoning from the white face makeup. Other people said Sharaku was my father. They said that after this first failure he renamed himself and went on, and the proof that he had been Sharaku was that he never painted a big face again.

I don't know if that was true. He told me much, but not that.

It was true about the faces, though: my father could draw anything that moved and much that didn't—dancers, elephants, oarsmen, mountains, gods, and devils. Waterfalls and waves stopped for his brush. Fuji showed its one hundred moods. But he never made a face. Eyes, nose, and mouth—for him these were only a few short, sharp lines, and that was it. Maybe the gossip was true and he thought faces wouldn't sell. Maybe he wanted distance from his past. Maybe he wanted distance from us all. Henceforth, to him, we had no faces, only burdened backs and sinewed buttocks, slim thighs and crinkled toes and dancing torsos.

Oh, but such bodies we had. Such glories were in them. They were our prized possessions. By these bodies, we were making ourselves into people. Before I was born we were not quite human, according to our masters. The *bakufu*—a tent government set up on a field of war two hundred years before—kept the Tokugawa Shogun in power. But as the eras passed, the *bakufu* remained. There were no wars; we didn't fight with swords. We fought with words and pictures. Our pictures and our little storybooks cost pennies. But they had a strange power. They gave us news, gossip, celebrity, mementos. They celebrated the only pleasures we were allowed—kabuki theatre and love affairs and the small indulgences for our bodies.

The Tokugawa could not attack us directly; there were too many of us. Instead the enforcers attacked the messengers, our pictures; they called them decadent and tried to destroy them.

Think of all that clanking samurai power directed at these fragile sheets of paper. I want to laugh. Pictures and words don't hurt anyone, except for those who are afraid of history. Rock, fire, scissors: these paper worlds go on.

The *bakufu* aimed their laws at our insubstantial world. There were to be no pictures of the Tokugawa. Any reference to how they came to rule was punishable by death. Famine and flood might ravage the country, but to note such calamities would be a criticism of the Shogun, who ruled celestial events as he did lesser beings. Therefore they were not to be noted.

We appeared to obey. We told ghost stories and repeated legends from times past, and went to plays about the love affairs of great courtesans. We put our faith in unnatural creatures, demons and gods and ghosts. Our gossip travelled through whispers and yellow-back novels. We sang and danced and devised outrageous dress. The *bakufu* bogeymen uttered ordinances and staged clampdowns. They did not stop us, but they kept trying. They were a constant backdrop to my life, from my first squalling complaints through my middle years until I was almost old enough not to care. Then, suddenly, they were gone. But that comes at the end of the story.

This is the beginning. The tiny tenement house. The mat on which we all lay, side by side; the soot-orange sun at dawn.

My birth was both lucky and unlucky. Lucky because I was born in the centre of this magic. First my father's words defined me, and then his pictures did. And unlucky to be under the thumb of another, weightier, power. And a daughter. In that terrible time. Lucky and unlucky.

That is Ei's story.

My first memory: I lay on my mat in the damp dark and the cold of whatever small room we shared. My father was working by the light of an oil lamp. Then he stood and blew it out. He opened the door to the night. White snow was emptying out of the heavens on us, thick as feathers. The snow erased the rooftops with its soft white brush, leaving only the thin, dark outline of tiles.

He lifted me in his arms and we went out to stand under the sky. We looked up. The snow fell straight down without fluttering, freighted, through the barren trees. There were no leaves to catch it. It melted on the lanterns: too warm. It fell around his feet and more snow followed. It blotted the ground, sopping up its colour, and then melted, making the packed earth gleam.

I lay in his arms, warm, with the cold, airy flakes landing on my eyes, my cheeks, and my lips. Tongue out, I tasted them. Laughed at the cold, and the warmth of him. How safe I felt! How loved! We were one being.

The snow was a gift. I licked my lips, where it tasted sweet. My father stared and sighed. I thought it was for happiness, for holding me. Now I know differently—he was puzzling how to catch it on the page—but then I was safe in illusion.

"What time is it?" my mother called.

"It is the Hour of the Rat," he said. "The hour of romance." Then he muttered under his breath, to me, "Or the hour of avoiding romance." He sighed and looked up, searching for his favourite stars. But they were hidden.

Illusion is shaken, a little.

"Even a courtesan might delay awhile," he said, "before necessity compels her to a client's company. Examine herself in the mirror or tidy the empty glasses. But not for long: this is the hour. The hour of tyranny and love."

What did he mean?

"Are you coming inside?" my mother called again.

Here my father laughed. I knew his laugh better than my own. It was a laugh not heartless but mirthless, a laugh that saw everything and presumed nothing. He was no romantic. He sucked at the hard tit of circumstances and made a game of it. He laughed as if he were a free man, and he laughed with rue because he wasn't.

"Not yet! I hear the crier coming."

"So what?" cawed my mother. "He's not crying for you."

We heard footsteps, footsteps slapping the wet stone. The crier rose out of nowhere with a hood on his head and ran through the streets, stopping on bridges to make his announcement, then covered his head again and ran on. He was a nameless runner for *Kawara-ban,* a small broadsheet that sometimes appeared. It was illegal: we were not allowed to know the news. So he ran at night, perhaps to alert us to famine in the north. Or rice riots in the south. Earthquake or fire at the other end of the roads, in Osaka or Kyoto. Arrests and sometimes deaths. Scandal about corrupt officials of the town. Some people said these stories were nothing but rumours and gossip. But we who watched the roadways into this huge city—the largest in the world—could confirm the disasters by the trail of starving peasants coming to Edo.

The *Kawara-ban* man came closer. I could see his dark form through the curtain of snow. I thought he must be afraid. But my father said no, he was not afraid. He was doing his job.

I know now that this was not true. Of course he was afraid. We were all afraid: fear was required of us. Failure to feel fear was an offence under the law. But some *seemed* not to be afraid. My father was one of these. He too did his job.

Now we could hear the crier's voice. I understood the tone of the words but not their meaning.

"Look tomorrow! It will be posted. A new edict. New prohibitions. Artists and writers take care. Look tomorrow!"

My father held me more closely against his chest. He prayed. We went to bed.

Daylight had come. A layer of white was on us and on every surface. It was beautiful. I scooped up light balls of it and pushed them into my mouth. We stood by the signboard and my father read aloud, stopping frequently for emphasis. A crowd of women, unable to read, formed around us.

*Behold the Senior Councillor's new edict. He speaks with the
authority of the Shogun.*

*There have been books since times long past, and no more are
necessary. Year after year people have applied themselves to useless tasks, including even picture books, and have obtained large
fees for their products. This is thoroughly wasteful.*

*Newly published books will be regarded as strictly undesirable
if they are depraved or a medley of unorthodox ideas.*

Amorous books are not good for public morality.

*Wicked children's books ostensibly set in ancient times will be
regarded as undesirable.*

*We will censor all matter intended for publication, including
picture books, readers, and novels. The sign of the censor—in
the form of a circular seal with the character* kiwame—*must be
stamped onto the drawing for the print after inspection and then
cut into the printing blocks.*

*Those pictures that do not pass the censors will be seized and
burned. The blocks will be destroyed. Persons who disregard this
order will be accused in court.*

*If the necessity to print a new book does arise, inquiries must
be made at the City Commissioner's office.*

*There will be no news reporting. You are reminded that this
was decreed in earlier times. However, it continues. There will be
no "true records" such as those that can be rented from lending
libraries. These are baseless rumours and will be seized. The lending libraries will be closed.*

"Blah, blah, blah," said my father to the women. "Here we go. I'll just get
on to the end for you."

They shifted and protested: they wanted to hear it all.

"I'm skipping all this part," he said, pointing to columns of characters.
"After this it degenerates into a harangue."

*The Senior Councillor repeats his determination and asserts the
rightness of the Old Way. We are losing the distinction between*

the esteemed and the despised. You people desire to imitate your betters, and to raise yourselves. This must end. We will root out corruption and laxity, and enforce austerity and morality. We shall rid Japan of private interest, and the destructive powers of passion and desire.

That was the end. He turned around and made a deep theatrical bow. The people were caught between fear and laughter.

3

THE SEVEN STARS

WHATEVER MY FATHER DID, he did with a kind of double, lunging in but also holding back, as if he were his own shadow. He loved the crowd, but he also liked to stand aside, watching himself, the entertainer amongst us, remarking on how it looked. He saw himself eating or lying, making love. He was hugely amused by himself and all the rest of us. He was an artist first and last, an ordinary man rarely, in between.

That night he went inside, put me down, and lay beside my mother.

"What did the edict say?"

"No more pillow pictures. No more picture books. No more libraries."

My mother shrieked and covered her head with a cloth.

"Be still, woman!" He yawned, as if it were not important. It made her hysterical.

For a time he had made his living painting calendars. He delineated the long months and the short months; they changed every year. But an edict had made it illegal for common people to own or sell such a calendar. Calendars could be issued only by licence of the Shogun; the Shogun alone was responsible for counting days and months, for celestial movement and changing seasons. He issued the only calendars that were allowed. Who could afford one of these official calendars? Only a lord or a lady.

But my father had not despaired. "A calendar is a handy thing. People want to know what day it is. It's a good market, and we won't give it up. There is a way."

He began to make calendars that looked like simple pictures—a rooster or a chrysanthemum. Hidden inside the swirl of the flower petals or in the rooster's feet were the characters giving the number of days. The townspeople would spot these and understand, and even enjoy the little game. The officials failed to notice, and we were saved, for a time.

But now it was books—picture books, storybooks, history books. Our mainstay.

My mother wept. "The *bakufu* have taken away the last thing. The last strand by which we cling to life . . ." She had her own dramatic flair.

"Just a moment!" said my father. This was a thing he often said. He had borrowed it from the kabuki stage. It created a dramatic pause, heralded a grand gesture. A wordless grimace and a moment to make strategy.

He jumped out of bed and pounced, legs and arms wide apart. He made us laugh. "We will make a new thing that he hasn't thought to censor yet!"

We felt reassured; we would get around this one too.

We children all went to sleep. It was the best way to keep warm.

Another night:

The Old Man was working. It was rude to call him that, but that is what he was. Forty years already when I was born. Most men died by the time they were forty-five. I was with him. My mother had put the three older children down on the mat and lay sleeping beside them. She would wake up very early, when he was just lying down, and pluck at him to come to her for sex. This was not wise: how did they feed us four children who had already made our appearance? I never knew. But she was an impetuous soul. She must have been to marry him.

From my close proximity I could smell my father's frustration.

"Look at this picture—it's hopeless. Hopeless." He acted out his feelings: artist flings down brush, covers eyes with fists.

I looked at the design. It was a view of the banks of the Sumida River, which ran through our city. There were tiny people and ox carts, bridges and boats everywhere. Not bad, I thought. He smacked it.

"Where is the life?" he cried, rhetorically. "You can't smell the tannery downriver or the incense from the temple; you can't hear ferrymen grunt as they're poling on the river."

He was harsh with himself. There were hundreds like my father who lived in that world and painted it, making shop signs, theatre sets, and the woodcut prints that were cheap and for sale everywhere. Since he had displeased his master and was discarded, we were on our own. It was difficult; there were always others, more willing, to do any work.

For a time he was a middleman of peppers. He bought red peppers from a peasant and sold them from his back. And sometimes he found a private commission for a laughing picture, one that told a little sexual story and was useful in its way. Artists were in fashion, out of fashion, only as good as the day's work—that was their lot.

Once in a while he was famous, then he couldn't sell. This was the way; he could not keep a good name. He had taken a new one recently. He called himself Sori.

I liked the picture. "It is good," I told him. Still, he did have a point. It was maybe too pretty.

"What about the cries of the men being flogged on the grounds of the jailhouse? Fifty times for the light sentence, one hundred for the heavy? No no no no no. How about that glimmer of lantern light in the black canal water? I want the people who look at my pictures to hear the angry sob of a nighthawk"— that was a riverbank prostitute; I knew them already—"taken by force!"

He stomped around.

"You can't feel the rain."

He was wrong there. You could feel the rain. His rain was good.

"How to capture it all? I want it, want it. I need to learn. But how can I? There's no teacher for what I need."

I held out my arms to be lifted. I tried to melt into his body.

He walked in small circles and patted my back. It calmed him. The proper teacher was his ears and eyes.

"I know it's in me. But how many years before I find it?"

With a father like that my mission was clear: someone had to look out for him. Even now that he is long gone, if I close my eyes and breathe deeply I can bring him back. I can feel, in the muscles inside my thighs, his back and waist, where I clung to him as he jogged along. I feel the sweat of his neck on my arms. I lay my chest along his spine; his arms twine behind his back and turn so they prop up the sling, and I sit in the crossed palms of his hands. Oh, seduction. Oh, that safe nest of cupped fingers on my bottom. The warmth of them, the stir that only many years later I would know was sexual.

In my ears there is still the cold slosh of water against a wooden wharf and the charcoal sellers' shouts in the alley. And in my nose I hold the musty air of autumn, the bitter chrysanthemum, the wet, smeared leaves on the stones. All of it, all of it now gone, a paper world, a weightless world, a world of mad colours and things that died.

He didn't have to say I was the one. He knew it and I knew it. The others belonged to my mother. Together we made the rounds of the city, with me slung on his back. It was a wonderful world. The bang of clogs over the arched bridges was music. Beautiful objects were being made in every doorway: silk and velvet cut in patterns; hair combs and painted lanterns; baskets, bowls, and cards of celebration. Firemen ran by with long poles on their shoulders; bannermen shoved us into ditches so the daimyo could pass. The ghosts of dead servants lived under the bridges, and sword-bearing gods leaned out of the clouds.

WE LIVED IN SHITAMACHI, downtown, in two rooms, each one six tatami mats in size, in a single-storey terraced house made of wood. This was the Low City, built on marshy land claimed from the tides, criss-crossed by canals and bridges. In the sun it was pretty, with bamboo overhanging the shacks and rushes along the waterways. The doors of whitewashed warehouses shone, and pilot boats pushed their way up the mirrored surface. On summer nights the dark water clucked invisibly from every side. There was the soft *burr-up* of frog and *coo* of roosting bird. But in winter it was dank and comfortless.

Farther down our alley, tucked away, were a storytellers' hall, a barbershop, and a shooting gallery. This last was mainly an entertainment for lovers. My sisters and I used to watch the men put their arms around the ladies' shoulders, showing them where to rest the shaft of the arrow. At the end, with its back to the water, stood a small temple to the God of the Harvest, Inari. Wild cats lived on that water margin, feeding on rats and garbage. I liked the cats very much, and their stealthy ways.

Beyond the alley were shops and stalls. You could buy anything: a bolt of indigo cotton, wooden bowls, cutting tools of every size and shape, mulberry paper, straw sandals. Raw voices were always hawking, shouting to make way, or crying down abuse on animals. Everything moved by—people and barrows and horses and mules and more people.

The High City loomed over us. On top of the hill the castle stood, in a huge empty space. People said its dungeon used to be higher than the distant peak of Mt. Fuji, three days' walk away. But it burned down in a fire, and most of the Low City too. That happened before I was born, and before my father was born. But we knew the story. Flames ate the bridges and trapped the inhabitants between the canals so they couldn't escape. On windy nights you could hear their ghosts screaming still.

From the castle, moat water trickled down to join the Sumida River, which ran down to Edo Bay, where the patient fishermen stood on stilts. Beyond the bay was a wide world of water—nothing more. My father said there were other countries and other peoples in a great world beyond. It was hard to believe him.

We were at the starting place: from here, foot roads led to the far points of our country. We had no idea of its shape. Maps were illegal for us. Townsmen were not to know where the limits of the Shogun's power might lie. But we could follow the dark ribbon of the Sumida against its current, northward.

That being the only journey we could make, we often made it. The Sumida was wide and powerful. The water gleamed despite the garbage it swilled away. The banks of the river were worn smooth by constant foot traffic and the loading of boats. Those banks divided the city itself from the water. They were a long strip of playground, a free place somehow agreed upon by the *bakufu* to belong to us, the disreputables. I would sit in the ferry as it plugged along and watch. Down on those banks I might see anything—fortune tellers, beggars, children flying kites, women dancing.

THE NORTH SEVEN STARS formed the Great Dipper. My father showed me how to find them in the sky. We looked along the line made by the outside of the bowl. Followed it to see Myoken, the shining eye of all the gods. Myoken was constancy; it was the writers' star. My father worshipped it.

I remember the night he decided to rename himself. This time his name would honour the North Star: it would be Hokusai.

"We will follow it," he said.

Beyond the reach of our few *mon* fare, we walked. (Always.) Too big to ride on my father's shoulders. As we walked I could hear the river chug, could hear his feet on the stones and the wailing of cats. But I could not see much. It was late afternoon, winter, and darkness was already on us. Women stood around their outside cooking fires, children tugging their skirts. There was the pounding of a wooden club on barrels, a girl fulling cloth. A rowing song echoed on the water.

We walked on. We came into light, lamplight from teashops, bookstores, a man with hot coals in an iron pot. On we went, and the city dwindled to marsh and then began to rise again. We came to the kabuki area. Here were the great theatres with their waving banners, pushing crowds, the thundering drums announcing a play about to begin.

"Kabuki is just as wicked as our pictures. But they'll never shut this place down," muttered my father. "They wouldn't dare."

But the theatre was not respectable either. Actors were like us—not officially people. They were restricted to this part of town, in the heart of the city. Still the rich merchants came, and their wives. The poor came too, going without a meal to buy the ticket. Even the noble ladies came, in disguise. They fell in love with actors. I had often heard those stories. Banned, and therefore popular. That was the joke.

"I used to paint here," he grumbled, "before you were born. The actors, the wrestlers—I hated it. You have to sit in the audience. You have to be a reporter."

Two of the slender boys who were training to play the parts of women in the kabuki theatre came giggling along.

We listened to their squeaky voices.

"He said he would give us one gold if—"

"You didn't believe him, did you? Don't be an idiot."

I agreed. One gold *ryo* was enough money to buy rice for one person for a full year.

The other one started to wail in a high, breaking voice.

"You're not supposed to cry; you're an *actor*. All this is a *play*."

"But I'm hungry." The smaller boy plucked the other boy's costly coat sleeve. The first boy hurried him along. The wind was blowing and the lantern was swinging overhead, giving its gaudy light. I watched them go. I was hungry too. But I had a father and a home. Boys like that lived in the part of town where children were sold as prostitutes.

I was so tired. It seemed I walked through sleep into wakefulness, from darkness into light. Ahead I saw a street bobbing with lanterns. We had arrived at the Nightless City, the pleasure district. We had walked from poverty into the jolly, gaudy plenitude that turned men from serfs into new, free creatures. Men, not women. I didn't even hope for the women. They were always servants.

I heard the drums, the wailing singers, the shrieks of laughter. I stepped more quickly, holding my father's hand. This was the Yoshiwara, the licensed quarters, where pleasures prohibited elsewhere were magically permitted as long as a tax was paid to the *bakufu*.

My father was in search of work.

I loved the Yoshiwara. In the Yoshiwara, we townspeople were kings—better than kings, if we had a little money. We stood by the docks. Boat after ferryboat pushed off, the high curved bows and sterns looming over us, the oarsmen with their long poles standing up in the wind and shouting to one another as they steered out into the clear. There was a lot of traffic. Travellers, labourers, bored samurai—all of these flocked northward into the wind as the sun began to set. The men would stay until they were shooed out and the Great Gate locked in the hours before dawn.

In the Yoshiwara, pleasure cost money. Money bought silk and velvet futons and food, music and sake—and women. The women collected the money, but they never kept it. They gave it to housekeepers and brothel owners, drummer boys and caterers. The clients too were bled dry, then ejected by the guard. But that would be later, after the long night of pleasure. If we ever came here in the day, we would come face to face with these defeated ones trudging south. But now it was evening, the best time, and we climbed over the rounded bridge with the Seven Stars above us and the houses of pleasure laid out in front.

On Nakanocho Boulevard, the main street, paper lanterns cast pools of red light on the wet snow. The noodle shop with its cartoon—"Fortify Yourself Before the Deed!"—was dark. Cauldrons that had boiled all day, rattling and steaming, now crouched half-seen on the burners. Next door, Waki's tattoo parlour was also dark, but Waki himself lay on the floor in the rectangle of streetlight under his door curtain. My father stopped only a few steps from his ear.

"What are you doing, Waki?" He nudged him with his toe.

It was plain that he was sleeping. But my father hated to see anyone idle.

Waki came up to sitting, all elbow. "I am concocting a design of dragon's tail and thunderbolt entwined. It will take hours to do the needlework, but it will be astonishing." He smiled with his eyes closed, envisioning it.

"Ah," said Hokusai. He loosened my hand and let me go. He stretched, soaking in the air of this place.

Waki lifted his curtain to let us into his shop. He had a high table there for his customers to lie on. He lit a small oil lamp. His designs were pinned on the walls. My father liked Waki: he was a simple peasant who had come to the city from the southern provinces to make his fortune. He stood beside his curtain, bowed, and gave his spiel automatically when we entered.

"I was born to a family of embroiderers in a village in Kyushu. I am good with a needle. I trained on the thick velvet and brocade that went to warrior families. By contrast, skin is a pitiful fabric."

We nodded as if we had not heard this before.

"But for one thing." Waki rolled his shoulders back and then shifted side to side, making eyes at me. "The movements of flesh! Such possibilities! You see—I can drape the dragon's body over the man's left shoulder and down the arm." He pantomimed. "The round muscles over the shoulder blade bulge, and so does the dragon. The sharp bone of the elbow becomes the arrowhead point of the dragon's tail."

"It would take you hours to create this tattoo—but it would be marvellous," agreed my father.

"I'll give it to the next man who comes in the door who can stand the pain. What should I charge? One *ryo* in gold?"

"That's one month's wage for a labourer."

"But he won't be a labourer. One thousand *mon*?"

"That's five days' wage."

"Not too much, do you think? For my artistry?"

"Not too much if they have it."

A man stepped into the doorway behind us. An umbrella was tipped low over his head. Only his thin, wrapped calves and box-like body were visible; his face was in shadow.

"What do you want?" said Waki sharply.

The man let the umbrella tip back and stepped into the lamplight.

There was no need to speak. The Chinese character for "dog" was tattooed on the stranger's forehead. There was only one place he could have got it: in the *bakufu* jailhouse. It was the mark of a criminal.

"Take this off," the stranger rasped. What had they done to him, to his voice?

Waki said he could not. The tattoo would not come off. That's why they put it there. To mark him forever.

The man came closer. "Then make it the colour of skin, so it won't show."

"I can't," Waki said.

He was afraid. I felt the fear.

"I would end up in jail myself."

The criminal cursed and roughly brushed the curtain aside, stepping back out into the street. He turned towards the end, where the low-class brothels were, and ran. We stared after him.

"Pity the women who are too poor to refuse his business," said my father.

I noticed he had sympathy for women, especially when they were not in his family.

Waki turned down his lamp. "I'm closed anyway," he said. He shooed us out, looking nervously down the street after his fleeing visitor.

"Turn your mind back to the fantastic dragon, conjure the scallops you'll draw for scales, and hope it puts you to sleep," Hokusai said.

Next door, Mitsu hovered over her shop counter. A man in a black travelling cloak stood with his back to us, looking at the goods. Mitsu's large mouth stretched and twisted. She had thick, dark brows and her eyes had huge black-rimmed bags beneath them—another socket, another brow. My father always said she looked like she wore actors' makeup; she exaggerated her expressions to go with her moods. She used to be a housekeeper in a brothel, that's what he said. She knew her business.

"What this one would do! Oh! Don't you want to see?" She lowered her eyelids and rolled her pupils skyward. Dildos made of turtleshell winked in a wooden case under her fingers. Elegant dried seahorses lay side by side on velvet. There were also cowrie shells, which I had seen my father use to pour out medicine for my mother when she was about to give birth. And in the very back, a wooden box contained a bear claw, used to stroke the pregnant stomach. For the right customer she would lift the cloth that covered all these. But he was not the right customer. He turned to us and I could see that he was as poor as we were. He turned away. She pressed her lips together and pushed out her chin: she covered her precious toys. She levelled a look of scorn at his back. She turned the look on us.

"What brings you out tonight? With that one?" She jerked her chin at me. She hated children. We weren't good for business.

My father was shabby; he was thin. I was proud of him, and I thought he should be rich. I did not know that being a great artist meant forgoing a thick mattress or a fine meal. I learned it soon enough.

I stood up straight and glared at Mitsu. If she was going to insult him, she would have to deal with me.

"Looking to see what's new," said Hokusai evasively.

"New? It's all new. No one likes old things today." She shrugged, and he nodded: in this, she was right. "The public is fickle," she said.

He wore nothing to distinguish himself from the trudging crowds of poor who thronged the streets of Edo. This made him stand out in the Yoshiwara, where everyone was dressed to show off. But he was not to be scorned. He was not a drunkard or a spendthrift. He didn't go into debt to buy courtesans, starving his children. We starved anyway. He was a window shopper. That was free.

"I made a nice little design of girls catching fireflies," he began. She looked bored. "And women caught in the rain on the bridge . . ."

Mitsu grunted. "That one you could sell to the shop that rents oiled-paper umbrellas. Let them put their sign on it."

He sighed. "It's a thought. I could design umbrellas. Now that the publishers have stopped printing books, since the edict."

"Temporary. It's only temporary. The *bakufu* will let up soon. They never pay attention to us for long." She scoured my father's anxious face and seemed to take a kinder interest. "Why don't you try famous courtesans looking in mirrors? That's what people want."

He groaned. "Everyone does that. Utamaro does that."

She shrugged. "Well, then, you have to do it better. Even the wealthiest are difficult to please these days. They don't think it's smart, anymore, to spend all their money in the Yoshiwara. They all want a bargain." She said this with disgust and followed it with a hissing sound. She folded her hands righteously. "Yes, my dear fellow, I do believe you have missed our golden days. Business is very difficult, very difficult."

Her jowly face swung side to side.

"You've got to do something to make yourself stand out," Mitsu was advising my father. "I'll tell you what—"

He wouldn't listen. He never did, to my mother or to anyone. A gust took the lantern, and it cracked against a roof pole, sputtering. The gaudy light swung back and forth, back and forth. We stood, both of us, looking at its red-edged shadow. Then we moved on. In a teahouse some other artists bought us tea. My father wouldn't take sake. We sat and it was peaceful there, with the movement of hopeful travellers in the street, the occasional stately passage of a fine courtesan, the undercurrent of drums from the brothels, the low murmur of the waitresses. The voices that roared up in sound and then abruptly cut off, as if the singer had fallen down a hole.

It was nothing Mitsu said that helped him; it was walking here, being here. It was the fever of money flowing and the wanting. It was the people my father wanted to make pictures of—not the prostitutes, though he'd done that, or the actors, the famous people. It was the ordinary ones—people who worked with their hands and their bodies, the ugly and misshapen ones, the funny and beleaguered ones. That's what he wanted. But who wanted to buy those pictures?

4

THE *Yakko*

WE HAD COME TO THE YOSHIWARA in the late afternoon. We sat on the side of the boulevard waiting for the parade. It hadn't started, but already people had gathered. It was the third month, and the day of the Lantern Festival parade. Every teahouse on the boulevard had hung a lantern with blue-and-black patterns under its eaves. The courtesans and their attendants would march in their giant costumes with royal pomp from the brothels to their places of assignation.

My father had his sketchbook. He commanded me to stay right there! Then he forgot about me.

The courtesans came out of the high-class brothels next to the boulevard. There was a man with a great iron spear in front to lead them and then a lantern bearer, although it wasn't dark yet. They stood with their child attendants in their brilliant kimono of silk and velvet in colours so deep I thought the seas and the skies had been emptied to make them. There was a cart with more women, their faces painted white, playing samisen. Drummers began pounding their rhythms to speed the heartbeats. Acrobats flipped in a series of circles, like the wheels of an ox cart, from hands to feet, hands to feet, all around the cluster of exotic women.

The first childish girls wore pounds of lustrous stuff, but they were small potatoes compared to the top rank, who towered on clogs as high as my forearm was long, with hair like wasps' nests speared with many golden sticks. The top courtesan, the *tayu*, was stupendous. Everyone gasped to see her. She paced with infinite slowness, balancing on one foot most of the time, while a man walked behind her holding an umbrella over her head. Then more followers—the housekeeper, the teahouse workers, and then another courtesan in her enormous shoes and her enormous hairdo.

I ran along beside them. I quickly caught up because of their special step, the figure eight, which meant they had to swing each foot in two circles and then out behind in a jaunty kick before planting it. It made them very slow. Some of the courtesans were very fresh and new. I tried my best to catch their eyes, but I could not. I was not certain they were human. The children in their entourage were, I knew, because they pushed each other and wailed. They were not allowed to look at anyone. I ran back to my father. It wasn't the performers he was drawing, of course. It was the watchers.

Amongst the watchers, and the subject of my father's brush, was a blind man with his cane.

He was bald; he had shaved himself as a sign of his blindness. This was the custom. And he was massive. His head was like a large egg sitting tipped back on the top of his neck. The oval of his chin jutted forwards and the larger oval of his crown slid backwards. His eyebrows were dark black, thick, and short, and they curled over his squinting eyes like sleeping dogs. His prominent ears were immensely complicated whirls of flesh. On one of them he had hung his rosary; I suppose it was a good place to keep it, if you were blind. You would always know where it was. He had big strong hands like paws, and these he kept aloft, as if he were afraid of misplacing them too. The wrists were high, and the backs of his hands and his long, fat fingers flopped softly.

The instant I saw him I hated him. I hated him because he made me afraid, and my father had instructed me never to be afraid.

There were two ways of living for blind men. One was to be a money-lender. A blind man was the only person amongst us townsmen who could buy a licence. Handling money was a despised activity, officially, and the *bakufu* assumed that this shameful occupation would keep the blind in their place.

But who cared about the official position? Money was running wild. Merchants were not ashamed to exchange it. They were, every year, louder and prouder. They dressed in fine coats and sported like lords. The real lords, we heard, were threadbare in their homes as well as in their hearts. Surviving on loyalty, duty, and the labour of others was harder and harder for the high and mighty. And so the blind moneylenders were busy. There was demand for their services. And they too became rich. Rich enough to eat and drink and spend a night at the Yoshiwara, to buy a courtesan.

But this particular blind man was not wealthy. There were a few other ways of life open to the blind of our city. These were hairdressing or otherwise working with the body. One way was to be a masseur. I decided that the blind man worked soothing the muscles of sumo wrestlers. That explained why the beefy hands—draping off his wrists in front of his chest—flexed and pulsed while the rest of him was still. He was watching the parade intently. The expression on his face was assessing, appreciative, like the faces of the sighted men beside him. He was thinking of skin, of flesh, of heavy men's bellies slapping against thin girls' thighs: I knew it.

The slit of visible eye was white; he had no pupils. Maybe those were rolled up to the inside of his head. His lips were apart, and top and bottom together made almost a circle; they too were fat and short. His nose was broad and stopped above his lip, leaving a wide, blank space there. It was a blank space that was the same as the blank space that was his entire face.

He could have been praying. But I doubted it; he didn't look religious. He was sucking in the courtesans' presence; he smelled them, he heard their breath, he felt their tension. He was taking them into his body.

It gave me a cold feeling. The women could not hide, even from the sightless.

ANOTHER TRIP NORTHWARD. I was older now. I ran alongside as he strode to the dock. I jumped from the shore onto the ferryboat he was boarding, taking my chances over the span of cold, dirty water. He put out his hand to steady me without really looking. I sank down into the bottom of the boat between his knees to keep warm.

It was nearly winter.

We stepped back onto land and, hunching against the wind, headed away from town towards the Yoshiwara.

The publisher's shop was just outside the Great Gate. I peered across into the brothel quarter. The street was grey and wet. The moat was brown, stirred up because of the rain. One courtesan was picking her way home, clogs covered in mud, bare feet white with streaks of dirt. Courtesans were not allowed to wear *tabi*, socks. Mine were not clean, but at least I had them. It was a strange hour, before midday, the Hour of the Snake. Normally no one of any importance was around. But today the caterers were lugging crates of tofu from the shop. Mitsu was washing her front steps, and men from the neighbourhood association were stringing lanterns amongst the bare branches of the trees.

My father took a seat at the teashop next door. The waitress set a cup of tea in front of him and gave me an almond cookie. Hokusai was cold, dirty, and thirsty. But he could not drink; his mind was occupied. I wanted him to at least put his hands around the warm cup. He told me to be quiet. I made myself small.

A balding, worried individual appeared beside us, polishing the top of his head with a hand, the hair there being sparse; maybe he thought it was dust and he was trying to rub it off.

"You disappear for weeks on end, and now you come to dig me out at my grandmother's teahouse?"

"If I don't 'disappear,' how can I get my work done? I have new designs."

The publisher paced to the door. "If I had any sense I'd drop you."

My father dimpled in a way calculated to charm. "But you won't because I'm good, correct?"

"Let's see what you've got. Then I'll tell you if you're any good."

My father bristled, but he opened his satchel. He put the designs on the table out of my reach. I could feel the tension. The bald man came and stood over us. The pictures were of courtesans under the moon, courtesans with flowers, courtesans walking by the canal. "Hmmm," he mumbled reluctantly. And "Hmmph" and "Hmmmph."

More pictures, then: of foreign men riding on horseback—Koreans, they must have been. Of teahouse girls.

"Give me lovers' suicides," said Tsutaya.

Hokusai lifted some papers. Boys gathering leaves. Children at the seashore. Tsutaya cleared his throat with impatience.

This man was an adopted son of the great publisher Tsutaya Juzaburo, whom the artists still lamented. He had died ten years before. The artists said he was a genius. I had heard the men talk about him. Myself, I thought he was a fake. He was the son of a brothel owner. They were mean, greedy men, I knew that. His father had had a bright idea, that was all. He bought the rights to publish the *saiken* guidebooks, with their tiny writing and columns full of symbols giving a prostitute's rank, how much it cost to buy her for a night, and what she would do.

The *saiken* were popular. Here is why: because when a *tsu*—that is, a sophisticate—comes in the gate, he wants to know about the courtesans for sale. He buys one of these little books. You can see him walking along, his head bent over the pages, his ears red with excitement, his breath coming shallow and fast. He could collide with a lamppost, or even with the famous courtesan Hana-ogi on her way to a teahouse, and not know it.

We watched them often enough, my father and I. My father would yell out, "Fool! Reading the map when you should be enjoying the view."

The guidebooks sold not only to newcomers but to regular customers as well, because they wanted to know how their sweethearts stood up in the ratings.

And naturally the *saiken* were of interest to the prostitutes themselves. They had to look themselves up to discover if their value was rising or—more likely—falling. They were always getting older, and as they got older this was noted in the *saiken,* even though the ages were off by a few years. The guidebooks didn't exactly speak the truth because they were made for advertisement. They didn't exactly have the best interests of the customer at heart. They represented the best interests of the Yoshiwara merchant.

So the little book would say something like this: "Misty Moon is eighteen years old and has rounded breasts but a slim figure and teeth with a space between the first two. Her look is demure, but her temperament is fiery . . . Easy to please and passionate in her response . . ."

This was a load of night soil, but never mind. You had to buy the book to read it, and everyone wanted to read it. And if you'd already bought one you probably bought another and another, because you had to have the latest. The *saiken* had to be edited twice a year. New girls debut, and old ones die or—rarely—retire.

Of course if you knew anything you knew that the *saiken*'s truthfulness was limited, to put it nicely, because Tsutaya had a lot of people to please: the brothel owners, the teahouse owners, the clients themselves. But the *tsu* didn't think of this. He read and his mouth gaped and his mouth watered and he believed.

It takes no genius to make money publishing that stuff. In fact it takes a certain stupidity. And this wasn't even the first Tsutaya, but a pale son. Why should a man like that have power over my father?

I glared at the publisher's head as if I could put holes in it. I fidgeted. He didn't say yes, but he didn't say no. What was so difficult? Hokusai was as good as and better than any other artist Tsutaya published. But there was one thing about my father: he made no effort to please anyone but himself. "I won't pretend to love doing what I hate doing."

Our needs were modest. He hardly ate anything and wasn't a gambler, and he worked from early morning until late at night. Earlier, Tsutaya had encouraged him. Now he tried to tell him what to do.

"Now that one—that could work. Take that girl, isolate her from the surrounds, take the other people out, lengthen her out, and show her looking in a mirror. Then it will sell."

Hokusai's face turned red. I pressed myself alongside his legs. He gathered his drawings. He made ready to leave. I pressed harder into the side of his thigh. Tsutaya folded his arms in the way of a stubborn boss. I was ready to provide a distraction by running away when a girl appeared in the doorway.

She saved us all, this apprentice courtesan.

"Who let you out?" snapped Tsutaya.

The prostitutes weren't supposed to go outside the gate. But the gate was just a few yards away, and the guard was watching her.

"Excuse me. I am very sorry to disturb but—"

"What is it?"

"I am to get the very special tea leaves that O-Fumi wants, to please her client who has made an appointment to see her."

She bowed respectfully and spoke with an elegant, clear, high voice. I knew right away she was new: she was funny-looking, gawky, and nervous. She had a thin neck and a face that tipped up, as if she had questions for the whole world. That made her heavy knot of hair topple over one ear. Her feet were bare, her nose was long and red at the tip, and it was running.

Plus, she was different. Her language marked her as nobility. The usual apprentice prostitute was a poor girl from the country sold into this life whose bumpkin accent was disguised by witty Yoshiwara slang.

Tsutaya snorted. "Wait. My mother will serve you."

She bowed again. She was very graceful. "Your mother? That would be excellent. But could you please let her know that I am in the shop and need her help?"

Tsutaya laughed, including my father in his smirk. "If it isn't Lady Murakami herself."

She inclined her long neck. "I beg your pardon, sir, but I am not entirely certain we have met," she said, with courtesy so exaggerated it was an obvious slap in the face.

Tsutaya looked down at her. He looked through her to the street. On the Edo side of the bridge, the city was teeming. But the gate to the pleasure quarter was empty of people. This did not improve his mood. His voice was ice.

"*Yakko!*" he said scornfully. "You don't know me, but you soon will. I know every house in the Yoshiwara. I know the inmates, the housekeepers, the owners, the entertainers, the caterers. I know them all and their reputations. In fact, I make their reputations," he said, "because I publish the *Guide to the Green Houses*. You plan on surviving here? Take note of me. I can ruin you. If, when you debut as a courtesan, I give you a good write-up, you will have plenty of customers. If I say that you are not pretty—and you are not, by the way—things will not go well." He grinned, enjoying his little lecture. "*That's* who I am."

The girl had listened. When he was finished she sank slowly and beautifully to her knees, placed her hands on the ground, and bowed. "Please accept my humble apologies," she said.

She stayed face down for a long time. We were looking at that large knot of hair; it was shiny and fine, and wisps of it came out at the sides. When she looked up her face was a picture of humility. Her eyes melted with sorrow. Or did they? They had intelligence, and something more—a deep spark, like coal in our hearth that continued to glow under the ash.

I grinned. She was not really sorry, not at all.

I don't believe Tsutaya saw the look in her eyes. He didn't lower his gaze that far. But something irked him nonetheless. "Get over here," he said.

The girl hooded her eyes. I knew she wanted to refuse this rude order. And I wanted her to. I hated the publisher now. I could tell my father did too. So much for the sale. We would have to do without this man.

The *yakko* couldn't, however. She was trapped. Unless I did something. I ran for the door.

"Oh no, you don't!" my father shouted, running after me.

My tactic worked. Tsutaya was momentarily amused.

"If you are not a good artist, you are at least the best mother in the Yoshi-wara!" he called after Hokusai. We were out the door when I heard him speak to the girl again.

"You will not do well here," he repeated. He would keep his temper and settle for a cooler cruelty. "After all, your face does not offer the onlooker the perfection of symmetry, nor your body a pillowy peace."

Saiken talking. I guessed he was already working on his write-up.

"You have one thing going for you, as far as I can see," he said. "And that is your excellent manners."

She returned to her face-down position, from which, naturally, she could not speak.

"Rise," he said.

She stood. My father and I watched her without seeming to watch. Wide-apart eyes, long nose, tiny mouth. Hers was a trouble face, my mother would have said. Not biddable, anyone could tell.

"I think she is charming. I would like to paint her," Hokusai said.

"You think people want to look at that?" Tsutaya snorted.

She was very thin. Her long legs and back formed a slight curve; her too-big kimono puddled at her feet.

"Her spirit is quite unquenched. She has humour too."

The girl looked down as now even my father discussed her face, her nature.

"And grace. Look at the hands—large but lovely," my father was saying.

"Maybe you think so," Tsutaya shot, "but your pictures don't sell, Sori II."

"Sori II is not my name."

The two men glared at each other: standoff. Tsutaya looked away first.

We went back in. My father sat down again and raised the teacup to his mouth. The teacup went down. The tea was cold. He looked over his designs. Then he raised the cup again. Again it did not get to his lips. The publisher rubbed his poor hair. He peered at the seal and signature on the new paintings.

"What is your name now, then?" he said with an air of weariness.

"Hokusai. North Star Studio. Do you like it?"

Tsutaya groaned. "People know you as Sori II. We've made your name. You can't change it now. Sori II is worth money."

My father grinned. "Why do you think I sold it? I needed that money."

The man threw up his hands. "But I'll have to launch you all over again."

"I'll put the two together on my pictures for now. 'Sori II, changed to Hokusai.' In time I'll drop the Sori."

In the end Tsutaya reached into his belt for money and bought two of the designs. The transaction only took a few minutes. My father didn't count the coins; he never did.

By this time Tsutaya's mother had given the apprentice her tea. We all escaped together.

"Nice girl," the *yakko* said, and she touched my cheek. For old times' sake, my father hoisted me on his shoulders, where I rode, my legs dangling on his chest. I began to scold him for selling his name.

"Terrible girl," he said patting my leg, and we all laughed. We walked over the bridge and through the Great Gate.

"I have a new name too," said the girl. "They took away the name I had in the outside world. My new name is Shino."

"Well, Shino, if you think this girl is nice," my father said, "do you want to buy her?"

I was six years old and looked like four. People who didn't know us sometimes assumed my father was starving and needed to sell me. I was just the right age for that. But Shino didn't. She told me this later, often told me this—she noticed the way, as I rode triumphantly on his shoulders, his hands grasped my shins. And she thought he would never let me go.

She smiled and said she knew he was joking and hurried away from us down the street.

I kicked his chest. "Put me down."

He did and I ran after her.

"Ei!" Hokusai called. "Oh no you don't."

He ran to scoop me up; I screamed with delight, and he shuffled back to a bench like a monkey swinging me between his knees, scolding: "You behave or your father cannot work, and when your father cannot work, then you, not I, will be Sori II!"

Shino turned back to see his antics. I liked what happened to her face when she laughed, liked to hear that pealing. Then quickly she covered her mouth.

"Come here, new-named young lady, Shino, who before was someone else. Will you help me? Do one thing for me? Look at my pictures. See if you like them," my father said. "Tell us what the noble ladies want."

I knew what he was up to. He wanted encouragement now because Tsutaya had slighted him.

We sat on the bench and looked at his designs.

They were sketches of our city, the Eastern Capital. I knew all the scenes. One was the ferry docks by the river, with lovers saying goodbye as the boat draws in. One was the front of the kabuki theatre, looking down from above on rows and rows of round heads. The heads were pushed together like cabbages at the feet of two large men. The men were reading lines.

"I've seen the front of the Nakamura, but I've never been inside," I said.

"I should hope not," said Shino. She looked at each of the pictures carefully. Her little filly-face was sad, but glad to look: maybe she had been to these places before. But she was a captive now.

The street scene in the Yoshiwara interested her: the courtesans dressed in white robes for the summer festival, mustering for their procession. "So that is what it will be like," she said.

My father put himself in his pictures for fun. Always he drew an old man, bent and wrinkled, with no hair. Then he said, "That is me!" I don't know why he did this. It was not what he was. It was what he would become. He was old in years, yes, but not in himself. He was wiry and full of energy and his thick, black thatch sprang out up from his scalp like grass.

"Look at others who are published and tell me if these are not better," he challenged.

The apprentice courtesan laughed. "Of course I don't know tastes," she said, "but they look very pretty to me. I have seen such pictures in the castle, not only here in the Yoshiwara."

"You see? What did I tell you? The noble ladies want this stuff," my father said.

It was fun to be laughing with her. I had no friends at all, only sisters and now, a brother. With them, I fought. He showed another page.

"This one is the Nagasakiya, where Dutch traders stay when they are in Edo."

I sucked in my breath when I told her. It was a daring picture, I knew. We were not supposed to see the barbarians. It was a test; she might have scolded us or turned away.

She did not, but examined the picture closely.

"Were you there?" she said.

"We were!" I babbled. "I was riding on my father's shoulders as he sketched. I could almost see in the windows. When the red-headed men appeared, a roar went up!"

"Oh my, are you always so brave?" she said with a curious smile.

5

THE STORYTELLER

IF MY SISTERS AND I were not grinding seeds for pigment or bringing clean water from the well, we might sneak into the back rows of the storytelling hall at the end of our alley. It was a long, narrow building and it was quite easy to hunker down amongst the packages and feet of paying customers. We tried to keep out of sight of the manager so we wouldn't get kicked out.

I loved these men who recited our legends in the making. The storyteller that day was wild-eyed and powered by some inner magic that created silence around him. I arranged myself in the aisle so I could peer down it. He warmed up by making the voices of a dozen people come out of his mouth, one after another. He shook a rattle to announce the suspense of the moment. He swung his body low on bent knees, circling flat hands on a level as if he were grinding corn. He only needed to start talking and I was still as a stone.

> Snow fine and bitter as dust was falling. A young noblewoman stepped into her sedan chair and closed the door. Through the curtain her husband said goodbye.
>
> "You are going to the World of Dreams," he said. "Mind you don't fall sick from the lacquer trees."
>
> He laughed, this lord. It was an evil joke. A double row of lacquer trees stretched alongside the Dike of Japan all the way from Harajuku to the Yoshiwara. The lacquer was poisonous, and you could die of it. But he wasn't really talking about the trees. He was talking about the danger of her falling sick because of the work she

had to do. This lord had been displeased with his wife. He had sent her to the chief magistrate, who sentenced her to five years' service as a courtesan.

"We're lucky," one of the bearers said, lifting the handles. "The load is light."

"Hey, she weighs no more than a few bags of rice," said his partner.

They began to run.

Inside the box, the young wife jostled from side to side. She could hear the bearers' broad, bare feet hit the wet stone. They could have been slapping cheeks or buttocks. Slap, slap, slap. They did not stop. The fifteen-year-old wife of Lord Yoshida shrank inside the folds of her silk and velvet kosode. She might be going to her doom, but no one was going to hear her howl.

They took the highway along the dike. She saw the lacquer trees through the split in the curtain. At the top of Primping Hill the bearers shouted and stopped and set down their load. The older one addressed her from the other side of the curtain.

"From here you walk. No one is allowed to ride into the Yoshiwara."

The young wife pulled back the curtain and craned her neck to see. The road zigzagged with teahouses on either side. At the bottom and across the water was the bridge. The World of Dreams didn't look like much. It was just a few square blocks, surrounded by moats, in a marshy area. She had been there once on an outing with her parents. Families with children often went to see the festivals. The place she remembered was more like an amusement park with clouds of cherry blossoms and a parade of exquisite women.

She stepped down, holding out her hand for help. The Bridge of Hesitation arched across the moat. She saw the Gazing Back Willow tree, where lovers parted. On the other side was the guard. She walked up and over the hump of the bridge. She had her naginata with her, a long, thin pole with a sharp curved blade at the end. The guard stepped out of his guardhouse.

"Surrender your weapon," he told her.

"Must I?"

"All those of the samurai class must surrender their swords. Even the women," he chanted without looking at her.

"Why?" she said.

"It is because samurai and commoners are equal in the pleasure quarter."

"Don't believe it," said the bearer, who had come up behind her. "Everyone knows why you can't bring any weapon inside. It's because the women are so unhappy that if they had a sword, they'd kill themselves."

The guard had a narrow, tall skull, which sank down to wide cheeks, so his head looked like a gourd you might find sitting in a field. His name was Shirobei. It was always Shirobei. Every man who lived and died in that position had the name of Shirobei. A tuft of spiky silver hair stuck up from inside his uniform. His chest moved as if it was alive, and a sharp nose poked out. It was a white fox—and it was in his shirt. The young wife screamed.

"Don't be afraid. The white fox is a God of Luck."

She wrapped herself more tightly and made a haughty face. "Let me in."

"The gate is locked. It's the Hour of the Rat."

"That's why they've brought me now. So no one would see."

"What's your business?" said Shirobei.

"I'm coming to the House of the Corner Tamaya," she said.

"Are you coming to stay?" He peered at her. It was a novelty these days. A yakko, a noblewoman sentenced to serve as a courtesan.

"So what was it?" he said. What disaster had befallen? "Famine, fire, flood?" Those were unlikely to affect the nobles. "Disgrace, treachery, kidnapping?" No? She must have brought it on herself, then. "An indiscretion with an actor?"

She held her chin high.

"We used to get ladies like you here," he said. "But not for quite a while."

He unlocked the gate. He took her weapon. On his face was an unreadable look. If she had not just learned that it was absent *from the world, she would have called it pity. She shrugged the shoulders of her kosode closer to her throat.*

"Thank you." She bowed a little. He bowed. She straightened. She walked past the guard and looked back, saying goodbye to everything.

She did not regret the husband who had the power to discard her. Her parents, if they did not die of shame, would be there on her return. For five years she would be a Yoshiwara courtesan.

The audience groaned in sympathy. The storyteller turned his back and took a drink of water. He gave us time to shift position and munch our rice balls before he started again.

A man was waiting, wrapped in a cloak. He was the proprietor of the Corner Tamaya. He put his hands on the yakko's shoulders. He looked her up and down. He turned her slowly front to back and back to front. It seemed he might unwind her cloak right then, but he stopped. He put a hand on her cheek and turned it slowly one way and then the other.

The storyteller had taken on the Yoshiwara dialect. His voice was now arrogant and snide.

"Not much of a bargain," he said. "They told me you were beautiful."

"You see the truth," she said.

"I only took you because you were a gift."

"Perhaps one gift more than you deserve?"

He reached for the clasp that held her hair and pulled it out roughly. He put his fingers in and drew out the tresses. They were long, so long. His fingers were like a comb; the hair kept coming until he let it drop. It reached her knees.

She raised her chin. Proud, almost defiant. She knew her hair was lovely. He looked as if he would slap her. But something— perhaps her fine clothes—stopped him, and he contented himself with glaring.

She bit back more words: if you don't want me, let me go. She told herself, *Don't talk back, don't talk back. How many times had her parents tried to teach her that? Hadn't they said her tongue would be the death of her?*

"Itz gonna cost me money to keep you. I hafta get you bedding too. Did you bring any kimono?"

"They took me from home with nothing."

He sucked air and walked in front of her down the boulevard. The quarter was marked out in squares, the streets in a small grid. The broad street in the centre, Nakanocho Boulevard, went straight for a short distance and ended at the moat. Branching off to right and left were smaller streets. Edocho 1 went off on the right side and Edocho 2 on the left. The next was Ageyacho on her right and Sumicho on her left. "All of these are green houses. The last street here'z Kyomachi. Itz where the poorest prostitutes live, izn it? See? You're lucky to be with me. Wait here; I've business to do."

The yakko stood waiting in the cold, just in front of Mitsu's shop. The layer of white snow was thin on the ground. She saw it covered blades of green that had already, too keenly, sprung up. But it was cold here, much colder than at home because of all the water.

From inside her shop Mitsu peered at her . . .

Mitsu? I knew Mitsu. She was really in a story? I worked my way forward a row or two. Miyo and Tatsu pulled on my coat from behind and made faces. They were going home. I shook my head. I put my hand back on my chin and rubbed it, my thumb on one side and my finger on the other, like an old man, my mother said.

. . . peered again, and then walked out to stand silently in the doorway. The yakko brushed off the light, high dressing of downy snow that had settled on her clothing. Her thonged clogs sat half-buried in the white fluff.

"Do you have any fresh tabi?" *said the yakko to the shopkeeper.* "I need them. These are wet and my feet are very cold."

"That's not what I sell," *said Mitsu.* "And anyway, you won't be wearing socks here."

The yakko leaned against the post of the wall, reached down, and picked up one of her feet. She rubbed it energetically with both hands. The foot was very white.

"But you are wearing some," she said.

"That's different," said Mitsu. "I'm retired." She noticed that the yakko's hands were white too. Her face was white. "You've never been here before, is that it? Izn it? Never come through the Great Gate? What are you doing here?"

"I've come to live at the Corner Tamaya."

"Ooooh," said Mitsu.

The storyteller's hand went to his mouth and his eyes bulged. I burst out laughing. It was a perfect imitation.

"I've heard about you. You must be the disobedient wife of Lord Yoshida."

"How did you hear?"

"Gossip," Mitsu said. "Rumour. We hear everything."

The yakko hung her head.

"You aren't the only lady here. But you're one of the few. It used to be that the courtesans were high-born and elegant, but now we're all a little cheaper. Everyone tries to save money, even on their dreams."

The young wife put her footsole down in the snow. She winced. She picked up the other one and lost her balance, nearly toppling.

"Courtesans go barefoot. That is the rule."

"That's a ridiculous rule," said the yakko irritably.

Mitsu raised her finger to her lips. "The bare feet are beautiful and desirable, izn it? You'll get used to it. Just remember: the Yoshi-wara is all backwards. That's because it's the pleasure world."

The yakko went silent for a few minutes. Mitsu stood staring at her.

"What did you do?" said Mitsu.

The pale white girl-woman inclined her head. "What do you mean?"

"You know. To get"—Mitsu sliced her hand in a theatrical gesture—"sent up?"

"*I disobeyed my husband.*"

Murmurs went through the crowd. They could see why that had got her in trouble.

"How?"

"*I . . . I went to the theatre.*"

It was a lie. She had raised her hand to him, but so great an offence she would not own.

Mitsu gasped. "The theatre! Thaz all?" It was not exactly allowed, but some women did it.

"*He flew into a temper and the guards pulled me away. They took me to the magistrate.*"

"What magistrate did you go before?"

The yakko pulled her coat tighter around her chest and buried her cold hands into the opposite sleeves. "Sadanobu."

"Bad luck!" Mitsu caught the yakko's arm and held her a minute. "Bad luck," she said, "to come before that one. He's not as pure as he makes out. And he'll get you for it."

The yakko began to walk back towards the moat, skidding in the snow on her clogs, hurrying, her arms flailing.

"You won't get out now," called Mitsu. "Your time is set."

The yakko stopped. She picked up a stone and threw it into the water. It made a hollow plonk *and disappeared, leaving ripples of perfect roundness in the black water. Then she went still, as if frozen. She was all white now, except for her beautiful garment.*

"Itz strange, izn't?" Mitsu said. "In real dreams you don't have so many rules. But these are not real dreams, they're—" She gave a gusty breath. "At least they are real dreams, but they are not our dreams. We live by playing roles in the dreams of others. They can buy their dreams."

The proprietor came out the door. "Wherez she going?" he shouted. "Come back."

"She isn't going anywhere," said Mitsu. "She has become a ghost."

That was the end. Everyone moaned. People shouted for more. The storyteller vacated the stage. My sisters were gone. When I found my way home, my mother was angry. No one had time to answer my questions. I knew in a way that stories came from real life. But could they come this close to us? Was that my *yakko*? My Shino? Could it be? I sat in a corner and rocked myself and pulled at my chin.

"Look at her! She's doing it again! She's going to make her chin even longer."

THE NEXT TIME we were in the Yoshiwara I ran off, looking for her.

"Ei! Come back." Hokusai put down his brush with a clatter of annoyance and ran over to scoop me up: I screamed with delight.

"Worthless child!" he said, loudly enough for anyone to hear. "Why am I saddled with this wild thing?" He ran bowlegged back to his travelling mat on the ground and scolded: "You stay still or your father cannot work, and when your father cannot work, you cannot eat!" That was his favourite line.

And then Shino appeared.

"May I take her to the caterers? I have to pick up some cakes for tonight and take them back to my house," she said.

"Take her!" he said. He didn't look up from his page. "By all means, take her."

That's how I got to see inside her high-class brothel.

6

THE CORNER TAMAYA

THE CORNER TAMAYA was on the corner of the boulevard and Edocho 2, the second big street of the Yoshiwara. It was built of wood, with three steps going up from the walk. The entrance hall was filled with red cabinets and silk floor cushions. There was an ebony Go board and vessels for incense. "These are from China," whispered Shino.

"How do you know?"

"They're like the ones we had at home."

To one side was an alcove with a low desk in it. There a woman sat on her heels, looking harassed. She was not young, but her clothes were heavy and ornate, layer on layer of velvet and patterned silk. She was doing three things at once: writing, giving orders to a small girl, and throwing her voice behind her up the stairs to order someone else. Her name was Kana, Shino whispered, and she was the housekeeper, a former prostitute who had married the boss.

"Here you are, Shino," she said bitterly. "Back at last. Hurry with those to the kitchen." She didn't look down far enough to notice me. I was very short.

We went back to the kitchen, which was warm and splashed with water from a well in the centre. Light came down through a vent in the roof. Shino caught the eye of a cook and passed him her parcel. On the way back we saw the bookkeeper, occupied with his abacus. She whispered to me, "He sold me my bedding. I had no money. I don't like it either—it's a rough cotton futon and all dull grey, nothing soft or smooth against my skin."

I didn't have a futon of my own; my sisters and I pulled one tattered thing back and forth between us.

"He said, 'You're an apprentice. What does it matter what you sleep on? When you are accepting clients you will buy beautiful bedding.' He wrote down the cost in a column beside my name. 'This is your account.' But there were so many charges against it already! 'I just got here. What are those?' I asked him. He ticked them off. 'A month of food. The bedding. Tips for the bearers who brought you here.' Do you get that, Ei? I paid for my own trip to jail."

She laughed at her story, and I watched her face to see if it still split up the way it did when I first saw her. It did.

"When I came here I didn't understand money. In my home the women didn't handle coins. Except, maybe, when we sneaked out to buy pictures."

I handled the coins my father paid no attention to: *mon, momme*. I pointed to the ones in her palm. "I know some," I said. There was a squared one. The large brown ones had a hole; those were the ones the moneylenders kept tied in long laces, where they sat at the foot of the Ryogoku Bridge.

"You can help me, then. You worldly thing."

I was delighted.

The upstairs was one large space around the staircase. In cubicles between thin screens, the courtesans slept; their doors were curtained. I could hear their voices. When one screen opened I saw a small cooking stove and a teapot and some folded bedding. There was the room of the great *tayu* Hanaogi; there was the room of the second-best, Fumi; here was the small room where Shino lived, beside her.

A rumpled-looking man with greasy hair emerged. He looked at Shino frankly and she lowered her eyes. She was an apprentice, under sixteen and off limits, for now.

As he passed, a courtesan appeared behind him. When he turned at the stairwell, their eyes met. They held each other's gaze as he descended. The courtesan gestured to her heart and sighed. The man's head disappeared from the stairwell. His footsteps passed the desk; there was the clink of coins. The courtesan's lip curled. "I 'ope your balls wither an' your dick falls off an' you never, *ever* show up 'ere again!" She whirled and was gone, behind her curtain.

Two other girls hung over the stairwell. "Headz up! He'z comin'!"

"He'z not!"

"Iz too."

"Znot!"

"Whadda *dra-ag!* Why duzn he *go?*"

"He'z in love!"

"Shee'z *good. Super* good."

Everyone giggled.

The courtesans crept to the centre window overlooking the street and watched as the man halted halfway down the front steps. He looked up to the second storey.

"Now he'z goin'. Look."

"Farewell, my sweet potato. My little shrimp. My dumpling—"

"Takao! Get out there," shouted the housekeeper up the stairs, "and see him off."

The courtesan came out of her room again, pulling her robe around her. She leaned out the open balcony. "The minutes will drag till I see you again," she lisped. "I'm, like, faintin' with pain to see you go." The last was a bit half-hearted.

The other girls groaned and elbowed each other. The housekeeper thumped up the stairs and hit one of them smartly on the side of her head.

"Takao! A little creativity, pulleez."

"So sorry. I *yam* trying, but I'm *zaus*ted. I never sleep till it'z day, and then it'z so noi-zy!"

A cross-looking beauty stepped out from behind a screen. On seeing us her face became kinder.

"Oh, Shino, there yu are. C'n yu come and make me some tea and help me clean up? Come . . . But whooz that *chi-yuld?*"

So this was Fumi, the second-best. I had read about her in the *saiken.* I had seen her picture, or what passed for her picture. I had seen her parading on the boulevard enfolded in her mammoth robes. She looked thin and hunched.

"This is Ei!" pronounced Shino in her bell-like tones, pushing me forward. "She's the daughter of that artist Hokusai who is painting along the boulevard. I said she could come with me."

"How kind yu are, Shino," said Fumi, looking me over absently and putting a hand on my head. "I fear it will only do yu harm. But the urchin can come too."

I sat on the floor.

Fumi had a low black lacquer chest and two round mirrors on handles. Holding one in each hand she looked this way and that to see the back of her head. "Need that hairdresser again. Too bad I canna 'ford it." She had a small brush, which she offered Shino, instructing her to powder her neck. Then she gave Shino a hairpin to tuck up the hairs that had escaped and fallen onto her nape.

"Your old man'z an artist? We usta have one here watchin' our every *move*," said Fumi. "We were, like, *pozen* all the time. He watched how we dressed and when we played our music and when we looked at the moon— evrythin'. But he duzn come here anymore. Maybe he'z, like, scared he'll get fined or go to jail"—here her face became tragic—"or end up on the White Sands or even, like, banished. Can you 'magine? Jus' for painting us. It'z 'cause we're so *evil*." She raised her eyebrows at me. "So here I am—all in my glory—and whooz to see? Only these yobs."

"You're beautiful anyway," said Shino.

We were all gazing in the mirrors, as if we couldn't look directly at her face. From where I sat the mirror was too bright, reflecting the sun. I couldn't see her at all.

"I know," said Fumi, looking contentedly in the bronze circle. She moved aside. Now I could see my own face behind hers. It was an awful sight. "But beauty'z not everything."

"You think so?" Shino's face was unreadable.

"Oh, yeah. Men say they wan' beauty," Fumi said. "They dream aboudit; they pay a fortune. But what they really wan' is kindness. Yu'll do fine in here 'f yu're gennle and considerate. Yu've just got to forget everything that'z for *yu* and remember everything that'z for *them*."

Shino moved around, setting up the kettle on the little grill.

"I'm no good at pleasing," she said. "I didn't please my real husband. So how can I please a false husband in the pleasure quarter?"

The courtesan twitched her lips in her mirror. It might have been a smile.

"That's a very good question. Jus' keep yur eyes open," she said. "Yu've godda brain. Yu'll finna way."

After that, if I was lonely or bored when my father worked in the Yoshiwara, I'd go to the Corner Tamaya and ask for Shino. One morning when she'd been up late and I was up early, I even crawled into her bed and lay there beside her. I was curled up in the warmth when a crowd of the other women came in to get her.

"Yu up, *yakko*? C'mon, geddup!"

They pushed past the screen, about five of them; behind them I could see Kana.

Shino had been sound asleep and woke up confused. But she sat up. Her hair was down in a soft, long braid that lay like a rope in the bed.

They giggled.

"Lookit her! She'z so, like, stiff. She'z, like, a lady! She'll, like, never gedda man. No one'z, like, ever gonna wan' her," one of them said.

Kana hit one of them on the back of the legs. "You're just ignorant country oafs! Shino knows a lot. A lot. You should take advantage. She knows writing and music; she can draw, she can dance. She'll do jus' fine. Fumi thinks so anyway." She pulled the futon off us. "C'mon downstairs, *yakko*. And bring yur liddle friend. It'z time to eat."

Shino protested as she got up.

"I don't like to be called that. You've given me a name. Can't you call me by it?"

"It's jus', like, easier to call yu the *yakko*," yawned one of them. "Besides yur so . . . yur, like, so . . ."

"I know I am," Shino said quietly.

We got up. Everybody clattered downstairs to the kitchen.

It was the one day a month when the prostitutes took it over. Normally they sat back on their knees, as if they had no interest in food, while clients filled their stomachs. But I had heard their stomachs grumble. Today they could eat as much as they wanted. They elbowed one another to grab the bean curd with corn, the fried fish, the white radish and eggplant in miso, and the bits of grilled chicken. Their mouths dripped with sauce, and they sputtered as they spoke in their funny dialect.

"Fumi says being beautiful is not the most important thing here. She says even if I'm not beautiful, I can be successful by being good," said Shino.

"Fumi is, like, todally *wrong*. Being beautiful *iz* most important," said one of them. "Izn it?"

They said that a lot. "*Izn it?*" I had started to say it to my mother, to tease her. It got my father in trouble for leaving me in the brothels while he worked. Still she didn't ask that I stay at home.

"Even if I were to believe you," said Shino in her careful way, "and I am not certain I do, can you tell me who determines what is beautiful?"

I slurped my soba noodles. The artists did, I thought.

"That'z a very good question, *yakko*," said Fumi.

Everyone laughed. She was supposed to call her Shino.

"Nobody decides. It'z not for, like, deciding. It'z just for, like, kno-owing. Duh-uh!"

"That's not true! Men decide."

"They doan."

"Do too."

"Do not!"

"Who's beautiful is just, like, obvious. Like Hana-ogi." She was the top courtesan.

"Or Fumi."

Kana was thoughtful. "But the weird thing is it, like, *changes*. Like the whole idea of who's beautiful and for what reason *changes* year to year. I c'n remember . . . Like, now the girls have to be thin. But before, when I was first in the biz, the famous girls were round."

"Never! I doan believe you. Yu mean, like, fat?" That was Takao, stuffing her face.

"Yu doan remember 'cause yu're too young, but yeah, it's true—like *round*. The girls were, like, round."

Everyone made various noises of disgust.

"And men liked it," Kana added as an afterthought.

Everyone laughed.

"So who decided we hafta be thin?"

"I tell you who decided. *We* decided," said one girl.

"We did?"

"Yah. *We* make the fashion. 'F I wear this, like, bamboo-leaf pattern in my kimono and let my red underskirt show, and 'f I tie a purple-and-green obi around, really wide—like, way wider than anyone else—and I go strolling down the boulevard, then the artists paint me, even the noblewomen will think thaz a new style an' it'z gorgeous. Izn it?"

"'Member when Hana-ogi went to the Spring Festival dressed like a man? They thought that was beautiful too." Everyone laughed.

"Yah, maybe yu're right. We decide."

"That is, like, so cool! We're, like, the *evil* ones, but they wanna dress like us? Even the little girls in the samurai families?"

"And talk like us. They copy our words, like *iki*—"

"Because we're so clever. We set the styles. And we're *fuh-ny*—"

"We're *fuh-ny* till they suddenly decide we're very bad for their *health!*" Everyone laughed again.

"Well, we are. Bad for their health. Izn it?"

Everyone laughed more, and some leant sideways on the floor, they were so full.

"Not to mention *our* health." Kana looked pointedly at one girl. It's true she was very skinny. And pale. And she kept coughing. "You don't look so great, Sanae."

"Doan say that!" she wailed. "If they think I'm sick they'll sen' me home, won't they?"

"We might all hafta go home if Sadanobu enforces these rules they're talkin' about."

"But they doan really mean it. They'll *never* shut down the brothels."

"The only way we *close* 'em down is if we *burn* 'em down."

"Mmmm, great idea," murmured someone.

More laughter.

Our stomachs were bursting with food. We were lying around groaning.

"So what did we decide beauty is?" said Shino.

"We didn' decide."

"But we c'n give you the list."

Fumi recited. "Best between fifteen and eighteen years of age."

I thought most of them were a few years older than that.

"The skin must be pale pink, like cherry blossoms."

Their skin was not pink but sallow; they never went outside.

"The eyes must be the shape of a melon seed. Nose depends on the face—not too large, not too small. Mouth should be very narrow across, and lips puffed as if a wasp has stung them. Eyes large and very black in the centre. Eyebrows close together."

The girls fell silent, each one reflecting on how far away she was from the ideal. I did too.

"The teeth must be white and the nose must be gradual. The ears must be long and far away from your face, not fleshy."

"Oooh."

They curdled at the thought of fleshy ears.

"When you lift up your hair, the nape should be clean and your neck long."

"How do you know all this?" said Shino.

"'S written in a tablet, and we're measured. We've all bin assessed."

"Waist must be very narrow and legs long in proportion to the back. Top of the head flat, like you can rest a plate on it."

A couple of them stood up and put plates on their heads and tried walking. The plates slid off.

"And don't forget the feet—a lovely arch."

"And the toes should curl up!"

Here all the women put their hands over their mouths and giggled. Shino didn't get the joke. Neither did I.

Fumi whispered, "'F yu have curled-up toes, it means that yur a wanton woman."

"I am not," said Shino indignantly. "Izn it?"

Everyone roared. Fumi patted her leg. "Good girl," she said.

I looked at Shino and she looked at me. Her eyes were nothing like the shape of a melon seed. They were flat on top and curved on the bottom: they looked like little boats sailing across a placid sea. And her nose—the slope was not gradual at all but rather hasty. It had a big bump in it too. I put my hand on my chin to cover it because I knew how it stuck out.

"Fingers!" said the nice one. "Fingers must have tapered ends and be long and supple."

"Got that one." Shino had graceful long fingers. We all looked at them. They didn't seem enough somehow.

"The *yakko* will become more beautiful as she gets a little older," said Fumi.

"Not possible. Your basic face can't change."

"Yeah, but the rules c'n change. F'r instance, it used to be yur eyebrows had to be far apart, and now, it's easy to see, the most beautiful thing iz to have the eyebrows close together," continued the older courtesan. "We can pluck some and get them to grow t'wards each other. I've seen it done." She paused. "And yur face will grow into this nose."

Shino did not look hopeful.

"Wait. Doan give up," said Fumi. "Think of those hands."

Shino held up her hands. They looked very nice to me.

"They are large," said the courtesan dubiously. She bent a finger back. "But so flexible!"

"I play the samisen."

"And she makes paintings," I said. "She can write many Chinese characters too."

"There, already 'z better news! It's as Kana says—you have talents! We poor girls have no talent, nuthin'. Probly you write poetry?"

"I like to write down my thoughts . . ." Shino ventured shyly.

They all fell over laughing.

"Oh, no. No, no. No one wanz to hear a prostitute's thoughts."

Shino led me back to my father and let go of my hand. He was crouched as usual and chuckling to himself as he copied the antics of a trainer and his monkey with his darting brush.

"Go," she said, pushing me. "I will see you again soon."

"But, Shino," I whined loudly. I wanted to see my father's reaction when he knew she was near. And sure enough his head came up, his face coloured and softened. He put down his brush—he never did that for anyone else—and scrambled to his feet. He was barely taller than her, and while she made herself taller, like a sapling straining for sun, he made himself shorter, swaying and bending his knees.

"It is the beautiful *yakko* herself," he said. "She has kindly returned my daughter."

"She is much obliged to you for letting Ei entertain her in her quiet life," said Shino.

They both laughed softly. I could feel the currents running between them.

"I wonder if you would be walking on the boulevard some afternoon," he said, "and I could thank you properly."

She inclined her head just slightly. She seemed to think about this. "My time is not my own. But it is just possible I could find myself getting tea and treats for Fumi the day of the coming festival. She is very fond of the tea in that shop where we first met."

7

THE MAD POETS

IT WAS THE EIGHTH MONTH, and one of those warm days before the cold set in. The Mad Poets group sat on the bank above the Sumida. My father was there, with Tsutaya the publisher, Utamaro the artist, and a jack-of-all-trades writer called Sanba. Sanba had the best cosmetics store in Edo; he sold the white lead paint the actors put on their faces. That was handy because he wrote plays. He also wrote critiques of their performances. As well, just to keep it all going, he sold a popular elixir of immortality that he had invented. He made a lot of jokes and kept the others laughing. There was also Kyoden, author of yellow-back novels, which he sold along with smoking materials at his tobacco store. And Waki the tattooist, who now made beautiful little drawings and poems.

The courtesan Yuko carried a telescope; she kept lifting it to her eyes. It was trained on the distant racecourse at the edge of town. She murmured the name of the horse her lover had bet on. If it won, her lover would buy out her contract and free her. She believed that. She was silly and a bit pathetic but not a bad poet.

> Like a courtesan's
> vowels the green strands
> of a willow tree
> stretch out extra long.

It wasn't true what the brothel-keepers said: that people did not want to hear courtesans' thoughts. Courtesans were very stylish. All Edo was keen to know the details of their lives in the Yoshiwara. And everyone went there, even though it was forbidden. They came in disguise, people from all walks of life. The pleasure district was a great vat of soup that way, and even though the *bakufu* insisted that the higher classes disdain us, it turned out that the samurai wanted to mingle with merchants and their daughters found it exciting to sit down with peasants.

Because they were so strange, these proximities were titillating. Waki the tattooist sat beside Akemi, a merchant's daughter. Her father was paying the bill, which meant we had plenty to eat. Everyone was drinking wine from stemmed glasses, making like Europeans. They were planning their next publication: the poets would write and the artists would illustrate a book, which the publisher would print. It was all very convenient.

Below us in the riverbed were wide, dry spaces on either side of the water. A dance troupe had set down a mat, and the women were tuning up their instruments. Soon they would perform. From our position on the bank above we had a good view.

I rolled in the weeds listening to the cicadas and the crickets. Their lifetime was nearly over; soon cold would silence them. When anyone looked at me I crossed my eyes. That wasn't very often. The Mad Poets were completely involved with themselves, timid when sober but now drunk and boasting. The serving girls were about my age and didn't want to wait on me. The poems were always about sex. "More so than the maiden flower which is charming from the front I prefer the purple trouser plant best seen from the rear."

It was my father's verse that made the poets laugh: purple trouser plant, ha, ha. I laughed along with them.

Hokusai looked up as if he'd just remembered I was there. Did he think I was too young for little rhymes about woman-fleers? I made a face at him. Give me a break, Old Man. I heard this kind of stuff all the time. It was nothing to me.

He went back to his composition.

I decided to make a painting. I got a brush and paper and painted an inlet with a little sailboat crossing it. I wasn't very happy with it. Something was wrong with the distance and the shapes. I couldn't make it appear on paper the way it was in front of me. I took it across to my father, who showed me how to correct it. He sat up and paid attention then.

"Now make a poem that goes with it," he said.

I started writing something about the opening being narrow, and when they saw it they laughed even harder. Their minds are nowhere but in the gutter, and I told them so. "That's not what I meant," I said. "I am ten years old."

"You are ten years old when it suits you," my father said. "And when it suits you better, you are twenty."

I told him I had no idea what he meant, *izn it,* and he told me to stop talking like a courtesan; I certainly did have an idea what he meant. I said, in the voice of a nighthawk, "Hey, hey, Old Man. How about it?"

Everybody laughed. I felt pleased with myself.

"Has she no innocence, your daughter?" said one of them.

Hokusai just looked at me as if he was seeing someone new.

"Look at the beautiful hornets," said Sanba, adeptly diverting him. "Yellow and black, with such long legs. Watch they don't sting."

"Too bad we've already done a book about sex and insects."

"The book did well," murmured the publisher.

"Without me it would have been nothing."

"You are so arrogant, Utamaro, my friend."

"I am arrogant because I am the best."

"You're not the best. You're only the most expensive," said Tsutaya.

"Publishers who buy cheap get what they pay for: the books won't sell, and they'll go out of business." It was true; Utamaro was on top. No painter in Edo could touch him. The common people loved his paintings. The *bakufu* did too. Even the Shogun's women loved his paintings, so Shino said. My father tried some in his style, but if you asked me (which he didn't), no matter how good those were they were still nothing but imitations of Utamaro.

"You won't be the best forever; new artists are always coming up," mused somebody.

"You mean those idiots who peek out from behind every screen in every brothel? Who crawl the streets like ants?" the great man droned. "They try to make up for want of brush power by dressing up their models in gorgeous costumes with painted faces. Whereas if I do a simple ink sketch, with the power of my brush, what I create will live forever."

Downriver from us, a humped bridge with many feet, like a caterpillar, rose over the sluggish water. On the high point, you could just make out a thick, heavily clad figure on horseback in the midst of the men with their swords. A daimyo's retinue was crossing.

"Look who's coming."

Everyone looked. It was Sadanobu. Sad-and-Noble, they called him. Famous author of edicts. Hater of the Yoshiwara and our lifestyle. He who— in the storyteller's tale—punished the famous *yakko*. Was it our *yakko*? She wouldn't say.

"No matter. He's not important," said Utamaro breezily.

Sadanobu had been councillor because the Shogun was a child. Now the Shogun was grown up and had taken over. As it happened the Shogun was more corrupt than we ever were. Things were back to normal.

"He can't be ignored. He's still got power."

"I wonder what he does with his time?"

"Keeps busy with his martial arts. It fills the hours when he can't make rulings."

"If he makes more, so what? We'll break them. Look at how many times they've ruled that there will be no publication of news. Notice how often *Kawara-ban* comes out?"

The little broadsheet and the criers who ran ahead of it announcing news had somehow survived the crackdown.

"The *bakufu* are cats—just choosing their moment to pounce."

"I've been pounced on once," said Kyoden. "That's enough. Thereafter I became a mouse: obedient to the Way."

Sad-and-Noble's men had come to the tobacco store and bought a copy of his yellow-back novel about life in the pleasure district. The councillor had read it himself, they said. Then his men had come back and arrested Kyoden. Kyoden was the leader of the literary world. Sad-and-Noble decided to make an example of him. He was sent up to the White Sands for questioning, and his old father too.

He was charged with making *ukiyo-e* and depraved books.

Kyoden suffered his punishment of fines and manacles, and he became even more famous. His book disappeared for a while. Then it came back into print, even though the blocks had been burned. But he didn't write satirical books anymore. At least not very often.

"Obedient? Is that what you call it? Gutless is what it is. You make moral tracts," said Sanba, "and once in a blue moon pop out a racy little novelette. You can't have it both ways."

"Why not?" Kyoden was grinning. "Sad-and-Noble has it both ways."

"He's not so bad. He started a savings bank for the poor. And during the rice riots he released rice from the merchants' hoarding places. He was even lenient to those who'd been caught doing violence to their betters." Waki said that.

"He hates *us*, though."

"That's because he's jealous."

Yuko brought down her telescope. She pushed out her tiny red lips and breathed a mournful "who-who-who." Her lover's horse had not won the race. "My hopes are dashed."

The men sighed in mock dismay.

She brightened. "But maybe it's better this way. I will write a beautiful poem about it."

"I ask you, how do you live with yourself, writing that rot?" Utamaro demanded of Kyoden. "And then you marry those *shinzo*? Those little girls are not even legal in brothels!"

Laughter, and they all lay back on the hillside. They called themselves old men—Kyoden; Hokusai, who was fifty years now—but they didn't really mean they were old men. Only Utamaro truly *was* an old man. He had no wife.

"I marry them to save them from lives as courtesans," said Kyoden.

The two of them doubled up together.

"I mean it!"

"An act of charity it is not. You marry *shinzo* for two reasons. You lust after little girls," said Utamaro. "Then you pump them for information to use in your books."

Kyoden only laughed. "And you? Who do you lust for? Little boys?"

Utamaro just waved his hand. He did not deign to answer.

"I may be false to principles," said Kyoden, "and to most of my friends. But there is one thing I'm true to. I'm true to type. I'm an Edoite—just let me live one more day. I'll write to the *bakufu* tune. I'll write to sell. It's called the Way of Survival. When I have enough money, then I will write what I want to say."

"And when will that day come?"

"Maybe never. When do Edoites have enough money to buy back their virtue?"

"Good question; a purchase of that nature would be very expensive."

The Mad Poets chortled away, and wet their brushes, and wrote their verses. They knew everything. They had seen it or done it, or they knew someone who had done it, and it was all funny. They had high-flying opinions of themselves, and they never stopped trying to slice one another's kite strings in order to keep their own sailing highest.

"I feel for all men who cannot afford virtue," my father said.

They sniffed, suspicious that he was putting himself above them. He was painting a dead duck with an abalone shell. He never wanted to make the kind of pictures the others made.

"I suppose you can be sympathetic; you don't have much to lose," said Kyoden.

My father grinned amiably. "Not much to lose. That's the secret."

He wasn't the most popular artist in Edo, it was true. But he did sell his prints to the Dutch, and that made people jealous. It was impossible to insult my old man. He believed he would one day prove himself to be greater than all the others. So did I.

At the foot of the bridge, the ranks broke around Sad-and-Noble and he stopped. He seemed to be looking right down on us. The samurai milled around. There was some holdup with his horse. His foot must have been caught. Clumsily, he dismounted and began to walk in our direction.

"Speak of the devil!"

"Look at the has-been slumming it down here in the quarter!"

I agreed with those who said Utamaro was wrong. Sadanobu might no longer be senior councillor, but he would never lose power: his grandfather had been Shogun. They called him a hypocrite because he loved the brothels and the drinking life, even though he preached against them.

We stared as he loomed up. The tobacconist murmured, "I wonder if he's still reading my books."

Laughter broke out, and it carried in the air.

"No, he isn't," said Sanba. "He's going to bed early because he has to get up early to practise jujitsu with his sensei. That's before he delivers lectures on Confucian fealty. No time for reading."

"No more writing either, I guess."

"I really do wish I'd published that miserable little novel he wrote when I had the chance," murmured Tsutaya while they all watched the large, clumsy man. "You know he offered it to me? But he was just a sappy young lord who was going to inherit some faraway domain—who cared? I passed on it. Now I hear he's destroyed it."

"Don't believe it. No writer ever destroys his work. He's got a copy," said Kyoden. "A secret part of him believes it will be discovered one day, and he'll be seen as a genius."

"Probably the loyal retainer has it."

"I remember one line," said Tsutaya dreamily. "'The truth dawned on me: words of praise that had been showered on me were nothing but flattery from those who wanted my favour. I had neither talent nor good memory.'"

Everyone laughed. "He got that right."

Now Sadanobu was within earshot.

The Mad Poets all turned their backs and became fascinated with the troupe of dancers in the riverbed. I saw that Waki was trembling, and that sweat came from his temples.

We felt, rather than saw, Sadanobu stop. He was breathing heavily. He was big, and from the side he bulged like a pregnant woman.

"I have a message," he said. Nobody moved. "A message for the man called Utamaro."

"No such man here," Utamaro called out. "No such man at all. The artist of that name is an immortal."

More heavy silence.

"When you meet him next"—heavy irony here—"kindly tell him he should take care. He treads close to the line."

"Close to the line? With what?"

"His pictures of the courtesans. He makes their faces known, as if they were heroines of legend. As you all know, the brothel world brings shame on our realm. It has long been forbidden to put out pictures of these evils. He has been warned." The heavy man was out of breath.

No one said anything. The retainers folded Sad-and-Noble back in their midst and set off.

When the horses' hoofs could no longer be heard, the laughter began.

"You see?" Utamaro preened. "I am the best. That proves it."

No one rose to the bait. The wine was gone. A chill rose from the grass. I felt it through my kimono. The waitress kneeled on the bank picking up glasses. The birds pipped; it was dusk. A sadness welled. Yuko sat with her hands folded in her lap, with no expression on her face. Only Utamaro went on.

"Let him say what he wants. I know I'm safe. I've been painting these women for how many years? So many. And never been touched. Kyoden was arrested because he used words. Words are flagrant and can't be ignored. But pictures," Utamaro was saying, as we all packed up, "pictures can be as I please. Strictly speaking, they are forbidden, but that means nothing when it is a question of greatness."

"Bring your picture, Ei," said my father gently. He lifted it and looked at it carefully. "It's not so very bad. We might be able to put it in the book."

I SAT WITH SHINO IN HER ROOM, making characters with brush and ink. She was heating water for tea on the small grill. She was a proper courtesan now. She'd debuted and had her own clients. Her contract would have been up, but she had debts and she had to work until she paid them off. No matter how careful a courtesan was, the debt built up and ate the earnings. She was always tired, but she tried to teach me manners. Right now she was telling me not to peek around the screen that divided her room from Fumi's. But I was doing it.

I saw Fumi's bare back. I saw fat fingers parting the hair on her beautiful nape and beginning to knead her flesh. She had called in the masseur. It was the blind man I had often seen in the crowds watching the courtesans' parade. I poked my head farther in. His pear-shaped face wore an expression of rapture. I doubted it was because of her matted and stiff hair or her thin shoulders. I doubted it was even her smell.

"Ei, away from there," Shino hissed. "Here—tea! Sit and we will have conversation."

I withdrew and sat squinting though the crack. The blind man's backside looked like a big sack of rice and his fingers were pale parsnips. His white eyes rolled up. He smiled as he heard Shino, confirming my suspicions. However softly she spoke to me, her voice caused that look to drift across his otherwise remote face.

His hands moved down the senior courtesan's spine. Fumi grunted. He pushed his thumbs in between the bones. She made a soft moan. Shino pulled me away. We sat across from each other with our teacups while she tried to lead me in a polite exchange: it was her mission to teach me charm.

"The cup of tea is so very warm in my hands and helps to keep the cold at bay."

"It does, and so does your smile on a winter afternoon," I answered automatically. I added, "I hate the blind man."

"You will regret that. The gods do not smile on those who despise the afflicted."

I could have argued that I didn't hate all blind men, only this one. He was trying to steal her. Shino belonged to my father, even though he could not pay to be her client. And to me. I knew they met. I didn't know how or where; they were secretive. But she was right that I regretted my hatred. It was so fierce and hot it had drawn him here. It was like a branding iron, which, as it hissed, clamped to its target.

His footfall came from the corridor.

"Where is the *yakko*?" he said, though he knew. His voice was penetrating, making up for his blank eyes. "I have something for her."

Shino gave me a glance. She tucked her heels under her hips and rose, with perfect grace, opening our screen. He pulled a sack from his backpack. "It would please me if you would take this and prepare yourself a meal," he said.

"You are kind," Shino said, "but it is quite impossible for me to take a gift."

"It's a fish," he said.

I heard a giggle come from behind the screens. I knew what the other girls would be saying: "Hear that? He brought a *fish*!"

Little whoops of merriment echoed down the hall.

"Smelly, *izn it?*"

"He'z in luv . . . He wants her, *izn it?*"

He heard, of course. He was blind, not deaf. The mockery made Shino even more polite.

"It is so considerate of you," Shino said. "A fish is the one thing I could not refuse. If I had a place to cook it. But alas I do not . . ."

"You will find someone to cook it for you." He thrust the packet at her and she took it from his hands, bowing low, although he could not see.

He stumped along the corridor and felt his way down the stairs, hilarity following.

"You can'd cook that thing in yur room! Id'll stink, wone it?" some girl shouted through the wall.

Shino professed delight with her gift. Then she presented it to me.

"Take it home. Your mother will prepare it."

"I *wone* eet' id, 'cause it came from *that*." I knew it infuriated her when I talked brothel talk.

I took the damned fish and put on my padded jacket. We went into the hall. In the next room two *shinzo* were playing a game of cards. A man emerged from a closed screen at the far end.

"Who's that?" I was curious about everyone here.

"A publisher's censor, a *gyoji*," said Shino.

I hadn't seen one before, had only heard of them. The *gyoji* turned his head as he descended the staircase. He had a small beard. Government men usually had small beards. He hadn't even tried to disguise himself.

"He's a spy!" I said.

"You're so harsh!" chided Shino. "Have compassion. He used to sell prints from under the counter, but now he has to inspect them. He had no choice. We all live in the same world. We do the best we can."

"I am too harsh, but you are not harsh enough." Then I relented: "You're tired."

She cast me a reproving look. "You yourself must become very tired, with such passions."

"Okay, then, what *is* he doing here?"

"The same thing the others are doing."

"He is our enemy and a spy for the *bakufu*—and he also patronizes the brothels?"

Her face got that infuriating look of amusement, the one she often got when I—or my father—was most aroused by injustice. "Look at it another way. How can he be a censor of the art of the brothels if he hasn't visited one?"

"My father hates *gyoji*," I said.

"Ah," said Shino, "but he is harsh too. And no excuses for him: he should understand life more than you do."

Shino ruffled my hair.

"A *gyoji* is simply a man. A man in fear like all the rest. He is forced by fear to be a spy. If, even while he's inspecting pictures, he's making an assignation with a courtesan," said Shino, "he sees no conflict. In fact he sees a continuity between the two. He has his feet in two rivers."

"One flows one way, and the other, the other!" I pressed one leg forward and the other back until I toppled sideways against the wall. A petulant female voice rose up complaining. They lived in a house of paper. I picked myself up. "Stupid way to stand."

"He must be careful or the current will take him, true," said Shino. "But we are all forced into difficult positions."

"You aren't. You are good."

"How can I be good?" Shino laughed softly. "I am a courtesan."

"The pictures are beautiful. If I was in charge, I would want pictures made."

"But if you were the powerful, you would not see things the same way the artists do. You might suspect that the pictures told stories against you and your ways."

"A picture can't do any harm. It's not like a man with a sword."

"Is that what you think?" She shook her head. "Then they are smarter than you are."

"To be afraid of a picture?"

"Oh, yes." She had walked me to the door. She was making me leave.

"What can a picture do?" I said, to keep her.

"You are asking me to think as they do," said Shino, exasperated. "I can only guess. Perhaps they are frightened not of the picture itself but of the thoughts it gives rise to."

"Thoughts are invisible, like ghosts," I said. "They can go anywhere. They won't be stopped by men with little beards."

"Maybe not, but men with little beards will still try. Ghosts, and thoughts, seep in, and before you know it people lose respect."

"People laugh at Hokusai."

"Yes, and he wants them to. Perhaps laughter will get him through."

"He will get through because he is stronger than the *bakufu*."

Shino put her finger on my mouth. "You are passionate, child. But you are foolish. I know this trait, because I was that way not so long ago. And look what happened to me!" She gave that light laugh.

"My father fears no one, especially not the *bakufu*."

"You can't say such a thing."

"My father says it."

"Your father also is unwise," she said firmly. "Before, he could get away with his crazy ways because he was not very popular. Now his name is growing. Everyone knows it. The *bakufu* choose whom they punish. Always it is the most famous."

"He says we'll leave Edo."

She seemed to brighten. "He's not at home in the licensed quarters. Not anymore. And you shouldn't be either."

"Wouldn't you be sad? If we left Edo?" I watched her face for signs and saw nothing. "Who do you love more, me or my father?"

That made her laugh. "You're too bold. You speak of adult matters."

"Tell me."

"I'll tell you this much: he asks me the same thing." Then she looked embarrassed. Her low-lidded eyes went blacker than normal, and her narrow chin ducked into her kimono. She drew in her lips, and the long tip of her nose dipped modestly. She reached up a hand to her heavy topknot, as if it too were destabilized.

As good as an admission.

"If we had money we could pay your debts and buy your freedom," I said. I said it without thinking.

She chided me gently. "Your father has a wife and you have a mother."

"But he doesn't have a courtesan—except you."

"He can't afford a courtesan, not even a plain one like me!" She laughed. "I won't be leaving the Yoshiwara anytime soon."

"Unless a man buys your freedom."

"He would have to be a wealthy man. And a wealthy man would have his pick. He wouldn't want me."

The blind man's bland, attuned face swam into my mind. But I knew he was not wealthy, so I was relieved.

I took the fish to the painting room my father rented sometimes in the temple, when we had lots of work to do. The apprentices were busy. I put it on the hibachi. Its skin frizzed up nastily and stuck to the grill. Its flesh fell off the bones into the fire. The apprentices laughed at me. I was hungry then. I was left with a skeleton of many tiny bones, each one of which could catch in the throat and choke me.

I decided I was not a cook.

8

The Dancing Lesson

IT WAS THAT DAY OF THE MONTH when the prostitutes had free run of the kitchen. Kana was out; she wouldn't sit with them, she said, and watch them stuff themselves.

The girls dug in.

"Thaz *rich*. She's already fat, and we're so skinny. *She* duzn like to see *us* eat?"

"Oooh, passa tofu."

"Doan take it *all,* hey."

"I wone, I wone, just one more . . . oooh."

There had been a fight in the brothel the night before. Yuko was holding a cold cloth over her swollen jaw.

"Can yu b'leeve this guy? He wuz such a *yob*. I wannud to throw him out, but I wuzen strong enuff. I mean why'd they let this todal *yobbo* in here? I told him if he didn' stop pushing me I'd get Jimi to come. But he woodn *lissen*. An' I had *nuthe*n to threaten him with."

"You need somethin' hard or sharp, or poinned."

"They woodn let us have stuff like that in here."

"I spose yu culd use yur meer?" said one of them, sucking a finger.

"My meer? But whud 'f I broke it?"

"Then yu cdn see yourself."

"Whud a relief!"

Yuko dove across the table and slapped her. "Very funny!" she said, putting the compress back on her chin.

"At home," Shino said slowly, "we were all taught to defend ourselves. My brothers as young as ten had swords. Women were taught also, just in case."

"In case what?"

"We might be attacked by a friend who suddenly became an enemy. We might be accused of disloyalty and have to kill ourselves. My father said we should know how to kill even a friend who was seated having tea or walking with us. There were special *kata* for these times."

"What were they called?" said dreamy Yuko.

"Oh, let's see: Rain and Thunder, the Monk's Walk, and Walking Talking Between Friends."

"Didja have a sword?"

"I had a long pole with a blade on the end, yes. My *naginata*. But now"—she gestured towards the Great Gate—"Shirobei's got it. Anyway, you don't really need a sword. You can use almost anything to defend your honour—a cooking pot, even."

They all laughed like crazy.

Shino reached into her hair and pulled out her metal *bin-sashi*. She held them up in front of her face: "You could even use your hairpins."

"Ooooh!"

She jabbed with them in the direction of one girl's eyes. "Go away! Hssss!" She feinted and jabbed again. The girls looked blank. Then they looked impressed.

"Sort of like that," Shino murmured sweetly, putting the pins back into her hair.

But Yuko got a glimmer in her eye.

"That's *wizard* . . . Can you teach me?"

They were drunk on food. That's how it started. They went up to their rooms and pulled the pins out of their coifs. Rolls and rolls of straight, black, oiled hair fell on their necks. *Bin-sashi* were about ten inches long and came to a long, sharp point. The higher ranked the courtesan, the more she had. Shino had six now. Fumi had eight. On days when she was dressed up, they were all in her hair. Shino's were lacquered red; she had a taste for pretty things and she had bought them, adding to her debt.

I had none and had to borrow. The thing was long and thin in my hand. It was not heavy or strong but very sharp.

"This is a *feebul* weapon."

"You think?" Shino said.

The first thing she taught us was how to pull out our hairpins swiftly and subtly. You did this crosswise, the right hand pulling the pin from the left side of the head and the left hand pulling the pin from the right side of the head. You did it simply, with no extra movement, quickly removing the pin from the hair and sliding it up the sleeve, turning the wrist; you swept it across your face with conviction. This could be mistaken for a gesture of vanity. That was the point.

We practised. Shino showed us how to keep strong but flexible fingers. She moved her pins in circles. It was easy to imagine them as small knives, for instance.

"We could do a dance with them," she said.

She held one in each hand. She walked around in a circle, dipped, went backwards. "Always keep them up close around your faces," she instructed.

Fumi was laughing.

"Close to your face. It's no good out there."

"We shuddn cover our faces. Our arms should only be a frame to them. Remember what Kana says? 'The face is a picture to be seen and enjoyed.'"

"Just so. But if you don't protect it you'll get hurt!"

That made sense to them. "Remember when that yobbo broke Takao's nose?"

"An' after, it didn' heal straight? An' she hadda go home?"

"He said he was sleeping when he did it. Just rolled over and cracked her on the bridge of her nose."

"I never believed that," said Shino softly.

She showed each of us how to hold a hairpin so it lay inside the palm of our hand and extended underneath a finger, almost invisible. She showed us each how to walk slowly around in a circle, preparing our weapon, sliding it into our palm. To cross our arms and shoot a fist each way—a block. To strike a balance on one foot with the other tucked behind the knee. This was called the Crane.

"This my father taught me. He never imagined where I'd find those lessons useful," she said sadly. She showed us how to lunge forward with our hands out front and jab the hairpins into an ear, or both ears, one on either side. "It is not necessary that we ever turn our skills on anyone. Just to have them makes us feel stronger, izn it? Only to save your own life," she said.

The women loved it when she used their talk.

We were all together making circles with our hands, circling, dipping, rising from and sinking gracefully, we hoped, to our knees.

Kana came in.

"*Whatz* going on here?"

Shino did not lose a step or a breath. She expertly slid her hairpin inside the palm of her hand and up her sleeve.

Fumi slid the pins back into her hair and smoothed it.

I found that my obi was coming loose and was suddenly involved in the knot.

"I am just teaching the girls a little dance my mother taught me. It is what the noble girls do on festival days."

Kana loved to hear about what the nobles did. And if the girls at the Corner Tamaya knew a certain dance, it meant they could raise the fees. "It's about time you came around," she told Shino, patting her shoulder. "I am so pleezed," she said emphatically, and she walked back downstairs.

Officially sanctioned, we began to practise in earnest, stepping quietly, neatly, one foot just a little way in front of the other, in a tight circle, the way Shino showed us.

"We should do that three times a week. That way we can improve," Shino said, remembering her sensei.

I continued walking like a tiger on delicate feet but placing each one firmly down so I could not be pushed off balance. We all began to do this and there was excitement in the room. The very idea of defending themselves made the girls dizzy.

Shino could remove her hairpins in a swift gesture, turn her head so the elegant nape of her neck showed to her opponent, who was no doubt so captivated with her grace that he did not know a weapon was being pulled on him, and turn again, wielding the pins at eye level.

"Practise hiding your pins in the folds of your kimono, with the sharp tip braced under your middle finger. When you've got that, I'll show you how to shift the hairpin along so its end protrudes just so"—she put it out a lethal four inches—"beyond your fingertip."

When we could do that we practised moving our hands in circles at our chests, our sleeves falling back from the wrist. It appeared to be a dance, but it was a block; firm arms protected our chests, and the sharp tips of the hairpins were ready to shoot for an eye socket.

"Yu c'n do *sum* damage with theez," said Yuko approvingly.

Shino watched us, a sad pride on her face. "As a girl I excelled at this. My father wanted me to protect my honour. Then he let me be sentenced for damage to his own."

Her hair was in damp wisps beside her temples. Our laughter stopped.

"Perhaps the lesson has gone on long enough."

Later, as we stepped out into the verandah, Shino got the nod from Kana. "Helping the other girls develop grace is good."

"Oh, yes," said Shino. "I can do it often if it pleases you," she murmured in her best submissive voice.

As I left I heard Kana tell the younger girls: "If you learn to move gracefully, as Shino does, you will be so alluring to your customers that I'm sure you can pay your debt more quickly."

9

GOODBYE

IT WAS THE NEW YEAR'S PUBLISHING PARTY in the *ageya*. The walls were hung with red-and-yellow banners announcing the new titles in big black characters. Everyone was there—booksellers, artists, publishers, courtesans and clients—in clouds of smoke. The sleek brothel-owners stood at the back. The massive blind man was there, his head above the crowd. I pushed past prostitutes whining for drinks, coming up against cut-off strands of conversation. I was lost in chests and waists, pushing people away so I could stay near my father.

"He's a straw man and he will get his throat cut!"

"What are the numbers? Don't tell me stories—"

Onstage Utamaro was showing his Big Heads. Here was one of a famous beauty. She could not be named; it was forbidden by Sadanobu's new edict. But Utamaro had found a way around that. Her father had a company that made rice crackers. On the ground beside her sad oval face, as white as the side of the moon, lay a sack with the words "Famous Rice Crackers" on it.

"Each woman is a type. Her character is evident from the shape of her face and the way her features sit in it. This one is a flirt. This one is a quiet type." He pointed to his works along the walls. "Now the edicts say they are 'too conspicuous.' What does that mean? Are the *bakufu* art critics now? Too conspicuous for what?"

"For your own good, Utamaro!" jibed an onlooker.

"I take it as a compliment that my Big Heads are conspicuous." Utamaro held his hand in a fist with the thumb sticking up. He jabbed this thumb into his breastbone.

A voice came from a bearded man in the back. "Do you think this beauty is a person of note?" Spies haunted every gathering.

"Yes," said Utamaro.

"She is not. She is evil. She is temptation. Whether she is a courtesan or not. She is a walking cadaver. Beauties should be permitted in pictures merely to show how a man can lose his way and die."

"We are all dying!" shouted Utamaro. "That is the sadness of existence. I have shown it in my—"

The bearded man pushed his table away and left.

I reached my father's side. The *ageya* manager, Etako, pushed her dogface into mine. "You brought the little girl to an evening of drinking and coarse humour? Shame on you!" she said to Hokusai.

But Hokusai had no shame. "I am a family man, you know that." He grinned. Then he disappeared again.

Here instead was one of his friends. He had been at the Mad Poets picnic. It was the writer of satires who supported his work by running a cosmetics shop, Sanba. He bent to my level.

"Good evening, young lady."

I turned my head quickly to acknowledge him and then looked away. I was concerned about my father. Everyone was laughing now; Hokusai had climbed onstage and was capering around.

"Will he get in trouble?" I said.

"Not if he behaves himself," he said.

I hissed. He never did, especially not when he ought to.

Sanba pushed me to the front so I could see.

My father was showing off his new book, called *Tactics of General Firebox*. He had made the pictures and written the words. "In the far province of the west there is a great lord named Big Heart, having a revenue of a million tons of rice. His name is Lord Disorder. He loves all those things that give pleasure . . ."

Here he drew his hands in a curving manner, like a river flowing downstream alongside his body. He turned himself to face the back wall so he was visible in profile. He drew the curve out in front of himself, a sad bulge below the waist, a wide, flat chest, and a hard, dull profile.

I recognized the shape. It was Sad-and-Noble, the fat daimyo who had passed by us with his retinue as we sat by the Sumida. The room grew quiet. People shifted away from their neighbours. The men with little beards began to look extremely interested.

"And he loved sake," Hokusai read on. "Not content with the pleasure of hunting in the mountains or fishing in the sea, he amused himself by making men swim with heavy stones attached to their bodies, or making them run with naked feet on ice."

I could feel the tension in the room.

"That's enough, Hokusai," said Sanba. But that only encouraged my father.

Timid Waki inched up to the stage and took him by the arm. Hokusai shrugged him off and kept reading.

"Lord Disorder dressed his entourage in hot clothes in summer and thin fabric in winter." He shouted now, "Silver and gold were in his hands, like water in a river . . ."

Waki looked for help. He found it in the big blind man. The masseur stepped up and, reaching in his general direction, caught my father by the scruff of the neck. My father kept reading.

Sometimes a child can do things a man cannot. "Hokusai!" I said, in my best *yakko* voice. "What a shame it would be if you gave away the ending."

Hokusai turned sharply to me—I think I fooled him with my voices, for once—and the break was enough for the blind man to bundle him out of the light.

Waki returned to speak to the crowd. "Hokusai cannot read anymore. I am so very sorry. His words don't make any sense; no one would understand."

My father had vanished. I sat outside, swinging my feet and looking at the moon.

"It is late," said Sanba, coming up behind me. "Are you tired?"

"No."

"Is there someone who can take you home?" he said.

"Shino will come if she can."

"Shino? And take you where?"

"Back to the Corner Tamaya."

Sanba whistled. "You are very sophisticated. For a ten-year-old."

"I am twelve now." I said it scornfully, but I was pleased. No one had called me sophisticated before.

"Do you go to school?"

"My sisters go to the temple, where the priests teach them. But I—" I looked down in a show of modesty.

"You don't go with them?"

"I already know a lot of characters. And Shino teaches me."

"Impressive," he said. He was staring.

I know why he was curious: my frame was small and undeveloped; I had no softness. I was still taken for a child though I felt quite old.

"And if Shino cannot come?"

"She will come." It must have been the Hour of the Ox by then. "Unless she is engaged."

"Something may have come up," he said. He smirked.

I scowled. These jokes were so tiresome. I knew her work. It was no laughing matter. He looked repentant.

"Shall I wait with you until your father comes?" said Sanba.

"No." I stood disdainfully and went back inside the *ageya*.

In the back rows, the artists were talking about my father.

"Hokusai is pushing his luck. What has he done this for?"

"He's not usually so brave."

"He's a copycat. He copies Utamaro."

"He copies anyone and anything."

"He has a flair, that's it."

"Simply a flair. People notice him."

"Yes, except for the *bakufu*. They don't notice him."

"That's what he wants. To be noticed."

"He will be. And not in a good way. You wait. The worst is that he sells his prints outside the country."

"I wonder how he got *that* gig? No matter. They'll get him for it."

I went outside. I stood in shadow between the ovals of lantern light spilling on the outside wall of the *ageya*. I hoped I was invisible.

At first I thought about the blind masseur who visited the Corner Tamaya and gave Shino fish. I never hid my dislike of him. But he had saved my father from making bigger mistakes than usual by dragging him off the stage.

Why did he do that? He couldn't have been a fan of his art. It must have been for Shino. So the blind man must have known that my father was important to Shino. How important? What did he know? Did he know me?

A kind act from this loathsome man could only be explained by one thing: he loved her. So much, even, that he looked out for his rival?

I did not understand love. Apart from my mother, who had no time for me, prostitutes and artists were the adults I knew. For them, everything was backwards. Duty filled their day, and love was what they bought when they had money. Many wished for the opposite to be true. Shino was sad, but she had hope. She would pay her debt. Others seemed to enjoy the backwards life and just went on and on.

Hokusai, although a man and technically free, was imprisoned too. I knew he loved our thin, goose-necked, long-nosed, sad-faced girl-woman. I loved her too. But he could not have her. It wasn't because he had a wife. It was because he did not have money. He earned money, sometimes, but it flew out of our hands; I did not know how. Had Hokusai given up? Is that why he pretended to be carefree? Had Shino accepted it too? Maybe my father was not a rival to the blind man. Maybe—awful thought—the blind man felt sorry for my father. Maybe he had the compassion that Shino always said I lacked.

Hokusai would never truly accept the backwards rules of love, I thought. Hokusai couldn't do that. He was restless.

And restless was dangerous.

I shifted farther from the door to the *ageya*, passing the well of light, finding the next patch of darkness. My father could not accept rules. One day he would get too tired to pretend, and he would go mad and break all the rules. Perhaps even today.

I was cold. The new year should bring spring. But this one had come with snow on pine branches and glitter ice underfoot. The moat winked in the darkness between the rows of brothels. It was a deep blue, almost black: the lamplight did not reach the water. There was a narrow curve of moon above it. And as I stared I realized that I had found my father. He was sitting in the fork of a tree.

He looked small, like a boy who could no longer stand all his friends' bullying. He was yearning towards the dark, towards the place where it was silent, where no voice baited him. I started towards him and then stopped. That man Sanba was in my path.

"What do you suppose Hokusai is doing?"

"He's worshipping," I said.

"The moon?"

"No, the North Star. Myoken. The writers' star. The star of the brush. It is one of the seven stars that make the Great Dipper. There." I whispered, pointed, then I saw that he knew; he was teasing me.

"I didn't know your father was a worshipping man."

"Of course he is. We go often to his temple at Yanagishima in Honjo, where he was born," I said, amused that Sanba would not know so obvious a thing.

Away from the row of lanterns the stars became brighter. There was smoke in the air; they did not hold still. They were intense, but they flickered. They were covered. Then, in a moment of clear air, they emerged overhead in waves and currents, like graceful brush strokes of light through the dark sky.

He caught my hand. "Let's not disturb him," said Sanba. "It's a good hiding place."

But I wanted to.

"Father!" I said. "Old Man!"

"Hey, you. Oooo-eei," he replied, without surprise, or regret that he had left me, and without turning his head. "Come and look."

I loosened Sanba's hand. "Thank you," I said. "You can go now."

I climbed the tree and tucked myself in at the Old Man's side. We stared at the dark sky as the night went on.

I was a ghoulish child. It was the company I kept. But I was not gloomy; it was a glittery, feverish fascination with ghosts I had. I watched everyone flirt with death. I was always excited. I was difficult to tame; my spirits were high.

But that night of the new year I was wary.

I searched for one beautiful thing on which to focus my mind. And I could find nothing. Not the cherry blossoms on the boulevard—they were planted only for their blooming season, and then they were ripped out. I bled for those trees, that they could not put down roots. The yellow flowers too were hastened into bloom. Soon after, their thin stalks collapsed and they died.

Not Shino's long, inquisitive face and fluting voice: no, now when I saw her face I thought of her in the Hour of the Ox, when she rose from her mattress, dark circles under her eyes, a washboard of bones visible on her chest where the kimono fell open, holding a lighted taper.

"Tie up your kimono," I would whisper. "You look so cold."

Her chin drooped and her hair overwhelmed its spiky pins and pulled to the side of her head. Her red undergarments showed around her ankles. If I showed pity it made her angry.

"You are not allowed to show pity! And not even to feel it," she chided me.

My father said I was not to feel fear, and she said I should not pity: what could I feel, then? Anger. I felt it, but I could not hold on to it. If I felt nothing, what did that make me? A ghost?

This thought was agitating, and I twisted away from it, nearly falling from the crotch of our tree. Then I found it interesting and tried to get it back.

Perhaps I really was a ghost. How long had I been one? Who else was a ghost? Was my father? He was angry, yes, as he'd showed tonight, but his anger died. Then he was sad. Was it because he made things beautiful that were not, in truth, beautiful? And he did it so well! Beauty that pulled at the cords of the heart, the cords that ran down the back of the throat, beneath words, beyond words, straight to tears. That beauty owned him. It replaced flesh and blood. He would deny all of us and himself to serve that beauty.

I had always known it. I had learned in his arms. This art and the need to make it was stronger than love. But each time I saw the God of Art win, I had to learn again. And painfully.

Myoken was his master. His master said he need not eat when others ate. He need not sleep when they slept. He need not paint what other people wanted. He must paint what he was driven to paint. He must not perform the act of creation strictly for money, or for our convenience. He must dance to the master's tune.

And for all that, for all his laughing and carrying on while he did it, he never seemed to find pleasure.

I fell asleep leaning into my father's side.

Sanba was standing under us.

"Hokusai, it would be good for you to disappear for a time. Utamaro has been arrested."

My father's arm tightened on me. He was silent for a minute. Then he called down, "So you tell me. And do you know what I answer? I feel for my friend. But how can I disappear? I am not a spirit, nor a demon! I am flesh and blood."

Sanba gave a short, sharp laugh. "I think you will find a way, if you want to stay alive."

We went to Shino's house. It was early morning. The customers were gone and the girls asleep. Kana let us in, even though she was not supposed to. We slept there, in Shino's room. Days were quiet in the green houses. Kana was kind, but she said we had to be out by the Hour of the Sheep.

Shino came to the door with us. I saw her put her foot into her sandal, and as she did so I saw my father doing the same. For some reason the sight made me want to cry. Her small, delicate foot, a servant of other people's desires. His callused, dry, and thick foot, ready for the roads. My stomach rose up and I was sick.

Shino cleaned me up. "I don't want to leave," I whispered to her.

Why was it, for me, so sweet within the thin walls of the bordello? The sadness spoke to me and piled up the woes of the courtesans with their foolish grace. It was like sour plums I could lick and lick, tasting salty and sweet. It made your mouth raw, but you came to crave it.

It was late afternoon and the crowds were building. "Go to Waki's tattoo shop. He will be frightened, but he will let you in. Stay there while the streets are full of people. Make sure Hokusai leaves Edo before dawn," she told me.

"What about me?"

"Maybe you too. You and your father can both disappear for a while."

My father was quiet, for once. He stumbled, holding me with one hand and Shino with the other.

We said goodbye.

We slept in the back of Waki's shop and were up at dawn. The vomiting, the drunken songs, and the pleading of the small hours had barely died away. Only labourers rose at this time. The cleaners of the night soil had only just departed. The cats, my friends, were fighting over fishbones thrown out the kitchen doors of the brothels, but except for them, the street was empty. Waki had some money that the Mad Poets had collected.

"I'll drop it by the jail for Utamaro," said my father.

"You're crazy. They'll be looking for you."

"No, they won't. Not at the jail. It's the one place they won't dream of finding me."

Waki and my father laughed then, arms on each other's shoulders. Hokusai and I walked the length of the street. A tipsy samurai went into the house of straw hats and returned the one that had hidden his face. A child followed him. It was the job of this child to convince the samurai that the amount of change he was handed back from the merchant who had rented him the hat was too small for him to be concerned about. He should leave it to the hat renter, who would share it with the child, who would return a share to the courtesan, who would pay it out in tips to the *yarite* and the food provider. I knew all that—knew how money and much else flowed in this world—and it made me happy to understand.

At the Gate, Shirobei retrieved the man's swords. Then, hatless, momentarily recognizable to anyone, the samurai moved quickly to the top of the bridge and over the hump. The brown-skinned men with brooms followed, disappearing over the hump of the bridge. And we too followed in the wet streak their cleaning had left.

We humans are like snakes, boneless. We glide along on the earth, our scales rustling in the grass. We shrug off that skin, coming out green and new. Again and again we do this. Because of these sheddings, there is no sequence. You are a child and then a dried, wrinkled old woman, then a child again, then worn to ancientness, and then once again renewed. Your life can move two ways at once, as you grow old and grow young, folding back on itself and running alongside in the opposite direction. The snake may look as if it is not moving, but it is. All parts of it are equal. All parts of it are present. Life seems flat, ordinary. But a few moments of your childhood, or a few days, will be imprinted and stay with you in every detail, every year, reappearing in that new or lasting in that old skin, forever.

Sometimes the world or time itself goes quiet in honour of some change of state. This was the case now; it was the beginning of the end of my childhood. Dawn waited as we walked. I looked back. My father did not.

Part 2

10

To the Sea

FOR TWO HOURS AFTER WE SAID GOODBYE to Shino, my father and I walked in silence towards the eastern edge of Edo. Then we came to the jailhouse at Nihonbashi, surrounded by its moat and thick wall. The wall was topped with metal spikes that pointed inward. It was as if some entertainment was to take place there; families and friends of prisoners were lined up by the gate, and vendors sold rice balls and tea.

"Such a popular place. Look at everyone trying to get in," said Hokusai.

Over the walls we heard bravado shouts like the ones you heard outside the kabuki theatre from actor-warriors. This was correct behaviour. No one cried in pain, although there were muffled thumps. No one screamed in fear when led away. Everyone knew that.

We stood in the line and asked to see Utamaro. I was feeling fear, that forbidden thing. My father was not so brave either, but he was angry, which gave him strength. He was right, and Shino, Sanba, and the others were wrong: no one was looking for Hokusai here; the *bakufu* weren't interested in him. Not yet. They had the famous one. We were able to talk to him, on the other side of the high window in the holding cell. We brought the money that the others had collected.

"Are you there?" said my father. "How are you?"

"How do you think?" came the outraged voice. "The cell is cold and airless, and it stinks. This place is full of criminals."

"Well, it's a jail," said Hokusai.

"I never imagined. They charge you money for everything, even for a little space to sit, even to move away from the piles of shit."

"We gave money to the outcast in your name."

He grunted.

"You will get out."

Then Utamaro said, "The only things that escape from prison, besides farts, are tears."

We laughed and nodded, unseen by Utamaro, on the other side of the wall. This too was appropriate behaviour under the circumstances: to make a joke.

Utamaro went on, "There's nothing of beauty here."

"Ah," said my father, "I am sorry." I suspect he felt pity then, that other emotion we were not allowed because it took away from the pride of the one who was pitied. I stifled mine. But it was strange to hear Utamaro talking that way, his voice fluting up from the cesspool on the other side of the wall.

"Don't be sorry. In a strange way it is restful. There is nothing I care about."

"People say you'll be released before long. You're being made an example of, that is what they say."

"Of course, it's what I expected. I am the best."

"Yes," my father agreed. "You are the best."

"They will punish me so the rest of the artists can see. Probably I will have to live on as an example of one who has been dealt with."

My father and I walked on. He held me by the hand. "We're getting out of here. We're going to the sea," he said.

We came to the Punishment Grounds on the edge of town. The smell of death hung over them. The tattered bodies on stakes were not recognizable as human anymore. One had been pulled down by the dogs that gathered here; they were fighting over it. In the dirt there were some heads too, which I could hardly recognize because the crows had been at them. More corpses were coming in: we saw the outcasts carrying heads on a pole.

"Pickled in salt," said my father, "so they don't escape the punishment that comes after death. Do you understand? The *bakufu* preserve them first so we can all see the criminals rot here." He loved to tell me these details. "But you don't need to look."

"Of course I'm going to look if you keep telling me!" I knew pickled plums. But pickled heads? Were they also sweet and sour? Certainly they were wrinkled.

The walls of the High City dwindled behind us while the splendid white cone of Mt. Fuji winked ahead. We were now on the Tokaido, the road to Kyoto. It took us past the Ichibee bookstore. This was a favourite place of the Dutch scholars, the *rangaku-sha*. Hokusai knew the owner, and we went in. The bookseller gave us tea, and we rested. Then we looked at the books for sale. There were many guidebooks and pictures of famous places along the big roads of our country.

"Who is buying these?" my father said.

"Pilgrims. Everyone is a pilgrim now. They come in pairs and in dozens. At certain seasons they come in armies. They're going to Ise or all the way to Fuji-san. That's why we moved our store out here."

"Such an outpouring of religious feeling," murmured Hokusai. He fingered a booklet with pictures of the two rocks at Ise that were said to be married. They were tied together with twine. There were prints of fields and wide marshes full of grass and open hillsides. There was also a picture of a cozy inn along the way to Ise. Two beautiful women stood in front of it.

The bookseller burst out laughing.

"On the way, perhaps. But on the way back the pilgrims are carousing and fornicating and committing every sin on the list. They've been washed clean by their visit—might as well start over." He shook his head. "My wife wants to go on one. I tell her, 'Would I let you? Are you crazy?' Not with what I've seen! People just want to be on the road. Any road, going anywhere."

My father picked up one book after another.

"Famous places," he said slowly. "Not famous faces. That's what they want to see now." He had a look that I knew, the look of an idea dawning.

Then he said, "We're going out of the city ourselves. As far as Uraga."

"You know you cannot take her."

"Why not?"

"No women allowed out of Edo."

"She's not a woman. She's a child."

"A *female* child."

My father looked at me; this idea had not crossed his mind. I was afraid he'd send me back. "I suppose. But she's my helper."

"Do you have to get out?" said the bookseller. "Is it so important?"

"Maybe yes, maybe no. Have you seen my new book, about General Disorder?"

The bookseller said nothing more. He led us out the back of the store, crossing the little courtyard to his house. He told us to wait in his tearoom. When he came back, he had a set of boy's clothes and a pair of scissors.

I screamed when they let down my hair and cut it ragged over my ears and brow. It stuck up from the top of my head like a wiry brush. But I was happy to take off my kimono, which was dirty and binding. The boy's pants were loose at the knees but narrow at the ankle; the top hung just to my thighs, tying with a sash. I had a coat to go over it. I couldn't see myself, but my father was laughing and so was the bookseller.

"They'll never know!"

And they didn't. When we came to the sentry post that marked the exit of the city, everyone had to stop. My father showed his pass card. The guards looked down from their tower.

"Why are you going out?"

"To see my wife's mother in Uraga."

"And this one is?"

We were on the muddy road below them. My father jerked his head in my direction. "My son," he said. "He's my apprentice."

"Pass."

We walked on. I felt curious; the cool air filtered across my scalp. I was light, as if I'd forgotten something. We'd left my girl clothes in the bookstore!

"When will I get them back?" I said. I didn't miss them much, but I could see people thought I was a funny-looking boy.

"When we go home again, we can stop."

We passed a drummer with small gongs tied to a belt around his middle. He had spread a mat on the grassy ground beside the road. He was dancing, and as he twisted, tassels with small, hard knots at the ends played a tune on the gongs. He banged on the skin drum in his arms. All the while he had his face fixed on an audience of three who sat on the edge of his mat.

I pulled on my father's hand and we watched for a bit. Hokusai made a little drawing of the man. We did not throw coins into the small collection that was on the mat.

"Can't we give him a coin?"

"That would be an insult."

But I could see the man's lip turning up. "He wants one."

"He may want it, but it will demean him to take it," said Hokusai.

We set out again on the road. I was tired and night was coming. All of a sudden this long walk did not make sense to me.

"Are we fleeing Edo?"

"Never," he said. "We are quitting it. I'm tired of the city. Everyone there wants money."

"Is it because you have debts?"

Hokusai was offended. "What do you know about debts?"

"Shino also has debts," I relayed.

"People pay plenty of money for my work. My work is popular. I sell to the Dutch traders. No, it is not because of debts."

I chattered on. "Shino has to pay out money she earns to the waiters and for the sake and to the housekeeper." She didn't pay the hairdresser because he loved to fix her smooth, endless black locks. I didn't mention that. "She even has to pay for the makeup she hates. She has to share her money with the other courtesans, and she gives some to the teashop where she meets her clients. And to her family also; she sends some home every month. She even gives some to her husband, who sent her to the chief magistrate," I said. "That's why she has debts."

"Her husband is a wicked man who only wants money now that she is a well-paid courtesan." He stormed ahead of me in his bowlegged way, fuming. "Why should Shino's husband get her money?" he muttered as he stomped ahead. "He sold her, in truth."

We marched along.

"You see, that's just it. People sell anything. What they love. Their labour. Then they take the money to the next place. Each time it changes hands, the money becomes dirtier. It is an abomination," he said. "Someone admires my print, they give it a value in this dirty money. I don't like it," he said to the road in front of him. "So I don't pay attention."

We passed a man with a slow donkey. He stared at my raving father, pitying me.

"How can you not pay attention? We need money. Without it we'll get debts too."

"I won't give coins the courtesy of my attention. I don't know their names. They are evil spirits."

He was faking. He did know their names. But his hatred was real. It was another of his ways to be different. Everyone else liked money. Waiters and cleaners picked up coins from the gutters. The courtesans pretended they didn't see the folded papers that were left by the tea sets. But they were very quick, as soon as eyes were turned, to unfold and count the money.

But I didn't believe this was why we were leaving Edo.

I ran to catch up. "Is it because you have to hide from the *bakufu*?"

"Hide? Me?" He snorted with scorn. "You must be crazy."

That silenced me. I was bad for having angered him. He was moving quickly. But now I stormed ahead.

It was a revelation to be able to move.

In the city we were stopped at every turn. There were crowds you had to dodge. The canals had small, crowded bridges. Our district was closed by a stockade with guards. Locked gates divided neighbourhoods from each other. Every way forward was blocked. You had to dodge and dart.

Now as far as I could see there was open space.

I began to feel the wind.

I set off past women carrying faggots on their backs, fishermen with two baskets over the sides of a horse, pilgrims in white. It was fun to run in boys' trousers. I imagined that there was a face on the back of my head, and it was making huge and hideous expressions at Hokusai. My eyebrows—the ones on the back of my head—were pinched together. My mouth was stretched into a square, my tongue dangling from the middle of it. My eyes were crossed, the pupils down and in the centre, looking down my nose. I was the villain. When Hokusai peered through the crowds ahead to see where I was, this mask-face would leer back at him. Hah!

But when I looked back, he was gazing off in the distance. Indifferent to my insolence. I was ashamed. I thought of something to frighten myself. It was a habit I had. I learned it from his stories. First the pickled heads. Now I imagined again that he might sell me.

I hung back and found him. "Would you sell me, Father?"

He gave that rattle of scorn he was so good at. He let his lower jaw drop, and he forced the air out so it hissed and stuttered as if it were going up a rusty old pipe. "I would not find a buyer."

Was I so ugly? So useless? Hadn't he just said I was his apprentice?

I ran ahead of him again and hid in a clump of pines. I watched him.

Hokusai bounced and zigged and zagged along the road. He stopped to sniff the air. He talked to himself, or to absent me. Or to nobody: he needed no excuse to keep talking. He was like a crazy person, it was true. I wished I could run away and not have to follow him. But his voice reached me in my hiding place.

"At the sea we will look outward." He sounded not at all angry. "It will bring peace."

His pleasant voice wooed me. I couldn't leave him. Maybe he could have left me, but I was not prepared to wait and see. I fell in step beside him.

Night was falling as we came to a crossroads.

"Will there be money at the fishing village where we are going?" I asked.

My father gave me a stern look.

"I have told you we are leaving the city because of money," he said. "Would I take you to a place where money is also the god? No, there will be no money."

"How will we eat?"

"We'll trade my work for lodging. We'll take our food from the sea and the earth. We'll sleep in the homes of your mother's family."

We trudged along.

"The Shogun's men won't find me in a fisherman's hut!" he blurted.

Hah! I knew we were fleeing. It was just as Shino had said. But I understood we were not to say so.

"I'm tired of the pleasure quarter anyway. Everyone's working there. I want to see the other famous places."

The next post town was ahead. We found an inn where they fed us and let us sleep in exchange for my father making a scroll painting of a Buddha. We went to sleep on clean straw.

11

Barbarians

THE NEXT DAY THE ROAD AHEAD was just as long. I looked at the people going by on packhorses, but I did not ask my father if we could have one. We moved aside when the *kago* of the rich merchants hove up behind us, carried on the shoulders of men whose eyes and arms bulged. After a long time we sat beside the road. I lay in the grass while my father drew three fat peasant boys running with a kite in the field.

"Where is the sea?"

"I told you. We're nearly there. Can't you smell it?"

I sniffed. It's true the air was different. Salty.

"You'll like it. It's a great beast that sleeps and wakes. It roars and it moans and it is its own master."

"What about your publisher?"

"I want no more publishers. I will make poetry cards and sell them on my own. I will make volumes of laughing pictures for rich women."

Farther along we came to a teahouse. Beside the teahouse was a workshop where a man and his family were carving the thumb-sized wooden charms we called *netsuke*. Hokusai sketched them. I picked up the charms—a fat Buddha, a fox, a sleeping cat, a stove. I wished I could have one. I could hold it in my palm and tighten my fingers around it. I could hide it in my sleeve when I got my kimono back. We all hid our valuable things, not because we feared their being stolen, but because we were not allowed indulgences. Our luxuries were invisible, like the paintings merchants commissioned for the linings of their coats. We were inside out.

Clouds came over and the sky was threatening. It was still only the third day of the new year. Spring, but not warm. Soon it would rain. We came to a post town, the dark buildings tight and seamless against the sides of the road—inns and stables and, up a few stairs, a small roadside temple under red arches. We would have gone in to sit by a warm stove, but something was happening. A man who made straw shoes for horses was setting up his barrow. A noodle vendor lit a fire under a big vat of water. I saw peasants leading lame children, blind ancients, pregnant wives.

"What shrine are we coming to?" I asked the noodle man.

He laughed. "It is no shrine at all. The Dutch traders are on their way to Edo to present themselves to the Shogun. The procession will be here by nightfall. One of them is a doctor of medicine."

The Dutch, alone amongst foreigners, were allowed to trade in our country. Hokusai said it was because they were prepared to step on their holy book. They did this to assure the Shogun that they wouldn't preach in favour of their Christian gods. "It seems a strange reason to trust someone," he told me when I asked. I thought again of the time I had seen the red-headed devils through the high window of the Nagasakiya when my father went to sketch the picture. I remembered the roar that went up when they came out the door in front of the crowds. These were also men, I realized, to whom money was a god.

A captain of the Dutch had come to our house. He asked Hokusai to prepare two scrolls showing incidents in the life of a Japanese from birth to death, one for a female, one for a male. These were for the first in command. The price he offered was 150 *ryo*. The captain also wanted a second set, for himself, and offered the same price. He said that the entourage would remain in Edo only ten days more, and that the work must be finished by the time it left.

The sum was enormous. There was dancing in the studio: as usual we had no money and the red-headed barbarians were going to save the day. But the time was short, and we all had to work.

My sisters ground the pigments and dissolved them in water. As the youngest I cleaned brushes and ran errands. My father drew funeral processions and weddings and festivals, imagining what the foreigners would want to see. The students positioned themselves along the length of the scrolls and filled in the colours where they were told.

Even so, it was too large a task; someone always had to be working on the scrolls, and so we rarely slept. Hokusai did not want to compromise his high standard. "We must tell the Dutch that we cannot have the scrolls finished in ten days' time," he said finally.

I was the messenger. Captain Hemmy with his frizzy cloud of sun-coloured hair leaned over me and boomed that the Dutch had no more time in the capital and would have to leave without the scrolls. I ran back to the studio with the dreadful news. But my father only grunted and continued his painstaking drawings of temple bells. Nothing, not even cancellation, would disturb his work.

But luckily for us, the Shogun delayed the foreigners' appearance before him. One day and then another, the Dutch waited to be called to the castle. We all continued to work on the scrolls. It was as if the Shogun was helping us, but of course he would not have if he knew. He forbade this trade.

Four days later we finished the scrolls.

I ran to the Nagasakiya with the news. We were asked to bring them that same day.

The *opperhoofd* was very pleased with his scroll and produced the gold *ryo* exactly as had been promised. But Captain Hemmy put his spectacles down his nose and set the scrolls side by side. He compared his to his superior's, unrolling them together, inch by inch.

Hokusai looked up and looked around. He made a little musical noise with his lips. He farted.

"Both the same? Both from your hand?"

Hokusai did not deign to answer.

Captain Hemmy let his spectacles fall off his downspout of a nose to his chest.

"I believe mine are copies," he said. "They are inferior. The price should be exactly one-half."

It was a terrible insult.

Without speaking, and with enormous dignity, Hokusai wrapped up his kimono in the front of his thighs and cleared his throat with that hiss I knew so well. He stepped forward and carefully, even gingerly, rolled up the second set of scrolls. He did not bow. He took me by the hand and we walked out. The large wooden door closed behind us, and we were back in the streets of Japan.

At home my mother took the 150 *ryo* and asked for the other 150. My father showed her that we still had the second scrolls. "He tried to cheat me."

She screamed. "You have the airs of a lord and the ways of a peasant! Why are you so proud?"

"You know nothing."

"We need this money. Half of it is spent already."

He shrugged.

"Do you deny it? Look at this child. He is hungry!" She pushed my little brother under his nose. I guess we girls weren't hungry?

You couldn't escape their fights in our small rooms. My sisters and I wormed our way into the corner and covered our ears, but the shouts penetrated all the same. "Where is that useless older brother? He should be bringing money into this house!"

"Woman, beware! Curse the children of my dead wife," Hokusai said, "and you will bring down demons on your head."

"And you, Tokitaro"—she called him by his birth name to remind him he was nothing much—"you love the dead and not the living. You love yourself and not your faithful wife. One hundred and fifty *ryo* would save this household from great misery."

I prayed that she would be silent. But the woman sailed out in gusty lament, moving in circles like a hawk in a gale. At last she exhausted herself and collapsed.

"You waste yourself in rage," he said. "But I forgive you." He spoke gently. "You cannot help it. You do not understand me, and you will never understand me."

My mother wept.

"Which part of our poverty do you think I don't feel?" Hokusai said. "The cold and wet? The shabby garments? The way I work through the night? The way this child runs errands, as I did as a boy? The way, even though my mastery is accepted all over Japan, we have meals of rice alone?

"You may think this is misery," the Old Man went on, "but there's something worse. That's when a stranger—a barbarian—holds me in low regard. When he says I have not done my best work." He was good, that far. Then he lost it. He flung his arms out and stamped. "Anyway, he is a bad man. He is not a good person. Unpleasant airs emanate from him."

"They eat beef, is all," she said.

"I don't care what they eat."

"You don't care what *we* eat." She ripped through his words with a shriek.

"I care about respect."

"You cannot eat respect."

"Yes, I can."

He popped his eyes, sat with knees high and feet crossed, slurped and burped and rubbed his stomach. I fell into a giggling heap. My older sisters hated him for teasing my mother. She began to moan. My younger brother sat staunch with his eyes on the pathetic little fire in our hearth. Sakujiro was so quiet. My mother slung him around from hip to hip like a bag of rice. He was a mystery to us all. But I suspected he was not stupid.

"See, Wife, that's your problem: you can't laugh."

"Laugh?" my mother shouted. "No, but I can cry."

That made an end to it for an hour or two. But then he asked her to serve him an empty bowl at dinner, and she did. He sat with his chopsticks, lifting his invisible dinner to his lips, smiling and winking at me, the accomplice.

"Your hunger may be in your big head, but you can't pull off your magic with me," said my mother. "Mine is in my belly."

It was simple: Hokusai lived on invisible things, the good as well as the bad. It was an unfair fight, I knew that. He had a genius for taunting. He used words nearly as well as he used a brush. He was an actor. His ghost stories went to bed with me and his jokes woke me up. I understood the Old Man; my mother didn't.

I felt superior to her. My father and I both did.

That night we went to the Yoshiwara, hoping for a glimpse of Shino.

The next day it began again.

"Your daughters are cold because we have no coal for the fire. Your son . . ." She pointed to the boy. He was poking the fire with a little stick, expressionless. He was a spooky kid, I admit. Even she had no words for him. "You paint all the beautiful ladies who are for sale, while I, your virtuous wife, have only one kimono—"

"Oh, this is tiresome, tiresome," he said. He had been up all night. He spoke quietly while bent over a sketch. "For the sake of argument let's call this misery. What I am saying is that I prefer misery to humiliation."

"Why?" she said. "Humiliation is nothing to me. Humiliation is a mosquito to be waved away. Misery is in the bones."

"Your ideas are from the old times, from the peasant times, the distant past," charged Hokusai. "You have no pride. Pride is in the spirit; where is yours?"

But later, when they lay on their mat and were lovers again, he spoke tenderly. He rolled her frontward and back again, like a package, to get free of her wrapping. He propped her on her knees and knelt behind her. "Do it this way and you'll be in the pictures," he said. "Isn't that what you want?"

"It is not the laughing pictures I want to be in!"

"But I can teach you." He laughed and she cried. Then she wheedled. I was young, but I had heard many women wheedle.

"Tell me, Husband, don't you wish you had taken the 150 *ryo?*"

Shino would never have said that.

THE NEXT DAY, LO AND BEHOLD, Captain Hemmy and his Japanese escort appeared at our door again. I was sent out to tell their translator that my father was too busy to see him.

"I understand," he said. "But we are very patient."

They sat by the door all day. When evening came I admitted the translator. He bowed very low and asked forgiveness for suspecting Hokusai of making a copy. Captain Hemmy had reconsidered. He would like to have his scrolls and he had brought the money.

My father didn't want to sell, I knew. But my mother's sheer volume had made an impression. "You will have to inspect the studio books," he said to me, "to see if the scrolls are still available."

I went to the other room and played with the cats for a long time, and then I brought the scrolls to where the translator waited and so it was done. We paid our debts and my mother was happy for a time, and when he laughed, she laughed as well.

Later the news came that Captain Hemmy had died on the long journey back to Nagasaki.

"Oooh! Do you see? Do you see what happened? I told you so!" said Hokusai. And oohed and aahed. "Do you see? I told you he was full of an evil spirit. It overcame him, and he is gone. Probably he had an imbalance of the four grains. He was filled with bile. Even the Western medicine could not save him."

Hokusai prayed, he chanted, he took his Chinese herbs and breathed incense. He wanted to expunge the Dutch captain.

I sometimes wondered what happened to the scrolls Hemmy bought when he died. No one knew. Maybe they travelled to Europe with one of his party. Perhaps they were sold there and started the fame that would make our life a little easier, before it made it much more difficult.

12

The Waves

NOW IT WAS FOUR YEARS after our first encounter with the Dutch. We sat by the side of the Tokaido, amongst the peasants and noodle sellers. We had decided to wait to see the barbarians again. Hokusai sketched. I had a brush myself, which I used to practise characters. By the time the noodles were cooked, the procession had appeared. At first it was a cloud of dust, far down the road. Then it was noise—drums, whips, neighing of the horses. We were supposed to kneel and bow, but my father wouldn't, so instead we moved back from the road into the rushes.

Two policemen were at the head of the procession. Behind them, oxen crawled and horses cantered. The drivers shouted. The porters trailed along like bent hooks under tubs of foodstuffs and a cookstove. Then came a giant black piece of furniture, borne aloft on men's shoulders. It was covered with a red cloth written on in gold: this was their counting house.

The bearers stopped. The palanquins jolted to a stop with the curtains open. The barbarians' heads poked out; two of them climbed down to see what blocked the road. They were very tall and dressed in heavy black coats with hats like stovepipes. Their skin was pasty white, and copper hair hung from their chins and grew under their noses. Their eyes were cool and lit from within, like the eyes of wolves.

They opened their baskets of linen and their cooking pots, and they set up their bizarre furniture, tables and chairs. The bearers began to prepare tea. A lacquered black sedan chair shook and out of it came their leader, like a tall puppet. He sat for his red devil meal of tea and cakes while the doctor began to look at the sick babies and old women.

My father approached. The translator glanced down at him: a peasant, dusty, on the road with other peasants.

"I have a question. Your scientists say that the world is round. Is it true?"

"Yes, it is true. We have sailed all around it in our ships."

My father had many more questions, and finally three barbarians spoke to him and showed him the instruments they aimed at the sky. The moon was round; he could see that. Maybe everything was round. But if it was, then what about straight lines? Where did they come from? And how about the directions to the stars? Did those directions change when you were in a different place in the world? Was the sky possibly round as well? It would change everything.

The answers did not convince him, but Hokusai thanked the Dutch and told me we had to hurry on. It was getting dark.

He explained it all to me when we found a teahouse that would take us in.

"If this is true," he said, "there can be no straight lines."

I didn't believe it. Straight lines were everywhere. You just had to look.

"We will find out for ourselves. We are going to the horizon. We'll see if it is curved."

URAGA WAS A SMALL FISHING VILLAGE under a cliff, with sand shores. We had come out of the long bay that led to Edo. Now we looked out to the open sea. We walked to the far end of the shore, where there were some fishing huts. No one lived in these huts anymore; only a few old men and women walked the beaches with their eel spikes.

"I am Tokitaro of the family Nakajima," said my father to one of them. They welcomed us. In one of their huts we put our bundles. My father sat on the beach and stared out at the sea, which he had told me was a great beast.

"What are you looking for?" I asked. There were no boats coming in, and none going out. Only the waves and the far horizon.

"Do you see that line? Where the water ends and the sky begins?"

"Yes."

"That is the edge of the world. If the world is round," he said, "that line must be curved, not flat. Tell me what you see."

I looked at it very carefully. "It is a straight line."

"You are wrong," he said. "It is round, but it is very, very large—so large that it looks straight to us," said Hokusai. "But it is a curve that is very wide. We are not far enough away from it to see the curve, not here."

"We can't get any farther away," I said.

"Then we will have to change the way we see."

Hokusai wanted to paint the waves. He sat for a long time trying to catch them at the right moment. But they moved too fast and were always dissolving in front of us.

"Nobody paints these things," I said. "Paintings have people in them."

"Yes, they have, but they don't always need to."

"Oh," I said. I could see that he was planning more changes.

He was. He would make the people along the shore tiny, and that would show that the waves were big. He had the people all ready. Along the way to Uraga he had sketched peddlers of pots, toys, and baskets with their wares. Now he copied them onto a drawing of the shore. He made tiny offshore waves that arched like cats. He added himself, the old man.

I was certain that it was not the kind of painting people wanted. I said, "Who wants to see just the water and an old woman carrying sticks in a pack on her back?"

There had been light in the sky, but night was falling. My father walked at the edge of the water. He turned and walked into the water, then he turned his back on it and towards me. He did this again and again, like a child, returning to safety and then going deeper and deeper each time.

I could see the lightness of his skin. I could see the white rim of water where it rose up. I could not see the water itself, because it was dark. But I heard it growl, the great beast. I was afraid of it, and of what it could do to my father. I tried running in it, but it sucked at my legs as if it would drag me down, and I jumped away.

He went deeper and the water picked him up and moved him. In the dark, it became invisible, but it still moved him along. I thought it might carry him away, and I began to whimper. My father had drifted. The foam was white or grey and occasionally came up and covered him.

A fishing boat appeared, coming in for the night. It came upon us suddenly, out of the dark. I imagined that the distance between me and the edge of the world was a scroll unrolling.

The boat appeared and then disappeared, rhythmically, as if in a dance. The men inside it were riding the invisible. Wind, or the pushing of the water, brought them in towards me. I watched to see where they would land, at the bottom of the scroll.

Foam swallowed my father time and again as the beast tossed. I stood on the sand. I thought that if I stood there at least he would come back to me. I moved back and forth along the shore, trying to be at his landing place when he finished his dance in the claws of the beast.

My father ran back and forth, echoing the motion of the boat as it rocked up and down on the waves, out far and high up. He ploughed with heavy feet, then was loosed and skipped, then turned as if he carried weights, then pushed sideways as if he had to push crowds out of the way to get where he was going. The water was black paper. He was the brush. His strokes were making a figure. What was he drawing?

I watched a long time. He drew many characters with his body. He stopped and started as if moving to music. He strove to remain erect. He strove to stay above the waves. His body used every muscle to articulate itself. It came to me that he was drawing his path. Perhaps it was his message to me.

But I couldn't read it.

I called out to him, "Old Man, come back." He did not answer. I even wheedled: "Old Man, I can make you some nice tea . . ." The water made him deaf. "Hey, you! Get the hell back here!" I tried. "You ugly thing!" Nothing.

I will remember this forever, I thought. I had no idea what forever would be. I did not know what my life would be, but standing there behind my father as he danced with the waves, I knew that I would always watch him tumble, would always think the ground underneath me tumbled just as the waves did. I would never trust that solid ground. I would face the tumult, scanning for the shadow man I loved. I was his child, but he was mine too.

We grew up early in my time. We learned about sex and the women who sold themselves in the Yoshiwara.

We were with the men in the studio when they painted the erotic prints. All those pictures of couples grappling, of women forced down to the mat—as if we didn't hear it at night too, in our houses.

We knew about the hardness of life. I took charge of the money when my father couldn't or wouldn't. I heard my mother saying the words that would make him stop loving her. But that wasn't the moment that turned me from a child to an adult. It was that day, in the waves. Me hollering after him like a mother.

When he came in at last, I asked him what he was doing. I gave him my boy's jacket and tried to warm him. He was so excited he didn't notice I was cold too.

"Puzzling," he said. "I'm trying to understand. I know I'm here and there's motion everywhere and there's motion against the motion. I know that the foam and the water are two parts of the same thing."

"Are they?"

"Yes," he said. "Like ghosts and live people. Like spirits and demons. It's fluid and it's like smoke. It may even be like clouds."

"That's good," I said, although I did not understand.

I went farther down the beach and asked a fisherman's wife if she could give us some supper. My father would make her a sketch, I said. And he did, of her husband pulling in his nets. She was pleased. She loaned us two mats and two cotton blankets for the night. Then we went back to our little hut.

In the morning, when the sun began to emerge out of the water, my father was up again. He crouched on his heels at the shore and watched the fishermen push long skiffs through the advancing waves to get away through the crashing surf. When a boat shot through the wall of water, he cheered.

Then he watched as wave after wave broke.

The wind was high. It ploughed a furrow in the water. This was the beginning of a wave. The wave rose higher and then it was too high for itself. Before it broke, it began to pour. Clear water ran smooth as satin from the top froth to join in the indigo swirl below.

After a long time, Hokusai stood. He put his feet in the wet sand at the water's edge. He walked in deeper; his feet sank a little into the sand.

He whooped with delight.

At noon it was warm. We splashed ourselves and then we lay down at the edge of the sea. The fisherwomen had big hats and covered themselves. We were showing our skin.

"It is difficult to bear the cruelty of one's own people," he said.

"What are you talking about?"

I felt the mixture of heat from the sun and cold from the watery sand on my body.

"I will have another chance. I will do better next time," he said. Then he ran out and tried to jump the next wave.

I felt life endless ahead of me. There would be next times and next times again and again, lifting us up and ploughing us under.

We stayed there all that day and the next. He grew braver about the sea. "It is a beast, but I can tame it," he said.

"I don't think so."

He went out farther and the froth curled around his skinny chest.

He couldn't swim, so I had to follow him. I couldn't swim either. As I reached the place where he was, he went to his knees to greet the water. I followed, trying to stay standing. The water sucked me back, trying to pull my flesh from my bones. He let it knock him. He went sideways and straightened himself. I spit salt out of my mouth.

"We will come to this life again," he said.

The wave slapped him.

He went deeper, turning sideways. Now he was standing in a blue-and-white water spiral.

He fell.

The wave pounded him down to the sand. It scooted him forward. He was rolling. He had no control. He was in the wave.

Gone.

I stood. I waited. I watched for him to come up. I waded a little closer to where the water stopped its slide forward and began to slide back. I stood.

He popped out of the wave and slid forward on the sand.

My two ankles were there like bamboo stems. He grabbed hold of one.

I decided to try it. I lay in the shallows, letting the water push me. The wave from behind was cloudy, then clean as it curled down.

The motion of the water pushed me down.

I was very cold and frightened but happy: I was playing with my father. He was all mine. I wondered if he was thinking about Shino, or about my mother, or about what he did with one and the other. I wondered what he thought of me and then realized that I knew: he did not think of me. He was used to me, that was all.

So it fell to me to think of myself. What was I like? I was not in the habit of thinking of myself as separate from him, from anyone. I was ugly, I supposed, but I was smart and ready with my tongue. And with my brush I could do whatever he expected. That seemed to be enough.

Later in the afternoon he came and sat on the sand and waited for the wind and the sun to dry him.

"Now we will go back to Edo," he said.

I was disappointed. "I thought we were going to live here."

"One day we will. But for now I must go back."

"Why?"

"I have to find a publisher and make prints and sell my work."

"But you said we would live here. And you would trade your sketches for food."

"Did I say that?" He looked genuinely puzzled. "It's no good. I can't. It won't satisfy me. It's not the real world."

We stood up and began to walk back.

13

HOME AGAIN

IN THE YOSHIWARA IT WAS SPRING. Carters with bursting cheeks walked up Primping Hill with cherry trees in tippy wheelbarrows, clouds of lime green on thin grey stems. The wheels rumbled, hollow, up the mound of Hesitation Bridge. On the downslope the men ran around in front and pressed their backs against the barrows to stop them rolling out of control through the gate.

Once across the wooden bridge the carters fanned out along the boulevard. They got out their shovels and started digging. I wondered where the trees came from. What nursery, what little paradise fed them until it was time? When the trees were in the ground, they would look as if they'd been there forever. In one week the little drop balls would be swelling and opening, and in two the seashell pink would be awash over our heads and all the parties would begin.

Mitsu, the gossip, came out of her shop. She pointed at my haircut and covered her mouth, giggling. My father got right down to business.

"Where is Utamaro?"

Her eyes expanded with relish.

"At home now. But things are worse, worse even than when you left!" she said.

I could see my father rock back and set his eyebrows up. Oh, yeah? She was too dramatic, Mitsu. The wrong person to talk to now. She loved bad news. You had to take everything she said and hold it under cold water for a minute.

"Scandal, scandal." She stopped to catch her breath.

"Brigands! They broke into"—she named one of the mid-range brothels—"and ransacked the place. They raped two of the courtesans and cut one of them in the neck. It's terrible." She lifted her great big, knobby finger and waggled it. "Oh, this district is going to the dogs. In older days, you know as well as I do, these types would be stopped at the gates. Now we can't even catch them when they don't pay their bills."

Next door, sweet-faced Waki was working on a back tattoo for a fireman. He left his client lying on the table and came out to greet us. "I will do an excellent job," he whispered to my father, "because once you get one fireman coming to your shop, you get all them."

I realized then that it wasn't the design that made him happy; it was the strong, masculine fireman lying there. He lifted his head and winked at us. He winked to show that he could take the pain. And Waki returned reverently to him. Here was the man-fabric he had been longing for.

Hokusai was agitated with the news but not unhappy. "That is the city," he told me. "Always changing, always tragedies." We had been gone for only a few days. Already Utamaro was out of jail and robbers were attacking the brothels. He smiled and tilted his head this way and that. The birds, the flowers, the cats in the gutter—they all got a smile.

We walked on to Etako's inn. A man stepped in our path at the door.

"To what do we owe the pleasure?" said Sanba.

"I have returned to the world."

"I suppose you missed me." He included me in his smile.

"Not at all. It is only necessity," said my father. "I must be in the world."

"Well, the world has got a little darker since you left us," said Sanba. He jerked his head towards the corner, where a man sat writing on a scroll, scowling. He made sure, swift brush strokes, stopping every few seconds, dipping his pen and admiring his work. As he wrote he reached out absently to grasp a little cup in his thick fingers, quaff the contents, and set the cup down.

"Who's that?"

"Out-of-work samurai," said Sanba. "He's about to hector us. There are more like these every day."

The man finished what he was writing. He stood and raised his voice over the noise of the crowd.

"Edo is becoming a place of moral disorder," he shouted. Actually he was reading his own words. "Moral life has been thrown into disarray. It's a disgrace!"

"First they come to enjoy our fun, and then they try to redeem themselves by pronouncing us evil," said Sanba. "Sad-and-Noble's work goes on."

The samurai was using all those ancient words that were supposed to be our hallmarks. "Virtue and benevolence have been lost through treachery!"

"He's a moron," said my father loudly.

The courtesans nodded in the corners of the room, making assignations. "Whose treachery, love? Have you had your heart broken?"

"Love is all you think about. Look at you! Playing at love. Working for your own gain. What kind of men are you? Spending your money on prostitutes and drinking. No one is loyal. No one is serving his master. What has become of the Way of Tranquilizing the People?"

"Too true, I say. What *has* become of it?" said Sanba. "Maybe it is becoming the Way of Waking Up the People?"

"You glorify your bodies with silks and luxurious bedding. You worship beauty as if it was"—he sputtered—"as if it was a power in itself."

It was. Even I knew that.

The samurai went on. It wasn't only us he raved against. He reviled Edoites of every stripe. "Lords borrow money from the moneylenders. They even take the stipends of their samurai to pay their own debts."

"You tell the lords the error of their ways. You won't find them here," murmured someone else.

"Only their spies."

Howls of laughter. I began to smile. Like my father, I felt good to be there. For me it was safety to be in the melee.

"Where are the customary boundaries between the esteemed and the despised? Washed out! Down the gutters. These divisions are in *nature*." The man slapped his thick palm on the tabletop. "What of the Way of Principle? Passion and madness have thrown things into disorder. All you do with your days is struggle between gain and loss . . ."

He was still shouting as Etako ushered him to the door. On the threshold he came face to face with a woman with a towering helmet of hair pierced by lacquer ornaments, wrapped in a cut-velvet cloak of purple and green leaves. Standing on clogs that boosted her ten inches off the ground, she loomed over him.

"And women's hairstyles are far too elaborate!" he cried as a parting shot.

Hana-ogi VII gave a languid smile. She was the reigning beauty, the top courtesan, the most expensive and the one whose hours any man in Edo would kill to buy. "I'll read all about it when you publish your book," she said, gesturing to his scroll.

"Pay for your tea, please," said Etako.

"Do you see what I mean? Money, money, money?" the outraged guest asked the crowd, grabbing for his pouch. "The whole city is nothing more than a huge brothel. Everyone wants everyone else to pay, to pay, to pay. In the old days we had no need of money." He threw coins in the dust. Then he went out into the street and disappeared into the throngs coming over the bridge and through the Great Gate.

We went to visit Utamaro in his rented room above the printshop. His skin was sallow. He was stooped. His wrists were lashed together with leather. A woman from next door had brought him sake; she bent to help him sip from the cup.

"Awkward, this," he said. He had adopted a little toss of the head to speed the liquid on its way. He showed us where his wrists were rubbed raw. At night the woman pushed the thongs aside and rubbed oil in the skin. Sleep was impossible except for snatches of half an hour, and in those he only hovered below the surface of his waking mind.

"We feared for you in your examination on the White Sands because we know how proud you are. But you are well," said my father.

Utamaro lifted his hands and dropped them. "I was let go," he said, "if you can call this free."

"Better than behind the walls of the jail."

"You're just glad that it isn't you whose hands are trussed," Utamaro said.

Hokusai was silent. How could he respond to this bitterness?

"You would not be able to paint. Even though you can paint left-handed and right-handed, you cannot paint no-handed. Even you, Hokusai."

"My father can paint with his toes," I offered.

Hokusai shushed me with a look.

"He can paint with his teeth."

"I get cramps," said Utamaro angrily. "I am older than you are. I am an old man."

"We are both old men," said Hokusai.

Utamaro lifted his wrists again and let them fall heavily on his knees. "They will remove these shackles physically, but they will always be on my wrists, heavy as the name they call me: criminal," he said slowly, adopting it. "They have killed me."

"No, Utamaro. Not you. You cannot be killed. You are immortal. And you were never afraid."

"I am not afraid. It is not like in your ghost stories. It is not like that—dragons and snakes winding up at you out of the smoke of burning bodies. It is not like that. That is not fear."

"What is fear, then?" said Hokusai.

"I can tell you how it starts. It is an evil worm growing within, and because it is growing, you must deny it, and always be boasting."

My father was listening carefully. His friend had been pulled down. The man was crumbling. I felt the desolation of it.

"And how does it end?"

"It doesn't. It simply becomes a part of you. It saps your strength. Perhaps there is no end," said Utamaro. "Perhaps the end is . . ." He raised his hands to show that he meant death. "There is no honourable way to live with it."

Hokusai said nothing.

Utamaro smiled. "They said you made great sums of money selling to the Dutch."

I sucked air through my teeth.

"Only once, and it was soon gone. Four years ago. Not great sums."

"Yes, they were." Utamaro twitched his head again to get the hair out of his eyes. "I will be honest. This success of yours eats into my gut. It is wrong that the Dutch take your work. I am older and I am greater and I speak for the people more than you do."

"Not true!" I piped, but my father said nothing.

"How is it, Hokusai, that you are free? It appears that when you break the rules, it is not a problem for the *bakufu*. Why is that, I wonder? Because you are a peasant and your art is the art of peasants? Because you are unimportant, I think. Or is it because of those noble ladies? Your courtesan has a powerful family. Is that how you get your ability to slip away unnoticed when trouble comes?"

"Perhaps," said my father, "I am a ghost."

"Yes, I think perhaps you are," said Utamaro, jerking his head towards the woman for her to bring the cup to his lip. It was like a ballet, the way he guided her hand with his eyes, opened his mouth in a narrow, elegant slit, and then quickly flicked his eyelids. She tipped the cup suddenly and then brought it back again. A slug of sake went neatly into the slit, and he swallowed.

"How is it for you, child?" he said. "Will you slip away as your father does and manage a kind of freedom? Will your plainness, your strange lack of femininity, save you?"

He had never looked at me with any interest. I was not what he liked in a girl, or especially a woman. Had he been studying me? Why did he ask?

"What will you do?"

"She has some promise as an artist," said Hokusai. "She will help me."

Utamaro shrugged. He looked back at my father. "Those with children believe they will be immortal. But you are nothing special. You think you are, but you are not. You are like all of us, swept along with events. Without power, and without recourse. Carried along."

He raised his strapped wrists and rubbed them on his forehead, scraping the skin so it came away and blood ran down between his eyes.

AS SOON AS I COULD I RAN, dodging vendors' carts and the gawkers and dawdlers, to the Corner Tamaya to see Shino.

As usual Kana was guarding the entry. She was adding up all her expenses in the account book. It was hard to imagine her as a beautiful courtesan. She was unkempt now and thick in the waist, harried and coarse, but somewhere in her heart she had feelings. She smiled to see me. To her, I was just some local kid who liked to visit the kitchen. She did not suspect me of having thoughts. I hung by her desk. I saw a receipt that said a new girl was the property of Jimi. The price he had paid for her was written: two *ryo*.

"Quite inexpensive, at that price," I said.

Kana snatched away the receipt.

"She is not intelligent," she complained. "And anyway, she is addicted to opium. I don't know why we took her."

"Maybe you wished to be kind," I said. It was fun to prod her this way.

"That is just it! Kindness! You are a perceptive child, aren't you? That is why we are not profitable, not anymore. People don't understand how risky our business is. How we take these girls in—where else would they go? We train them. Look how beautiful they become, and how useful. Of course, anything could happen—they could get sick and die. So they do. And there is our investment, gone into the graveyard. We have very little profit. We work seven days a week, and the customers are so badly behaved!"

"It's awful," I said.

"And the policemen! Every time they're short of money, they come by the door. They accuse us of some small infraction of the rules and stand by with their hands out. Really! Do you see this column? This alone is for bribes!"

"And now robberies," I prompted.

"Just as you say! Fortunately that was not our shop. Oh no, they'd never get in here, not with the boy on the lookout." The "boy" was a wizened old man with a cane who took out the sewage.

Kana looked around and beckoned me closer. "But that, shocking as it was—robbery! rape!—is not the worst. The worst, the very worst, is that my husband keeps on having sex with the girls. It shocks you, I'm sorry. But you are growing up in the middle of this. You've seen it all. I told him no! I told him I would leave this place, I don't care where I end up, if he keeps on with it."

I composed a look of sympathy.

"Because," she said, and now a look crossed her crabbed face, a wistful look, a look of hope followed closely by one of defiance, "my daughter . . . We sent her away. To my parents. She cannot live here. She cannot even come to visit, surrounded by all this lechery. Only if he runs a clean shop will she ever see her parents again." Kana's eyes welled and she blotted the figures she was making in the long expense column. "Otherwise we will close the brothel. Just close it down. I am thinking of starting a rice shop instead. That at least would be profitable." She pulled her handkerchief out of her sleeve and wiped her eyes. She touched my arm. I had listened.

I tipped my head towards the stairs. It wasn't allowed. "Can I go?"

"Run along."

14

Caught

IT WAS LATE MORNING, a quiet time in that world, and upstairs Shino and the girls were practising their "dance."

They had reason now. There was not so much laughter. They walked like tigers, soft-footed, the way she told them to. Their metal hairpins—those that in all the pictures stuck out of their piled-up hair, indicating their status in the hierarchy (the more hairpins, the more you cost)—were expertly hidden inside their wrists, pushed into their sleeves of their kimono. Their eyes were fierce. Shino led. She glided and thrust her hands into the eyes, the ears (one on each side), the soft hollow under the chin, the heart of her invisible opponent. Jab, jab, jab, block, punch, turn—quickly, like a bird pecking, in, out—and then the pins were invisible again, shrugged away.

"Do not hesitate. If you strike, strike to kill. If you can't succeed, don't go forth. If you go forth with ambivalence, you will not succeed." She moved so smoothly her unpinned hair lay flat over her shoulders and undisturbed down her back. She showed no effort; her step and her long spine were elegant. She was a good teacher—methodical, patient, and firm. I stood there, loving her. Maybe she didn't suit the stated requirements, but she was beautiful.

A long, exhaled hiss marked the end of the *kata*. The girls relaxed their fierce faces. Shino nodded my way. She had known I was there. Of course she had—felt sweat off me, probably smelled the road and even the salt water, maybe my longing for her. Sensing was part of her skill. She bent her neck in mock deference: I was still dressed as a boy. In her eyes I saw she was glad we were back.

"Ei! Just in time. You can help us. Let's see how strong you are," she said. "Reach out and strike me. You're going to try to force me backwards."

I reached out. I put my hands on her shoulders. I pushed backwards. She was just a whippet, thin as a stray dog, but long. She had her hairpins at my throat in a flash; I didn't even see her move. One elbow had blocked my hands and the other fist was under my ribs. I was off balance and fell away from her.

The courtesans clapped discreetly. Then they kicked the tails of their kimono out from under their feet and got to work. They tried blocking and punching, making it all look like noble deportment. They sank to one knee in the usual way, head bowed, but rising thrust one forearm in a block and slid the other hand, pin extended under the middle finger, deep under the ribs of this imaginary man. They rose and brought their hands together, pins out so they could stick directly into a man's ears while they knocked his chin with a knee.

"Keep your weight forward. Use your centre—surge up, but stay in one small knot of force," Shino was saying. "Then you will get him away from you. Don't let your arms stretch out so he can twist one; keep your elbows in."

We were carried away with ourselves. We didn't hear Jimi in the hall. Nor did Shino sense his entry. She failed her own lesson. We all failed the lesson. He grabbed my shirt—thinking I was a boy, I suppose—and threw me backwards. He collared Shino, clenching her kimono in his fist and shoving it into her throat.

"What the hell are you doing?"

The prostitutes stayed in role. Whimpering and squealing like so many little pigs, they dropped to their knees and pitched forward in deep bows, hiding their faces. Their hands dug comically in the heaps of hair to put their hairpins back in place. Except for Shino.

"We are having our dance lesson," she said calmly, seeming not to notice that she was being choked. She did not look down. She gazed at Jimi, her black eyes serene. There was that unquenched thing in them again that I'd seen the first time I met her, when Tsutaya insulted her. I suddenly wondered what her real name was, the girl who saw no reason to submit, and who had bought herself this sentence.

"Dance lesson!"

Jimi did not see into the depths of her eyes. He was not a subtle man. But he sniffed something; he got a whiff of it. He was a big fish in the waters of other people's helplessness, a scaly predator. But for a brief instant, he suspected his power over the girls was a charade. A shadow crossed his face. His eyes scoured Shino. He saw only a *yakko*. He could not see his prostitutes as capable of anything. If he had imagined they were learning self-defence he would have laughed. He knew something was off balance. But he could not grasp that it was him.

He lifted his right hand and slapped Shino across the face. A sharp tool in his hand, a blade to cut his tobacco, sliced her jaw. There was no blood at first. Then it seeped out the edges of the clean cut and stood.

She swayed. She had no other reaction.

He loosened his hand from her collar.

The blood filled the gash and slowly, minutely, began to overflow. He examined it with mild interest. I knew what he was hoping—that he hadn't marked her and brought her value down. "You've done something to your face," he murmured.

Shino tidied her kimono and twisted her heavy hair rapidly, pinning it in place. Without his noticing, she edged out of range. Then she touched her cheek.

"I am so sorry. It's a rather wild dance," she murmured. "It's meant to follow the drinking competition. It occurs near the end of an evening, as a prelude. That's why the hair is loose." She began to put her pins back.

The others remained on their faces. I was on the floor myself; I didn't want to see.

He must have thought she got off too easily. "Insolent bitch," he said, lunging forward to take her elbow and twist it behind her back. But Shino was not there. He lost his balance. She knelt, slipping her knee behind his. He tumbled over her onto his side.

For a minute he lay there. Impossible to say how it had happened.

Shino was kneeling beside his head. "I am so very sorry," she said, "so clumsy. It is my mistake."

He might have exploded, beat her, if she showed nerves. But she didn't. "I only meant to bow to you, but as I moved forward you did too, and we collided. I do apologize. I must have caused you to tumble. Please, let me help you . . ."

She looked at me over his back, and in this moment, when her life could have ended, when her life did, in fact, take a nasty turn, I swear she raised one eyebrow. Then she cocked her head: get out!

I ran. Street urchin with the hair of a boy, no one cared to stop me.

We waited all day for news. Mitsu finally came back to the tattoo shop where my father and I waited. She said Shino was lucky.

"She was not hurt."

"Not hurt?"

"Only a scratch. It will heal in no time."

"Only Jimi was hurt. *Izn it?*" I said, to make my father laugh. He didn't.

"What else? Give us the news."

But Mitsu was in no hurry. She was not going to give up her moment in the spotlight so easily. She sighed and smoothed her hair, asked for tea; Waki brought it, dainty and concerned. My father wore a look of stone—not allowed pity, not allowed fear.

"She was lucky. Oh, she was lucky. He could have killed her. He may yet have scarred her for life. Unknown how it will come out, that cut. *Izn it?* As it is, she is only—" Mitsu took a giant breath, stretched her eyes and pushed them out, forced her lips down at the corners, and blew out a big O.

"She is what?" Hokusai stood on one foot and then the other. What he could not show in his face he showed in his calf muscles, his thighs, his arms and fists; they clenched and unclenched. I had been vomiting. It was my fault; I knew it was my fault. I wished she had killed Jimi. I was sure she could have, with those hairpins. But I would never tell.

"She is bruised. Where he beat her. Around her arms and back. Where it will not damage her worth. The others are caring for her. They have sent for herbs and bandages. They have secured a spell: a paper on which is written a list of each of the grand shrines of Ise. She has eaten this, and the bleeding has stopped."

It seemed very recent and accurate news.

My father paced. He knew something of Western medicine and did not believe in spells. On the other hand, he did not disbelieve them either.

"How do you know this, Mitsu?" Hokusai squinted.

As the boulevard gossip, Mitsu knew everything about everyone. She never had to explain. She looked wounded. Did we not trust her account?

"I have my ways," she said. "I have been in the district a long time. Longer than you have. Longer than any of you.

"She was teaching the others to dance. To be graceful, you know. Kana, she's my friend, the *yarite*. I knew her when she was only a poor-class prostitute. Kana feels guilty. She encouraged her. Shino was only trying to help. But the dance got rather wild. Jimi thought they were plotting somehow. Kana protested Shino's innocence. She truly did."

Mitsu looked very important. Very sober. "Kana has saved Shino's life. She will be punished for insolence only, even though Jimi somehow—*inexplicably*—hurt his back as he was attempting to stop the commotion." Mitsu stretched up her terrible eyebrows and pulled down the edges of her mouth. Like a villain in a kabuki poster, she was. She was lavish with the horror of her message.

"All the same he tied her to a post and threatened her with his whip. He punched her. The courtesans were all crying, begging him to stop. Can you imagine? *They were only dancing.* What possessed the man?"

I knew what had possessed him: that serene and inner defiance in Shino's eyes. She had stood up to him, and in such an elegant way that it made him feel stupid.

"And what could the man do?" Mitsu could be heard repeating to all and sundry. "His prostitutes all stood up for her. They said they were all at fault, and if he punished her he must punish all of them. And he couldn't punish them all without going without a week's income, maybe even ruining his business. I know, because I'm a businesswoman too. He had to listen, especially to Hana-ogi."

We were unfreezing, my father and I.

"That is all very well, but ... but ..." The eyebrows were working, the eyes popping, the lips stretching. I cursed her theatricality. I wanted the news as calmly as I could have it. "She won't escape unharmed. She won't get out of this one. You wait. This is not over. He hates her, always did. She's a troublemaker. *Izn it?* Even now he is walking down there"—she jerked her head to the far end of the Yoshiwara, towards the low-class canalside brothels— "looking for a good price for her."

In an hour the news came to us: she was sold.

"Her new owner is very mean," Mitsu said, "and the women do not look healthy." Kind though she was, you could see the gleam in her eye as she fed on our suffering. "But it is not all bad," she added cheerfully. "Now the blind masseur can afford her. You know he has been in love with her for years."

WE WAITED A WEEK and then went at twilight to Shino's new brothel.

It was a two-storey house, flimsy and unpainted, on a back street beside the dirty moat. The musty water gave off an odour. There would be no high Chinese chest, no velvet draperies. The women from these places did not dress in finery or promenade to the teahouses in the late afternoon. They sat inside the lattice on display.

And there she was.

The light was on her face but not on us. We stood to one side, nearly touching the verandah, looking at the little crowd as if we were inside with the courtesans, not on the street with the window shoppers. She was perfectly composed. She wore thick white makeup, and I couldn't see the cut Jimi gave her.

A man crooked his finger.

Shino got up off her knees and walked, knees locked together, feet swinging out behind just a little, making the ends of her kimono sway like a tail, to the edge of the verandah. She looked over at us but gave no sign of recognition. She murmured something to the yobbo. Her manner was not very flirtatious, and the yobbo lost interest. She backed away and sat again.

The blind man came around the corner. He positioned himself in front of her, just as if he could see. His face was up, his ears wide, his fat tentacle fingers waving. The yobbo backed off. Mitsu had guessed right: the masseur had become Shino's client.

I visited her new brothel when I could.

It sat at the far end of the rectangle of land that was the Yoshiwara. There, the drained marsh reasserted itself; the street was always muddy, and as summer advanced there were mosquitoes. The proprietors didn't bother with coloured lanterns or flowering trees. Each dark door was the same.

Just before noon most days, I could catch her when she emerged. Down here, beside the well and next to a tiny burial ground, was an old Buddhist temple, its red paint worn to flecks. It was a quiet place: no one else went there. I followed her, but she asked me to wait a little distance away while she prayed. When Shino came away she smiled.

"What is this praying? I never knew you prayed."

"I have made mistakes," she said. "I must pray to the gods for the strength to control myself."

I waited, weaving in and out amongst the leaning gravestones of this famous courtesan or that. They had been buried here, once, with pomp, I supposed. But no one kept their graves. I spoke over the headstones, holding her from going back to her brothel. "One little mistake," I said. "You didn't hear him coming."

"Oh, more than one. I have let the heat of my temper get the better of me."

I did not see that as a mistake.

"Remember what I said," she instructed. "When your anger goes out—"

"Your fist stays in." I frankly did not see it.

"You must not feel pity for me."

"I know. Do you have open-kitchen days? Are the other prostitutes funny?"

No, she said. And there would be no more classes in self-defence. "You can practise in your mind and no one has to know," she said. She said she had quelled the demon of pride. She had learned to behave according to her station. "There is always someone watching."

The blind man came often. He was possessive. I understood that he had a name, but I would not use it. She didn't use Hokusai's name either. "Your father," she said to me sometimes, as if he were a man she did not know directly. She never asked me why he hadn't stepped in. We knew the answer: to buy her, he would have needed money. And although he sometimes was well paid, sometimes there was no work. When we had money it went quickly. Where to was a mystery, and he became fierce and scornful if I asked him.

Meanwhile the sad, wispy woman alone turned up in picture after picture. Anyone could see Shino was the woman he painted walking under willows, holding umbrellas, waiting for lovers.

"You have one who watches you and one who sees you," I said one day. "The blind man watches and Hokusai sees." But the blind man's watching was hopeless because he had no eyes. And even though my father saw her truly, saw who she was, he could do nothing.

"Maybe it's the opposite," she said. "The blind man sees me truly, without eyes, while your father only looks and sees the outside."

"One puts you on paper and the other puts his hands on you."

"Rude girl."

I had nearly made her cry and I was glad. I was cruel. The blind man was her livelihood now, her only client. Shino had to treat him with deference. She made this her discipline, her spiritual training. If she made him happy, with any luck he would see her through her term in the Yoshiwara.

"He is taking the training to be a moneylender," she offered. And then later, "He cannot come to me because he's saving his money to buy the licence."

I believed she had given me that message so I could tell my father, and I did.

UTAMARO JOINED THE MAD POETS AGAIN. His handcuffs, the chosen punishment for the "seated classes," as they called us, were off. But his hands hung heavy in front of him like useless things in which he had lost interest. His skin was yellow. His hair had fallen out. The bridge of his nose, the famous proud, high bridge of his nose, was bony.

The boulevard gossips said that Utamaro was too tired to go on. They said that he had given up, and that all he wanted to do was speak about the old days.

Then suddenly, he was dead.

He died of the handcuffs, people said.

They talked of nothing else.

No one dies of handcuffs. He was an old man already.

He died of the humiliation of the handcuffs.

No, he did not. They could not humiliate Utamaro.

But he couldn't paint with them on.

They'd been removed.

He died because he did not want to live.

15

THE BLIND MAN

THE CITY WAS FULL OF BODIES. Not only thrashed corpses and pickled heads, but quick bodies, wily and always in motion. The tattooed firemen raised their ladders showing cleaved buttocks and stout necks. Courtesans sat in windows with their kimono sitting wide over pale, round shoulders. The standing legs of throngs in the temple markets were like thickets of bamboo. If you paused going over a bridge, a dozen arms pushed you forward from behind.

Bodies were the spokes in the wheels that made the city roll. One day I'd watch a pack of girls learning a new dance. The next I'd catch acrobats in front of the theatre somersaulting to bring in the crowds. Boys flew kites in the riverbed and even the courtesans got out to play on festival days, batting at shuttlecocks. These bodies were my father's subjects. His brush was alive with them. Skeletal old men, tubby children, winsome girls, monks in prayer—whatever moved attracted his eye, and the movement went straight from his eye to his brush to the paper.

Carpenters and bricklayers heaved up their loads in the streets, adding storeys to our cramped buildings. The old ways cramped us too. We could not be contained. Even scarred Shino in her verandah with its wooden pickets would rise again. She would have a blind moneylender for her lover.

I saw how life was punishing and how bodies took the brunt of it. At the fishmarket I watched an exhausted old man drag his lame leg, dodging the brown, healthy young ones as they tossed a giant tuna back and forth. His wife tidied the shellfish on their cart: she was smaller than me, but her hands—scarred from the shell edges, gnarled and swollen-knuckled—

were brilliant, arranging frilled shells in exact lines. Those wrinkled fingers flashed; they darted like swallows, showing their ugliness only when still.

Women's bodies swelled like fresh fruit and withered just as fast. In the public bath I watched covertly as the married ones took off their clothes. After the evenness of youth, female bodies gave away to folds of flesh, rolls in the thighs, scrawny ribs. Yet each woman was proprietary, scrubbing off her dead skin, patting her pink, moist folds.

If he had nothing else, a man had his own body. A woman too had her body. At least until she took an adult shape. Then, most likely, a man wanted it. If he took it, he gave it back worn and used. I watched these things and, perhaps without knowing, decided that I would be the kind of woman men did not want.

My own body was dressed again in girls' clothes. I was fourteen and ugly. So everyone said. My jawbone was wide, breaking my face out in a diamond shape. My chin protruded with a round knob. They called me lantern-face. I worked in the North Star Studio. I was the errand girl for Hokusai.

The day I remember, I had gone with him to the bookseller's stall. I rested at the side of the street. I did this as often as I could. If there was dust, I drew in it with my toe. If there was mud, I used a stick to make my lines. If there was paper and a brush and ink, I made sketches from life, just as he did. This day I wandered off and hung around the fruit seller with her trays of watermelon until she gave me a piece. I slurped it down, and the thin, red juice drooled down my cheeks; I spit the black seeds up into the air. Shino would have been scandalized by my manners.

I stood for a while in the crowd gathering in front of a man who sold perfumes. "Almond blossom," he shouted. "Almond blossom." The sweet, delicate smell was lost in the charcoal fumes from the *yakitori* stand and the sweat that rose up amongst the bodies. Then I went back to listen.

My father was showing Tsutaya his new work. He'd made a design of a boat harlot, slumped in a corner and wrapped in a black headscarf. It was meant for an album of Edo courtesans. These were the lowest of the low; they worked in the cold, damp anonymity of the canals. The blacks and reds were deep, saturated on the paper.

"I don't think so," pouted the publisher. "It's so dark. Anyway, we don't need more courtesans. It's more difficult every day to get these things by the censors."

That annoyed me. The truth was I'd painted in the colours myself, after Hokusai made the outline.

He brought out another: *Tipsy Beauty.* The courtesan was drunk and leaning over a black lacquer box. I'd had a hand in that one too.

Tsutaya laid a heavy hand on my father's shoulder. "You're bound and determined to show the dark side. Fine, if it suits you. But I can't sell 'em. Not like this. Not unless I find a real connoisseur."

I went to the back and watched the woodcarvers; if the publisher bought our designs, these men stuck the paper to the cherrywood to transfer the image, and then cut the lines into the block. Their carving tools were crescent-shaped or knife-straight, in sizes from baby finger to fist. The carvers were tucked cross-legged into low desks, digging out tiny bits of wood and blowing them off the edges of their knives, cutting the fine lines of our writing as well as every sensual curve of the figures. I marvelled at their dexterity. They nodded silently to me, never losing concentration.

When I came back, I could see that my father hadn't made the sale.

"Why doesn't he publish you anymore?" I said.

"He's afraid I'm bad luck," said Hokusai.

It was his good luck that had made Hokusai bad luck. His good luck was that—with Utamaro gone—he was now the most famous artist in Edo. How you could be both famous and poor was still a puzzle to me, but that's how it was. His bad luck was that he was popular with foreigners, and the publishers suspected the authorities would turn on him. The Dutch were back in Edo, kept secluded in their strange house with its windows above eye level. Patient crowds stood along the bridge opposite. Every day, reports went out about who went in and out the tall door. Scientists and students of *rangaku.* Famous actors and courtesans, even Hana-ogi. It was she who sent word through one of the apprentices that Hokusai's old clients were again looking for his work. The *opperhoofd* wanted to see him.

"Tell him if he wants to see me, he has to come to the North Star Studio," said my father.

I don't know why he insisted on entertaining important people at home.

Our studio was like the scene of a crime.

It was only one room, identical in size to the adjacent room, where we lived. At least we no longer slept on the same mat. We all had separate mats, but they lay side by side, touching, around the hearth. In the morning we ate our food on the same spot. There were two of us females, my sister Tatsu and I, and the boy Sakujiro left at home: my older half-brother had been apprenticed to Nakajima the mirror polisher. It was the same family my father had been apprenticed to once, but he had not taken on the work, or the inheritance (another stick my mother used to beat him). Still, the Nakajima family remained curiously interested in us. Although my father—thinking himself too good to stand in the long hallways of the castle and rub the bronze so it was perfectly clean at all times—had flown in the face of their generosity when he was a boy, my half-brother had been conscripted to do the job. His labours brought in a little money—more than any of ours would have—so no one complained. My sister O-Miyo had married one of my father's students. Tatsu and I worked in the studio. My mother took Sakujiro to school. The boy was her greatest pride, and he knew it.

The "studio" wasn't big to begin with, just six tatami mats in size. The sides were packed with chests holding prints and studies. There were always students working with us, sitting on the floor or at low desks, drawing from life. There were chickens, monkeys, and rabbits in cages around and about. Someone usually had a bird in a cage or a fish in a bucket, and the cats—my pets—were always prowling and ready to pounce.

It was noisy too. O-Miyo returned to us by day, bringing her crawling son to the studio with her. He poked the cats with sticks and spilt the paint on purpose and laughed. I did not like that boy.

The work took over everything, and it brought us nothing: that is what my mother said. My parents still fought. My mother would not give up. She could not believe she wasn't going to get what she wanted. They fought because my father was bad about keeping track of money. And he spent it on his own entertainments, whatever they were—painting parties, a little gambling. Nothing out of the ordinary, but she felt he was cheating her. And so the noise of their shouting added to the screech of the caged birds and the sound of O-Miyo scolding her son and my father's mad, crazy laughter.

He kept us entertained. He painted with his left hand and with his right.

He could paint above his head or, by reaching between his knees, on the floor behind him. He made paintings with his fingernails, laughing while he did it. Just now he was writing a book called *Strange Food*. He played around with rice, soups, sake, tea, cakes, vegetables fresh and dry, crustacean eggs, and he sang this little song about sake:

> *At first the man buys the sake.*
> *Second, the sake buys the sake.*
> *Third, the sake buys the man.*
> *There is no limit to the way sake leads to disorder.*

IT WAS AUTUMN AND THE WIND BLEW the fragile awnings—*bang, bang*—against the shopfronts. The Mad Poets sat outside the teahouse by the Asakusa temple. I had a slate with me and was practising my characters. In the road, a thick figure appeared, wrapped up against the cold. Sadanobu. Again. The artists followed him with their eyes.

"Why does he come around here?"

"He's haunting us."

"Maybe he's ready to publish his novel."

But the jokes were thin.

"Maybe he too is frightened," said Sanba. "He wanted to make history. But history makes itself. And it will not make him look pretty."

The wind came down through the housetops and made the lamps swing. The glow passed over Sadanobu's face, uneven, orange, white, then gone. It passed over all the other faces, simplifying them, making them stark.

"I do believe he wants to tell us something," said Sanba.

Sadanobu moved in closer and, in that curious way of his, placed his body at right angles to become a silhouette, a caricature—soft paunch, hard chin, big nose. He took no notice of the jibes. His voice was low and reasonable. "I come to give a warning. A warning for the one they call Hokusai."

The Mad Poets were not to be intimidated. "There is no one by that name. Hokkubei, Hokuba, Hokutsu, Hokuta? I don't know who you mean."

"There was an artist of that name, but he sold the honour to a student."

Sadanobu appeared to laugh, silently, into his large belly. It rose and fell.

"Hokusai should know there are laws against giving details of Japanese life to foreigners," he said.

Then he moved on.

I looked at my father. He took a drink. It had come. What would we do? Nothing, apparently.

THERE WAS A DISCREET KNOCK and the studio door slid open. Father became alert, showing no sign of recognition but going slightly pink.

It was Shino.

Her long, thin face had become sharper during her days at the low-class brothel. The scar on her cheek had healed and sat just along her jawbone, almost invisible. The great bundle of hair wrapped on top of her head and pierced with several pins seemed to have stolen the energy from the rest of her body. The wide sleeves of her kimono and a thick obi dwarfed her figure, but the narrow lower skirt clung to her legs and pooled at her feet. She still looked too genteel for the life she led.

How had she come out of the Yoshiwara? She must have been on business, but what business?

I went to her. I had not seen her for months. My father snapped.

"Ei! I asked you to look at Mr. Bohachi's drawing."

"I did. It's not very good!"

The master gave an elaborate shrug. But he couldn't hide his smile. "Do you see," he said to Shino, "how she becomes more and more like me?"

"I thought I would take Ei to the bath, if you can spare her," said Shino.

Tatsu and O-Miyo looked annoyed. They minded my special treatment.

"Why should she be excused? She has work to do."

"She will discuss work with Miss Shino."

"Why always Ei?" muttered Tatsu. She scowled as I edged to the door.

"You are too old to whine, Tatsu. Get to work," said my father.

And we were gone. At the feet of the bridges mendicants were chanting and holding out their bowls: "Praise the Sutra of the Lotus. Praise the name of the Founder." They brought with them a scent of country air; they had parcels of mountain herbs tied around their necks. A mad-eyed soothsayer crouched with both fists holding a long bowl between her legs. "See your future," she called. Shino dodged her, refusing apologetically.

"I don't want to see my future," she said. "If I can't change it, why should I be warned?"

When she said that, I imagined the worst.

"Is there news? Is it bad?"

"News is whatever we make it," she said. "We must always be hopeful."

Life in the Yoshiwara was changing her. In the sunlight I could see wrinkles at the corners of her eyes and furrows beside her nose. Her beautiful hair did not shine as before, and the knot was wound in a way that looked several days old.

We reached the bathhouse. The entrance was marked with a carved wooden arrow; the sign read, "Adults, 10 *mon*. Children, 8 *mon*." Shino counted out the square-holed coins. The men's bath was next door, and the wife of the man who ran the men's bath ran the women's bath. The men's assistant peeked around the wall into our bath; he needed soap powder, he said. But I think he wanted to look at Shino. She was someone you wanted to watch. She was still taller than me. While we both lacked beauty, she had grace. I was short and bowlegged, like my father. My chin stuck out when I asserted my will, which was often. But Shino was quizzical, with that piquant face and frequently downcast eyes. Men liked that. They were misled to think she was meek.

We got our washing cloths and kicked off our sandals, untying our sashes. We squatted with small wooden buckets and scrubbed under arms and between legs, splashing the suds onto the polished wooden floors. We doused off the soap. We stepped carefully along the slippery wooden platform and tested the steaming water. The bucket boy eyed us.

"Too hot, is it?" he said. He was always polite around Shino. Everyone was. "Too cold?" Other women banged on the side of the wooden tub to get his attention: not us.

"A little more hot would be wonderful. You are very kind," she said.

The women looked up for a minute to hear her accent, before they went back to their pressing conversations.

Across from us were two wives, weirdly featureless, with no eyebrows and blackened teeth, complaining about their mothers-in-law. One had a good one, but she was old; the other had a nasty one who was unfortunately young and stood a good chance of living for many years to come.

"I wonder how mine will be?" Shino said bobbing her head significantly in their direction.

She had in her indirect way told me two things: that she would not be going back to the old husband, and that she would marry. I sucked air between my teeth. "Are you really going to marry? How can you?"

"I received word. My husband has died." Her face was impassive.

"So you don't have to send him money?"

"His brother now claims the money," she whispered.

An old lady bent like a scythe came to the edge of the tub. She had no teeth. Shino stood to help her down to the water. The rinsing boy came up and took the hand away from her. "No, you don't," he said. "That's my job."

Shino sat down again. She scooped the steam up against her cheeks. She closed her eyes. It was what she did when she was thinking. Or crying.

"But I could be free to leave the pleasure quarter. The blind man—as you call him—has offered to pay my debts."

I blew across the foamy surface. I slapped the water. "Hey, you! Cut that out!" said the married women in unison.

"In return for?"

"He would take me as a wife."

The rinsing boy was pouring water on the bent woman's back; she had small, round moxa scars all over it, from the burning of herbs we practised for healing. I stared gloomily at her.

"If that happened, would you be glad for me?" said Shino. "It would take some time . . ."

Why would I be glad, if she was crying? Why, if she was glad, had she said she didn't want to know her future?

"It is the best possible outcome," she said delicately.

I snorted. She was pretending to discuss with me what was already settled.

The woman beside Shino dropped her washing rag into the bath. It floated a minute, absorbing the water, and then disappeared. The bucket boy came, all gallantry, and dove into the deep. God knows what he saw down there.

"Better than what?"

The unspoken possibility of my father buying her, keeping her, freeing her sat in the air between us and then sank into the hot water as well. It would never happen.

"There you have it," she said. "*Izn it?*"

Someone again asked for more cold water from the bucket boy.

"No! No cold!" I said. I wanted it as hot as Shino did. Soon I would get out and scrub, then get back in again, one layer smaller. Shino too was nearly ready. Her face had become pink. Her skin had plumped out: maybe she was blushing; maybe it was the hot water.

"I think you care for him!" I suddenly accused. "That blind potato."

"But why do you hate him?" she said at the same time.

"Why?" I could list reasons: his hands; the unarticulated, dark shape of him, like some huge sloth leading with his nose, picking up her scent from his position amongst the window shoppers; his low, insinuating voice; the doggedness of his attentions.

"Blindness is an affliction," Shino said righteously.

"Oh, and must we love him for it?"

"We must not despise him for it." She turned her back and climbed out, modestly making her way to her scrubbing towel. The rinsing boy was ready for her back. I listened to the talk. It had turned from mothers-in-law to hairstyles.

"I had it done by someone new; it's not quite the same," worried the first woman.

"What happened to the girl you liked so much?"

"She went back home to the provinces, I heard. Her father is ill."

"It's always like that when you find a good one!"

I had to get out. When I did, I turned around and was right in front of Shino, who was cooled and rinsed and now returning.

"By the way," said Shino, "he has a name."

"I don't want to know it."

As always when I was clean, my clothes felt old, and I could detect their smell. I suddenly hated being poor. I had to be proud and not feel it. I had to be more noble than my mother. But I wanted to weep. I sulked and scuffed; I looked everywhere but at Shino. I said nothing, punishing her, until we turned the corner near our house. Then what I had been thinking came out of my mouth.

"Does my father know?"

"It is what he hopes for."

That was too much. I went cold, as if that rinsing boy had doused me right there, out in the open, fully dressed. "No," I shouted, there in the street. "You ask me a question: Could I be happy for you? The answer is no! I could not. If you marry him, it will be nothing but another form of slavery. You know it!" I hated Shino then. She was too proud to say to me that she was poor, that she had to survive. I would have scorned her if she did.

At the studio door the cats called to me and switched their tails with vehemence: no one had fed them. I put my foot under the male's belly and lifted him. I ran my palm along his bony spine and then tossed him away. He prowled the edges of the room until someone's elbow struck him and spilt an ink bowl. The cat hissed; Tatsu picked him up. He drooped on either side of her hands, his feet splayed in protest. She slid open the screen and threw him outside.

I watched my sisters—innocent of this whole life with Shino. I heard my mother amongst the cooking pots outside. She was a crash-and-burn cook, and a messy one. Hokusai sat like a happy, wiry Buddha in the centre of all this, entranced with something that was flying off the end of his brush—a goddess emerging from clouds.

I saw clearly in my rage. We worked, and he created. He alone was happy. And I—oh, lucky me—was his favourite. The one assigned to my father. My sisters felt that, and it made them dislike me. But they didn't know what it was like. I had no one but him. And he was changeable and, when he wanted to be, a mystery.

It was a burden to be his chosen one. My mother knew about Shino, but my sisters didn't. Hokusai's friends and the Yoshiwara people knew about Shino. I saw them together. It made me an outsider where I should have been an insider. This was my family. But as I folded my legs to sit on the floor beside a cold-shouldered Tatsu, it did not feel like it. He had taken away my family and made me his alone.

And now he would allow his beloved Shino to be taken by the blind moneylender. This made me see his ugly side. As if it weren't bad enough to have all of us propping him up—and him with a courtesan—now he would let the courtesan be sold off because he couldn't afford to keep her.

How did Shino and my father see each other? I had no idea, but I was certain they did. Did my father keep another room? Was that one of the ways he spent his money? Did they go, the two of them, to even lower-class brothels so the blind man did not find them? How had they come to the decision that lack of money would separate them, that Shino must be sold once more? "It is what he hopes for," Shino had said.

So they had spoken of it. Yes, marry the blind man, he must have said. I can't take you. Here is your lucky chance. A new life any broken-down prostitute would be grateful for. Was that what she was? The elegant, fierce, always patient Shino?

I hated Hokusai then. Why had I been given to him? To him and his lover, who did not even really belong to him? Why didn't my mother want me? I didn't want her either, that was true—but hadn't her rejection come first? My father chose me to help in his studio. Did he ever love me? Or did he just need help? Nothing really lasted with Hokusai. Everything was shed, everything changed; he moved past. It all went in the service of his great passion, this making of pictures, this making of fame. His brush he jealously guarded. And mine too: I could see him laying his hand on my work. It was my duty as a girl to help my father; it was our duty as a family to uphold this man's little kingdom. Which he mismanaged.

Here was one thing I had in common with my sisters, then: we were broken by his ambition and tied to his work. I must try to love them, I thought. How would they escape but to marry another of these men who eat people's lives?

I drew a series of round, fat stomachs of men and the ripples of flesh over their ribs—one of my father's specialties. "The best mother in the Yoshiwara," they called him. He reached his brush over the edge of his desk down to my level and corrected a line. I wanted to cry. I remembered Shino's instructions and tried to arrange my face in a pleasing manner. I was never successful. Still less, today. I thought, not for the first time and not for the last, If I have to be different, then I will be different. Not like my sisters—willing to marry. And not like my mother, bleating about how it was impossible for her to get what she wanted. That went without saying. Now I thought, Not like my father either. He was a bad father and a bad lover.

Shino and the blind man would marry. If no other way was found. It couldn't be helped. But not me. I saw what came for women, and it was not going to come for me. I could avoid it; I could be an artist. As for the love of a man for a woman, in my parents' marriage it had brought suffering. That was obvious. But with Shino there had been devotion and a measure of joy:

I had seen it. It was not legal, and it was not to be bought and paid for, but it existed along the canals and in the dark corners of the teahouses, under the lacquer trees—it was an outside love, an outlaw thing. I would be loyal to that. I believed in it, even if they didn't.

Crazy, I suppose.

I looked at the line he had put with his brush on my paper.

Much better than my own.

I studied it. My father could still give me something precious. He could teach me to paint. To learn from him, I did not have to believe he was a good man or a fair man. I had talent. I would get what I needed, and then perhaps I could escape.

16

SANBA

SHIKITEI SANBA CAME TO THE NORTH STAR STUDIO.

I was near the door as usual, the gorgon at the gate. Hokusai waved his hands amongst the students, intense, comical bald head gleaming in the lamps that lit the dim space. We had moved by then to rooms near Ryogoku. A huge fire had ravaged miles and miles of Shitamachi terrace houses the year before. Our tenement went up in flames, and many pictures went with it. But new shanties, papered with the wrapping from sake barrels because wood was in short supply, grew like mushrooms. They had the advantage of being clean, at least when we moved in. Now a student lived with us. Our pots of paint, our menagerie of restless caged animals about to be drawn, our stacks of paper covered the floor. Cats, made homeless by the fire, circled outside. I tossed our food wrappers their way, and they licked up anything with the smell of fish.

Sanba bowed low to speak to me. Could he come in?

He was that man who spoke to me at the poetry parties. Parodist, drama critic, and seller of face cream.

"Have you come to sign up for painting lessons? Or to see my father's work?"

"Perhaps I have come to see you."

"I doubt that."

"Can you show me some paintings?" he said, bowing again. "What is your name again?"

"My name is O-ooo-ei." I made the sound that meant "Hey, you!" I had begun to prefer it to my real name. Its street sound matched my raspy voice.

I sounded like a frog in a stagnant pond, my father said. It was part of my general unattractiveness. Did someone once put a hand around my throat and try to squeeze the life out of me? I don't remember. Shino had tried to teach me to sing, and in singing, to let go of the screams that I never let out, she said. She coaxed my natural voice to emerge. Not much better. It was low and brown, like the chestnut paste the confectioner squeezes out of his paper cones to make little pancakes. At least I would never sing along with the high-pitched women in their baby tones.

But Shino was not in my life now. I had not seen her since the day she took me to the bath. At fifteen, I was the rasping cricket.

And here was Sanba, leaning over me.

"What is it you are working on so furiously?" he said.

"At the moment, I am writing accounts," I said.

My father was teaching me to read and write the way men did. Women learned a less complicated set of characters because they had such limited free time. It took years to acquire the educated script. I liked it; it was convenient for him that I did, because that way I could keep track of what we were owed. What we owed, more often.

It was fun learning the characters. We had games to speed us along. Two sailboats made the number five, and pine trees made the character for "jewel." Each line of the numbers two, three, four, six, and seven was part of a drawing. A mouse sitting on a jewel for the God of Plenty, and flying bats. Nothing was wasted. I learned the character for "mirror maker" by tracing my father's drawing of a chubby, cheerful fellow whose rounded head and shoulders and thighs made a triangle as he sat on the floor with his wire brush, rubbing the surface to make it reflect. Hokusai had told me how, when he was apprenticed to a mirror polisher, he could never look the ladies and lords in the face. So he peered into the mirrors and saw them over his shoulder, and they never knew he was staring at them.

"I am very sorry to disturb you then, Ooooei. O-oei? That is not a name," said Sanba. "That is a call. Like a bird call."

"It is what my father calls me," I said. "It is easiest."

"And when he calls, do you come?" said Sanba. I think he must have seen the evil humour lurking under my disguise as faithful servant-girl.

"If I did, he would not have to call me so often, would he?" I said.

He laughed.

"And then I would have another name, wouldn't I?"

"I wonder what it would be."

"Ago-Ago is another he uses." I saw him examining my knobby chin. I thrust it forward.

"A sign of strength," he pronounced. "You haven't said if you remember me."

"I remember," I admitted.

"I am looking for someone to illustrate my books."

"You know his work," I said.

"Yes, but I want to see some."

I was beginning to think this was a fishing expedition. But I pushed my account book behind me and we picked our way to a corner of the workshop. I knew exactly which pile I wanted to penetrate.

I pulled out Hokusai's designs, laying them carefully one by one on the floor, then lifting each one and putting it away after he had seen it. Here was the boat harlot: he still hadn't sold this one. She was curled up in the stern with her head wrapped in black and her arms tucked inside a blanket. You could feel the cold and wet. She looked like Shino—who would never behave that way—but then, all his women did. I showed him a couple of night views of Edo.

"These are nice," I said grudgingly.

"Tell me what you like about them."

"Oh, well, the designs and the colours," I said. "But mostly I am happy for the lies they tell."

"Lies!" Sanba laughed. "Surely not."

"That's what they're for, isn't it? For instance, when the painters make scenes of night they show it as if you could see everything. But really you can't see everything in the night, because it's dark. So that is a lie."

"That's not a lie," said Sanba.

"What is it, then?"

"A technique."

"Just as I said."

"You're very absolutist for one so young."

I didn't like to be argued with. I flipped through the pictures with my fingers. "You don't think so? Look. In the picture of the *netsuke* workshop, he shows all women working. That is not true. Only men work there. But men are not so interesting to look at for the people who buy prints. So he makes women in those jobs."

"I see."

"Do you want to see the surimono?"

"Yes, please."

These were poetry cards that Hokusai made on commission to commemorate a birth or a death, a festival or a new year. They were delicate—beach at low tide, groups of figures amongst the weeds and shells and rusty anchors of the shore, glimpses of distant Fuji. These were influenced by Western art, and by what the Dutch wanted.

Sanba looked at these—the faraway objects painted smaller than the ones in front; the curved horizons. "He has completely changed," said Sanba. "That is brave for an artist who is not young anymore."

"He changes all the time."

"What is he working on now?"

Recently he had been making books of *manga*, which was another way of saying "everything in the world, and how to draw it." He took the sketches that he made at parties and made a collection of these pieces of paper, and from that came a little book for beginners that showed them how to draw. The simple pictures were often ones he had used in teaching me. I liked to think that he imagined them for me, bowlegged, bad-tempered girl that I was.

The pictures were of crabbed little people struggling to lift a barrel or stir a pot, of fat people, old women, drunk men, blind pilgrims. He used no models. He had seen them once, or maybe we had seen them together, but I forgot and he never forgot. And this first book, *How to Draw*, was a good seller. That made everyone happy, especially the publisher.

"Right now he's making a book dedicated to Japanese women. Each one will be in the grip of a powerful emotion, and each at a different stage of her life."

"Maybe he's too busy, then."

"I don't think so." I said. "We take anything on. What is it you want?"

"I'm thinking of writing a new version of *Chushingura*, the Forty-seven Ronin. You know this famous story. I want to add scenes that are not known. There's going to be another kabuki play of the story. Do you like kabuki?"

I smiled. It was something I rarely did. If you're not pretty, why try? If your eyes are not almond and meek but round and high, with tight lids stretched over the bigness of your eyeballs. If your bulging lids cannot contain the rude health and impertinence of your spirit. If your legs when pressed together would allow a good-size cat to slip between the calves. If your hairline begins far back on your forehead, which swells with more brain than a woman deserves, and your chest is bony and a glimpse under your blue cotton kimono offers only jutting collarbone. I was suddenly acutely aware of these things and shut my smile.

"Yes, I believe I do, but I have never been to the theatre."

Sanba continued to look at me searchingly. I thought he was going to say something more, but he didn't. My father was pretending to be engrossed in his work. I reached for some designs he had played with years ago. "This is how Hokusai would show the Forty-seven Ronin. Shall I tell you?" Everybody knew this story, but not our twist on it.

"Please," said Sanba.

"The daimyo Takumi no Kami had many loyal followers. But he also had an enemy, Kozuke, the Master of Etiquette. The reason for this secret hatred was that Kozuke had fallen in love with the daimyo's wife. He wrote her a declaration, which she treated the way a virtuous woman would, showing it to her husband. That was why the daimyo Kami raised his short sword against the Master of Etiquette."

"Really?" said Sanba. "That's a very interesting change to the story."

"After this, the overlord commanded that the daimyo Kami kill himself, and so he did. Therefore, his forty-seven loyal retainers had no jobs and had to become wave men. That means they rolled back and forth with the waves because they had nothing to hold them still. Are you paying attention?" I said.

"You're teasing me!"

"Not teasing but testing. Are you listening?" It was fun to talk to him. I was good at amusing old men. I played this way with my father.

"This Lord Kami, who had drawn his sword and had to die, you will remember, was very much liked by his retainers. And it was not his fault that he had raised his sword because he was upset about his wife. So his retainers made a plan and waited for a very long time. Then they would carry it out and get revenge on the overlord."

"Revenge! What is that?"

"You know. A special kind of noodle. It is eaten with broth."

This was a pun—inspired, if I may say so. My father and I made puns all the time. Sanba liked it and we started to laugh.

"Look at this one. It is the print of the ronins' attack on the overlord. It's night, but we can see everything. It's what I said before. A trick. That's what painters do."

"Trick people or lie or tell the truth?"

"Well, truth or lies." He was twisting my words so cleverly I was getting confused. I giggled. The painting students and my sisters looked up. My father scowled. We moved out into the alley.

"And I will tell you another thing if you are very interested," I said.

"I am."

"There is something very personal in this for my father. But you have to promise never to repeat it."

"I would never repeat gossip," said Sanba.

"Now that is a lie."

"My lies are just like the lies you see in your father's paintings, merely pragmatic." He was flirting with me. I had been slow to recognize it because it had never happened before. But that's what it was.

"Ah," I said. I was flustered. I decided to tell him the really important part. "This bad Lord Kozuke, who was *in reality* not Kozuke but Lord Kira, was the great-grandfather of the mother of my father."

"The great-grandfather of your father's mother?" He rolled his eyes and counted on his fingers. "How many generations back?"

"Four. Or five. So she says." In fact my grandmother often insisted on the nobility of her background. But something had put her amongst the peasants. She never explained what.

"That is a distinguished thing. To trace your ancestry to someone in the story of the Forty-seven Ronin."

"I suppose," I said dubiously. "But he was the villain. The wrong ronin!"

He laughed again. "That's quite an admission. Lucky I'm not a spy," said Sanba.

"I knew you weren't. They're fatter and have better clothes. Often they have small beards."

"Ah," said Sanba, "it's true."

At this point Hokusai got to his feet. His brow was wrinkled. He came to the door, wiping his hands. "O-ooei!" He smiled vacantly at Sanba and jerked his head for me to get inside. "O-ooei, can you look to the students?"

"My father will talk to you now."

"Good grief, my friend," said Sanba. "She is—what?—twelve at most? I wonder how the students like to be tended by her."

"She is fifteen. And they should like it. She's rather good," said my father with satisfaction.

They began to talk business.

"I am going to write a new vendetta storybook, for which I will need pictures," said Sanba.

"Ah, one of your formula cheapies? Whose work will you copy this time?"

"Not yours; no one would want it."

This was their way: to insult each other, and themselves, as often as possible. And they put their heads together. My father called my mother to get tea, and the two men stood happily side by side, at the door, pointing and comparing and nodding. I sat down and began working on the design for a set of combs.

17

ANTICS

WHEN I WAS NOT MUCH OLDER my father left our home.

First he went to live with his friend Bakin, whose novels he illustrated.

"Woe betide Bakin," my mother laughed. "Hokusai will bring chaos to his home with his dirty clothes and dishes."

The more successful my father was, the less respect she showed him. "Confusion reigns when Hokusai moves into your mind," she said.

He stayed with Bakin only a few months. Maybe they did drive each other mad. Or maybe he had finally taken Sadanobu's warning to heart. There were signs of another crackdown. Soon we saw my father at the door with his woven backpack and pilgrim's hat. He announced he was setting out "on travels." It was a clear, chilly day in early spring, with green shoots and the promise of blossoms.

"I hope you have your rainwear packed in that," my mother said angrily.

He did not, I could tell. There was no room in his pack, and he would reason that he could get a coat along the way when he needed it, maybe by trading a sketch or painting a lady's fan.

"Why are you going away?" I asked.

"To see things I can paint," he said.

"If you stand at Nihonbashi, all the things in the world will parade in front of your eyes," said my mother.

"Not the fisherman on the bank of a quiet river at dawn," said my father. "Not a rocky waterfall between pine trees. That I can see in Chiba, not in Edo."

"These are not the subjects of painting," said my mother with all the haughty air of she-who-knew-nothing. She believed, as most people did, that the only true subjects of painting were the sights of Edo, the fashions worn by the beauties, and the actors with their giant scowls.

"You are a critic now as well, are you?" said Hokusai.

I felt the cut. My sympathies, which were naturally with him, swung over to her. He who lived on respect gave her none. I had seen so many women bob around uselessly, trying to please men with foolish smiles, taking the low seat at dinner, walking paces behind. My mother had once tried; she did not like the result.

"A better one than those fools who call you an artist," she sniffed. She fought with more cunning these days, having learned a deadlier style from him.

"You know-nothing daughter of the slums."

Hokusai, who loved to call himself "a peasant of Honjo," nonetheless taunted her with his suspect high birth. Sometimes I wondered where this man had sprung from. Humble roots or noble, or some unholy mixture? Was his father Nakajima? Had he truly been born from one of the descendants of the enemy in the case of the Forty-seven Ronin? *Whack, whack* went my heart from one to the other, like a shuttlecock swatted with a racquet, back and forth. *Whack, whack*. It made me dizzy.

Waterfalls and quiet dawns my mother had not seen herself, only heard talk of. Like everyone she was curious to see the wonders of our country and go to the ends of the national roads that crossed right here at Nihonbashi. I knew she hated her life of drudgery, which she often said was brought on by us children and of course her husband. I added to my "never marry" vow the determination never to have children.

With my father's absence, I was abandoned. After her bitter announcement at the public bath, Shino had gone silent. I did not go to her brothel for fear of seeing the blind man. Had they married? Would they have children? Courtesans did not, usually. Something to do with the precautions they took when they were working, and certainly the abortions they had, made babies impossible. I was glad.

"Are you travelling alone?"

Hokusai smirked and said, "I left sketches and instructions for Mr. Kenma and Mr. Oburu to copy. You must supervise. Bohachi accompanies me."

I argued. Mr. Bohachi was a student of the North Star Studio who had worked for the city government and was now retired. He was too old to work and had plenty of money to pay for lessons, but could he walk miles at my father's speed? He was younger than Hokusai, who was over fifty-five years old now, but he would have no idea how fast or how far that old man walked. "You are jealous," my father said. I was.

And so, they left. We daughters were to run the studio.

My sisters took my mother's part in all quarrels, which was odd because they were born of Hokusai's first wife. They were older, halfway in age between my mother and me. O-Miyo behaved like a cow, making big eyes and swinging her lowered head winningly towards her husband, Shigenobu, still present in the studio as a disciple—and a poor one!—of my father's. And she indulged that son of hers, who had graduated from tormenting the cats to stealing neighbours' food and laundry.

In the studio, chaos reigned while Hokusai was on the premises. His drawings piled up in the corners like dry leaves. The money he made was left in its little envelopes here and there: we never knew what happened to it. On the now quiet, now curiously flat days that followed my father's departure Tatsu went through the piles of drifted paper in the corners, sorting the dried banana leaves that had wrapped sticky rice from the sketches of children playing with shuttlecocks and the brush paintings of ravens. Tatsu was hard-working and sensible. I liked her, but she tried to boss everyone and often succeeded. She was well organized. But this did not make her a talent, something she failed to understand. Meanwhile, younger brother Sakujiro continued his important education and my mother tended to him with something like love.

I finished work that was owing. I copied out sketches of trees—cedars with bushy branches going up; willows with thin, wispy ones trailing down. Odd, awkward drawings of women's hands and feet. He never did those well. Did he forget that women had use of these tools? The thatch roofs of sentry houses. Waves and beaches. Seeing these curling, crawling water ghosts, I remembered how my father and I had played in them. My heart was broken that he had left me with the women.

If I stayed face down over my painting I escaped the worst of the chores—cooking and disposing of dirt. Youngest girl but older than the boy: it was a position from which one could abscond, disappear, and I did my best.

Shopping was my forte, setting me free on the streets for an hour or two. I loved to walk, and to breathe the wind off the water. Occasionally I caught a glimpse of myself in a polished bronze shop mirror. I didn't seem to be as ugly as they said. But who could tell what others saw? I modelled myself on the cats, which had no idea what they looked like but lived in their bodies with complete, insouciant pleasure. I sometimes even took the ferry up to the Yoshiwara, stopping to see Mitsu and Waki but never hearing a word about Shino. And I dared not ask.

My father took his time "on travels." The leaves were blowing sideways out of their branches and the nights were cold when we heard he was back in the city.

"Like an animal to his den when the cold comes on," my mother muttered with satisfaction. He had yet to darken our door. And he did not: we suffered the indignity of knowing he was back in the city for three nights before he appeared.

One day his shadow landed on my paper. I felt his warmth over me in my cold corner. I began to trace his outline—the top of his head and the small bulges beside it that were his ears. Circles: everything is made of circles, he had told me. I crouched low over my paper and did not look up at him. I heard him laugh with pleasure. He nudged me in the back with his knees—our little signal of secret connection. I kept my eyes down so he couldn't see my tears.

I had learned to make the characters for heaven and earth, and so I made them carefully, first one and then the other, with my brush and I could feel that he was pleased. "Where did you go? How did you return?"

"We walked one way the whole time—forward," he said, smiling. "We never went backwards." It was our joke.

"So is it true the world is round?"

"We didn't get far enough to find out—we'll try another time," said the Old Man, and he and I cackled with laughter.

IT WAS WINTER. Cold but dry, the earth dead and hard as rocks. We needed money. My father went to Gokoku-ji, a temple on the edge of the town. He announced that he was going to paint an enormous picture. His disciples cleared a space in the centre of the square—seventy tatami mats by fifty. Tatsu and I were enlisted to push back the people to empty the square. In that space we pasted many sheets of paper together to make one enormous sheet. People stood around the edges gawking. Hokusai brought out a sake cask that was full of *sumi* ink. He had made a broom from hollow stems of the reeds that grew along the river. Lifting his enormous "brush" as if it were as heavy as an axe, pushing it along the paper like a street cleaner, Hokusai began to paint.

He made a circle, then he lifted and spattered the pigment. He made circles within circles, and straight lines next to curved lines. We knew he saw his subject in his mind's eye, but we did not know what it was. From where we stood, there were only broad and broken lines.

He twirled the broom on its brushes and put a foot up behind him, dancing. The more people laughed, the more he twirled. I worked my way along the edge of the crowd as people shouted out their guesses.

"It's the coastal highway. The black spots are the inns where you can have a waitress!"

"It's the mountains to the north."

Arguments broke out.

"No, it isn't."

"Yes, it is."

"When did you ever see a mountain?"

"There—in the two lines that meet in a peak."

"That's not a mountain, it's a roofline. No, it isn't a roof—it's a broken branch . . . it's an eyebrow."

People pushed, craning their necks, but from the flat ground, they could not see, any more than I could see, what my father could see in his mind. In the crowd were some of his artist friends. I also saw government spies, and I saw publishers. I saw the priests who commissioned altarpieces and lamps from us. They circled. But the drawing was too large to be read.

The first to climb to the temple roof were the firemen. They shimmied up the pillars and clambered on hands and knees over the roof tiles. Hokusai swooped around with his broom.

From the rooftop the firemen shouted, "It is the Daruma. It is the Buddha!" And it was. The crowd roared. How had he kept its giant proportion in his mind? He was a genius, so they said. He took his bows. And collected the coins that were thrown.

Sanba was there, not impressed. "A simple matter. Anyone could do it."

So much jealousy amongst these silly men! "Then why didn't they?"

"They wouldn't stoop to it."

"You mean they didn't think of it."

"It's not even so original; there have already been giant paintings by the monks Kokan and Hakuin," he said. "He did it only to make money."

"Is that something to be ashamed of?" I flared. "We need money. Don't you?"

Sanba touched my arm. "You are his loyal daughter; of course you would say that."

"I am. And if you are our friend, you are loyal too."

I knew that any artist might have done it for money. But Hokusai didn't. He didn't care for money. He cared not much more for us. He did it to be known. He cared for fame. I would go along: I had to. But I understood finally what I'd glimpsed the night I tasted snow in his arms. This ambition, my father's desire to be great and known as the greatest—not the *bakufu*, not cramps of hunger—was the true danger.

18

THEATRE

ON AN AUTUMN AFTERNOON when I was sixteen, Shikitei Sanba looked over my shoulder as I drew the fine temple hairs of a courtesan and her maidservant, who were pictured side by side, in parade. He stood there for several long minutes. I tucked my chin, fierce in concentration.

"Something I can do for you, *izn it?*" I said. We spoke the chic Yoshiwara dialect to amuse each other. Shino wasn't around to stop me.

"You can let me stand here unmolested. I am interested in what you're doing, that's all."

I thought of Sanba sometimes when I lay down at night and wanted pleasant ideas to ease my mind towards sleep. I would recall his presence, the way he included me as no one else did, even excluding others, as if he and I had an understanding. Prickles of warmth would come over my chest and climb up my neck.

Sanba and my father had a curious friendship based on rivalry. Sanba boasted that he was the only man in Edo who could live on his earnings from writing. Hokusai said that Sanba was obsessed with sales and cared nothing for quality. He said that Sanba was a hack, that his writing was trashy and borrowed from his betters. According to Hokusai, it was always the cheap imitations that sold and never the genuine. Anyway, if Sanba was so successful, why did he run his cosmetics store, offering secrets of eternal youth?

"Maybe because he really knows the secrets," I said.

It was true that Sanba sold cosmetics—black powder, red paste, whitening creams—just outside the Yoshiwara. He was the authorized and only dealer for the very popular Immortals' Formula Longevity Pills. On top of that he had invented his own makeup base, called Water of Edo. My father scoffed and called it eyewash. "He gets it out of the river. No limit to people's gullibility. They buy it in a bottle!"

But other artists had stores too, like Kyoden with his tobacco. Hokusai himself once sold condiments on the street. I began to suspect I knew why he mocked Sanba in particular. Despite the hack vendetta stories he produced on a regular basis, Sanba was a true original.

A cynic who believed in nothing, it seemed, but his own promises of eternal youth, Sanba had tight lips and frowsy hair. His dry jabs made everyone at the North Star Studio laugh, even my mother. He had credentials too, for having been persecuted. Before I was born, he had tangled with the fire brigades. Our flame-scarred citizens worshipped firemen, who were brawny but none too smart. When Sanba satirized them they attacked his home.

This brawl had given him his start and made him famous. The authorities punished Sanba instead of the troops. He was manacled for fifty days. He showed me his wrists. They bore the badges of honour of the sitting classes, scars where the leather thongs had torn the skin. They were the same as those on Utamaro's wrists.

"I celebrate them," he said. Waki had made tattoos of cat claws around the risen, white tissue that circled his wrists and wound up his forearms. Surprisingly muscular forearms.

I wouldn't see him for months at a time. Then in a minute, like today, just as I was finishing the hairline of a Beauty, he would appear.

I moved my brush minutely, as I had been trained to do. Sanba leaned against my back. I could feel his bony shins on either side of my spine. "Let me take you to the kabuki."

"I'm working."

He spoke to Hokusai. "Give the girl a break. You work her too hard. Anyone would think you can't get on without her." He coughed his small, practised cough.

He knew how to twitch Hokusai's pride. I blushed and bent farther over my painting. He said in a loud whisper that went in my ear and also over my head to Hokusai, "She's got to see some of life, *izn it?*"

It was eleven o'clock in the morning, the Hour of the Snake. The clouds spun across the sky, lit from above as a sharp wind came in off the sea. Smoky yellow and grey moved off, leaving a clear, cold blue. Sanba strode ahead making instructive comments, as this was for my edification. His voice was bigger than his frame.

"'Edo is the land of splendour, and without it there would be no place to sell things'—have you heard that famous line?"

I had.

"It's mine," he said. "I said it first." He tried again: "There are three places where one thousand gold *ryo* change hands during the space of a day. Can you guess what they are?"

"The fishmarket is one," I said.

"Yes."

"The Yoshiwara must be another."

"You are too smart."

I pretended I didn't know the third.

"And the kabuki district."

"Ah." I scuttled behind him.

"Come up, don't lag!" he commanded. "You are my companion, not my servant."

The Yoshiwara had burned to the ground. Again. We picked our way over the wasteland of broken timbers and ash, and discussed the rumour that the inhabitants had burned it down themselves. Certain courtesans had been charged with arson. Sanba was on their side.

"Good riddance to the place," said Sanba. "It's not what it was. No fun at all unless you like brigands wearing black hoods."

He showed me a cellar where, he said, prostitutes were tortured. The house above it had collapsed. "It won't be the end of the cruelty," he predicted. "The owners have been given permission to relocate for a year, and they're ecstatic. Things will be even worse: there won't be any rules in the temporary quarters."

We passed the area designated New Yoshiwara. Brothel houses were going up faster than shingles could be found: like our tenement, they were sided with the sake-barrel wrappings, a paper in abundance at all times. A troop of blind people with shaved heads moved together across the rough ground, singing out directions to one another.

We got a ferryboat along the Sumida, and Sanba stretched his arm along the gunwale. "I'm taking you from one evil place to another," he said.

The Nakamura: I had walked by it many times, but I had never been in. It was not only for lack of money but also for lack of time.

"It's where I am most days. When the orchestra plays the first strains of music I'm in my little seat close to the stage. Although sometimes more goes on in the audience than it does on the stage. I get splashed by water and mud. I never go out to get food. I just wash down a few bean-jam buns with tea. I never get tired of it."

"Why?"

"It's an immersion into the whole business of being human, that which Buddhists tell us is of no importance."

"I take it you are not religious."

He laughed.

It was opening day and tickets were free. Men were beating the drums from the turret of the three-storey wooden theatre. The outside was hung with prints and advertisements and paper lanterns. We pushed through the sellers of sticky rice balls, hot teas, eels, and souvenirs. The crowd was mostly men, but there were a few women. A lady of the court hid her face under the deep slant of an umbrella, finely ribbed and dyed a beautiful eggplant colour. Members of Danjuro VII's fan club were lined up with his crest on their kimono, on their headscarves, even on their umbrellas. They were already shouting out praises.

"Nothing to do with the show. They've got their opinions memorized," said Sanba.

Facing the crowd, on the verandah of the theatre, were dancers with scarves tied under their chins. They fluttered fans from cocked wrists. Women were not allowed to perform. These were men imitating women.

"Even so, the law demands that they be unattractive," murmured Sanba, "to protect our morals."

We were in no danger.

A man with a yoke over his shoulders sold watermelon. Sanba bought me some. I loved its colour, red verging to crimson to pink, the crunchy flesh, the sweet juice, the black shiny seeds and the way you could spit them.

No one had ever bought me anything just because of a gleam in my eye. I ate and slurped and spat happily. As we waited, the *kago*-bearers pushed through. Sanba carefully took the watermelon rind from my sticky fingers.

"Here come the investors," Sanba said. "If the play is popular, they'll be rich men. Or they'll be paupers. It depends on what I say."

He gave his little self-mocking grin.

Out of their sedan chairs stepped the sleek, well-dressed men. They checked in all directions to see that their heavy coats were being admired, then shrugged the silk up their shoulders, shook out the folds, and faced the theatre. They nearly pawed the ground with their feet, so eager were they to get inside. I saw the investors' pasty, broad-cheeked faces and knew they were very nervous. I thought one or two of them gave Sanba a glance.

"You see how a cosmetics seller from the wrong part of town can get a little power?" he said. "They recognize me. They want a good review. But oh no, no, no. My good opinion can't be bought," he said.

The front row of people pressed closer and closer to the verandah, where the shapely male dancers minced and flipped their fans. Guards came to push them back. Sanba pulled me out of the way. A manager crooked his finger at us from the side door, and we were in.

In our box seats Sanba's knees were crammed against the barrier. Mine didn't reach. Above us were wooden timbers and more boxes where women sat fanning themselves from excitement. Below was the pit where labourers camped out with food for the day. I looked down on a mass of turning, tilting heads, ear to ear and nose to nape—I couldn't see between them. A long wooden ramp stretched overhead from the back of the theatre to the stage. This was the *hanamichi* where the great Danjuro would appear when his moment came. His fan club was going wild behind us. Actors, like us, were not officially counted as persons, but if Ichikawa Danjuro VII was not a person, I thought, he must be a very rich horse or cow.

Sanba bought me a booklet to explain the play. The paper was soft and the pages clung to each other. I held it to my chest and hoped he would let me keep it.

"I was going to take you to see a play of domestic realism," Sanba laughed, "but I thought perhaps you had had enough of that."

"Rude."

"Instead we will see a play about severed affection. The plot goes this way: A woman declares she is out of love with her lover and urges him to discard her, but she does not mean it. She is doing this for his good. The lover does not understand her sacrifice and murders her. Her ghost comes to haunt him, with the intention of protecting him, but instead it drives him mad."

I still went to storytelling halls when I had time. "I know a lot of ghost stories," I said, "but that sounds more improbable than most."

"Do you think so? On the contrary. Those reverses are all too familiar to me. You see, Ei, your father has not prepared you for life. You only know reprobates. You are sheltered from the disastrous hypocrisy and conventions of proper people."

The story made no sense, but I loved the roaring, the postures, the applause, and the abuse. I watched the way the actors' faces worked while painted white, with red lines across the cheeks. I forgot the dragging hours and lived inside the wrenching, overdone lives. When it was finally over and we got out into the tainted sunset, I felt as if I had two sets of eyes, my usual and a new set. I towered over my own body and looked down from above. Sanba and I had screamed and suffered as one. Now in the cold, damp air I moved closer to his body. And he pressed against me, once, and then moved away.

Would I like to meet the great Danjuro VII? Who wouldn't? I climbed the stairs to the actor's dressing room on the third floor feeling proud: everyone treated Sanba with respect. "Welcome, teacher. Come and see, give us your thoughts. What did you think?" they asked.

At the top Sanba called out. The door opened and there was Danjuro the man, diminished to a fraction of his size. The costume was gone, he was perspiring, and the makeup was tacky on his face. Sanba produced a cloth from the folds of his kimono. "Would you mark this cloth for her?"

The great actor took the square of cotton, opened it like a book, and laid it on his two palms, flat. He looked at us.

"I see sparks flying."

"You see no such thing," says Sanba. "This is Hokusai's daughter. I am saving her from toil."

Danjuro raised his painted eyebrows. The effect was large in the narrow doorway.

"I hear the great artist uses his daughters as models for the *shunga*—"

"That is mere gossip," said Sanba shortly.

"Gossip!" said Danjuro. "Shikitei Sanba complains of gossip?" He laughed, and his laughter floated over us like a ticklish, escaped feather.

I reddened.

"Better to stop talking and give us your face print."

"Of course. I am your slave, critic," said the great actor. "What will you write about my performance today? Never mind. Don't tell me." He turned his eyes to me. "And what do you think of the play? Will it succeed?"

I had nothing to say.

"It's not a great play," said Sanba, "but that may be in its favour. There is an appetite for these ghosts. It is the times."

"They take everything your man here says with deep seriousness. I see the audience reading his reviews even in my finest moment," said Danjuro. He began to laugh, Sanba with him.

People called for Danjuro to appear. But he was in no rush. He held the square of cotton. Then rapidly and fiercely, the actor pressed his face into the cloth as it lay stretched out in the palms of his hands. He pressed the cloth into his face, and his face into the cloth, and held it very still. Then, in a moment, he lifted it. He passed the cotton to me. His features were on it. Eyebrows, nose, lips, cheek gashes. It was a print, a seal of his face.

Sanba and I went to a restaurant on a boat tied up along the river. It was dark and dank and narrow. I suppose it was a place where no one would see us. And that seemed important, all of a sudden. Angled walls—we were down in the belly of the boat—and dark wood made it cozy. Sanba lit me a pipe with a match string he held over the tip, and passed it back. I inhaled deeply and felt the smoke burn my throat and my eyes. I drank some sake. The owner approached; he joked about picking up women. He must have meant me. Sanba was apparently the expert. He had come here before with a girl. This delighted me: I was glad to be in experienced hands. The owner fed him more than sake and soya beans—he fed him questions that Sanba could dilate on for the entertainment of those few men slurping their noodles at the bar.

"Hey, Sanba, if I want to seduce a Buddhist nun, how should I go about it?"

"Confidently," he said. "They are amongst the very easiest." He coughed and downed more sake. "Women become nuns on impulse and later are hungry for male company."

"But it's against their religion."

"Not at all," he said. "If the Buddha cautions against sex, it is because most people develop attachments. To fornicate is sweet and good. Just remain detached and there is no harm."

I swayed on my heels where they dug into my buttocks and sucked softly on the pipe. I loved the rough, scalding smoke in my throat. It was like doing myself a violence, but one of strange comfort.

When we had eaten Sanba said he would show me where he worked. We walked to a small upper-floor room; a futon was on the floor. But something that had been said earlier had not left his mind.

"It is true what Danjuro said, then? Hokusai uses his daughters as models for the *shunga*?"

It was true; we modelled, in a way. But it did not merit such shocked gossip.

"Then you are not entirely innocent?"

"Not entirely." I smiled.

I was untouched but not unseen. If I had lost something it was a gradual loss and not one that was thrust on me. It was true—I had been research for the *shunga*. It wasn't only me but also my sisters, when they were younger. We slept in one room. My father had seen our kimono open to reveal thighs, buttocks sometimes. My breasts, which hardly existed, and the buds and folds between my legs—all these had been examined.

I did remember my mother hectoring from the step-down kitchen: "Why bother the girls? Go to the brothels for that. Better still, you have a wife." But she was always instructing my father, always finding fault, telling him in a shrill voice that he had done something wrong. This wasn't any different. The voice simply announced that this examination of Ei or Miyo or Tatsu was an irritation to her, and while it might be a matter of convenience to my father, it wasn't—what?—good manners, or in keeping with her ideas of current style, or a thing you did with your family.

But scandal? No.

I was willing to help. Lying on my back, my legs waving as if I were an overturned beetle, I laughed, and so did my sisters. It was all for the pictures: my father had drawn my parts with great precision, afterwards comparing them to pictures he had seen in the Dutch anatomy books then circulating in Edo. My mother, far from being old-fashioned, the way he accused her of being, had an idea of privacy that would exist only in the future. We lived in small rooms; we were all there together, day and night. We heard one another and smelled one another and saw one another. I took my sisters' clothes. They stole my drawings. We all searched for the coins my father earned and lost.

I untied my obi in front of Sanba.

And yet.

It left me open. To him and to others. I had given something away before I knew I had it. I had to take it back so I could give it properly.

Sanba said to himself, "I seem to have made the decision to deflower Hokusai's daughter."

"Don't 'daughter' me here," I said. "I am Ei."

"So you are," Sanba said to me. "Relax."

Difficult when under duress. "I'm trying," I said.

"Don't *try*, whatever you do," he said. "That makes it worse."

He touched me under my robes. His fingers were not soft but hard and probing. But they had expertise, I had no doubt. He knew just how to work through the furrows. My skin shrank. I hid my face. In hiding I came upon the smell of him, his chest, his kimono. I liked that part. I just didn't like him touching my private places to try to make something happen. I didn't want him to know how I worked.

But he continued on. I did not live up to normal performance standards. There was my reluctance to be known. There were some shocking parts that hurt. But somehow we got through.

And then I fell asleep, deeply. Sanba woke me from it and walked me home. I carried my square of cloth with Danjuro's face print on it. At home I slid open the screen and the cold air entered the room.

Hokusai was still working. He did not look up. "You are home smelling of tobacco," he said declaratively. "And relatively safe, I suppose."

"Relatively," I said.

We both lay down until morning.

THERE WAS NEWS IN THE YOSHIWARA. So Mitsu told me when we dropped in to her shop. It concerned the courtesan Shino. The blind man had written a letter to the owner of the canalside brothel saying he would buy out Shino's contract. I acted as if I didn't know. "But that's not all! Oh *no,* that's only the start of so many complications!" That owner had asked for a certain sum to pay her debts. Then Jimi, her original owner, stepped in.

Mitsu laid her hand along her jaw as if she had a toothache. She grasped her countertop with one hand; the magnitude of the announcement might blow her off her feet.

"What complications?"

"Kana and Jimi say they still own her."

"Jimi doesn't. He sold her," I said idly. I peered inside the display case wanting to see the seahorses, whose grace and fragility I loved. I wondered if I looked different since I'd been with a man, and if Mitsu would notice.

"He claims that he didn't, that he was just punishing her, that he was about to take her back. He claims that she has debts with him too. He says he was acting in anger and the sale is not legal. He says the Corner Tamaya still owns her."

"Then why don't they take her back?"

I watched my father's face to see if he flushed or showed guilt. He did not.

"It seemed it would all fall through. And here with a man willing and ready! A shame, *izn it?*" But, no surprise, money will solve it, the blind man will pay. He's panting for her."

It was rather graphic even for Mitsu, and I was rewarded with a slight flinch by Hokusai.

Mitsu moved out into the light of the street. I followed. "Jimi and Kana are insisting that they always loved her, that she was like a daughter to them. This is all for the benefit of the blind man, who can be milked for more and more money."

She finally looked at me. She was alerted to a change. "Something's different," she muttered.

Hokusai's lip curled. "How long will this take? She will not be beautiful forever."

I laughed in his face. "The masseur is *blind,* Old Man. Does he know that she's beautiful?"

"He knows," said Mitsu. "His eyes have not, but his hands have seen her."

Why did we say these words? They were hurtful to everyone. We were silent and moved apart. Mitsu developed a furrow between her eyes. Then she clapped her hands, like a babysitter calling the children.

"Never mind! Shino is making history. She's the only woman in the Yoshiwara who has been sold three times and will be free by her twenty-seventh birthday."

So Shino would marry. She could dress in plain indigo cotton, woven in stripes, like any townswoman. To our shame, neither my father nor I expressed gladness for her. We walked on with Mitsu still talking.

"Oh, and *that'z* another thing. The blind man has family! Like worms they've crawled out of the woodwork. Just a poor dumb masseur stumbling around the pleasure quarters and he had nobody, but now he's a money-lender"—she brushed her thumb and forefinger together—"we find out he's got parents and a brother, all living in the suburbs." This little cynical snip of life amused her and she started to laugh, and tears wobbled on her cheekbones.

"So where is Shino now?"

Mitsu lifted her shoulders slowly, grandly, and dropped them. She fixed her dark pupils on me. "I don't know."

I went to the canalside brothel at twilight. Shino was not sitting behind her lattice. I was thankful but apprehensive. I asked one of the other women where she'd gone. "Corner Tamaya," the white-faced shape said out of the side of her mouth where she knelt in the lamplight.

At the Corner Tamaya, Kana opened her arms to me.

"A woman you've become, *izn it?*"

"It is." I was happy and blushing. "How do you know?"

"I can see it. You have a secret smile."

I smiled, not secretly.

"You've come to see Shino. I know. You are so happy for her. But she is not available."

"Oh."

"She's getting ready. This is her number-one day. Her last parade. Yes, her debt will be paid, you know. She will go out of the pleasure quarter a free woman. We wanted to do this much for her."

"What is she doing?"

"The hairdresser has come. She is putting on her makeup. Putting on her lovely kimono for the last time." Kana opened her hands once more to show there was no limit to what the brothel would do for her. "Then she will give it away. She will give away her bedding too, tonight."

I couldn't imagine anyone would want it.

The retirement parade was a ritual, although it was rare to see it. "Go on, now. Come back in a few hours and you'll see her."

I stood by the side of the boulevard. They came out of Corner Tamaya at twilight, the courtesans Fumi II and Yuko walking on either side of Shino. She did not stumble on this, her last public march, but smiled faintly, distantly straight ahead and held her chin up. The apprentices came behind carrying boxes of "gifts," and the "boy" who carried the waste, that pathetic old man, paraded last.

There was a crowd.

"There she is, the *yakko*. Can you see the scar?"

"She walks beautifully, *izn it?* There won't be one like her again."

"She deserves her freedom. She was kind and good."

Retirement was a kind of death to a courtesan. A good death: an end to that life of serving men. Her name would die too, I supposed. I wondered what name she would take tomorrow. She would be an ordinary woman, and she would leave the Corner Tamaya as a daughter left her parents' house, to go to her new husband—that is, after he had handed over the money. Tomorrow there would be no more Shino. Who would she be? I wondered.

My friend looked neither right nor left. Her eyes saw no one: they weren't supposed to. She looked straight ahead into the future and did the figure-eight step with perfect balance. Each step ended with a little circle kick out the back, which signified her tossing off this world of debauchery.

I meant to go back home, but I couldn't leave her. I went back to the Corner Tamaya and coaxed Kana to let me inside. Shino was not allowed outside that night, in case she ran. I came in to see her seated in front of her oval mirror while Fumi shaved off her eyebrows. It was the custom for married women. Fumi soaped the arch of soft black hairs that had always informed me ahead of time of Shino's mood, whether it was dangerous or not. Then she pulled them out, one by one.

"You'll have a wide forehead, to be in the wide world," said Yuko. The women tittered.

"Your hair will be down and you will wear the blue stripes of the townswoman."

All these good wishes! Hanging over the screen were a wedding kimono of white silk and a dress for after the ceremony, made of red silk. The blind man had given the fabric. His family waited for her. They had come to dinner to meet her the night before, and she had charmed them with her koto and her dance. She had spoken to them of poetry and religion, just as she ought.

"You shuddv *heard* her: she wz fabulous. We listened behind the screen," said one of the apprentices. "The way she *talks* 'z music!"

The last part of the ritual took place in the kitchen. The maids brought a large bowl of water. The Yoshiwara was marshy land, originally. Before leaving it, a retiring courtesan washed its mud off her feet. Shino's feet were narrow and arched, unblemished. They would be clean when she started her new life.

She sat on a stool and put one foot in the bowl, wincing from the cold. We each took a turn, soaping one foot and then the other. Yuko tried to remove the bowl; a fresh bowl of rinse water was on the way. She slipped and nearly fell, catching herself on another girl's shoulder. That girl pushed back. Shino dipped her toe down and sent a perfectly aimed spray at Kana's face. I put my hand in the bowl and swept out a great wave.

"Aeeii, you little shit! I'm soaked!" Fumi got control of the bowl, dumping half of it on me. "Let's wash off those sins!"

"You're terrible! More water!" Everyone was splashing and sliding across the wooden floor and laughing.

I got no chance to ask Shino what her mother-in-law was like. I heard that her dowry belongings had been carried to the in-laws' house already: her box of shells, her white face paint, her black brush and tweezers, even her long pole with the blade on the end, the *naginata*, reclaimed after these years from Shirobei, the guard at the gate. Now they had everything but her. I hoped it was true what they all said, that the family would accept her as the daughter they needed. After all, the son they had to offer was damaged goods as well, wasn't he? I begged Kana to let me sleep over. My father would think I was with Sanba. But I wanted to stay at the brothel as I had when I was a child, one more time.

And I did: we lay on her mattress.

"What name will you take?" I said. "What was your name before?"

"I will not retire my name. I have discussed it with my husband. The young wife who was sent here is dead. But Shino is not. We have enough name changes in our lives, don't you think?"

In the morning we rose late. Her new white feet she put into socks. Socks! Allowed for the first time in nearly ten years! Her feet had always been cold. We wrapped her in the new kimono. She grasped me by the shoulders as soon as she saw me and asked me to carry her bedding to the women on the canalside. "They need it," she said.

The ceremony was nearly the same as a funeral. Jimi and Kana had lit torches at either side of the door, to signal the departure of a dead body. The blind man and his brothers came to the front door with a palanquin. Kana tossed rice grains in the little carrying box to purify it. Then Shino stepped inside, and the porters lifted it for her journey back across the Bridge of Hesitation. I saw no more of her.

I missed her terribly for almost a full year. But when the date of her marriage came around again, I stopped hating her and began to understand what it is to stay alive. We ourselves were working from dawn until the light fell. I thought I might one day see her at Nihonbashi or near the theatres, her hair tied and hanging down her back, loosed from its artificial courtesan's mound. It was one reason I loved to do the outside errands. But Edo was so enormous. I supposed there was little hope of our meeting by chance.

19

THE PAINTING COMPETITION

ON CERTAIN OCCASIONS Sanba dropped by the studio, diffident in his plain black kimono. Could I come to the theatre?

Once, after we had made our plans, Hokusai looked over and said, "You think you are pulling one over on your old man, don't you?"

"No, I don't."

But he didn't stop me.

In the theatre I entered the melodrama of my times. I watched depraved sons and greedy merchants. I liked the warrior plays, stories set in the long-ago past but understood to represent the politics of Edo. Evil murderers, virtuous wives: I loved the suffering the actors put up onstage. I shouted along with the mob. Sanba called me a true believer.

After, to calm ourselves, we sat and smoked. I critiqued. I'd say an actor was heaven to look at or getting long in the tooth. A writer must live with his head down a mole hole. Or the costumes made my mouth water. "I just like to hear you talk, Strong-jawed Woman," Sanba would say. I could make him laugh, especially if I drank sake. And if he drank sake, he wanted to take me to bed. I must have pleased him a little, or he wouldn't have kept asking. I'd creep home before dawn, when the stars were still visible, in the Hour of the Ox. My father would unfailingly be hunched over his work.

The Forty-seven Ronin project never materialized, not with Sanba. My lover was always behind on his deadlines. He liked it that way. When he really needed to produce he took a room over his publisher's office. And if that didn't work, he went into hiding. He emerged, sometimes weeks later, with a finished manuscript and a desire to celebrate. He found his home distracting because he had a small son. I didn't know where he was most of the time.

But I knew he'd reappear. We sat in little bars on barges along the Sumida. We walked along together—slowly, because Sanba suffered from gout that made his feet and ankles hurt. I drank with the crowd of printmakers, writers, and hangers-on—my father's friends, or they would have been, had he taken time to hang out with them.

I was happy then. I was a known entity: Hokusai's daughter, Sanba's lover, an apprentice artist. So what if my ears—like my father's—were meant for a person twice my size? If I was afflicted with the inability to be compliant? This body gave me pleasure, and Sanba too.

A miracle had happened. Life had opened a place for me.

MY FATHER WAS POOR AND PROUD OF IT. I began to understand why. It was his image, and it helped him become famous.

One day a furnisher for the Shogun came to the North Star Studio. This in itself was astonishing. More astonishing was that Hokusai took a dislike to the man and said he was busy. "I come not to buy a painting," the messenger told me. "I come with an invitation." He looked as if he wished he didn't have to.

Hokusai was not painting, but he was thinking about painting. Sometimes this took a long time. He sat on his mat in full view of the messenger, who was kept kneeling in the doorway. It was early summer. Our clothing was thin, plain cotton. The messenger remained on his knees, in his bright, padded jacket bearing the crest of the Shogun. Eventually Hokusai waved. The man could speak.

"I bring an invitation to join the Shogun Ienari on an afternoon of hunting."

"Hunting?" my father murmured, very low. "I will show you hunting." He asked me to bring him his outer robe.

Hokusai clad the subjects of his paintings in sumptuous velvets, but his own outer robe was shabby, had been worn many times, and was never cleaned. I reached it where it hung over the top of the screen, noted its odour, and carried it to my father on outstretched arms. I hoped to demonstrate to the messenger of the Shogun the necessity of showing deference.

Hokusai took the coat on his knees. He stretched out the collar and squinted at it. He made a quick jab, two fingers held like pincers. He gave a grunt of satisfaction. He peered again, running the fabric through his fingers. "Ah!" he said and again jabbed at the garment. "Mmmm!"

He was hunting a louse. I tried to see the messenger's face, but I couldn't. He didn't move; I didn't move.

He caught a dozen, crushing the barely visible creatures between the tips of his thumb and forefinger with great noises of satisfaction. He seemed to be alone in his world. To interrupt would bring a shower of abuse. The messenger, accustomed to self-abasement at the palace, waited. Hokusai hunted and pecked, hunted and pecked.

Finally he had had enough.

"Hey, you! Ooo-ei," he said. "Is there a messenger waiting?"

"Yes, Father."

"Tell him I can see him now."

The invitation was to attend a falcon-hunting party at the tidal gardens. The painter Buncho of the Shirakawa clan would be there, and the Shogun wanted an impromptu painting competition. This was the heart of enemy territory. Sadanobu was fond of Buncho. Suddenly Hokusai was jovial.

"I would be delighted. One request: may I bring my daughter?"

The messenger bowed. "We provide you with as many servants as you need."

"No, no. No servants. Only my daughter can be trusted with my brushes."

I didn't mind the long walk to the hunting site. It was the live chicken that annoyed me. Hokusai strode resolutely, bowlegged, in front. I came behind with the ink, and the squawking covered cage that bumped against my shins. People averted their eyes, as if I were burping uncontrollably. Behind me the Shogun's servant carried the roll of paper and a large mop.

Our destination was the marsh at Tokyo Bay, near the mouth of the Sumida River. Ienari had become Shogun at eighteen; he was over forty now. Sadanobu's reforms had affected him perversely: he was dissolute, quixotic, and indulgent. He had built a brothel inside the castle, lattice and all. All of Edo knew he often cancelled his afternoon appointments to take a falconry day in the marsh.

The tide flooded in and out through a narrow water gate. A huge pine tree grew at one edge. It was famous because it was 150 years old. Irises with fat purple flames were in bloom. Riding trails threaded around a little teahouse. A small mound representing Mt. Fuji was there for ladies to climb.

The Shogun's retinue stood by, with mounted warriors and standing warriors as wide as they were tall. Ienari himself beckoned us on, smiling and lighthearted; he looked like a fat boy. We trudged over three bridges that zigzagged through the tall grasses. They stood in water a foot deep, the pillars supporting them iced with salt.

I felt the nearness of the sea. The tide was coming in. At the sandy edges of the water little crabs scuttled. The sun was hot, and as the water rose, the marshes began to glint, like metal. The birds couldn't hide—not the ducks along the soft edges of the sandy earth that bordered the pond, or the small birds with yellow wings that were perched on the tall spires of sea grass, bending them.

The falcon sat on Shogun Ienari's wrist with the sun flashing on its majestic little metal helmet. It was chained and clad in feathered leggings. The Shogun wore an elegant deerskin glove. Everyone stood as in a trance. In the silence you could hear the insects. Hokusai scratched his ass. Buncho, the official artist, stood straight and looked at home surrounded by lords. Sadanobu—paunchy, hard-nosed, softer, somehow womanish—stood nearby. He looked at Hokusai with a curl in his lip.

There was a murmur, an instruction somewhere in the ranks.

No one flinched.

The chicken made a ghastly screech, as if it were being killed.

Ienari alone laughed. My arm ached from holding the cage. I lowered it a little.

My father jerked his head at me: up, up. I raised it.

I had no idea what he was planning. But my irritation was great enough to make me forget my fear. My father played a dangerous game. These lords, and the Shogun himself, were impulsive and could have had us in prison for impudence. Did Hokusai play the game because of his pride in his samurai background or—remembering the "Hokusai, a peasant of Honjo" sign he put outside the door of each of our dwellings—his pride in being simple?

The chicken squawked again. I switched it to my other arm. Ienari gave the signal to free the dogs. They bounded off magnificently. Splashing and barking and tearing first in one direction, then in another, in zigzags, circles, they scared up the birds: herons, larks. Up from one clump flew a crane. A crane! Symbol of good luck.

Then Ienari lifted the hood off the falcon. He released the chain. The predator trembled on the regal wrist. We all held our breath at our sovereign's brilliance, which was really the bird's brilliance, the brilliant threat of nature. The artists stood waiting. My arm ached. My chicken scratched. I lifted one foot and then the other. The platform squeaked. The water moved beneath. The grasses swayed, and bird cries tested every fibre of the falcon's being.

Then Ienari gave the sign. The predator shot forth like an arrow, pierced the heart of the crane, and brought it down. The dogs splashed towards the corpse. The falcon returned. Ienari stroked its neck lovingly.

Another crane flew up. Again the falcon went out to murder the bird of good luck, and again the dogs went mad for the blood.

There were larks, too, caught that day. There were others; I tired of it instantly. At last it was over. The Shogun's party repaired to a restaurant, where the cook prepared the crane in the ritual way. We made our way up to Senso-ji temple, where the art competition would take place.

Senso-ji was our home ground, which gave us an advantage in the competition.

Buncho went first. He made a brush sketch of the tidal garden we'd just left, the platform where Ienari had sat, the soft grasses of the marsh. His brush never varied in speed, never flipped or stabbed. He finished his sketch and remained still for a few seconds. Then he bowed extravagantly. The falcon deigned to turn its ears, keen enough to pick up the scratching of the brush while tucked inside its pretty helmet.

Minions lifted the paper and held it up so everyone could see. They sighed in appropriate awe.

Ienari paced back and forth. His step was heavy and rigid. His face showed a past of self-indulgence and certain gratification. The day would unroll as each one did: he would have his way, and there would be death and obedience and worship and pleasure. What did it matter? He had been too young; he had earned nothing. Even amongst Shoguns there is earning and not earning, there is worthy and worthless.

"You now," he said, barking in Hokusai's direction.

Hokusai's large ears were turned upward. He appeared not to hear the ruler. He gave a soft whistle. The falcon glared and did not turn a feather. He was teasing the bird. He was trying to make it lose its concentration; by his very nonchalance, he was spreading insurrection.

Sadanobu cleared his throat regretfully. He seemed to say, I could have had you all wiped out, back when I was senior councillor, and I didn't. I am too soft-hearted.

Ienari laughed at the stubborn little man as he stood in his poor robe with a roll of paper. "Come now, will you make us wait?"

"Oh," said Hokusai agreeably, "is it my turn?"

I hung my head, waiting for the axe to fall. Failure to fear, a crime for which Sadanobu had often had people convicted, was written as if on a placard over my father's head. But it was not failure. It was refusal.

Ienari laughed.

Hokusai fumbled for his brushes. He took the roll of paper. He stepped forward, his forehead wrinkled with pleasure. The retainers' faces were grim. Ienari appeared to be charmed. Hokusai hummed a tune. I was wobbling under the weight of the stupid chicken cage. Its inhabitant was obviously the only bird there that did not know how to behave. Flapping around in its cage! Feathers coming loose. Loud squawking. It had no idea what it was doing there, and neither did I.

Everyone was watching Hokusai. Oh, he was famous, that was true; even the Shogun had seen his pictures. The very fact that we were here showed the change in Edo. The refined Noh theatre and the Kano school of arts were losing fans amongst the aristocrats. The officially despised, tawdry, and cheeky Yoshiwara culture had never been more fashionable.

Hokusai rolled out the paper. I had put it together the day before. It was fifteen paces long. The ends would not lie flat. He gestured to the guards: You stand on that corner, hold it down. You on the other.

Ienari laughed again. Then he gestured to the guards that they should do as Hokusai wished. "Go," he said to them, and four of them went.

I bet he hadn't laughed like that since he was a nasty little boy putting worms in the maids' noodles.

Sadanobu's teeth clenched. But as the samurai clinked and rattled in their armour to their spots on the paper, certain nobles began to follow the Shogun's lead and titter.

Hokusai scooped up the air in front of his body with his hands, indicating more laughter, more laughter. And the laughter got bigger, and now the corner-holders themselves were smiling sheepishly and it was not laughter at anyone—it was just laughter.

I put down the chicken's cage.

Hokusai took up his mop. I mixed the blue indigo ink with water in a pail. He bent down and soaked the straw ends of the mop. He walked over to the paper, eyed it from this way and that, smiling to himself, waving to me.

Buncho, beside Sadanobu, straightened up from his deep bow. I saw his elegant, understated work and I saw something else: he too was smiling.

Hokusai got down on all fours and pushed his face near the paper. He lifted his mop from the bucket. A drop of paint fell from it. Sloppy. He looked at his audience and smiled. Then he lowered his brush to meet the paper at the exact point where the drip had fallen, beginning his work there.

Everyone could feel the change: he was unaware now, of the birds, the sky, the temple market, the waiting retinue. It did not matter that the Shogun was there. There were no more airs or poses. He began.

He painted a long blue line, walking with his mop the length of the paper. He pressed the giant brush, and twisted it, and pressed on the other side, getting the most of the ink. He created a long, wavy blue line. Even the chicken was quiet. I had been speaking to it. I had reassured it. But it was false reassurance; I did not know what its fate would be. Was it to be some sort of sacrifice?

Hokusai jerked his head at me. "Oei!" he hailed.

"Old Man!" I shouted back.

My next job was to produce the red ink, and this I did, with more water and a bowl.

"Oei! Bring the chicken."

I opened the cage door. The chicken went berserk, flapping and squawking, but didn't get out. I fished around in the cage with my hand. The chicken fought for its life and I could not get hold of it. There was a moment of chaos. The falcon sat disdainful, its head turned away. The dogs were sorely tempted, but they held. I finally got the flapping thing by its two legs and pulled it out of its cage, not without a great deal of raucous poultry noises, some soft cursing, and a cloud of small white feathers.

Hokusai came to me, his robe tucked up into his belt so you could see his scrawny thighs. I transferred the frantic flapping thing into my father's hands. The bird hung upside down. Mine won't be an elegant death, it seemed to say, not like those that had been rehearsed here so often. But it was resigned to it and ceased to flap.

Hokusai reversed the chicken so it was the right way up. It took two of us to dip its feet in the red paint. We got them good and wet. Hokusai walked back to stand at the top of his samurai-pegged paper with the wide blue ribbon waving along it. Then with a great flourish, he threw the chicken into the air. It was too much for one of the dogs, which broke and had to be beaten.

The chicken could not fly. Its wings had been clipped. It settled on the paper and ran. It ran with its paint-soaked feet down the blue and then back up the blue. It saw my father's feet and veered off, ran back and jumped into the sky, and flapping hard, elevated itself a few feet and escaped out of our vision. But it left its red tracks all over the painting, brighter at first and then fading out to faint stains.

Everyone looked at the paper.

Hokusai presented his work to the Shogun.

"There," Hokusai said, pointing at the paper. "The Tama River in autumn."

The Shogun was delighted, and everyone cheered and clapped.

We walked home alone. We were weary but happy that we had won the competition.

"Oei, Oei," he said. "Hey, you. You did well."

"Hey, hey, Old Man," I said. "You too."

IT BECAME PREDICTABLE. I went with Sanba to his writing room, wherever that might be. He had a little mattress there and he would lie down on it, shifting to find a less lumpy bit. When he was settled, he would pat the space beside him and I would lie down. I'd fit myself along his body, he would grunt and pull me closer, part my wrapped kimono, and seek with his bony legs the length of me.

I wormed closer. He put his mouth to my ear, the back of my neck, my shoulder. His lips were warm but his body was chill. I was strong and limber but not much of a furnace. No words escaped me, just a yelp of happiness, now and again, when he stroked me.

What did he think about, making love to Ei? He knew me when I was six. He saw me grow up. In the studio he had seen drawings of my body parts. This was nothing unusual. I believed that he chose me for my spirit, as my father had. There were thousands of lower-class prostitutes, nighthawks, and temple singers: women for view and for sale. But one has to pay even the lowliest of these. One does not have to pay the daughter. But of the daughters, why Ei? The others were worth more, weren't they?

Whatever else, I had no shame. I was healthy and young and there was truth to me. And maybe it had brought me here, where I was happy.

"You surprise me, Ei."

"I do? Why?" I said, digging for compliments.

"You are not humble." His little cough, as always.

I fit myself neatly on top of his penis, which, I am happy to say, stood hard and at a good angle. I sat on his lower stomach, backing up a little on my hands and legs. His face was directly beneath my face, his breast directly beneath my chest and my tiny, upright nipples. My knees were on either side of his hips. I squeezed them and rolled him a little, side to side.

"By that you mean I ought to be," I said.

I threw off the blankets. My eyes were used to the dark by then. I wanted to see the curved lines of his body against the blanket. I wanted to see everything.

When I rose from Sanba's bed, weary and collecting my clothes to go home, I often thought of Shino. I had become a woman now. I wondered if she wished she could see me, if she still hoped that I had become elegant in speech and thought, like her. It was the only sadness in my life for those years. She was gone and there was no chance, in that teeming city where the townspeople had no second name, that I could find her.

20

DISCIPLES

I WAS NEARLY TWENTY. Sanba and I walked in the Yoshiwara late one afternoon. It was a festival day, and many people were gawking. But a wall of black clouds started to mass over the low, wooden buildings with their barred windows and unmarked doorways. Rain began. Umbrellas came out—orange, mustard, green, purple—their mounds and spokes sprouting and knocking one another, and water splashing off at angles. Everyone had one but us. We skipped under the eave of the *ageya*. Thunder, a great bang of it, had all the visitors taking to their heels. The rain pelted. The thunder grumbled as if it might move away but then cracked again overhead. Then lightning—I liked to look at it, roaming the sky, snarling, letting out its white, flickering tongue. We stood, inches from the driving water, under the eave.

Between flashes I told Sanba how my father claimed that once, travelling the Tokaido, he had been struck by a bolt of lightning and thrown into a field. He lay there and could not move for a long time. After that he named himself Raijin, after the Thunder God, for a while.

We waited it out, craning our necks and saying "Oh, my" to each bolt. Finally the rumbles and sparks ended. We stepped out. The crowds had vanished. The rain fell sullenly. We ran through the mud puddles to a tiny teahouse.

The teahouse walls, an earthen red, glowed in the lamplight. There were four seats. We squeezed in beside two young lovers. A child-sized woman stood behind a counter. It was low down, set on the earthen floor of an old kitchen that had once been outside the house. Her daughter asked us what we wanted. Sanba ordered *matcha*, powdered green tea. We revelled in our snug hideaway while outside the rumbling came back, stones rolling across a tin roof. The woman chattered: how loud it was, and how the people had fled. How all the courtesans must have stopped work—it was bad luck to have intercourse during strong winds and great rain. Thunder over lovers could shorten their lives. There was no escaping the Thunder God. The end was coming, so why run? *Izn it?*

Sanba said that it was true. "The end is always coming, as long as you believe there is one." This piece of irrefutable logic was lost on the teashop woman, who was truly frightened. He laughed.

I felt the clay teacup against my lips and the inside of my mouth, and the rich, thick pea-green tea. We were snug; we were protected. Wisdom dictated in such a storm to choose a low place and a low attitude where nothing stood up high to challenge the gods, not even your words. Yet here was Sanba showing his disrespect. "You tempt the gods," I said to him.

"I'm not laughing about the storm," he said. "I'm laughing at you."

"Why?" I said.

"Because you are a kind of joke. The gods have made you a great painter, and they have made you a woman too. They have made you better than your father. It is a cruel joke."

"What are you saying?" I said. The storm rummaged around in the invisible sky above us. "Not better than."

"If not better, then you might as well not bother," he said. "Stay at home and get married." He knew that was repugnant to me. He gave his little cough and smiled cruelly.

More silence within and more rain without. Two slow, very slow, tears worked their way out of my bottom eyelids. I did not blink.

"Perhaps I am wrong," he continued. "Maybe it's not a joke but a tragedy. Whatever it is, I won't be around to see it." The rainwater ran over the clay tiles and dripped down the wooden pipes beside the house. I could hear it everywhere.

The lovers got up and went out.

The tiny woman with the round face and the tense smile wiped and wiped her counter again. She dried and polished her dishes. Her daughter worked beside her, and finally they stood still, side by side. It was quiet in the sky. The storm was spent.

We walked into the street. The air was a shade of violet. There was no one out. It was a private time. At the long end of the row I saw a woman step tentatively from her house, her umbrella tipped down over her chalky face. She was far down the row of green houses. I stared into that distance. I wiped my face and found it wet. A feeling had just come over me: that my life was like that scene, a fearful, half-hidden thing just visible down a narrow, dark street.

Then the owners came out one by one and lit the big lanterns, and the orbs of light marched one by one down the row; Sanba went one way and I the other. I asked myself again, Why am I different? Why not like other women? Why was I doomed? Was my father the danger?

This was a new thought. My father was my teacher; I honoured him, and I did not resent him. Only when I was angry did those feelings come to me, and then I pushed them away. I was duty-bound to him. I didn't like Sanba saying my father was bad for me. Perhaps he was jealous of my father's hold on me. Must my feelings for Sanba conflict with my feelings for Hokusai?

And was I truly a joke of the gods?

HOKUSAI HAD LITTLE TIME for the students who came to us. He collected some of them on travels. They lived in Nagoya or Osaka, and they took their classes in the form of letters mailed back and forth. Others became part of our life and our family. He gave their work a cursory glance and passed it to me or Tatsu. Shigenobu, the husband of O-Miyo, wanted to do things his way and had no patience with my father's commands. He and my father quarrelled and parted, but O-Miyo and her brat still came to us.

A man named Eisen came to the studio then. He was of samurai background. He excelled at Beauties and wasn't bad at landscapes either. My father did not teach him but gave him tasks, pictures of his own to copy. He did this to all the men, but with Eisen it was somehow worse. He criticized the affable giant loudly about little things: the speed with which he applied his paint; the mannerisms that—to be truthful—all the disciples had. They had to develop personal tics as they tried to follow, but still distinguish themselves from, the master. Hokusai would not allow Eisen to progress. Eisen was decadent, my father said. He drank and kept a brothel. True, I said, but it didn't stop him from making ravishing pictures of courtesans.

"He must learn to do proper views of bridges and of deities; it's what we need. We don't need any more of those Beauties! You can do them, Ei!"

Before long, Eisen left our studio.

A few disciples who reached a high standard were offered, for a fee, a derivation of Hokusai's name. We had Hokki and Hokko and Hokuen. We had the beautiful Hokumei, a merchant's daughter. We were for a time a studio of women. There were three daughters and Hokumei. She was ready to submit to my father's will, or I should say whims. What else could she do? The North Star Studio was the only studio that worked with women. And we daughters had no choice either.

He saw it differently, of course. The Old Man would sit and sigh and draw furious designs, and pass them out to us where we worked, and complain in a light-hearted way that he was outnumbered. "I am your slave," he would say. "I only work here. You are the boss!" The opposite was true, but this cajoling kept us happy.

I HADN'T SEEN SANBA FOR WEEKS and then a *gyoji,* a government worker, came to the studio. He sat alternately chewing on his lower lip and trying to catch the upper mustache in his teeth. I was working on a design for a laughing picture: a servant was ravishing the wife while the husband looked on. Officially banned, of course, it would sell well. The government man watched, his breath hissing in and out. He suspected he was being made a fool of—but it was always so difficult to tell, wasn't it? Finally he said, "Did you hear that Shikitei Sanba is ill?"

I felt a shock, dull and pointless, as if I had been hit with a rubber mallet. My father kept his eyes on the painting in front of him.

"We have not," said Hokusai.

"Oh, yes." The *gyoji* was happy to share this delicious morsel. "He had a chest cough that would not go away and now . . ."

I knew that small, dry cough. Everyone in the theatre knew it too: it was his stamp and seal. It came at intervals, a measure in his speech, a gesture giving weight to some pronouncement. Surely this little habit was not evidence of sickness. Did the *gyoji* know Sanba and I were lovers?

"Perhaps he has a cold or flu?"

"Oh, no. It is more than that. He is not expected to live."

"Who told you that?" I said fiercely. I wanted to trace the information like a rat on the floor and stamp it dead.

"I heard it at Kyoden's tobacco shop. Mitsu said the doctors told him there is something in his lungs."

"What doctor? The students of Dutch medicine? Or the Chinese doctor?"

Sanba laughed at the Dutch scholars, their boundless determination to decipher the body, which he considered to be a mystery that should stay a mystery. He believed in instincts; he believed in signs; he believed in crazy medicaments and potions, even those he invented himself.

"The Western doctor came and told him it was too late. He'll test the worth of his secret of eternal life, won't he now?" mocked the government man. He raised one of his sharp eyebrows at me and backed out the door.

I remembered the teahouse in the thunderstorm; Sanba had talked about the art I would make. "I won't be around to see it," he'd said.

My father was drawing fat men. Fat men squatting, fat men reaching, fat men bathing, fat men dancing. Fat men bubbled in a stream off the end of his brush. Then he stopped and reached over to me, delicately withdrawing my picture of the servant and mistress in jolly congress. He substituted a double page of breaking waves. He had begun it: in the bottom half of the pages, the wave flattened and became relaxed lines of black and grey over the white of the page. In the upper half, the waves were advancing and looked like plumes, the black brush strokes leaving the white of the paper as a blankness that came down with its own power.

"Finish," he ordered.

Work was like that for me: piecework, factory work. One minute I was draping bosoms, the next making froth on a big rolling wave. I barked out a protest, but it was useless, so I switched my attention to the waves. My tiny movements made black curves higher and higher on the page, matching his, diminishing in size, farther and farther off. There was no horizon; the waves filled the space to the top border. My back began to ache, so I stood and bent sideways. He lifted his head.

"Go, then! You're not watching, so it's better that you run off the way you always do."

That was so unfair I laughed. "Who helps you more than I do, Old Man?"

"No one. I know it. But you are thinking of Sanba." He pouted.

"I almost believe you're jealous."

This was so impertinent it was funny. He smiled his wide, innocent smile.

"Jealous?" he said. "I have three daughters and you're the last. If Sanba is unwell, I'll be stuck with you."

"You'll be stuck with me anyway. Sanba has a wife."

"Run and find him," my father said.

It was raining softly. I took the umbrella and my short kimono jacket and fled to the boat dock. I had no money. But I saw a ferryman we knew and begged a ride north. He jerked his head that I should climb in. The rain stopped and the clouds lifted off the horizon and great squared yellow bars shot sideways from the place where the sun was disappearing.

I sat in the middle, near the flat surface of the river. The prow broke it and the disturbed white undersides of the water folded back like a snarl. The ferryman stood high on the bow while his partner stood on the height of the stern, both with their long poles aloft. The back man pressed his pole down into the river bottom, leaning his whole weight over the end that drove into his sternum. They sang to keep in time: "Stroke! Make way! Stroke! Make way!"

As I travelled north the light sank bit by bit until those low horizontal flares were extinguished. The city was dark and glowering. There were small fires in teahouses along the banks; I saw lanterns lit and hoisted on poles over the shops that faced the water. The ferryman in the bow swayed, the hard bulge of his calf muscle, his bare legs in the cold. In his confidence he hung out wide over the water.

From the water rose that dank smell, and I remembered Sanba's nearness, an intimate smell that was easy to pick up through his black kimono. His face was always strange to me when we first met, even if we'd been together only the week before. Who is this codger? I would think. When I lay with him, he smiled on me with great sweetness and short-sightedness. His hands were cold. When he looked at my painting, I was nervous. I wanted him to like it.

"You use strong colours," he had said at first. Grinding pigments had been my job since I was small. I prided myself on the colours I made.

"Bad artists can have strong colours," I said. "That is of no consequence."

"It is. Colours count for a great deal. And you are not a bad artist. You may be a great one, and it will be a terror for us all," he said. "You also have a good teacher." I nodded. "But you must defeat him."

Twice he had told me I must overcome my father. "Then," he said, "we will all see your powers, and we'll shake in our sandals."

"Do you mean artists will fear me?"

"Already, already we do," he laughed.

I looked down at my hands. I willed the complacent ferryman to push harder, stroke faster.

"It's no fun to be the older one," he had said once. "You're young and have everything coming to you. I have had most of it. When you're an old woman you may have a young lover. Maybe then you'll understand."

I reached the Asakusa grounds. Crowds of men stood at the doors of the restaurants and teahouses. A street musician was remonstrating with his disobedient monkey, and a little crowd jeered. It began to rain again.

"Entertainment to the daimyo! See it here first. Watch what the noblemen and noblewomen watch in their homes in the High City." The monkey was dressed in women's clothes and had been taught to mince and play a flute. A boy passed a bowl to collect the coins that fell with a dull clink from dirty hands.

I pushed through the standing bodies, which were solid and resistant to my pressure. I made my way along the row of small houses with their closed screens right to the end and turned the corner into a side street, now mostly in darkness after the brightly lit market. Three, four doors in was where he would be. I came to a door: behind it I saw a single lamp burning.

When the screen opened I bowed. My umbrella bowed with me, hiding my face. "Is this the place where Shikitei Sanba is resting?" I whispered.

"Who are you?"

The woman stood erect, and her voice was strong. I felt her eyes making holes in my umbrella. I tipped it up and looked into the face. A woman older than me, but not a dragon. She drew in her breath. She rocked back a little, then forward. She knew the situation. She was enjoying her revenge.

"So the news has flushed out the lowlife," she said.

Her rudeness gave me strength. No need to repent, then. I raised my head. "I have come to inquire about his health."

"His health is not good. The signs can no longer be ignored."

It seemed an accusation, as if I had been ignoring signs, as if I were complicit in this illness. I let the umbrella fall and the rain come down on my head. I would drown if she wanted me to, here in the rain. But she didn't want that either.

"You might as well come in." She stepped back. I came over the doorsill. From the back came his voice. Vinegar, with angry wit. "Enchantress, are we entertaining?"

"We are not entertaining," his wife called hoarsely. "We are caring for the sick, and the sick is you."

"Ah, yes," said Sanba, and he gave his little cough. "We mustn't forget, must we?" The cough was stronger. But his voice was no weaker. The music of its bass, the rumble, convivial, the tickle of it, inviting laughter. He's not ill, I thought. He's the same!

She saw me take heart.

"Don't be encouraged," she said coldly. "Your eyes will tell you what your ears will not."

"If we're not entertaining, who has come in?" The voice of Sanba was a beautiful thing.

"It is your girl."

Silence from the back room. I could picture his sudden childish look of being caught out. His wife swung her hand sideways: go to him.

He was staring at the ceiling. I could see the glint of his bottles: he was using his own ridiculous remedies, his secret elixirs for immortality.

"My old eyes like it dim," he always said, turning down the wick.

His features were sharper than ever. His skin was a little yellow, his cheeks were hollow, and around his eyelashes there was a crusted crystal substance that made the lids sparkle.

"Sanba."

"Ah! She's right! It is my girl." His hand drifted out.

I was not a girl. I had been when we started. But now I was twenty-two.

I wanted to lie with him and curl towards the warmth of him. But he was hot; the air smelled bad. I was repelled, and anyway his wife was there. And where was the child?

"I tell you what I want," he continued, as if I had asked. "An outing. We will meet at the theatre," he said. "Buy sticky rice and take it with us to the Nakamura. But instead of staying all day, we will leave at dusk. We will take a little boat to the Three Forks and lie under the trees."

His wife stood just behind me.

"Get your father to release you. On the night of the full moon. It is how many days from now? I'm losing track," he said. "I lie here and try to open my eyes, and the days slide away from me. But I will be better then."

"Full moon is in five days."

"On that day I will meet you at the Nakamura. If you can manage to get away." His attention wandered.

I was forgotten, a leftover doll from carefree, cut-away days that had even then been entirely separate from his life, this wife, this mattress, this stared-at ceiling. I had no place here, and yet the voice, the profile in the dark—it was him. He was mine.

His wife dug her toe into my buttock.

"Go on, speak." She was asking me to bring him back.

"Sanba," I whispered.

"Yes."

"We're nearly finished the album of laughing pictures. You know, the story about the servant and the mistress who are lovers. And she dreams of taking to the road with him . . ."

We talked about our work this way.

He gave a little expiration of air. "I wish you luck with it," he said. He said it in a way that showed he understood everything: the work, the dream, even the toe in my tail.

"You are an artist, and it will never be easy," he said. "If you're lucky and if you're clever, you will survive. Promise me something."

What could I promise? Why would I promise?

"Anything. It will keep me hoping," he said.

"I promise to make the best colours in Edo," I said.

"Ah," he said.

The voice was captive, in his body and in that little house. I imagined I would steal it away. Wrap it in a cloth, in cardboard, roll it and put it in a scroll box. I would free it from this room and from this sickness. I would unroll it when I too lay on my mat staring up through the top of the house, staring into the stars and the sky, or where they would be if the roof were taken off, as if it were made by artists in that lying way, making the inside outside. His voice would be in the stars, and I would go there too. We would look down and see ourselves: tiny, finger-sized creatures in the maze of streets and screens and walls and alleyways and narrow canals that was Edo.

"Sanba?" I said.

He came back. "Yes?"

"If the day is not good?"

"Then we will take a raincheck," he said. As he said the word "raincheck," his voice cracked. It was just a small crack, through that low, masculine, scratchy voice. I heard it. As if he might, if he stopped, break down. As if the crust might split and something hot, scalding, true, deep, and violent would break out. I never knew what that something was, what he might have said if we had met as before. That was his goodbye.

My face was wet. The wife sat watching me with faint curiosity. She didn't trouble to be angry with me. The son, a handsome boy of ten, came in. Ministrations were in order. The patient seemed to sleep. I had only dreamed our long hours together, the white paint and the red slashes on the faces of the actors, the lying down and the getting up to go to the teahouse for sake. The grisly murders and black rages we had sat through, with him scribbling and me shouting, were ghost scenes. Real life, this tamed and vapid thing, this yellowed, patchy remnant, had taken its sad victory.

I wormed my way backwards out the door and over the threshold. I knew I had hoisted it only when I heard the rain falling on my umbrella like the crackling of some fire.

My father took one look at me and knew. He showed no emotion at what must have been, for him too, tragic news about a friend. He examined the page of waves and passed me a page of comb designs; to him it was boring work, but he could still bring a sense of fun. Could I? A comb was a comb, or was it a view of Mt. Fuji, a bridge, or a wave? Maybe a trotting pig. Pigs were a problem because they had feet. Better that it be a wave. There was a resemblance between a curling wave, its foam a white rim along its top curving edge, and hair pulled over a comb.

We worked in silence. The hardness in my father steadied me. He did not have to speak. What he had to say was palpable: What did I expect? People had wives—that was a given. People became ill. People fell by the wayside, foundered, and died. They were the weak. Sanba had fallen prey.

There was even a sense not of vindication, exactly, but of affirmation: my father had won. Shikitei Sanba, noted expert on the kabuki, satirist and peer, purveyor of the elixir of immortality, had been caught by the demons.

He would die, most likely. This was the dirty work of life; this was its not-so-secret destination. While Hokusai went on. He was sixty-two years old—by ordinary measure, already an ancient man. He would not die. Not yet.

We sat working. I felt the impermanence of our surroundings, my father's imperative to live. Work dried up. Censors got on your trail. Illness stalked. You had to reinvent, rename, and reposition. You had to fight off the oncoming threat. Outlive the others. My father was good at it. He was better than good: he was inspired. From those who were caught, he became detached, as if they might contaminate him.

But why was I thinking about my father? Sanba was leaving me. I could feel it. It was in the air. It was in the cock's crow that came before long: dawn. How many days would it be?

When I was too tired to sit I fell forward onto my crossed arms. I hunched over the floor, my eyes closed against the flesh of my forearms, and waited for my father to berate me.

He didn't. When his hand came, it was a surprise. It was a heavy hand, just there on my right shoulder, at the back near the nape of my neck. It was a kindly hand. A touch one might give to a fellow-in-arms. It was the hand of one warrior to another, admitting me to the whole of it: life, death, art. And survival, especially.

His hand warmed me. Then he nudged me upright.

I wiped my face on my sleeve.

He took the comb designs and looked them over. Hmm, he said. And, Haaa. Ahh. He liked them. I went out to the well and splashed cold water on my face. When I came back inside, he looked at me and seemed to see me afresh.

"You must marry," he said.

21

HUSBAND

THERE WAS ANOTHER PAINTER in the North Star Studio. His name was Minamizawa Tomei. He was the son of an oil seller. He was gentle, with the eyes of a child and a shuffling gait. He longed to work with Hokusai. But my father could teach only those who taught themselves. So I worked with Tomei instead and he relied on my example.

I liked him. At the sake houses after work, he was company. We listened to the women with their heads bent over samisen. He sang like a bird. We clowned together. Since Sanba's death, I was the punster.

My father asked us one question after we announced our intention to marry: "Why do you drink sake?"

"To let go of the hours of the day."

"Ah! I see!" he said. "Not me. I wish to hold on to every minute."

I was cruel to my husband. Some people said, "Oei is the daughter of a master and she laughs at the no-talent son of an oil seller." That is another of the scurrilous accusations of history, and I dispute it. I married him for friendship. It would have been worse if I hadn't.

I was young and felt old, as if I had lived a famous life already. I had been the companion of Shikitei Sanba, and people crowded our table after the theatre. But with Sanba gone, I was cut down to size, married to a man who would never add up to anything. He was gentle, it was true. He was kind; that was odd. Young women often have an unfair reaction to kindness: when someone is unfailingly so, they are not grateful. They begin to despise that person.

Ah, kindness, Sanba would have said. You hear about it—isn't it a kind of skin rash? Can it be got off with soap?

I shaved my thick eyebrows on marriage. This widened forehead, as we called it, was the only obvious change in my life. You could still see my frown; it was carved into my flesh. I still went drinking. I was missing love. I took to pulling strands of hair from the tight knot at my nape and chewing on them. I rubbed my eyebrows where the stubble grew back in. When I walked out in the morning to buy breakfast, Sanba's form—that particular slope of his shoulders and his languid, narrow gait—went ahead of me, stepping sideways out of the traffic into a bookshop.

I dodged into that nook where new volumes lay. I let my eyes run over the latest prints of Beauties by Eisen and Hiroshige—beautiful but without energy, without sympathy. Simpering, lank figures with bloated faces. My father was represented by his books of instruction: *Manga,* series VI and series VII. *Blind People. Skinny People and Fat People.* Good but silly. A horse bucking and a woman in black on high clogs, standing on the rope that tethered the horse. We were in the 1820s. He was perhaps fading. "Hokusai will not die," Sanba had predicted. "He will go on for a long time. He has ingenuity, and he has you."

Under the counter, contraband but available to everyone, were the *shunga* that my father, and I too, painted: couples grappling, huge nether parts waving in the breeze as clothes parted conveniently. Not like the sex in my marriage!

I was supposed to be grateful to Tomei for having me. But I dismissed him with a short expulsion of breath in the top of my mouth: "Ugh!" He brought me tea: "Ugh!" It was cold. He put brush to paper: "Ugh!" There was too much ink.

Nothing disturbed his good humour. He smiled, taking his eyes off the page and letting the ink spread out from the tip of the brush.

"Now you've ruined it."

He tried to kiss me when I was annoyed. Whereas I wanted to kiss him only when he was cold to me, and he never was.

"Come, let's go out to eat eel," he would say. "I have money today. We can walk along the riverbank."

My shoulders rose and I bit my lip. "You're bothering me. Can't you see I'm working?"

It was not his fault: it was only that he was not Sanba. He didn't know about Sanba, but he ought to have. People did. He didn't pick up clues from my experienced behaviour on the futon. But he was a child, a dreamer.

To add to my crimes, then, I made him a fool. I knew that. Some days I couldn't look at him. His delight with a piece of watermelon, the sticky, sweet water running down his chin—I had been that innocent before. The way he clapped palms with the man who sold divining poems written on little bits of paper. And that sheepish laugh, huh huh huh, his shoulders lifting as if they were strung up.

He was sympathetic to awkward children. He would spend an hour over sandals with a broken sole. "Throw them out!" I'd say. "I don't know why you became an artist at all," I said, standing beside him one day as he knelt on the road, picking up coals from the remains of a cooking fire that had been kicked over. "You aren't really interested in art." How had I become so stern? "You're only interested in broken things," I said in disgust.

"I *am* interested in broken things," he said. He smiled and I thought, He's going to say it's why he likes me! "But you are not broken, my pumpkin. You are strong and whole."

He had read my mind. Unforgivable. I made a face.

He kissed me. He loved me! Why? Why? I wanted Sanba, but Sanba was dead. In a candid moment I told Tomei that the way to get my love was to be cold. Mock me. "Only boil in secret and in the dark," I instructed.

But he boiled at low temperature, in no time and without shame. And then he boiled over. He tried to make me "vanish," the term we used in *shunga* for climax. Nothing. "It is not your fault," I told him, taking pity. He fell away from me. I was a bad clam, the one in the broth whose shell would not open.

I wanted to extinguish his love for me.

Of course, when you truly want that, you will finally get it. After a time Tomei smiled less on me. I was killing his love. Immediately I regretted it. "Don't give up on me," I would whisper to him after he fell asleep. "I'm trying."

THEN CAME THE TIME when the public did not want Hokusai's pictures. He had a bad year, and another bad year: all those years were bad. Troubles came to us and stayed. Have I enumerated the deaths in my family? The first was my father's son by his first wife; he, who like my father himself had been adopted by the Nakajima family, who were possibly his blood relatives, to be heir to the mirror-polishing business. But unlike my father, my brother had made a success of it. When he died, with him died the sum of money we got every year from his employer.

My sister O-Miyo, married to the drinker and gambler Shigenobu, finally ran for her life to the divorce temple. She returned with her son to live with the family. The boy was trouble. She sent him back to his father, but that was not good. His father did not like him either. He roamed the neighbourhood, bullying younger children and the harmless poor. I saw him try to choke the fee collector at the shooting range when he was not even ten. Then O-Miyo developed a wracking cough. She died when she was thirty. The boy was ours. My mother tried but could not control him.

And Tatsu. We watched her fail. I would squat behind her and wrap her chest in my arms to hold her erect while she went into coughing spasms. I tried to pass on the warmth of my heart, my strong spirit. Sometimes blood splattered out. She couldn't paint then. We missed her work and the way she organized us. The papers went into their former flyaway piles in corners. Her death was a disaster.

Hokumei, too, the merchant-class woman who had brought an air of delicacy and decency into our workshop, had her brief flight of productivity and then left us. I slept at home with my husband but lived from early morning until night at the North Star, where I ran the studio. I had a few students of my own by then. One was Mune, daughter of Hokumei. She became my friend and filled a little of the emptiness my sisters left.

As his women faded away my father stopped laughing. Fellow artists and even disciples seized the opportunity to rise against him. Eisen, whom he had rejected, was now succeeding. Hokusai accused him of taking work that should have been ours. Masayoshi accused Hokusai of being a copycat; a certain former disciple called Dog Hokusai forged our work. I had to write a letter to our Osaka publisher on behalf of Hokusai: "My disciple Taito II is selling his paintings as 'by Hokusai.' That is unspeakable. Please make it stop."

When my father wanted work done under his name, it was by me.

One day I came in to see Hokusai trembling on his side. He flopped his right arm out and shook it. It was loose, like a dead branch.

"How long have you been sitting there?"

His face twisted and his words seemed glued inside him.

"I yam p-pa-ar-lyzed," he moaned.

It frightened me.

"You are not paralyzed! You're moving."

"I caa'an stan up." He jerked around, trying to get to his feet.

I helped him stand.

"I waaan wal-kit *off.*"

He began to limp in little circles. I began to giggle. I thought he was clowning. I thought he had simply put his limbs to sleep by sitting.

"You're paralyzed but you want to walk it off?"

"I'm *wal*-kit off, *wal-kit* it off."

He dragged his legs and his breath was laboured. But he kept going, his face a mask of determination. I watched him. Then I knew. Suddenly he was the old man he had claimed to be since my birth.

"*Maa-ke* me sit. Sit!"

In those days he did not have a desk to work on. He used the top of a rice caddy. I pushed it in front of him and gave him his brush.

His brush was jerky and rigid. That made him angry. "You do it," he said. "Liiie tha, no liie tha . . ." He wanted the line of the back thicker; he wanted the curve under the arm thinner. "Liiie tha. Yes. No! No! Noo dry bru stro—"

That was how it began.

We thought the palsy might be the end of him. It seemed to go on and on: the great man in this paralytic, spitting, jerking state. He hated being incapable. I was the only one with patience for him. Together we made designs for books of his "famous painting style." I held his hand while he sketched mountains and trees and fishermen casting their lines into the sea—bald, smiling fishermen basking in the sun.

He told me a legend.

He sketched a bare hill and, behind it, a series of hills with narrow valleys between. "'S a grea' army through t' valley. It go-s to co-on-onquer far lands." He drew the army caught between snow-covered mountains, where nothing but rock, ice, and the small, dark tips of buried trees were seen. The army lost their battles. They even lost their enemy. But the general and his troops pressed on. The general walked. His horse walked beside him, exhausted because the snow was deep.

The general had no advisers left; they had fallen in fatigue. All he had were these rows of mushroom-like men—my father's arm was improving. He drew each face in the ranks under a shallow straw hat. The army stretched out of sight in the cleft of the farthest valley.

The great warlord was alone in the world. "So h' asss-k he horse. Unnerstan'?"

"Yes. He asks his horse what to do."

"Rii-t. 'E says, 'Ho-oorse, what you think? We go on? Or we go ba-aack?'"

The horse too was old. He had been waiting many years for this question. Now it had come.

The picture grew under my father's brush. He held his stiff hand with his good hand and drew lines. Each strand of straw on the soldiers' raincoats and each flagstaff, each rock or treetop protruding through snow, each small disc of hat in that huge army, he drew.

Ahead of the horse were no footprints. Behind him were the general and hundreds on hundreds of men. In his spine and the angle of his head and the way his eyes followed the ground, the horse from my father's brush expressed his weariness, his resolution, his careful retreat.

The men held their flagpoles high, but the fabric was tattered. Their small feet in black leggings wobbled on the uneven, trodden surface and amongst the footprints of those ahead of them. The warhorse watched the ground in front of him.

"If we go on, we'll be the conquerors; we'll be the emperors. We'll have gold and glory and be celebrated for our bravery." The general let the reins drop. "Or should we turn back? If we do we reach home again."

The horse did not have to ponder. It turned and began to plod home, riches and glory of no interest.

"Wha's vir-tue?" said Hokusai.

"Acceptance of defeat?" I guessed.

He shook his head.

"Fidelity?"

No. This made my father scoff. "N-nnn-no."

"What is it, then?"

"S-s-ssim-plishty."

Simplicity.

What was his message to me? That I was the warhorse—there when all else was lost? That I should forgo further battles, and further dreams, and head home? That "simplicity" should be mine—in heart, in art, in thought?

Would he do the same? Was he giving up?

It puzzled me, and I thought about it for many days.

I had no liking for simplicity. Tomei was simple. He reached for me, and when I pulled away from him, he smiled anyway and put his hands behind his head so he could watch me.

"Why are you watching me?"

"I think you are beautiful."

How could he? I knew I was ugly.

Another symptom of his simplicity was this: he could not see ghosts. That was lucky, because I never lay down with him without the ghost of Sanba alongside. It brought with it his familiar scent of leaves and pine needles, of something half-burned, a wood smell. I suppose it was the scent of Sanba's quack remedies. I loved it.

My husband was a gem, a genuine fine fellow. He was fond of life and free of anger. He was not conventional: he would have accepted anything I gave him. Yet I had nothing for him but a cruel streak that was entirely new to me.

22

FAMILY

I WENT TO VISIT MY MOTHER.

Her cheeks had fallen in on her gums. Long-suffering but never silent, she had declined to a garrulous, greedy poverty. There were no riches for her in the artist's life: she cared for neither prints nor books. She wanted food and warmth, which Hokusai disdained. He became gentle with her, as if she were an old dog.

She was at her sister's, bundled on a mattress. There had been a crisis. My aunt was crying. The cats were mewling and children stood in corners. My mother had fallen, standing in a crowd at the fishmonger's. She had to be carried home.

We sent a child for a bonesetter. He put his hands on her and said there was a broken circle in her pelvis.

"It must knit and mend. She must be absolutely still, or it will grow crooked and she will never walk again."

My father stammered his question: She appeared to be quite dead, but could she come back to life if she wanted?

"Western medicine knows about broken bones. But for broken spirit, the gods of Japan are better," said the doctor.

"She broke her spirit in a fall at the fishmonger's?"

"Earlier," said my aunt.

My mother moved.

"She 'eears us," said Hokusai. "Sh-she-shee sa-ay she will c-c-c-come ba.'"

"Are you a mind reader now, Old Man?" I said.

"I'm a *re-re-ree*-ader of faaa-ces."

"Then what is my mother's face saying?"

Hokusai hung his head.

"Talk to her. Maybe you can change her mind."

"I c-c-caan' t-taalk—"

The gods had taken away his eloquence when he needed it.

I became the translator.

"My father wishes to say, 'Wife, come back to me. My life will be better with you. I am not ready for you to die,'" I said woodenly.

Hokusai waved his hands. Apparently he did not like my love words.

My brother Sakujiro was there. He had become a solemn young man and adept at accounts, something unusual in our family. Yet humour was in his eyes; he clearly was Hokusai's son. He alone could tease me. "What would you know about love words, Chin-Chin? You who laughs at her husband?"

"You'd be surprised what I know."

Hokusai blinked.

"Maybe she is right to want to die," I said.

Sakujiro looked at me quietly. "You and our mother are one and the same."

That surprised me. My mother was an ordinary drudge who understood nothing. But I had her face, it was true.

"This is the one who cast you away," he said. "The one who said strong spirit must be broken. Now you would cast her away?"

"I don't cast her. I only want her spirit to rest."

My mother lay on her mat. Her eyes darted on the inside of her eyelids. My aunt nursed her. My father remained wordless. There would be no reconciliation.

What did she watch, inside those eyelids? The landscape of her life had been grey. There would be, on that curtain, no festival fireworks, no boat rides on the Sumida, no great processions, no ribald ditties, no laughter and cups of sake to warm her. No unfolding of red-striped velvets or canopy of *sakura*, even in the imagination. She would only see the inside of that sac that enclosed her. What did it look like?

I had seen my sister give birth. I knew colours—blood red, black waste, and the afterbirth with its rainbow shimmer. I had seen death too: the flesh-wrapped bones at the Punishment Grounds; the defiant, flat face on the march of the doomed; even fish at the fishmonger's. Fish were the last thing she saw—lying on their sides; silver, green, or blue, with arcs of pink; fading hour by hour as their cool, watery spirit ebbed away.

Most likely she was still watching the weigh scales; life was in the balance.

"Say loving things," I told my father. "The kinds of things you said to Shino. Say them, if you want to change her mind."

For once I had shut my father up. Hokusai opened his lips. They moved in silence. "I c-c-aaan't."

We both stared down at her. This object had produced me, then handed me off. I knew the reason. From the very start, she had recognized me: I was her. She had been wilful. And with what miserable outcome? She had sought to spare me.

"Poor Hokusai," they said. "Another wife to die on him, and now who will keep house?"

A HUSBAND COULD LEAVE HIS WIFE for being barren. But Tomei didn't blame me. To him, the fault was Hokusai's.

"Your father is your baby," he said.

More than once his simple logic hit its mark.

Still, nearly ten years of childlessness did not ruin our marriage. I'll tell you what ruined our marriage. It was food: the getting of it and the serving of it. I had thought we would be artists together, whereas Tomei wanted to be served his home-cooked meals.

I loved the food market. That's where I got our meals. It was divine. There were eggplants covered in miso paste. There were ruffled dumplings and crimson pomegranates and tiny grilled whitefish with bronze skin. Curled blush shrimp with their transparent shells and fine whiskers; shaved purple cabbage in vinegar; cubes of bean curd swimming in squid ink—it was all so beautiful. One day I had a little money from a commission. I came back with grilled fish and eggplant and deep-fried tofu squares, his favourite dinner. I was proud to be providing it.

But he tossed away the banana leaves that wrapped it.

"Why?" I said, my mouth full and open. The food was hot.

"You didn't cook it for me."

Did he want me to stand outside on the hard earth and bring him his plate on bended knees? "No, but I bought it."

"It's not the same. A wife cooks."

"Why would I do that? I am an artist who earns our keep."

Tomei began to shout and wave the broom around. "You serve him." He jerked his head towards my father's house. "Serve me too."

I did laugh then. Not at his bad art, but at his crazy idea that I would keep house.

Laughing at an angry man is never wise.

Usually when a husband was dissatisfied, he took a broom and swept his wife out the door. To be banished like that was lucky: he might have killed her. The punishment for a crime of passion—or is it a crime of possession?—was not severe. The babies remained with him, so all he had to do was get a new wife to care for them, while the first wife returned to her family in shame.

When Tomei reached for the broom, I decided to save him the trouble. I tucked my brushes in my kimono, put on my quilted coat, and slid out the door. I was very sad to leave the dinner.

There was a saying: "See a woman running in Kamakura, no need to ask where. Just point the way."

The Temple of Refuge was called Tokei-ji. A woman of a noble family had founded it, and its courtiers wore the imperial crest. It was the only way for a woman to get a divorce by herself. You had to run. If you reached the temple before your husband caught you, you were safe. The pictures we saw of this place featured a woman throwing her sandals ahead of her through the temple gates, her husband making a grab for her hair from behind.

I stormed through the crowds on the streets of Shitamachi. I felt the wind on my face. I felt alive. I was angry. I was often angry, but this time my anger was outside, free, in the world. How exhilarating it felt! To think that Tomei might divorce me. My pride was offended. This in itself was amazing. I took so much grief from the Old Man that I had not known I had pride. I crashed into a porter with a heavy burden and he screamed at me. My face was wet. I slowed. I needed to think. My life was at a balance point; it could tip either way—into disaster or back into tedium and mediocrity.

"Use your sense, Chin-Chin," I said. "Not your bile." Shino would have said that. "You are not being pursued by demons. Slow down."

I was not even being pursued by my husband. I knew that. And yet I felt like a fugitive. I had nowhere to go. If I stayed in Edo, I would have to go back to my home. If I presented myself to my family, they would tell me to go back: "We don't need another divorce! Look what happened to O-Miyo!" I knew what their advice would be. And so I did not seek it. I decided to go to the Temple of Refuge.

It was five stops along the Tokaido to Totsuka. At Totsuka you turned off the route and went over the mountains to Tokei-ji. I had to get there.

I couldn't get out of Edo alone. That was the law: "No women out. No guns in." I would need help. Who could I go to? I could only think of Mune.

It was winter and snow began to fall, wet snow that melted on the stones. I walked on, pleasantly invisible in the white downpour, which thickened by the minute. It muted the noise of carts and made people seem far away. A strange euphoria took me. I must have walked all day. I was walking away from all the confinement I had felt, for years. My joy at escaping carried me all the way to the Ichibee bookstore, where the *rangaku-sha* gathered.

In the warm glow of this little shop, scholars sat in groups with their domed heads and fluid draperies, drinking tea. They spoke of ideas. How different their world was to mine. I pushed aside the door and entered.

The owner, who had once given me a boy's haircut, had not forgotten Hokusai's daughter. He made me welcome, although the solemn scientists hardly slowed their gossip to glance in my wet direction—hair soaked and straggling, hem heavy. He gave me a chair by the stove and a bowl of tea.

"Is the master in good health?"

"Oh yes, indeed," I said, as I always did. His true condition was a secret.

Outside the snow redoubled itself, piling on the edges of fences and on the top of every branch and twig. A black cat hating to get his feet wet jumped from post to fence and then went under the awning.

Finally the door chime tinkled for the last time and the *rangaku-sha* were gone.

"Now tell me. What brings you?" said the storekeeper.

"I must leave Edo. I need help to get past the checkpoint."

"May I ask why?"

No one was allowed to aid a runaway wife. "Better for you if you don't," I said. "A student will help me if you can send a messenger."

The bookseller's boy trudged in with his pack of volumes on his back. He got a scolding for letting the snow get onto the books. His umbrella was so heavy with the white stuff he let it drop, he said. He was given another errand to do: to find Mune and give her a letter.

I slept as my father so often slept, draped over myself beside the heating table. Outside and in my dreams the snow fell and fell, covering my foot-steps. In the morning I was dry and warm, and the bell tinkled. In came a figure wrapped in a black travelling hood: Mune.

I told her where I wanted to go: Tokei-ji. "My poor Oei," she said. "I had no idea."

"Please, no pity. My husband does not abuse me. I abuse him, more likely," I said. It was comical, and we both laughed.

In Mune's sedan chair with its curtained windows the two of us approached the checkpoint at the edge of Edo. The bearers had been instructed to say that there was only one noblewoman inside. But the guards with their swords saw the effort it took the bearers to hold the chair up.

"Wait! You are smuggling! What is in there?"

I was ordered out and stood shivering in front of two boorish inquisitors. They hacked and spit and scratched their private parts. Clearly they sat too long with nothing to do but harass passing women. "Where are you going? Why do you try to leave with no papers? What is your reason?"

I wondered for the first time how my sister O-Miyo had managed this. I had never asked her and now she was dead. These men were beneath me: I couldn't bother to lie.

"I'm going to the divorce temple."

The men laughed. "Why?"

"My husband doesn't like my cooking."

They laughed some more. They grabbed me by the arm. "We should give you cooking lessons. That will keep you till he comes along."

"You will be disappointed. He enjoys my cooking so little that he isn't even chasing me," I said. "I don't sew either."

This time I laughed along with them. Mune slid her window open and coughed. We all went quiet. "Miss Oei amuses you. But she is a distinguished artist," she said. "She is my teacher, and I am taking her to a temple where she will paint pictures for the altar." She waved a letter. "Here is the commission."

The chief guard leaned out of his little wooden tower and waved us on. We hurried so we would be out of sight before they put their heads together.

About an hour down the road Mune gave me her heavy black headscarf and squeezed my shoulders. "I can't go any farther. But you will sleep in the inn at Totsuka." Then she and her bearers turned back and before long were invisible.

I began to walk again. The snow was a gift from the gods. It smoothed the path before me and filled my footsteps behind. I had not been out of the city since I was a child. It was not a day for tourism, that was true. But it was beautiful. I could see nothing of the land—or the water—on either side of the path. There was no colour in the world, only me with my black wrapper, like an unreadable character, an ink blot. I was going to an unknown existence.

Because of the snow a carter took pity and gave me a ride to Kawasaki. I repaid him with a sketch of his mule. I looked at the sea—white-whiskered, and getting more so. People passed me bent under umbrellas that were themselves bent under a fat cushion of snow. I walked on. My feet grew cold. I went to a teashop and warmed them. No one pursued me. No one wanted me back. No one knew where I had gone.

I dawdled, an ox between masters. A woman on her own. Thinking ahead to all the years of my life and savouring, in advance, the pleasure of being myself. I would go to the temple and make sure the bonds of the marriage were officially undone. I would bow that far to custom and law. After that, I would be free.

Kawasaki, in summer, was covered in barley fields waving to the sea. Now it was dry brown sticks poking through the blanket of a vast snow plain. I could not get as far as the inn at Totsuka in such weather. I begged a bed at a temple. The next day I took the ferry over the Rokugo River. I rode with a carter from Kawasaki down to Totsuka and alighted smelling of fish, the snow still falling blankly and without haste from a sullen sky.

Here was the inn Mune spoke of, just at the side of the Tokaido in Totsuka. A friend to the *ukiyo-e* artists owned it. Bunzo had bought scroll paintings from my father. If I introduced myself, he would take me in. But would he tell his other guests? Would they laugh at me? I did not want to break the spell.

It was easy to be unrecognized. It wasn't as if people stared and wondered. They just didn't see me. I sat hunched in a dark corner until the latest hour. I watched Bunzo amongst the guests. He was a good man and would be kind to poor women who showed up in storms. I let him assume that I was one of the usual fugitives. There was no danger of his remembering my face. Without my father, I was nobody. Luckily I had a little money, and I bought a place for the night beside the stove.

In the morning they gave me tea and a lunch of dried fish and rice. The innkeeper stood wordless in the doorway with his hand outstretched: a path led up to Kamakura. I took it, leaving the Tokaido behind.

The snow had stopped. The sky was blue. The path was steep but wide, trodden for centuries by courtiers, desperate women, and furious men. In places the snow was caught in the high pine canopy, leaving the ground bare. But in other places it was deep. I made the first footsteps, and these footprints remained behind me. I passed courtiers on the way down. They gestured onward: "Not too much farther! That was the steepest bit!" One gave me hot tea.

It was dark and the snow had begun again when I came to a small temple to the Fox God. There was a candle burning there. I stepped inside and rubbed my hands over the flame. I breathed into the cup of my palms and drew that breath back inside me: warmth. I stepped back onto the path and looked up. Finally I saw, just off the path, a set of steps leading up into the hill.

I climbed into the tops of the trees. There were lanterns. There was a temple roof. For the first time I hesitated. I had come all this way. Was I doing the right thing? I was discarding a man's protection in a world for men only. Was it foolish?

Yes.

But was I prepared to cook?

No.

Here was the gate. No one chased me. I did not have to throw my shoes ahead to assure my safety. I walked slowly and thoughtfully under its welcome roof and stood in the courtyard in silence. I could hear the nuns singing. I went towards the voices.

I don't remember how they welcomed me that night. How did I ever get warm? The marrow of my bones had frozen solid. I was wet up past my knees.

"Is anyone pursuing you?" the nuns wanted to know. They waved their incense over me.

"No," I said.

"It is a tribute to your great strength to arrive in such weather."

I STAYED FOR THREE MONTHS. I described my innocent husband to the Suigetsu kannon, a tiny female figure who stood beside the pool and gazed at the full moon in the water. "He is not angry. He is not violent. He does not drink to excess, and I have not been beaten."

The water shimmered; the kannon maintained her curious fraction of a smile. "What on earth do you find fault with, then?" she seemed to say.

"He does not see me. He wants me to cook and sew," I said. "He wants me to be other than what I am."

My grievances sounded petty even to my own ears. Other fugitives had bruises and scaldings; they screamed in their dreams.

"What woman expects to be seen for herself?"

I did.

"Does he berate you for being barren?"

"No, he does not. Yes, I am barren. I am glad to be barren. I need every hour of my day to paint." I found that I did have complaints about him. "He resents my work. He resents my old father. He fears me, and fear makes him cruel."

These merciful nuns heard and did not criticize me. They understood study and prayer, and they understood the need for silence. They alone allowed that art made its demands on my person. They had their methods to secure the divorce I wanted. They set about it. There was no contest. The husband had to file a letter of just three and a half lines. Tomei's epistle, written on thick mulberry paper in careful brushwork, arrived to join the hundreds of other letters kept in the treasure house.

"She is not a proper wife. I do not want her and release her. She is free to go where she likes and to marry whomever she pleases. She is useless to me."

I read it by the pool. The kannon winked. She had saved me. But I was to be called "useless." That was the price. I folded the paper and tucked it in my sleeve.

Spring came. The grounds were covered in moss; the old stones greened with it, the grasses luminous in their newness. I walked in the graveyard, where there were statues of famous nuns of the past. I wandered the gardens and painted the flowers—narcissus, hydrangea. I walked out to the harbour. It was April, the season for fishing bonito.

The bonito came on the Black Tide. The fishermen were out in their boats with their nets. I watched the waves; I walked beside them. I thought of my father and how he must need me. From the beach I could see Mt. Fuji, resplendent in its cape of dazzling snow.

Part 3

23

VON SIEBOLD AT NAGASAKI, 1823

ON THE FAN-SHAPED ISLAND in Nagasaki Bay, the Dutch doctor sat at his piano. His fingers ran up and down the keys.

The fingers were strong and long, easily reaching an octave and a half. At the end of a run he rapped each yellowed ivory hard, twice: this was meant to be a workout. A surgeon needed strong hands.

The music rattled in the stillness. The Japanese guards who knelt at the doors gritted their teeth.

The doctor was a prisoner. His back door was the Water Gate and opened onto waves. That was where the ships docked. His front door was the City Gate and led to the town of Nagasaki. He was not allowed to go out there. And few people from the town were allowed in through the gate. On the high wall beside it was a sign that said, in Japanese and Dutch, "No Priests. No Beggars. No Women." Smaller brush strokes added: "With the Exception of Prostitutes Bearing a Red Stamp in Their Papers."

Phillip Franz von Siebold was twenty-seven. He was tall and blond, a strikingly beautiful man, although so strange did he appear to the Japanese that they imagined him to be a demon. The upper half of his face was generous: he had wide eyes and eyebrows that sprouted above deep sockets; his forehead was flat, and his look was ready. Below the eyes his face was quite different: it became narrow and sensitive. His nose ran like a plumb line down his face, long and thin; his lips, also long and thin, crossed it but, happily, turned up at the corners. He had been smiling since he arrived. But the smile was wearing. He was impatient. The world outside the City Gate was rich beyond knowing.

He wore a uniform with epaulettes. The gold tassels on his shoulders shook. Up and down the ivories he went, fingers leaping, chin bobbing. He and the other traders of the Dutch East India Company lived on this man-made island called Deshima, at the very edge of the closed country of Japan. Von Siebold's job was to provide medical care to his countrymen. There weren't many of them left: trade had dwindled and did not justify the posting. Only curiosity did, and a collector's avid desire for artifacts. The Dutch wanted information about the Japanese; they wanted objects, pictures and growing things, trees and flowers. Phillip von Siebold was the perfect man to collect these.

If only he could escape his little island prison.

He had landed a month ago. When his mind returned to the wild sea journey, he planted his feet wide on the floor under his piano stool, as if the stool might buck him off, as if he had to ride it like a horse. Sailing from Batavia in late spring, the ship *Drie Gezusters* had been caught in a typhoon as it approached the southern tip of the Japanese islands. Von Siebold was lurching along the deck thinking he might die. When he saw a fishing boat foundering in the waves, with no sails or oars, he shouted: "They're going down! Can we hook them?"

"We might go down ourselves!"

"Try!"

The Dutch sailors pulled five Japanese from the water. The fishermen knelt on the deck and prayed as their boat was bashed to planks. Then they did a curious thing: they made a circle and shaved their beards and heads. They seemed to be in despair. They gestured: we wished to die in the water.

"You're saved," said the Dutch. "We saved you!" And they clapped their giant hands on the fishermen's dripping backs.

But the fishermen trembled and prayed.

A week later the *Drie Gezusters* sailed into Nagasaki Bay, to be greeted by a row of fanatical sword-bearing men as wide as they were tall. Guards took the Dutchmen's guns, and the rescued local sailors were marched away to whatever fate. Why? It was a crime to be rescued by foreigners.

The rulers of this shut-away place were perverse, thought the doctor.

While he was being searched for forbidden articles, von Siebold had looked around. The land, unlike the people, was gentle. Sheltering hills scattered with white houses surrounded the deep blue bay. The manmade traders' island sat like a plug in the basin of the harbour. His Bible he sacrificed ostentatiously to the Bible barrel, but he kept a smaller version tucked down below his belt at the small of his back, its title page ripped out. He didn't know why. He never sang a hymn or made the sign of the cross. The Japanese abhorred Christians. He had been prepared to stamp on his holy book, an act sometimes required of his predecessors. It would have cost him nothing. But they didn't ask him to.

Still, at the end of it all, they had nearly refused him entrance. The guards spoke better Dutch than he did; he was born and had studied in Germany and spoke with an accent. This made them suspicious that he was a German spy. He told them that he was a *yama-orandajin*, a Mountain Dutchman.

He got a fresh chuckle out of this witticism as he banged down an octave lower on the piano. All that fierce display to stop spies and Christians, yet they had welcomed him. He had got this far. In fact he *was* a spy, in a benevolent way, eager to endure his imprisonment on artificial earth and to submit to Japanese rules, if doing so would allow him access to their secrets. He had brought with him an electrostatic generator, an air pump, and a galvanizing apparatus, to impress the Japanese and encourage them to share their own wonders. And he had brought this piano, which he played every day.

Even his countrymen—the Dutch who inhabited the strange island prison with its low houses, enclosed courtyards, warehouses, and animal pens, with its salty smell of sea and rusted metal doors awaiting the next ship (not expected for half a year)—existed out of time. They dressed in what had been the court fashion before von Siebold was born, quilted velvet coats and black cloaks. When they went out into Nagasaki, which they did only with permission and under guard, they wore hats with feathers and carried Spanish canes with gold handles. They loved to impress. They were tall and the Japanese short; they strode while the simple Japanese farmers and townsmen scuttled. The Japanese were thin and the Dutch were fat. When they returned from their town excursions, they were even fatter because of the parcels they hid in the folds of their cloaks.

They smuggled in these goods under the noses of the guards, who appeared blind as money changed hands. The Japanese used to allow their copper, gold, and silver out of the country, but no longer. Handmade carvings and dolls and pictures—and objects of worship and ritual—were meant to stay home as well, but they found their way into the hands and the tea chests of the Dutch, and eventually home to Holland.

"God's grief, von Siebold, whatever the hell are you playing?"

One of the displaced Dutchmen stuck his face around the corner of the door: the partitions were so thin that the whole island was shaking with the music.

The young doctor raised his voice over the clatter. "It's a popular German song by von Weber called 'Invitation to the Dance.'"

The protruding square face arranged itself in a look of horror and then withdrew.

"Take pity, von Siebold! It's after ten!" His superior, the *opperhoofd* de Sturler, clearly already was irritated by him. This von Siebold enjoyed. He was competitive to anyone above him and jovial to all below.

He completed his last crescendo and closed the top of his piano. Another day had passed.

Walking out of the room and across the little yard to his home, he kept his eyes low so he did not have to acknowledge the young Japanese women coming and going from the Dutch quarters. These were the prostitutes with the red stamps in their passports. His countrymen were fat and old-fashioned, but they enjoyed rude health.

He got ready for bed. On each wall of his chamber he had hung a chart of the phonetic characters that small children studied in schools here, and he ran through them before sleep. He was hungry for everything Japanese—words, pictures, flowers, animals, bamboo chests, lacquer boxes, the practice of acupuncture, and the worship of many gods. And he would get it. Little by little.

He lay on his back, wide awake. He had a plan. His first step had been to offer to teach Western medicine to Japanese doctors. Lectures were at Deshima: a steady stream of respectful men came to the City Gate, and he welcomed them all. He asked only that each man bring with him a living plant, in rich loam so he could easily transplant it.

He had made a garden to receive these gifts. Tomorrow, early in the morning, when the sun first lit the edge of the hills, he would inspect it. The hosta would have added an inch to the height of its spearheads, and the buds on the maple tree might show a hint of orange. He would stoop and smell the crocus with its shy scent and fight back the longing for intimacy that often invaded him, as it did now. It was the sight of those evening women, the subdued clatter of their wooden sandals, that unbuttoned him.

But to the conquest! Tomorrow morning, after the garden walk, he would play the piano again to keep his fingers nimble. They were long and probing, like his regard: he maintained them like faithful slaves, well trained to answer the messages his brain sent. He was a young and inexperienced doctor, and one never knew when he would be required to commit an act of surgery. And the playing sent a message to the rest of the men: he was here, ready.

Thinking of this soothed him, and he slept.

And in the morning it all unrolled just as he had imagined. First came coffee and chocolate; then came inspection of the garden, which was growing, though not as fast as he hoped. The soil, dug out from the mountainside, was not rich. He would ask the servants to collect more pig manure and dig it in well. When he came in, he could see the Japanese doctors lined up early for his morning lecture. Wearing his first smile of the day, he went to greet them: he liked them more than he liked his fellow Dutchmen.

He moved amongst the long-skirted men, smiling and bowing. They kept their eyes down as if blinded by his height, his grace, his blondness. He enjoyed their admiration, the excess of politeness, the quiet, watchful eyes and quick brains, the fierceness of their will. They were as hungry as he was. They had studied Dutch for years, some of them—it was the "Latin of the East." They excelled in coded behaviour in their country and had agreed, tacitly, to play the necessary games to get what they wanted.

This morning they handed him their essays on subjects he had assigned: the annual festivals and their meanings, the confinement of women in pregnancy, the education of boys. Von Siebold read them quickly and asked questions.

"What do you do when a child cannot come out of the birth canal?"

"When a child cannot be born naturally, if he is caught inside the mother's body, we try to pull him out with hands and fingers. But some parts are too large. Either the shoulders or the hindquarters"—he looked up, quizzical; what to call it?—"the back end, the rear cheeks."

One of his countrymen issued a reprimand. The extrovert had used the expression commonly employed when speaking of a domestic animal. "No, no. That is not what we call it!"

"The buttocks?" said von Siebold helpfully.

"When the *bew-tox* be not out coming, it chances the child may perish," the Japanese doctor concluded, with a look of relief that was not in tune with the information he was delivering. But he was not released. Von Siebold interrogated him: Why not use forceps for difficult deliveries?

"We use not these tools, as women have an abhorrence of them," came the answer.

Von Siebold doubted that the women's will would prevail, even in such matters.

"The women tell you what to do?" he prodded.

"We decide. It is not good for use metal in the body."

"What happens, then, if the child cannot be extricated?"

"We will find what arm or leg we can reach and pull," said a comical fellow, making a pantomime of it. His fellows coughed. "Maybe will be cutting it off, and the child out come in pieces."

"And the woman?"

"Dies or lives, according to the gods," the student concluded. Von Siebold's expressive face showed dismay.

"Why do you not perform a Caesarean section?"

The operation was known here; von Siebold had read the notes of his predecessor.

"Oh no no no no. That is wrong, murder; gods not happy, and both mother and child pay price," said the Japanese doctor from his kneeling position on the floor.

Von Siebold gathered up the essays, informative writing that had bypassed the censors. He collected the little bamboo boxes of plants that the doctors presented as tributes, exclaiming over the ones he hadn't yet seen. Here was a tiny yew tree. And this one appeared to be a variety of cypress. This was a precious bonsai: it had been pinched and tortured, so it was only a very small version of itself. He bowed deeply and the men bowed back.

Later, he patted the new seedlings into place in his garden. He had magnolias and wisteria and varieties of pine. To each one he gave a small whispered blessing: take root!

AT NIGHTFALL, THE ISLAND WAS SO SILENT that he could hear the waves slurping at the Water Gate. At the City Gate the prostitutes presented their red-stamped passports to the implacable guards and went quickly in their hobbled gait to the men. He saw one clearly in silhouette as she crossed the courtyard. Pregnant. The children of these liaisons were adopted into Japan, but a Dutch father had no claim—and maybe wanted none.

No woman arrived for him. Restless, he sat and read the essays in stiff Dutch offering him the secrets of the people's customs, their laws, their history as they understood it, the art of healing by needles. He went to the toilet in the backyard. He had glued the chart of Japanese characters on the wall so he would not waste time there either. It was in this refuge, thinking over the day's class, that he resolved to persuade the doctors to perform Caesarean sections. He would do that by offering his best students a very special Dutch doctor's diploma.

And this would give him reason to apply to the *bugyo,* the governor of Nagasaki, for special leave to make daily consultations off the island. Lives would be saved and he would get out.

The next day, von Siebold expressed this plan carefully to de Sturler. The request was duly transmitted to the Japanese. A message came back, so courteous. No. We are very sorry.

They gave no reason. Von Siebold argued in his mind with the invisible *bugyo.* He had only Japanese interests at heart. Lives of women were being lost, or more important, one could say, lives of boy children were being lost. But he could not ask again, he knew that, and so he dug pig manure. He was kneading it into the roots of his hostas when a messenger came. The man was burdened with heavy braided armour, two swords, and a flag and standard.

He brought a written summons: the doctor must go to the home of a wealthy merchant who had been struck blind.

Von Siebold was only too happy. He put on his giant hat and his black cape, took the gold-handled cane and the black leather bag containing the surgical tools. With a samurai in front of him and a samurai behind him, he walked out the City Gate into the early morning and the town.

The first thing to hit him was the sound. He heard the guttural cries of porters pushing donkeys. Hawkers were singing in a higher pitch. Temple bells clanged. The life of the place hit him between the eyes: women wrapped in sashes and in fabrics of stripes and swirls; men running with tea caddies. A riot of country people selling faggots and birds in cages, turnips, and fish on skewers. Children of three were lighting fires under huge cauldrons. Fishermen with dark skin and bands across their brows had their catch in barrels. A procession of pilgrims all in white went by, chanting and looking at the ground. It made him laugh out loud. He was amongst—and towered two feet above—these preoccupied people.

He could have walked forever, but the merchant's house was not far away. The guards pushed von Siebold though the gate, in a bogus show of force intended to impress. At the door, a shy young woman bowed him in. The interior was dim, black-timbered with low ceilings. Von Siebold had to remove his hat, but he was still too tall, so he stooped and leaned to the side.

The merchant Kusumoto sat cross-legged on a Chinese cushion. He did not flinch under von Siebold's glare. The Dutch doctor could see that a whitish film was spreading over the man's eyes. It was a simple case of cataracts. At school he had watched the operation to remove them, but he had never done it himself. Nevertheless he told Kusumoto with confidence that he could restore his eyesight.

Modest and solemn, the daughter showed him out.

In his quarters again he asked the Malaysian servants to bring him the head of a pig. He could hear the squealing as they decapitated the animal. He had the head drained of blood. He sharpened his scalpels. He played his piano scales and blew on his fingers, warming them. "Be clever, be agile," he whispered, tapping them on the edge of his lips. He put on his medical coat.

In the operating room he cut into the skin of the dead pig's eyes, removing the coating over its still-warm cornea. He thought that he acquitted himself reasonably well.

"Are you a butcher now?" cracked de Sturler from the doorway.

"If I am to cure a man of blindness, first I must practise."

"Hmmm. You conduct a dress-rehearsal operation. Your logic is flawed, don't you think?"

"I don't, but perhaps you do?"

"The pig is a pig," drawled his boss, leaning into the room. "As it had no cataracts, its sight cannot have been improved. And even if it could, how would the pig tell you he could see better—or worse, in fact? This would be true even if it were alive. But on top of it all, the pig is dead." De Sturler slapped his leg and roared.

My superior dislikes me. It is simple jealousy, von Siebold thought calmly. He had encountered it before: men took offence at the excess of natural gifts he displayed.

The next day he marched off with his guards to Kusumoto's house with operating equipment and a brighter lamp. He was afraid. If he botched the operation, he would get no more favours from the Japanese. He might even be punished. He asked the daughter, Otaki, to assist. He would have preferred a man, but one was not available, and the girl was excellent. Even when her father's eyes were being peeled, she had qualities of repose and alertness that impressed him.

When the operation was done, Kusumoto declared that he could see perfectly. The foreign doctor had miraculous powers.

"Not so!" von Siebold insisted.

But word spread. The next day the Japanese guards were calling him the Miracle Doctor. Three days later he knelt in Kusumoto's receiving room. The merchant seemed to be proposing to give him Otaki. Von Siebold pretended that he didn't understand. He promised to visit them again. The matter was suspended.

As he left, he thanked the girl for her assistance. She was modest, murmuring over and over that she had done nothing. But it seemed now to von Siebold that she had held his hand and made it steady, and he noticed how very pretty she was.

He was allowed a little freedom. Several times a week he walked with only one guard through the market to the merchant's house to check on his patient. It became understood that he loved the girl, and she him. All of this happened quickly. In order to visit him at Deshima, Otaki produced her passport. There was the red stamp of the courtesan. The family seemed to say that she had requested this so she could serve the doctor. Had she been a prostitute before? Here von Siebold's Japanese proved inadequate.

Six months after his arrival at Nagasaki, Phillip wrote to his uncle in Holland that he was happy. (When had he ever been unhappy?) He said: "I have temporarily become quite attached to a sweet sixteen-year-old Japanese girl, who I would not willingly exchange for a European one."

WITHIN A YEAR VON SIEBOLD had permission to build a medical school in a pretty valley with a waterfall. He went there freely most mornings, lectured all day, and returned to the island at night. He had amassed a big collection of plants and added to it constantly. He sent new species—hydrangea, cypress, delphinium, cherry, iris—back to Europe every time a ship left. And he had objects. With the lower class of people, he found bribery successful in getting them to part with their treasures. With the educated, he made exchanges—his knowledge for theirs. As far as officials went, it was easy to convince them that they saw nothing by offering his expertise in questions of their family health.

Otaki came to the island. She was allowed to live with him, given her new status. Her presence was far more effective in his learning Japanese than the chart of *kana* on the wall of the toilet. He had been on the island only two years when she was on the table, labouring under his hands. The child was a female, and von Siebold loved both his wife and his daughter very much. He was sad that the two were forced to move off Deshima, but on this point the laws of Japan did not bend, not even for the Miracle Doctor. Mrs. von Siebold would live with her child in her father's home, and the child would belong to Japan. Phillip visited them every day. He now had a clinic under the whispering waterfall; the grateful Japanese built a house for him, and he stayed there many nights himself. It was strictly forbidden, but no one seemed to notice. Students stood in groups five deep to watch him as he did operations. "They hang on my lips," he told Otaki. She laughed because you could not say that in Japanese: it made a ridiculous picture.

Perhaps the only sour note was his relationship with the *opperhoofd*. A certain strain existed there. But even that seemed to be easing. De Sturler had spoken to him: soon the Dutch mission must travel to Edo to give tribute to the Shogun.

Von Siebold would join the procession.

IN LATE FEBRUARY THE SNOW WAS GONE from the hills, and the white tips of the hostas were inches above the soil. The buds on the plum trees were swollen and von Siebold's daughter was two years old by the Japanese count, which gave her one year at birth. Nearly sixty Japanese and three Dutch set off to walk the six hundred miles to the Eastern Capital. They carried food, silver, glassware, and furniture—including the piano—and many gifts for the Shogun. Von Siebold packed his tools—barometers, chronometers, sextants. He intended to measure and record everything he passed. A Japanese draftsman hired to draw the sights walked alongside. Von Siebold himself sat in a sedan chair and made notes as he, a European, one of only a handful ever to go there, passed through the forbidden countryside.

Word had spread. Peasants grouped by the wayside with curiosities: the miscarried fetus of an albino deer, a child with seizures, a beautiful shell. They stood in the rain and waited for hours.

The guards were at first suspicious and later lax, allowing von Siebold to get down, minister, and take gifts. One day the servants caught a giant salamander with a head like an arrow, a long spiny body, and a pointed tail. It was five feet long and looked prehistoric. Von Siebold had them build a cage and sent it back to Deshima with instructions that the servants feed it rats, which were plentiful under the floorboards.

He jolted along in his enclosed chair on the shoulders of the bearers for many days. Then suddenly, mystically, the white cone of Mt. Fuji appeared against the sky. He jumped down and got out his sextant to measure its height. There were murmurs of discontent amongst the guards. Von Siebold got back into his sedan, and they walked on.

But there was Mt. Fuji again. He insisted on being let down to measure it. The canny peak seemed to leap out at them, first from one direction and then from another. Eventually, not to upset the guards, he hid his sextant and compass in his hat and pulled them out only when he thought no one was watching. From then on, whenever he saw the mountain raise its perfect head, he stepped out of the procession and surreptitiously measured it.

AFTER WALKING FOR TWO MONTHS the procession arrived in Edo. It was April 10, 1826, he noted. Here, unlike in friendly Nagasaki, he felt like a freak. Crowds clogged the streets to see the three tall, red-haired barbarians. The Dutch were immediately closed up in Nagasakiya House to await their audience with the Shogun. Important scientists came calling. They were the *rangaku-sha,* and many had been newly named by the former *opperhoofd.*

Mogami was there. Genseki, the court physician, was there. Takahashi Sukuzaemon, the court astronomer, was now called Globius.

These men wanted books, and they brought documents to trade. But von Siebold knew you could learn as much or more from the images the Japanese made. His predecessor had bought a pair of scrolls from the painter Hokusai. One scroll was much admired and the other was considered to have had a spell cast on it: whoever owned it took sick and died. This Hokusai, von Siebold believed, was a court painter. He asked that he too be brought to the Nagasakiya.

24

Meeting

A LITTLE FELLOW CAME TRIPPING into our slum with a message: the Dutch Miracle Doctor wanted to meet the court painter Hokusai.

"Court painter!" I fell over sideways, laughing.

My father gave no sign he heard. This was his way, more and more often. But I was all ears. Maybe the red-haired barbarian would buy paintings. His predecessors had. Times were grim, and I remembered how in years before we'd briefly prospered on the Dutch trade.

The Old Man was annoyed that day. It was not a significant irritation. I can't even remember it. Maybe the message itself put him off. He never liked anyone important. Sycophants too had to be put in their place. Maybe he remembered the old insult from Captain Hemmy, who tried to buy the scroll at half-price. Maybe he was thinking of the bitter words between himself and my mother on the subject of that famous payment of 150 *ryo*. He was sentimental about her now she was gone.

For whatever reason, my father sat picking the rows of black paint from under his fingernails and refused to meet the Dutchman.

I came out of the house squinting. The daylight dazzled me; it was dark where we worked, so dark that now my father was lifting his pages up to his nose and peering at them. Feeling unsteady on my sandals and displaced—as if I myself were cut out of a book of pictures and pasted onto this scene—I set out.

I was a simple townswoman in her indigo blue cotton-print kimono and jacket, with a few coins and some papers tucked in her sleeve. Neat enough: hair wound tight in a bun at her neck, no makeup, not slender but rounded now. I passed through a market and bought myself some grilled eggplant and tofu mixed in a sweet, peppery sauce. Delicious.

I sucked my fingers, one after another. I didn't get out often enough. I concentrated so fiercely on my work. Now I could see changes out here in the big city—more countryfolk surrounded the vendors, if that was possible. Women in clusters crowded a fabric-sellers' stall where bolts of patterned silks and velvets were stacked up to the roof. There were wooden toys for sale everywhere, spinning tops and something you rubbed between your palms to make it fly up into the air. Howling dogs and competing vendors and chains of monks.

This was the life my father couldn't be without. I too could enjoy it. A man hailed me from across the aisle—the candy vendor Hokusai visited faithfully.

"How's your old man?"

"Excellent!" I gave my tight smile. It was an unfamiliar feeling on my face. "Better and better."

Only his friends knew about the palsy. The sweets were a regular delivery and part of Hokusai's plan to cure himself. I waved and strode past, breathing more deeply, on my errand to the Dutch, feeling proud. I thought, It is true that I am only a woman and I have a thrusting chin and a shabby kimono, but I represent the finest artist in the land, and this is the proof.

The guards at the Nagasakiya bowed me in. And I was in his presence.

The Miracle Doctor astonished me. He was tall and not red-haired at all. His hair was golden, like sheaves of grain. He had broad shoulders and a narrow waist and long, thin legs. His eyes were intense blue. He towered over me but bowed to my height, and looked at me openly, kindly.

My little lecture to myself had worked. I was not intimidated. In fact I was awash in his glory. I felt accepted by those eyes. I softened. My face came unstuck from its rigid, defensive expressions. My eyes cast modestly down, I found myself eager to talk.

"My father, the great master, is at this moment deeply engaged in a large work and unable to be here." Sanba had told me I had dimples in my cheeks that I could use to my advantage. I used them, probably for the first time ever.

The Dutch doctor showed no surprise. I was astonished to be speaking Japanese with a barbarian. And we understood each other! What he didn't say in words, he indicated with his deep-socketed eyes and giant brows, which lifted and lowered to add feeling. Oh, what a beautiful man he was. Hardly a man, like another creature altogether, a finer one.

Usually the Japanese did not examine him; he examined them. But this young woman stared openly. He could see her tracing his face, and he felt its difference from hers: his shaggy eyebrows where she had a small, thick ridge indicating she was unmarried; the caverns of his eyes, darkened with lack of sleep, where she had bright sharp stones that seemed to pop out of their lids.

Hokusai's daughter was small, and not as feminine as some of the women here, yet possessed of a certain charm. Her face was diamond-shaped, wide at the jaw with a square-ended, thrusting chin giving her an inquisitive look. She had large ears, and a voice pitched strangely low for a Japanese woman. She was not well dressed, which must have been an artist's affectation. Nor did she bow.

He found her lack of shyness refreshing and mildly challenging. She spoke to him as an equal, a thing he had never experienced before with a Japanese woman. She said her father was in his sixty-seventh year.

"An old man!"

"He has boasted that since I was born," said the daughter. "But now it has become true."

"What is he working on?" he said.

"Beautiful women not so much any longer." She became a little vague. "Peasants in the countryside, views of natural wonders . . ."

He asked to see some of Hokusai's paintings, and the woman said she would return. He went to his desk to take notes for the book he would one day write about the Japanese character. What was this pride in being old? He had heard it said that death was the high point of a man's life. And this lack of respect for conventions by the artist's daughter? They were eccentrics—if such a thing were possible in Japan.

So many contradictions! The government of course was two-faced. The announced strictures were extreme. Yet punishments were applied only in opportunistic circumstances. He was summoned here and then ignored. He was not to explore, but official scientists called on him with official questions. The Japanese navigated these layers without much difficulty. But he found them inexplicable.

Take Japanese women, for instance. The rare sophisticated woman ran a family inn or store. Others, earthier, were skilled in weaving or silk production. But even the most independent of them withered in the presence of a male relative. Women, he observed, had no social context of their own. They rarely appeared alone in public; it was positively Arab that way. Here was the greatest puzzle: there appeared to be no coercion. Women were willing partners in their own invisibility. Why was the Japanese woman so dependent, her very existence defined by obligation?

And yet, as seen today, why was the opposite evident, at least this once?

He put down his pen and laid his head on his Western pillow in his Western bed, carted all the way from Nagasaki. He might learn more from this strange daughter when she returned.

WHEN I TOOK PAINTINGS to the Nagasakiya, he offered me tea. And a sweet cake that I found delicious. The Miracle Doctor told me about his journey, about how, at each stop along the way, he had pulled out his telescope and looked at Fuji-san in its virgin beauty. He measured it again and again, and wrote down his observations while he was being carried in the sedan chair he called his flying study.

"But was the height of Fuji-san different, from different places along the road?" I said.

"Of course! It depends on where you are looking from."

This astonished me. I thought the mountain must always maintain the same height. He laughed to see my pondering. "Of course it is a trick of the mind. Don't you see?"

"The mountain is a god," I observed.

"It has no magical powers," he said shortly. "But it appears to change when our position changes. It is we who go up and down. So we were actually measuring not the height of the mountain but the lay of the land."

"I see," I said, and I was beginning to.

"I hid my compass in my hat," he confided. He was so proud of this contraption that he showed me the tall black felt with its pocket inside.

"Compass in your hat!" I was amazed. "Is it a brain you wear outside your head? Does it help you think?"

The Dutchman did not laugh. "I don't need help in thinking. Only in measuring."

He was marvellous to look at and so curious. And I thought he was good. He wanted to do good. But he lacked caution.

"It will not go unnoticed," I murmured, my face bending low in front of him.

"Unnoticed by whom? Your authorities allow me to do what I wish. My curiosity arises from my great respect for your people," he said.

"It is not for people to be curious." I used a term that meant a lowly person.

"I am not lowly," he said. "I am a scientist."

"The laws . . ." I began and bowed again.

"These laws are not serious. They exist, but no one pays any attention to them."

He elaborated.

"Laws," he spouted, "they are ignored. For instance, the law against smuggling. Everyone knows the *opperhoofd* goes out and comes back laden with trinkets. The *opperhoofd* is not searched." The doctor made a joke. "When he arrives back at Deshima he is very fat. Then he goes to his chamber and disrobes, and suddenly he is thin."

I laughed because he seemed to expect it. I said that he had learned to speak Japanese well. I asked him how he had done it.

"Hanging on the wall in my toilet I have a copy of the poem children use to memorize the syllables."

I cackled at the picture this conjured.

He looked startled at my outburst, but so was I. Why so frank?

"In my sleep, I work on vocabulary," he said.

"How?" Hokusai would be interested in that. If he could figure out how to draw in his sleep he would do it.

"I say word pairs as I'm drifting off."

We were suddenly struck dumb. Our conversation had got off to such a fast start; it had hurtled, and now we were embarrassed.

The doctor suddenly seemed to wonder about me.

"Are you married?"

"Yes."

"Did you choose the man you married?"

"I chose him after I met him in my father's art classes."

"This is unusual," he said.

"My father knows me well," I said.

"Did you study in the classes too?" he asked.

"I did, when I was younger. But now I teach the classes. My father is very busy. Hokusai had decided it was my job to pass along his method."

Silence. I could have told him more about that, but he didn't ask.

"Are you married?" I asked him.

"I have a Japanese wife."

It was a puzzling answer. Yes, he was calling her his wife, but at the same time he was saying she was Japanese, which seemed a qualifier. "Does that mean yes or no?" I asked.

"Yes," he said stiffly.

"Do you have a Dutch wife as well?"

At this he laughed.

"No, Otaki is my only wife. We have a child. I love them both very much," he said.

I was charmed by the way he said that. I knew no man who spoke of love so simply.

The doctor wanted famous views of Edo. He wanted festivals. He wanted pictures that showed our rituals. He wanted these in watercolour. I agreed that Hokusai would paint them. We settled on a good price. In exchange, he offered to provide us things from Europe. I said, as courtesy required, that we wanted nothing. Then von Siebold mentioned the colour *beru*.

Ah, now that was different.

I knew this colour. We called it Berlin blue. It was a new blue from Prussia, very expensive, very strong. It had appeared in our markets only a few years ago. Painters in Osaka used it for actor prints. Here in Edo, the rebel disciple Eisen was using it on fans. He was clever, that man. The grains of the pigment were very fine, and it printed more smoothly than our dayflower or indigo. Our blues were fugitive—they faded. But *beru* was long lasting.

I told the doctor that *beru* was too expensive. We couldn't even afford it for a painting, where we would use a very little. For a print it was unthinkable, because of the quantity we'd need.

"No, no," he said. "It can't be true. Nothing can be too expensive for the great master." He wanted to give me gifts. Though I demurred, again for manners, he produced a little *beru* right then. And some Dutch paper. And a pencil.

As I made my way back through the twilit streets, a little more lurid as dark grew, with performers japing, drums beating, hawkers insistent at the end of day, I wondered why he had given me the pencil.

I think it was because we had spoken of painting in the Western style, and of the straight lines used to draw buildings, pillars, and furniture. Von Siebold's draftsman used a pencil, and he thought Hokusai might use it to make his paintings.

But I used the pencil. First I held it lightly and reverently in my hand, knowing that his long, slender fingers, his surgeon's fingers, had touched it. Then I began making lines with a straight edge to draw in the scaffolding around my figures. Over the pencil lines I used the watercolours. The results were mixed. I had asked Hokusai to paint, but he would not.

"These are for the Dutch doctor," I reminded him.

"You do it, and get the students to help," he said. "Stupid foreigner. He won't know the difference."

25

THE GIFT

I RETURNED WITH PAINTINGS. Von Siebold smiled more kindly on me each time I saw him. He cleared the room of his learned hangers-on. We fell into conversation, as if we'd done this often.

He liked *Sudden Shower:* the peasants bracing themselves as a cloudburst broke over their heads. It was a common enough scene in Japan, but he didn't know that.

"An instant so fleeting only a genius could have caught it," I said, showing him the gestures of self-protection against wind and water, the onslaught so frequent in our land. I enjoyed the charade. It was a picture Hokusai had designed but left to me to put in the colour.

We discussed my father's genius. So unconventional! How refreshing his vision was; how, of all the Japanese artists, Hokusai was the one whose name would one day be known in Europe.

Von Siebold's secretary wrote down the particulars of the sale. The doctor smiled warmly at me, which gave me the confidence to ask my question.

"You are a learned man," I began.

He nodded. No argument there.

"In England," I said, "there was a great writer, name of Shakespeare. Do you know him?"

He was surprised by my topic. "Any educated man knows the works of Shakespeare. We studied him in school."

He struck a pose.

"'What a piece of work is a man! how noble in reason! how infinite in faculty! in form and motion how express and admirable! in action how like an angel! in apprehension how like a god! the beauty of the world! the paragon of animals!'"

Oh, he was like an angel himself. It was the one word of English I understood. I clapped my hands. It made tears spring to my eyes, that man reciting the strange words that rolled and tumbled together. The secretary chuckled. I had never heard the language before. Sanba loved Shakespeare; that's how I knew of him. Perhaps a few of his plays were read here, by the scholars in Dutch. But Sanba was no scholar; he was a scavenger of names and fame, and knew nothing of the man's work, only that he was great.

"That is wonderful," I said carefully. "Can you tell me about the man?"

"What?"

"Can you tell me, for instance, if this Shakespeare had a daughter?"

I don't know what question he had expected next, but it was not this one.

"A daughter?" he said. "He has been dead two hundred years."

"Yes," I said, "but . . ."

"Little is known about his life."

One of the other Dutchmen in the room came and spoke in von Siebold's ear. Perhaps he understood my question.

"It is possible that he did have a daughter," said von Siebold.

I smiled. "And she wrote for the stage also?"

No need for consultation this time.

"No."

"But she helped him with his writing?"

"No, no."

I was shocked and disappointed. "Why not?"

"Maybe she didn't know how to write."

"The daughter of the great master was not taught to write?" I had thought these Westerners were highly civilized.

"I doubt it. Shakespeare was a simple man from the provinces. This daughter, assuming there was one, may have learned to sign her name. Or maybe to write simple things, like a list of her possessions."

"She would not be required to help him with his work?" I had spent many hours imagining this woman. I felt certain she existed.

A light came in his eyes. He thought he understood me. So I was interested in the role in her father's life taken by this mythical daughter. His smile became broad.

"He went to live in London and left both wife and daughter behind," he said gently.

"Oh! But how did he manage without her?"

He tipped his head. He spoke as if not wanting to disappoint a child. "We are imagining this," he cautioned.

"My father," I said, and I knew I had given myself away but threw all caution to the wind, "my father had three daughters. Still not enough."

Von Siebold laughed. I laughed with him.

"Of Shakespeare's daughter, we have no information," he said firmly.

No information. I was stunned. I had not imagined a great life for her. Only a little one. But not that fate. To be utterly unknown. To have one's labour for the art forgotten. To have one's very existence in question.

"England is not like here. Shakespeare's work was not a family project."

"Not?" I didn't believe it. I sat trying to absorb it.

He was clearly puzzled. "What did you think she did?"

Sanba had talked about the great dramatist of kings and wars; the kabuki actors discussed him too. He wrote many plays, and to do that he would have had to have a daughter at his side. She might have helped with the work if he went out of town, on the road or gathering information. Or if he had too much writing to do at once, he would lay out the pattern and she—

"No one but the great man himself could have written the plays," said von Siebold. "No daughter, even if he had one, had anything to do with it."

I saw he had missed my point entirely. "Of course," I said. "And she would never have said anything but that that was the case."

He looked at me keenly.

"It seems a waste."

A dubious smile played around his lips. Was I teasing? "A waste of what?"

"Of her great talent."

He looked blank.

"In Japan we make sure that such skill descends in families," I said.

"Anyway," he said apologetically, "there is no such woman. We don't know that she was ever born."

I kept my teeth covered, as they were bad. My time was up. "I am very grateful for your thoughts." I bowed. I promised to be back. I left, disappointed but somehow stirred inside. I had not realized how backward these Europeans were.

I traipsed down the street deep in thought. Since I first heard Shakespeare spoken of as the man who understood great and small, I had likened him to the Old Man. He taught his daughter to write. When a child she was made to do errands for her father, and she did them willingly because she understood his art better than anyone. He shared his insights, his rages against the world. He was not a worldly man, because his head was in the clouds, and his daughter became sharp with tradesmen and competitors who would have cheated him. In this way the daughter was a true disciple, and always loyal.

Because Shakespeare-san was difficult. The master could be some kind of asshole; they often were. Had the daughter been of the same temperament as he—unwilling to please for the sake of it, hating pretense—she would have had to hide it. She would perform duties for her father not because of deference or duty but because if she didn't, the work would not be produced. The work was their livelihood. And she believed in its worth.

But this daughter—all right, if she did not exist, then perhaps I would have to speak of myself—this daughter herself was capable of great work. But she rarely had the time to concentrate on it. The more she helped Hokusai, the greater he became and the lesser she became. As he grew greater, she grew older. That was the real question. When would it be her time?

WORD CAME FROM THE NAGASAKIYA that von Siebold had a gift for us.

I went to pick it up.

"For your father," he said. It was a supply of the paint called *beru,* the vibrant blue that did not fade. In quantities enough to make anything we wanted.

I touched the packet. I rubbed the fine, fine particles between my fingertips. As the primary grinder of pigments in our house, I was fascinated. It would save me a great deal of work. It would also make wonderful sky and sea.

"I can't accept this," I said, pushing it back to him.

"Yes, you can," he said, pushing it back towards me. I was confused because his hands touched mine.

"Do you know the story of how it was discovered?" von Siebold said, covering this awkward moment.

"No." I passed a small amount of the pigment between my forefingers and thumb. I rubbed it onto the top of my hands, the way actors tested their white makeup. It went into the lines of my skin. It was that fine.

"Scientists made it by accident. They were trying to make red. Isn't that funny? It has iron in it, I suppose," he said. "Please accept it; I am eager to see what your father can do with it."

He had forgotten that I was a painter too.

He squeezed my hand.

I took the packet.

A WEEK LATER, I returned to the Nagasakiya. I presented him the first of the paintings: my father's print *A View of Both Banks of the Sumida River*, an older one but we still had a copy. He wanted a Beauty, a *bijin-ga*, so I sold him the silk painting *Courtesan Inspecting Her Coiffure*. We said it was by Hokusai, but it was studio work. I felt a little guilty. I had not had time to use the *beru* yet.

This time he showed his pleasure at seeing me. He smiled widely and took each of my hands in his.

The place was quiet; it was as if the Dutch had been forgotten, stranded in the midst of the clogged streets of Edo. His secretary served me coffee that was rich and bitter. He showed me his specimens. He had a collecting album, each page a little pocket into which was tucked a dried, pressed flower. We looked at a hairy primrose that grew only on a mountain in the Kiso Valley. He showed me dried blossoms of the early blooming Yoshino cherry, leaves of the Zelkova tree, a large *kanoko* lily, and some seeds of a hydrangea. That was his favourite; he wanted to name it after his wife, Otaki. He grew them on his prison-island and sent the seeds, and even the living specimens, to Holland. He collected tea plants as well and sent them to the Dutch islands.

"The exotica of Japan," he said dreamily, "going out into the world. Flowers, tea, your father's pictures, your ways, of which I will write in my book."

"Our ways are exotic?" To me they were harsh.

"Oh, yes. They are exotic and even bizarre to our eyes. But this will end, with the foreigners coming and our ways colouring the water as tea leaves do."

I smiled at his metaphor. It was something he was learning from our speech, I felt. "Will foreigners come?" I wanted it but could not believe it would happen.

"It can't be helped. They will come here from all over the world. The Shogun cannot keep the walls up around these islands forever."

THE SHOGUN TOYED WITH THE DUTCH. The official visit was delayed further. Crowds collected in front of the Nagasakiya. The Dutch were easy to see, in their locked house.

"The Dutchman told me about beautiful things that he collected along the road," I said to Hokusai. "He found a giant salamander, longer than my two arms stretched apart. Its head is flat and triangular, like a stone arrowhead made by the Indians of North America."

I had visited half a dozen times. Then I came home and told my father stories. I liked being the one with stories to tell. I repeated the one about the emperor Napoleon, who defeated the king and queen of France and who lost his power once he lost his wife. I told him about ice, and how it could be made and stored in a special box with electricity. I told him that there was a wild man with long hair who walked through the forests of the New World sketching birds that no one had ever seen before.

When I went next to the Nagasakiya to deliver pictures, the doctor had a question for me. On his journey to Edo he had left the expedition to visit a magistrate. He had discovered that after he left, the *bakufu* put the magistrate under house arrest. He was concerned.

"What law did the magistrate break?" he asked, sincerely puzzled.

"He talked to you."

"But many people talk to me! You are talking to me."

"It's true," I said. "It may seem that there is no law, or that no one obeys it. But don't be mistaken. The laws exist. They are kept secret."

He rocked back on his high heels. "Secret laws! What is the point of that?"

"To instil fear! The Shogun is a stalking tiger. The tiger can be very patient. His prey can mosey along or skip and run. It does not matter. Suddenly he takes a step too far and the tiger pounces."

He examined my face.

"You will make a note for your book that this Japanese woman has nonsensical and primitive fears," I said. "But you should take heed."

Von Siebold was taken with the women in the many pictures I brought showing our rituals, like *Two Women and a Boy at the Time of the Boys'*

Festival and A *Merchant Making Up the Accounts at the End of the Year.*

It seemed we had a friendship, despite our differences.

We talked then about slavery. The sale of the Negroes of Africa to work as animals on plantations in America. I said I abhorred it and I said this with disgust.

"People are not to be bought and sold," I said.

His hand twitched as if he wanted to take notes. "You display an unusual passion," he said.

In my visits to von Siebold I saw Mogami Tokunai with his imperial guards, also Mamiya Rinzo: these men made maps. They had official roles in the palace. My father knew them from the meetings of the Dutch scholars, but neither recognized me. As I passed them, I felt fear. Maps were forbidden to us. The Shogun received them from the gods. I supposed the men who copied these god-given maps had curiosity, like the rest of us. But at what cost?

One day I saw a man waiting in the courtyard of the Nagasakiya. The servant called him Globius. Many Japanese had asked for Dutch names and been given them. This new-naming was popular now even amongst the high-born. "Who is the man they call Globius?" I asked my father.

"You saw Globius there?" said Hokusai. He whistled. "He is the man who reads the stars for the Shogun." So it went as far as the stars, this eagerness for Dutch learning. I remembered what von Siebold had said about the Dutch flaunting the laws while the Japanese turned a blind eye. I disagreed. There was no blind eye. The eye blinked, but it missed nothing.

I made my thanks to von Siebold. Then I told him I had an additional, special painting for him. I told him that it was a gift, and that he should open it after he had left. I did not think I could bear to have him see it and not know I painted it. I had made it especially for him, painting it on silk, not the Dutch paper. It was modelled on a picture of a young courtesan my father had done ten years ago. I had the sketch. But I had turned her around and given her a face that showed how she felt, and even how I felt. I had worked long hours on this painting and I loved it. I called it *Promenading Courtesan.* I was proud of that painting and I wished it luck as it went out into the world far away, the world of Europe.

I held it on my two palms, stretched my arms towards him, and bowed. It was the way samurai bowed to their swords.

Von Siebold thanked me graciously. He unrolled it and looked at it carefully. "This painting is like a jewel," he said.

I bowed my head, just a little. It seemed he understood it was mine.

"Why is her head inclined sideways?"

"We often take this shape." To me it was a broken shape, but I did not say so. "She is on parade," I said, "in the pleasure district."

"I suppose it is a matter of training," he said slowly. "The women are subjected to much that is abhorrent." He was at his note-making again. "The Japanese woman," he said, "is quiet and obedient. She is always concerned with the welfare of others. Never with herself."

I wanted to fall over sideways, as I did with my father when something preposterous was said. I did not.

"You live amongst women," he said. "Truly, maybe you can help me understand. How can they be so selfless?"

Had he tried that opinion on my husband? Had he seen my sisters? Had he heard my mother lambaste my father? Perhaps I would have to agree with the Old Man: von Siebold was a fool. A likeable, romantic fool. He could never tell a real Hokusai from a fake.

I cleared my throat with a little cough. I wanted to speak frankly. But I could not. Here was a stranger to our land, and it shamed me to speak about our realities. And in what sort of code were we communicating? Was he speaking about the suffering of the women in the Yoshiwara, as I was? In short, I was at a loss for words. "Perhaps we are not taught that we have a self."

"Then it is good teaching. These women are so gentle," von Siebold pressed. "How is it created in them?"

I thought of the exhausting nights, rising and moving from one man to another. The training, from childhood, that men must come first. The small rebellions stifled, one by one; the self-denial turned to ritual.

"Through great brutality," I said.

He stared at me. "You speak like a monk."

I was happier because he seemed to be listening. "You don't see everything, even with that thing in your hat." I teased him as I teased my father. "*I* am not docile or gentle."

"No," he said, musingly.

This was always my problem: being a woman and not being one. It opened up some kind of wound. I felt raw. I felt desire. I backed away and turned my face down and to the side.

"How has the training of Japan failed in you? You're different. A bohemian, perhaps? The avant-garde? You're like a whole new species."

"Is the new species me? I often think it is the other." I was careful. You never knew who would hear. "Some men in Japan think they have the right to distort the habits and instincts of other human beings for their own pleasure. That is your courtesan you see there." I answered with a laugh. "I am not new. I am a very old species. Like the giant salamander. Unseen, but original. A woman who has not been domesticated."

"I suppose your father is responsible," he mused. "The court painter, able to be his own man."

He still thought Hokusai was a court painter! I shook my head. "Aren't the docile women odd? You talk of species. This woman," I said, nodding at my poor courtesan, "this species is against nature. It must forgo any pleasure of its own. It must serve, and suffer, so the needs of the male are filled. No animal is like this. This is the idea of selfish men. Where do they get the right?"

"Oh, my," he said. Or something like that. Had he seen my touch on the scroll? He asked no more questions. Of course he had much on his mind. But none of the paintings was signed. Hokusai always signed his work. You would think that even a foreigner would insist. But perhaps he thought we were protecting ourselves from the Shogun's laws.

When I came next with our last finished works, von Siebold confided that he had arranged to trade with that same Globius, the court astronomer. Globius had a map of the islands to the north. Von Siebold had a map of Edo, as well as a map of the whole nation of Japan.

"This will not be looked upon lightly," I protested.

"Why? Knowledge must travel!" His eyes lit with fervour. "People want to know. Laws that stifle the curiosity of man are futile laws and cannot last."

"But you yourself can't make an end to 'futile laws,' as you call them."

"It's only a map."

I had to tell him that pictures and words on paper inspired the rage of the Shogun almost more than anything else. I didn't understand it myself, but I had learned that it was true. "They are afraid of what is written with the brush. This is why artists are jailed."

He looked blank.

"They are afraid of years to come," I said. "They are afraid that eyes from another time will look back and judge them for the way we are. Did you pass the Punishment Grounds? The heads on poles, the flayed corpses on their wooden beams?"

"Yes, we did. Our guards said the display was to make us feel safe."

"Lucky you didn't see Hokusai amongst those remains," I joked.

"You exaggerate."

"No," I said as simply and as firmly as I was able. "You have not felt the awful power of Japan pressed down on you." And in my mind I thought, Not yet you haven't. I prayed he never did. "We sometimes also think the Shogun is sleeping."

Von Siebold's long, deep-set eyes flickered, but he smiled still. He felt he was above suspicion.

As we sat, envoys were discussing the shrinking copper trade. Doctors were gathering to make a presentation about acupuncture. These conversations were not known to anyone. They did not have a material being, so he did not have to keep them in his luggage. He said things into the air. He believed they dissipated like fog, like the spray off the waterfalls.

"I never did meet your father," said von Siebold, seeking my eyes as if through them he could see into my heart. He took one of my small hands between his two large, white hands. "But perhaps I have met the better part of the painting team."

My heart warmed. But I chided myself. He was flattering me? Or being flirtatious? "My father has been ill," I said, "but your *beru* has cheered him."

I wondered if I had thanked him enough. My father *was* improving; maybe the doctor really did work miracles. I walked away. I met two geisha coming in. They were entertainers who would dance and sing and serve them drink. Not courtesans, but a cut above. Still, he would not lack for stimulation.

That was the last time I spoke with him.

His much-delayed audience with the Shogun took place. Immediately afterwards, the Tokugawa were finished with the Dutch. They were no longer welcome in Edo. There was a rush to get them out. Von Siebold and his entourage marched out of Edo without the pomp of his entrance, the doctor a full head taller than the rest, with his long, kind face quite absent of expression. I was just a woman at the side of the street in the crowd when I last saw him.

Spring turned to summer. And here I was in the walled-in world. Despite his protestations of love for Japan, von Siebold would go back to his country. I consoled myself that he had my pictures. I pictured his life: he made visits to his wife and child every day; he had his school near the waterfall and the many Japanese doctors who learned the operations that had made him famous. He loved us, but he would be gone. "Our" pictures would go with him.

And now I had a little, high-up window in the walls.

26

Dark Years

LIFE, LIKE ART, IS FULL OF INCIDENT. Some people's more than others'.

My father's life, like his art, was broad, scattered with figures, events, characters, exertion everywhere—up planks and up mountains, across rivers, on platforms—twinkling and never dull. There was no emphasis. Everything was in competition; anything could distract the eye. A little man at the edge of the paper carrying a bucket will be given his humorous face and his odd posture to amuse. And in the centre a woman bid her lover farewell. These were equal in importance. The whole place is buzzing. At any time, in any place, someone was putting out for the audience, and none of this merited his indifference.

But my life was not.

Not that way.

My life was like a painting on silk, intense but softened. It was a dark splatter of blood on an empty canvas. Examined carefully, it was not just a splash but a cluster—figures pushed together, too close, against each other. These figures are distinct, they are technical, they are dark and deeply impressed. But they float in space, mere space, empty space that makes them severe. Beyond my immediate world was emptiness. Great events and signs were absent for years on end. Then they all came at once.

MY FATHER WAS NOT MUCH BETTER, although every day he rose to say that he was cured. The censors continued their attacks, and times were dark. Often, as I worked on small commissions, I returned in my mind to my conversations with the Miracle Doctor, and to the scenes he had conjured: kings and queens of Europe swirling in each other's arms in a place called "ballroom." A man in a great forest drawing the birds as they nested. Wild people wearing feather headdresses and building conical houses of animal skin at the foot of giant mountains, each peak as high as Fuji-san. The idea of the world beyond our gated and moated city gave me comfort, I suppose. I hoped too that one day I would come across Shino on the street, her shaven eyebrows and simple hairstyle leaving her face all the more visible. I even wondered if I had passed her, one year or another, and not known her.

We were sad, which was why my father and I maintained our little games. Hokusai massaged his tongue. He stuck it in and out, and I laughed at him. He put it to work again telling ghost stories. There was one about sailors who drowned in a typhoon. It took more patience than I possessed to listen to him, but I begged it from the gods. Suddenly he was all I had, and I was all he had.

"Their b-b-bodies were ca-arried aw-way by the w-w-waves! Bu' lader, much lader, their gho-oo-osts were seen in the w-w-white foam. And they were sin-sin-s-singing!"

His goofy laugh was stretched out of shape. I made tea of Chinese herbs for him, while he chanted—in his drunken way—the Lotus Sutra. He stood on his head and swung his feet; his balance was better that way. I had to duck walking across the room or get hit by a flying foot. He stood on one leg with the other folded on his thigh, holding the wall. He fell, like a rubber man, and could not get up. He moaned and spit. He got me to rub his feet and had the herbalist come to stick paper poultices on his back, with magical inscriptions written on them. He prayed to the North Star whenever he could see it. I made pigments while he made circles to retrain his hand.

His heart was sick too. He had taken on the name Iitsu, meaning "one again," six years before, in anticipation of a new life. But his renewed youth hadn't materialized. He was well past sixty in years, and most of his peers were dead. He had illustrated books; he had made instruction manuals; he had created *shunga*. He was tired of the city and its vices. He wanted to paint the seas and the skies; these subjects had been difficult to do, with our fugitive blues.

Now here was *beru*, a new toy, and the Old Man came slowly alive. He prepared for a day of painting by rubbing the muscles of his feet, stretching

his leg up to his nose, and hooking his arms around his back while opening and shutting his mouth. Our studio was quiet. Shigenobu was gone, my
mother and sisters dead, my brother apprenticed to an account keeper. The
men who had thought to learn from Hokusai had moved on. I got Hokusai's
ink ready and his water. He made a hundred sketches but his hand would
not do what he willed it to. He gazed at Berlin blue to spur on his recovery.

I told him about the compass in the hat. We pictured the Dutch doctor measuring the sacred mountain over and over, from different vantage
points along the road to Edo, and finding it unchanged. In his telescope
sacred Fuji winked from under a cloud or behind a bridge, through the
hoop of a barrel, under the curl of a wave. We laughed about this. Hokusai had the idea of drawing these views of Fuji-san. The publisher loved it.
There was a cult in Edo that worshipped the Peerless One. All the adherents
would buy the prints.

And now he had the blue that would make sea and sky resplendent. One
day he would be well enough to use it. But he had to learn to walk again.

I walked in the lawless open space along the riverbank, passing the hag-
gling drunks and the temple dancers. The water was low and the sun slanted
across it. Eagles swooped down on the stranded fish, then rose flapping over
the twisted, brilliant strands of water, leaving shadows on the surface. My
hands were stained turquoisey black with *beru.*

I had gone directly to my father's house when I left Tokei-ji temple. What
choice did I have? He needed looking after and I needed a home. No one
had asked for papers when I re-entered Edo. A bird leaving a cage must be
cunning and find the exact moment. A bird returning to a cage finds the
door ajar.

We were not selling much work. Hokusai did not paint; he could only
dream of the sacred mountain and the roads he would take to see it. My
themes were gloomy: a sketch of an attempted rape; my father as an immortal, playing with a pet toad.

Still, I had at least achieved a measure of peace. My cage was comfort-
able. In two years I had reverted to being an unmarried daughter. There
was no other choice. My father still suffered from his palsy. It was expected
that I keep his work alive. What did we live on? No one actually asked, and

if they did, they did not get a truthful answer. I affected a bizarre posture that kept people from approaching me, my head leaning steeply on the angle as if my neck had been broken. I scowled to show that I did not conform to female ways. I made my way around the city, to the publisher with designs, to the market for butterfish and soba noodles. I loved these errands. I had certain reasons for happiness: I was painting, and I had met the Dutch doctor.

In my dream the night before, the Dutch doctor was playing in the waves, the way my father did. I stood on the shore. The waves became higher and higher, and I walked up and down trying to keep him in sight. The waves swallowed the horizon, and then—even with his tall hat—they swallowed him.

It was a frightening dream and I couldn't shake it. I walked along with it still alive in my mind, marvelling at the way I had recreated the tall barbarian so exactly.

Above me the *Kawara-ban* crier appeared, running, on the Ryogoku Bridge. I climbed the bank. At bridgeposts, the moneylenders and the soothsayers sat like bookends. You could borrow from your earthly future or gaze along into your heavenly fate, one-stop convenience. The moneylender had his long loops, with the hole-in-the-centre coins threaded through the rope coiled in front of him. The soothsayer moaned and swayed.

The crier pulled back his black hood as he reached the top of the arch of the bridge. I saw his human features for a moment: haggard, pockmarked.

"A typhoon has struck the town of Nagasaki. The Island of Red-headed Strangers has been destroyed.

"The typhoon has devastated the surrounding country. Whole towns have been blown down. Many people have died. The ship called the *Cornelius Hauptman* has been crushed on the rocks. Its cargo of eighty-nine chests of stolen Japanese treasures will be seized.

"Hear me, hear me. The Shogun tells our people that the Miracle Doctor has been found to be stealing many precious objects from the Japanese. The gods have acted to destroy the foreign devils."

I followed him. I was frightened, of the news and of myself. The dream had told me this. How did it come to me, and from where? Was I, as some people said, a witch? I feared for the doctor. I feared for our paintings.

The crier came to a little storytelling hall. "This way to hear the story of the Dutch doctor," he said, holding out his hand for coins.

Many of us crowded in. I tucked myself into the back row amongst the packages and the cats, the way I had twenty years ago.

"You all know of the Miracle Doctor who lives on the Island of Red-headed Strangers in Nagasaki Bay," he said.

"Yes!" said many.

"No!" said others.

"He's a good man," some shouted. "He saved many lives."

The storyteller appeared and the story began:

The Miracle Doctor was well loved. So well loved that his superior officer was jealous. That superior officer complained to the powers in his country across the sea: the Miracle Doctor spent too much money; he went his own way, heedlessly. The powers recalled the doctor to Holland. He must go back home.

He was devastated; he loved Japan. He had collected many treasures to take with him—flowers and trees and a giant salamander. But there was one treasure he could not take with him. She could not be bartered for or hidden in a cloak. Two treasures, actually: Otaki, his Japanese wife, and their daughter. Their keeper, the governor of Nagasaki, would not take a bribe.

He sat playing his piano in his quarters on the island in Nagasaki harbour. He heard a loud noise. He went to the narrow slit that let in air and caught a glimpse of a surge of water reaching over the wall and spilling on the inside.

He didn't recall water that high. A storm was coming. He looked to the clouds: streaks of green. He'd sailed in a typhoon to get here five years ago. He was suddenly afraid he would not get away.

He thought of his lacquerware and baskets, kimono and objects of devotion. The small carved wooden toys and pictures of funerals. Books. Maps. He had filled the waiting ship with these treasures to take with him.

The storm lashed.

He went to the Water Gate. The guards were gesticulating at the edge of the water, their voices lost. The little sloops that went back and forth to the ships were foundering. The sky was black and yellow. The wind came into the bay as if down a tunnel.

The water leapt the walls of the island and splattered on the rooftop.

He called the captain.

"We must leave now."

"It's too late."

"But the ship?"

"We are trying to secure it."

I hadn't encountered this storyteller before. He was good. He had thick hair that stood up straight on top of his head, and a stocky body, and a voice that he could send out of himself so it seemed to come from a man in the front row, whom he had made into the captain. I was not so impressed, as I could do that myself. Von Siebold's accent he copied perfectly, and his voice he made high and womanish and sent it behind the curtain as if the Miracle Doctor were hiding. This was a good trick and made people laugh. The story captured my imagination and gave me time to think, to grow calm.

One day later von Siebold clung to a plum tree in his garden, trying to stay upright in the wind. He had transplanted it himself, and it was now ten feet tall. But even as he gripped its trunk the wind came down, sucked up its roots, and tossed it like a carrot upside down over the roof. He was thrown sideways against the wall. He roared with rage.

All of this the storyteller mimed. It might have been true or it might have been just an excuse for some crowd-pleasing action. People were leaning with him, and gasping, and it was a lot of fun, and they weren't too concerned about the poor Dutch doctor from what I could see.

Now he was wading, waves bashing the back of his knees. He tried to catch things flying by—bushes and flowers, the little wrought-iron bench, a watering can. But it was hopeless. The little plants were drowning; his Otaki hydrangeas were swept away; his primroses, past bloom and crouching out of harm's way, were under a foot of water; his lilies were sinking. And the seedlings were packed on the ship. Would all this be gone? A shriek came out of him. A vicious slap of water hit his cheek.

He did not understand: the sea did not come here; the sea was kept out by the wall. But the sea had broken through. Through the gap he could see the ship tethered, rocking, its sails bound tightly, its timbers creaking horribly. He prayed for the anchor to hold. He thought he would be swept away.

"What happened?" I shouted along with others. "Get to the point! You beat around the bush too much!" He looked me in the eye.

But he was not to be so lucky.

The typhoon had hit just in time to forestall his escape.

And it would have been an escape, that which only a few days ago had seemed banishment.

Suddenly he was sailing sideways, his feet above his head, to the western side, where he banged up against a wall of the warehouse. Inside the pigs and goats were bawling. The servants must be with them, he assured himself, trying to peel himself off the wooden wall. It was not for him to save a pig. The warehouses were being battered. He was being battered. How ridiculous to be imprisoned here, on a flat piece of reconstituted land, right in the eye of the storm!

Waves like mad dogs raced in through the breach in the wall, one after another, splitting on contact and shooting both ways. They tore planks from the side of the warehouse. These sailed away on the surface of the water and became weapons.

Where was everyone? Had they fled out the City Gate? No one came as crates of precious things begin to slide out of their storage places on sleek, glassy floors of water. Within minutes the near warehouse wall had softened and buckled. A high examination table floated out of the sickbay: this was where his daughter was born. His instruments—his acupuncture needles, a sealing jar of formaldehyde with a lobster inside—bobbed in the water. Tiles crashed off the roofs onto the stone.

He tried to walk, but the water picked him up and twirled him. Rain and wind blinded him. He was furious. He got down on his knees and crawled back to the shelter of the main house. His fellow Dutchmen were gathered there and stood watching as the pigs floated away, squealing in terror.

The audience loved this. What a diverting story! What a thrill to see this man, who had set himself above us all, caught out by nature and brought down. I was ashamed. This was our society; this was how we were—powerless, rumour-gripped, taking pleasure in catastrophe brought down by gods on anyone who tried to escape.

The ship was pushed up on the side of the harbour, damaged but afloat. The crates of treasures were unloaded and stacked to dry. The Dutchman survived, but the Japanese were not so lucky. Thousands drowned, or were hit by falling roof tiles, or were swept to sea.

The crowd stirred in anger, that the Dutchman's punishment should become their own.

Still, the Miracle Doctor who tempted the gods will be caught. He has not departed. The ship will take three months to be repaired. The garden cannot be salvaged. Von Siebold himself is trying to appease the gods by helping with rescue work. He travels in the towns, amputating crushed limbs, suturing gashes, and wrapping broken skulls.

Now something worse than a storm has come. It is the call. Under guard, he must go before the governor of Nagasaki to be interrogated. The authorities have seen that he was stealing valuable treasures. Granted privileges, the Dutch doctor has repaid the Japanese with treachery.

There was general gasping and outrage.

Von Siebold had eighty-nine chests and thousands of other items, animal, mineral, and vegetable. He says he does not know where they came from. He says that the cargo was loaded by others. He simply cannot explain the treasures, except that he knows they are his. All the while he is relieved, because the greatest has not come to light. He has it hidden deep inside his house.

But that is not the end of it. The plot grows wider. The most powerful men in the realm are swept into it. Takahashi the court astronomer, the man they call Globius, has been dragged out of his library and thrown in jail. He has traded maps with von Siebold; he himself may be a Russian spy. The plot has reached into the very heart of the castle.

People were torn between thrill and horror. They feared everything because in the end they suffered it, and they understood nothing because they were never given any reasons. Only the gods, shifting their furniture, could bring down such heavy punishments to earth.

And do you know the very worst of it?

The hall fell silent.

Von Siebold saw the guards turning a man away from the City Gate. He was cloaked for travel and worn out.

"What is wrong, my friend?" He peered into the grizzled face and saw bruises. He recognized the man: a translator from the Shogun's entourage.

"You have to watch out for these translators," called a listener, obviously a practised one, from the front rows. "They are always two-faced." I was immobilized with dread. This was a masterful story. It was too good to be invented. It had to be true.

The doctor invited the traveller inside to get warm. He had brought a warning: von Siebold's home was going to be searched. The translator himself had been arrested and beaten. "I was freed only because I promised that I would come here and find all your maps and pictures so we can use them as evidence against you."

"Then you must save yourself," said von Siebold. "But first we will make copies."

His most important map was of the Russian islands far to the north of our capital. The two of them sat up all night and copied it. The original he placed where it could be found. The copy he rolled in a can and stuffed in a hole in the log wall behind his piano. Here he also placed certain other papers, including pictures he had bought showing the Shogun's castle and secret rituals of our people. They were so valuable that he had not sent them to the ship to be packed: he imagined he would carry them in his clothing. He hid daggers in the flower containers, in case he needed to defend himself.

Two days later, von Siebold watched as the guards found his precious maps and took them away.

"Did they find and confiscate the pictures he bought from Edo artists?" I shouted. The storyteller looked through me as if he knew. But how could he?

"Not yet," he said.

The guards laughed at his hidden daggers. Then they sat down at the gates of Deshima and forbade him to leave the island. Every week the soldiers pull him from his desk and march him up to the governor's house, where he is asked the same questions. He refuses to admit he has done wrong. He names no one.

27

FLIGHT

I WENT HOME SLOWLY along our street with my packages. The wind whipped at the laundry—little children's shirts—that was strung on poles. The wild cats were out prowling for fishbones. The always curious neighbours squinted at me. One woman was at the well, raising a bucket by the pulley wheel. She pulled it towards her while the wind pushed it away. All of these details were clear in my mind.

A young woman knelt in front of a fulling block with her pounding tool raised high. *Whump, whump,* it went as she brought it down time and again on the cloth stretched over the block in front of her. She looked purposeful and even happy. Her baby sat propped in his bucket beside her. A larger child sat on the edge of the house swinging her feet over the mud.

Von Siebold names no one, I thought. I believed it: the man had character. But there were our paintings. Not signed, but perhaps recognizable as by Hokusai. Would we too be arrested?

The woman beckoned me. "There was a big noise from your rooms," she whispered.

My heart thumped.

"There was?" I said. I suddenly had no feeling.

"A man came out running," she whispered. "I haven't seen your father since."

Our screen had been left open. I stepped up. The wind was stirring the old bamboo-leaf food wrappers scattered on the floor. My father was on his elbows and knees with his bottom in the air, peering at a painting on the floor.

"Old Man?" I said. "Did you have a visitor?"

He did not reply. I saw that his hands were not moving. He was just propped there. I stuck my toe into his side. He did not move.

"Hokusai!"

He toppled over sideways.

Everything went black. I must have called for help: the neighbour sent her children for water while she ran to the apothecary. I held my father's head in my lap.

I waited for hours for a sound. Then he called for his *shochu*. He drank the potato liquor and pretended nothing was wrong. He said that he was sleeping, and what was the problem? But I knew who had been there.

The orphan son of my sister O-Miyo and Shigenobu had progressed from being a bully to being a gangster. True, he had learned from a master: his father had beaten my sister with his fists while she was making the evening meal. The boy had clung to his mother's kimono while Shigenobu threw cooking pots at the walls. He had forced O-Miyo to stand outside in the cold while he and his cronies sat around the *kotatsu* drinking. The boy's name was Shigeshiro. My father mumbled excuses: his parents had divorced.

"So what?" I used to say to him.

And he had come to us before, several times at this address.

My name for him was Monster Boy. Every time he showed up and stamped on our tatami with his dirty sandals, my father greeted him with a face wreathed in smiles and a handful of money. He loved him. Loved him silly. Never stopped.

"Old Man, beloved old father. Hokusai," I warned, "you are a fool. He is going to throw that money away after we work all day and half the night to earn it. He is the Leech Child." That was a figure of myth. He was born of deities but had to be cast out because of his actions.

That was the last time Monster Boy came.

"Yes, but you see," said Hokusai triumphantly, "look what became of the Leech Child. He was transformed. He is worshipped as Ebisu, one of the Seven Lucky Gods."

"Well, I don't think this one will be."

"He is a good boy. You must have patience."

I put my head in my hands. My father was so stubborn.

"I am going to set him up as a fishmonger."

"Old Man, you're dreaming. He won't do one day of honest work."

"Ei is a hard woman." He stared into the air as if speaking to an ancestor. "She hoards my money."

"You forget that it's my money too. I mixed the pigment. I painted the bridge and the cherry trees myself. I designed the women."

But I was not to mention these inconvenient facts.

"The apprentices will do the work if you don't wish to," he muttered, shuffling out to make water behind the tenements.

"You forget we have no apprentices at the moment!"

The young man had come back only hours later.

"We have nothing for you," I said.

"You have nothing, *izn it?*" he said, addressing my father, whom he found to be more receptive. "You are the famous artist, they say. You get paid a lot of money for these things. Where'z it gone, then?" He drove his toe into a pile of design sketches. I said to myself, Remember fear? How the bullies want us to feel it and we must not? Nothing ever frightened Hokusai but Monster Boy. His fear was caused by his love. This was a weakness in him, this longing to see something good in his grandson. I was not similarly afflicted. I stood over my father.

That day, when Shigeshiro was gone again and Hokusai was sitting by the coal fire, I put a cold cloth on his bruised cheek.

"Oh, he is a good boy under all of that," he said.

"You never felt that much love for me," I marvelled. "You old fool."

Hokusai did not answer for a while. Then he said, "I don't need to. You're strong."

So that was my problem! "You love him because he's weak?"

"He's my burden. He's my curse for all the things I've done wrong. He'll improve; he'll grow up."

"He won't, Old Man. He's a lost cause," I said.

So he had come again. "You don't fool me, Old Man. I know who's paid a visit," I said. Despite the disgusting fact that this gangster bully had beaten up on an old man with palsy, I was glad it was the devil we knew and not the guards.

When he had his potato liquor he was much better. Then I told him the bad news.

"I dreamed of waves last night and the Dutch doctor in them," I said.

He rubbed his cheek. He rolled his tongue. These were exercises. But I knew he was listening.

"More than that," I said, "today in the streets I heard the crier. There was a typhoon in Nagasaki and his ship has crashed on the shore, so he cannot leave Japan. And he has been investigated. All his treasures are confiscated."

My father was superstitious. This happens when you are sick and always praying for respite. He stared at me with rounded eyes. "You 'a soo-sssooo-ayer."

"I see things," I agreed. "But not soon enough. We are in danger. We have sold him our paintings. They may be on that ship."

WE ELECTED TO MOVE HOUSE, again. This time we chose a part of Edo we didn't know at all.

We had several robes each, a tea kettle, cups, and our painting things. I called a bearer for my father, an incredible luxury, and carried the rest through Honjo and then farther, to where the back streets were not so crowded. The little dark rooms that we stepped up into from a back street were identical to the ones we'd left. No one hailed me when I went out for grilled eel. We didn't even tell our publishers where we were.

But we were too starved for news to stay hidden for long.

"You always said the best place to hide is out in the open," I said to the Old Man one restless morning. "And no one will be looking for us in the place we are most expected. Can you walk?"

To my surprise he got to his feet easily. We walked across to the river, my father with his straw hat low over his face and leaning on the *bo*. We took the ferry to the Yoshiwara. Just at the gate was the big banquet hall.

The wooden noticeboard in front announced the event: "Today, Poetry Party, 3 p.m."

I loved the *ageya*. It was huge, one hundred tatami mats. From the street you saw only dark slats of wood with squared-off lattice windows made blank with white paper. If you looked up you saw the roof tiles on the first and second storeys, curved to ripple like small waves; the ends were impressed in the owners' crest—mulberry leaves under a temple roof. Bronze lanterns lined the wall that faced the street.

The inside was cool, freshened by the high roof with its slit opening for smoke. Filtered daylight fell on the wooden floor near the windows, but the centre was dark. I could just make out the racks on the walls, where the swords of visiting samurai lay harmless side by side.

As we entered voices chimed out, "Hello! Welcome!"

"Hokusai! Old Man, what are you doing? Have you designed any new prints? Are you working on a book?"

"No, no," my father said. "Nothing new."

"Never quite what one had hoped, this life," said the owner.

From the entry I could see into the kitchen with its cauldrons of steaming water, the iron kettle, the bucket and well. Cooks moved deep in concentration, their sweatbands printed with the temple and mulberry. The owners came hurrying with hands together to greet us.

They were the fifth generation; they had rebuilt the *ageya* on the ashes of the original after it burned with the Yoshiwara. We went down the hall to the "fishing net room," with its ceiling made of woven strips of wood. On the walls were paintings of Chinese children playing with kites, touched with gold leaf but sooty and dark. I lit my pipe. The press of bodies increased. No one said a word about our notoriety, or mentioned our friendship with the Dutchman who was now a prisoner of the realm. We were welcomed, the two of us.

Poor Waki the tattooist was showing his watercolours: he had no talent, but he was determined to make his name. After him came a literary-style brush poet, some parodists, more painters unrolling scrolls.

All afternoon we drank tea and ate soba noodles, my father's favourite. We ate pickles and grilled fish. As the light failed the waiters brought in tapers so we could see our fellow artists gesticulating in their hour of glory.

Finally it was night and the little candles on the low tables gave a glow that outlined every head, every set of shoulders, every forehead with gold so it stood out against the dark. The high ceilings rose above and through the air holes I could see stars. It felt like earlier times. I knew that this safety was a temporary thing, and so I loved it all the more.

Into our midst with a clamour of greetings and cries for drink came a group of scholars of Dutch. They had news.

"Court Astronomer Takahashi, known as Globius, has been arrested! He has been denounced by Mamiya the explorer!"

These were the men I had seen in the entry rooms of the Nagasakiya. "What for? What does Mamiya say that Globius has done?"

"He traded maps of the secret reaches of the kingdom to the Miracle Doctor, who would have taken them out of the country had not the God of the Sea risen up."

How quickly they dropped their sophistication and spoke with the old beliefs.

"Someone has informed on him. Someone he trusted."

The tailor beside me spoke. "These are the intrigues of the powerful, always trying to do each other down! Who cares?"

A sombre, downcast line of geishas moved in silently and disappeared behind the rolled blinds on the stage. Then the blinds were lifted to reveal them. I watched their white faces: how garish they looked. I recognized their special gaze, false but pleasing to men. I wondered how men could be so easily fooled, or if they were fooled by the geisha's forced delight.

The music began. I swayed in my own world, like the soothsayer at the foot of the bridge with the crowds clattering past her. I moaned too perhaps. We had been drinking all day. The smoke from the fires and the pipes hung in the damp air: my legs felt cramped. I stood and excused myself.

In the enclosed garden two old pine trees leaned together, one with a thick limb that grew horizontally, nearly on the ground, for the distance of ten long steps at least. This limb was propped up with bamboo crutches. I loved to stand in that little courtyard. There was a cat, winding himself along the wooden poles, then darting under the planks. Rain was falling; thunder came and, close after it, lightning, which set our fellow listeners to a frenzy of murmurs and oaths to protect themselves. Better yet, drink up.

Inside, the men came to lift the small tables away for dancing. My father and I paid for our food and pushed our way out through the sweating bodies to the street. The rain had stopped. Everything was shining through the fog. The lanterns at intervals over the narrow walk threw their yellow light down, making a pattern of light and dark.

We looked overhead for the Seven Stars. But they were not there. We had a long walk ahead. My father was slow and one leg dragged. He leaned against me. We were both silent as we breathed the night air and stepped in and out, in and out of visibility. The boatman was kind and took us up the river near to our new house.

IT WAS WEEKS AGAIN before I could leave my father. But some small work at last found us—a pair of demon quellers for a temple fair—and two students came to complete it. I made my way to the Ichibee bookshop, where the gossip from Nagasaki would be fresh. The postal runners had been slowed by uprooted trees on the Tokaido. But finally they had arrived. They had little news. I asked about von Siebold's wife. Was she hurt? And the child, who must now be four years old? No one knew. What about his collections? His paintings—our paintings (my paintings)? Had they been on the ship that blew ashore?

The Dutch scholars who gathered there were not sympathetic. They pronounced the Miracle Doctor's powers evil. He had committed many transgressions. Measuring the height of Mt. Fuji was perhaps the worst. These were men who had flocked to his door—publishers, medical men, merchants. Artists who had tried to sell him their work. How quickly they deserted their hero. It was, I realized, a form of self-hatred. The all-knowing Dutch doctor would now fall into the hands of the same powers that kept us ignorant.

"But I saw you lined up outside the windows of the Nagasakiya," I said to one of them.

"You must be mistaken."

I understood that these men thought there were spies amongst us. But could I be one? They went on listing his crimes.

"He had a detailed map of Edo."

"He had a linen cloak bearing the imperial coat of arms."

Collective gasp of horror.

"How did he get that?"

"Genseki gave it to him in exchange for medicine to dilate the pupil of the eye."

He had a copy of the Shogun's secret map of the island of Karafuto at the edge of Russia. The Europeans called the place Sakhalin and thought it was a peninsula. Von Siebold's copy was even better than the one held in the Imperial Library, they said. Mogami made it, and Mogami traded it. Now he had confessed and called von Siebold a spy.

But why had Mogami turned?

Because he himself was caught.

Mogami accused Globius as well. Globius had been discovered with a book about Napoleon and a map of St. Petersburg. This was taken as proof that he had been supplying Japanese maps to the foreigners. He had been thrown in jail. His teeth had been smashed in the initial beating. This was so he could not bite off his tongue.

The court astronomer's crime was punishable by death. He was under watch so he could not kill himself.

Ah yes, that pleasure would belong to the Shogun.

THE CIRCLE OF THOSE UNDER SUSPICION GREW. Soon, fifty people—half the learned entourage of the Shogun—had gone to jail.

The Miracle Doctor was taken in handcuffs on the long journey back to Edo. The old information that von Siebold had gone to school in Germany and spoke High German better than he spoke Dutch was dredged up. He must be a spy, they said. He had aimed his telescope and his sextant at Fuji-san. He had been in the Shogun's library. He was asked, again and again: "Are you spying for the Russians?"

"I have never met a Russian."

"Why have you stolen the linen coat decorated with the imperial coat of arms?"

"I have not stolen it. It was given to me."

"Who gave it to you?"

Von Siebold would not name Genseki the court physician or explain what they already knew: that it was given in exchange for the recipe for the medicine that dilated the pupils of the eye, so Genseki too could perform the magical eye surgery.

"Why did the court physician want your medicine? Is it superior to Japanese medicine?"

He knew there was a wrong answer to that one. All cures came from the divine, with the Shogun's permission.

"It will work with a little skill and your gods' permission."

"Why did you measure the height of the sacred Fuji-san if you are not a spy?"

"I propose no illegal use for this knowledge," he said. "I measured it for the pleasure of knowledge."

It went on for a year.

WE WERE NOT THERE to see the end. Our temporary rooms far east of Honjo were not far enough out of the way. Our trade with the foreigners—always an irritant to the authorities—had become an offence. One day a messenger from the Shogun came looking for my father. He unrolled a picture. It was one of the studio works.

"Why did you paint the walls of the castle and give it to the foreign spy?"

Hokusai was insulted. He had never seen this painting. It was one of those that were intended to illustrate how we lived. It was not very good, I knew. The black stone walls loomed and in front of them was a fire, that was all. In my mind it was a fire of woodcut blocks; it had to do with the censors. My father had never paid any attention to it, in truth, as I had painted it. And it just so happened that his symptoms were rather bad that day. "Thz pchr not me-me-my-mine," he said. "'Tz bad. You c'n see, no"—he rattled his hand as if he were signing his name—"n-n-no." He made the gesture for stamping. His eyes looked ill that day, round and popping. It was clear he could not have done the work.

I sat with my head bent and my eyes cast down: the gloomy, divorced daughter. When the messenger was gone I laughed and clapped, and my father rolled on his back and kicked his feet. What a joke.

Nonetheless, that night we walked out of Edo. We had discussed it: while one messenger might be embarrassed to accuse a sick old man and his strange daughter, the next might not. And now that it was known where we lived, there would surely be more visits.

Hokusai was feeling lucky that we had no possessions.

"You see, Daughter, we would just have to carry them on our backs," Hokusai said. He was markedly improved.

We turned our backs on the sprawl of wooden houses and the black, curving walls of the Shogun's palace. We took the ferry as far as we could. Then we began to walk, as we had walked before. We passed the jail. We passed the Punishment Grounds. There was a body on the cross. The birds were crazed with it. Strips of flesh lay around its feet, too big for their mouths.

Hokusai laughed. It was this laughter that had confused me when I was a child. He had compassion, but he was ruthless. He had no feeling for the dead but a great deal for the dying. The dead were completed. Only the dying were in pain. And the living.

I wept for the loss of my window on the world.

He made that gesture with his shoulders, bringing them up to his ears. It was comical. Defiance gave him energy. He was suddenly himself. He staggered and stuttered no more. He put his elbow in my ribs.

"The spirit of protest is in you, Chin-Chin. I breathed it into you. That is why you look so funny."

Tears ran down my cheeks. He shook me by the elbow. He peered into my eyes.

"What have you done? Did you fall in love with another man you cannot have?"

I began walking furiously.

We were on the Tokaido heading for the sea at Uraga. The Old Man did not hurry and he did not slow. He did not tire and he did not stop. Perhaps he leaned on that long stick of his, perhaps he pushed himself forward with it, but he maintained an excellent pace. At the top of the hill he turned around and walked backwards, fixing the city in his gaze. I sped up and passed him. When we came to the checkpoint he performed a perfect imitation of himself in his palsied state, staggering and slurring. I held him upright and became invisible, one of the nameless women who helped the aged. The guards waved us through. We walked until the city was nothing but a soiled spot in the distance.

I protested our leaving. "We won't hear what happens to him."

"Yes, we will," said Hokusai. "I'll return by night and hear the gossip."

MONTHS LATER THE MIRACLE DOCTOR was judged and found innocent of spying. His crimes were committed "in an excess of scientific zeal."

Takahashi, known as Globius, died in prison before the sentence of death could be brought on him, and his son was banished. Genseki the court physician was removed from his post, and his son was punished.

Von Siebold was extremely lucky: he was merely expelled. He left Edo in disgrace and was ordered never to return. I could not explain this clemency to the barbarian when the Japanese were so terribly punished, but perhaps the truth was what von Siebold had always said—that the laws did not apply to him.

Rumour said that back at Deshima, the doctor had searched the walls for the maps he had hidden there, only to discover that rats had eaten his cache. Incredibly, the crates of Japanese objects that had been seized in Nagasaki were restored to him. But—I asked my father—what about my paintings? Where were they?

"You must dream the answer to that," Hokusai said to me. "Otherwise we will never know."

I tried to dream, but I wanted less than the knowledge of my paintings' fate to see my tall, golden man again, he who spoke to me of Shakespeare and women's lives. Maybe my false pretenses were the reason why the dreams did not come.

I tried calling the paintings. What has become of you, promenading courtesan? Samurai horses? Some of you were seized, I know, because the picture of the castle walls was in the hands of the guards. Were you returned to the doctor, as the gossip said? And now where are you? Decorating the Shogun's inner chambers? In the belly of the great sailing ship returning to Europe?

In the fire?

But my inner eye remained closed.

In the depths of December, the Miracle Doctor sailed away from Nagasaki on the frigate *Jawa,* bound for Batavia. His wife and daughter came out in a small fishing boat to watch. They said that he carried their portraits bound into his shirt next to his chest, and that as the sails filled with wind, the Miracle Doctor hung over the rails and wept.

I wept too.

Part 4

28

Dark Days

MY FATHER STAYED IN URAGA and I returned to Edo. He was perhaps in danger, and we spoke of it as if he were in exile. But I think he wanted to see the ocean, and Mt. Fuji. He was ready to start the series he'd planned of the sacred mountain. I had to take such work as was available—nothing much.

The first thing I did was move back into our old quarter of Asakusa. There, I was not lonely. I could resume teaching some of my old students. I took my tea and rice and small grilled fish on the street. Breakfast, enjoyed before nerves interfered with my digestion, was my favourite meal. Sometimes I had a "dancing unagi," an eel grilled and then fried so it wrinkled. It was crunchy outside but, once the crust was gone, smooth and sweet on the tongue.

Delicious. I sucked each finger and let it go with a pop. I said good morning to the candy seller, who was my father's friend. I got back home just as the students were arriving.

Mune was still with me, and although she did not have the talent her mother had, she was a good painter. She had directed her friends towards me. I set them to work, sketching, copying, designing. I moved amongst them on my knees, edging the cats off the papers, telling them to be exact, making them repeat and repeat. We smiled together.

"You will learn to move the brush through the air without thinking, as a swallow moves its wings."

One of them would bring me lunch from the stalls—eggplant, if I was lucky. But it was expensive and I always demurred unless they insisted.

Sometimes pictures flew into my head. But a student would look up with a question. I tried to save the idea in my mind's eye. But the next day would be the same: no time to put my pictures on paper, full of teaching and commissions (thankfully, commissions).

The times were difficult, of course. Hokusai's old apprentices began to show up, looking for work—Hokuri, Hokuryo, and Hokusen. Even the pupils of pupils made their way to see me some days—Kakusen, who was a pupil of Hokumei's, and Keiri, who had studied with Hokkei. But I was on my own and strangely content. I did a series called *Lives of Flourishing Women*, thinking, for once, that I too was flourishing. Some people compared it to my father's work and said Hokusai was getting old. But he wasn't getting old; he was growing younger.

He crept into the city now and then on moonless nights, arriving by boat at the fishing piers at the mouth of the Sumida. From there, wearing a bumpkin's hat and leaning on the *bo*, he mingled with the crowds heading north on the riverbanks. He kept his head down, He chanted constantly to keep his palsy at bay. "*Atanda, atanda, atanda-bate.*"

In the alley the neighbour women might be sitting on the edge of one of the houses, keeping out of the way of their drunken husbands. They were not fooled by the hat. "Hey, hey, Old Man," they would say. "Old Man coming!"

He really was Iitsu now: "one again." "You are blessed to have such a father," said the candy seller, awestruck by Hokusai's great age of seventy years. He had left so many lives behind him. He had begun his magnificent series of views of Mt. Fuji. The cost of *beru* had dropped, so we could afford to have prints made in it. I thought of the blue eyes of my lost Dutch doctor every time we did.

IT WAS AN EARLY WINTER TWILIGHT. My students folded up their bundles and chimed their goodbyes. Mune was the last. She touched my hand affectionately. "You'll be all right?" were always her final words.

I pressed more charcoal into the *kotatsu* and settled under the blanket. I asked the boy next door to bring me tea. I now had a few hours to paint for myself. But someone coughed discreetly at my door.

"Who's there?" I threw my best low, masculine voice across the room.

"Eisen, come to see you." I heard his laughter. He was not fooled by my manly tones.

"Strange hour to visit," I said ungraciously, sliding the screen open.

Eisen's samurai background assured that he had lovely manners if he was sober, and impeccable manners if he was drunk. We both understood why, years before, he had left the North Star Studio, choosing to learn elsewhere. He was restless and talented. Hokusai had kept him down too long, and Eisen sprang up in the world once he left us. I supposed he had merely come to give me his news. These days he was successful. He too used *beru*—in fact, he had used it first. We spoke about the sudden drop in its price: now everyone would be using it. We chatted awhile, and as I did not offer him anything, he bowed himself out.

But not long after, in the late afternoon, Eisen appeared again at the studio door. In that hour we were all women, cleaning our brushes amid chirps of tired conversation. He looked around and took the mood of the place. "What are you hiding here?" he said, and, "Your cherry tree is ravishing." He picked up a cat and massaged it behind the ears in a way I took note of. "I am despondent. What are we men to do when the women refine their skills to such an extreme?" He stirred up the younger female students, flirting with even the plainest and shyest girl, who could not raise her eyes from the floor. Mune, confident in her role as lead student, played along. "If you are asking for advice, you might drink a little less and work a little more."

He inclined his large and shield-shaped head in her direction. I found myself charmed. His rough edge disguised polish within, just the opposite of most people those days. "Ah, I thank you for your kind observation," he said. "I am going to seed, it is quite true. I have decided, however, to put up no fight and to watch with detached curiosity as life's temptations get the best of me."

Titter, titter, went the ladies.

He helped me chase them out into the smoky decline of day, as if he thought one or another of them might take advantage of me. As I rolled up the papers he said, "Shall we go out for a little drink?"

I spoke more crossly than I intended. "You don't need any more, if you don't mind my saying so."

He saw that I was not amused. He apologized profusely and left. There! I thought. I have got rid of a pest.

But I looked for him the next day. When I heard his soft cough at the *shoji*, I opened the screen rather quickly, which action was not lost on him. He tried to hide his small smile.

If I was not mistaken, that look of pleasure was gladness in seeing me. He was a little disreputable, with greying hair, noble, thick brows cutting straight across and a hawk-like nose. His deep, resonant voice was clogged with smoke. He apologized for the day before.

"You mentioned, Oei-san, that I did not need any more drink. I have no wish to argue with a lady so assured. And I hope you will excuse my saying so, but I very much do. It is precisely when a man has had a lot that he has need of more. Don't you agree?"

He never used five words when fifty would do. How could I resist? And why should I anyway?

We sat in a teahouse and drank cup after cup of sake. I knew that my large ears burned red. I knew that my laugh—"ak, ak, ak, ak"— sometimes ending in a little explosion of smoke from my pipe, was not feminine. But I forgot how very unattractive these traits were. We talked about who was painting what, my father's Fuji series, which new prints we liked and which we didn't. He returned me to my door by moonlight and went off.

The next day I wandered into a bookshop to look at Eisen's work. I found his print of Hana-ogi VIII, the most recent incarnation of the great cour- tesan. She had a shovel-shaped face which was very much like his own. She looked haggard, dogged, and beautiful. I studied it with admiration. How did he do it? There was much said in the plain white space he'd left for her features, and much in her hectic clothing. He had far more feeling than his clever chat let on.

I picked up a directory he'd written of floating world artists and was astonished that he spoke of me: "Ei, the daughter, works under her father. She is an excellent painter."

Not many men would have said that.

The next time he came I offered him tea and called the boy next door to get it. He looked around at the little burner. "Are you cooking something?" he said hopefully.

I thought I should put him straight. "Pigment is the only thing I ever put on a burner," I said.

"Let's talk about your pigments, then," he said. "How do you prepare them? You take such care."

"It's my job."

It had been just a task when I first worked for my father, but now I was an expert and the process gave me pleasure. My colours were deep and clear, the envy of other artists. I had my own technique to get the paint thick and the colours dense. It was not a recipe I shared. I simmered the mixtures of lead and seeds as I was doing now. I added secret ingredients and then took a further step that no one knew of.

"Apprentices could do that."

"Hokusai likes it better when I do."

"I bet he does."

Another night he said, "Why don't you sign your Beauties?"

Maybe he was trying to stir up trouble. But I chose to believe he was only curious. "Why should I?"

"If you did, you might find out that you have quite a different style from your father."

"That is the question, isn't it?" My father worked in a thousand styles. "My colours are my signature."

"Why should your father take the credit for them?"

"Because he is Hokusai. He is Iitsu, at the moment."

"And you are Oei."

"I am his daughter. Helping him is my duty."

"Duty!" he scoffed.

That word belonged to the other side, the neo-Confucians with their old, repressive ways. We both saw the bankruptcy of that world. I admit I felt sheepish invoking it. Yet the new ways that we artists touted might change a great deal, but they did not erase the family.

"Maybe he takes you for granted."

"So he should. Unlike others"—a little dig there—"I would never leave him."

"You left your husband."

"That was different."

"Why?"

A pointless question. I shrugged. "A husband is dispensable if he is not loved," I said.

"Not many women would say that."

"Not many women would have the choice."

He laughed.

I continued. "A husband can be left, but a father cannot. He is always attached. And my father perhaps more than some. He made me an artist. He loved me despite my unbeautiful face and 'manly' nature." Of course, so did Tomei, but somehow that didn't count.

"Was Tomei not good to you too?"

"He was," I said. I knew it was unfair. "I have no answer."

"I'm glad you said that. Love is mysterious and there should not be answers."

By then we were tucked under the *kotatsu,* with its mixed cold drafts and hot spots, his head one way and mine the other. My fingers were curled around a teacup and his around a sake bottle. When he mentioned love I thought of the Dutch doctor. I thought of how my father had told me I always loved men who were taken. Was Eisen taken? I believed so. He had a wife. His hand was straying inside the collar of my kimono. It was not the least hesitant, making bold incursions inside my wrappings.

"If the two of you, Oei and Hokusai, were married, it would be different. You could be his silent partner. But you are not married! You are grown up, an adult. You should have your own name. You could be famous."

"What a ridiculous thought!"

"You are a better painter than he is."

I knew I was a better painter. Technically. More patient. More precise. Hokusai knew that too. But that didn't mean I was a great painter.

"Painting is not all of it," I said, pulling myself up to sitting. "He can draw and perform, and he imagines strange things . . ."

"Yes," said Eisen, "he is Hokusai and you are not. But you are Oei and he is not. You understand women, you can portray humanity, you have a finer line, and you cook excellent pigment!"

I nervously retied my obi. I thought of the examination the Dutch doctor had put me under: he'd said that Japanese women became powerless in the realm of the emotions. That was my realm. I knew what it looked like: deep red, blue you could drown in, the green of thick forests. I even knew what it felt like. Or I had known, years ago. Maybe I had forgotten. I was the painter of intensity, not a native of that world. Was I too powerless in that realm?

Eisen reached for his sake. "You are so unconventional in some ways, and then you are so conventional," he grumbled.

I took my pigment off the heat. It would now go underground for sixty days—the secret I was not telling him.

IT WAS A FEW WEEKS before I saw him again.

As the last of the students left, I pulled my winter wrap around me and stepped out the door. The air was chill; there was the smell of charcoal burning, and whiteness everywhere. The lanterns winked like fireflies all along the street. Suddenly he was there.

We took a ferry up from Yanagibashi to the Yoshiwara gate. The water was inky and the passengers silent. We walked side by side over the arc of the bridge and through the Great Gate into the pleasure quarter; our clogs beat on the hollow structure. I hadn't been down the boulevard for a long time.

Ahead of us were the dark, shuttered sides of the little wooden houses. It was quiet. I had never before seen signs in front of the lower-class brothels: "Discounts Offered for Special Services." We passed Mitsu's shop. She had become a doom crier.

"You, you come here! I want to talk to you," she said from her doorway. "Do you know?" she whispered melodramatically, her eyes huge, her lips stretched. "The end is coming!" She peered. "Do I know you?"

"It is Oei," I said.

"Ei! My child. Remember the golden days of the Yoshiwara? Long ago, the streets were beautiful. And people came here to spend their money. Now the *bakufu* are going to shut us down."

She was an old lady now. But in the lamplight she was just as she had been when I was a child. She must have had cataracts. Her eyes glowed strangely. Her skin was very white.

"Who is it with you? Is it your father?" she said, and then I knew she couldn't see.

"No. It is Eisen, the painter."

"Ah!" she withdrew into the darkness of her little shop. "Take care of the Old Man. The Old Man is in trouble. I knew he would be one day."

"The Old Man is far away, safe, in the countryside."

The doors were shuttered: people hurried in the gloom. Year by year the Yoshiwara was losing its allure. The great brothels were declining; there was competition from illegal houses in Shinagawa and other parts of town. It was no longer considered chic to spend all your money on a desperate love affair with a courtesan.

There was still, in the teashop, a display of bedding meant to tempt the yobbos—sumptuous red silk futons and sky blue sheets embroidered with rivers of gold thread—but it was covered in dust. We sat in the back, near the fire. Beside us was a courtesan begging her lover not to forsake her. She was watched by a patient young attendant. She was not young, but not old—probably my age.

She was elaborately decked out, her hair high, greased and punctured with lethal hairpins. Her face was heavily painted white, and her feet shone a chalky white too in the dark teashop. Her toenails were reddened with fruit juice. She shrugged her kimono back, and I could see a name carved in her shoulder. She had made her own tattoo this way, filling the wound with black ink.

It was the name of the man who was leaving.

Large tears stood on her pasty cheeks. Courtesans were famous for their tricks to make themselves cry "for love." They pulled out eyelashes and sniffed alum. But this one was sincere. He was probably her last hope.

But he thrust her away and stood up. Before he had gone three steps, the courtesan had given up on him. She buried her head in her hands. The lamplight fell on the gouged-out characters of her lover's name above her collarbone.

Her attendant extended a finger to touch the black scar. "You're gonna hafta change it now," she piped.

"Yeah, yeah," said the woman, rubbing it absent-mindedly. "I'll burn it with moxa and, once it heals, start over . . ."

And I thought, Here, I agree with the *bakufu*. The pleasure district is immoral. But not for the reasons they cited—that simple people enjoyed luxuries and forgot their woes. What was immoral was the suffering of the courtesans. Eisen read my mind.

"The doors of the Corner Tamaya are solid gold, but inside are plagues of flower and willow diseases. When the courtesans are sick, the owners put them in a chicken coop," Eisen said.

Eisen himself ran a brothel for a time, but it burnt down and he was not sorry: it was more than he could stomach, he told me. Anyway, he could not compete with the unprincipled ones.

"The brothel owners go out to sumo matches and the theatre. While they're gone the managers let in thieves and murderers, whoever can pay."

His eyes glittered. His hands were near mine on the table.

I said, "It is difficult to remain a decent person in these times."

"Interesting point," he said. "Would I have been more honourable if honour were easy to achieve? Would it still be honour?"

I laughed. "The difficulty is knowing the definition."

"I'm sure you are right and there's no hope for me," he said, raising his glass.

Candour was his appeal. He was close to the muck and the mire; he felt its lure, and its horrors too. Despite it all, he still liked to paint Beauties. We shared that.

"Here's to the great art you would make," he said, raising his sake cup, "if you were not held captive under your father's thumb."

He reminded me of Sanba. Was this the way to my heart, then? Through the traitors' gate that hated my subservient position to the Old Man? We talked until the clients came out the brothel doors and headed for the gate. Then we followed. The lamps were like stepping-stones in a garden of black. I looked for stars, but they were invisible that night, from that place. I ground my teeth at his word for me—"powerless." It made me think of my mother.

"I am not powerless. I refuse to be powerless," I said.

He gallantly took my arm. "Ago-Ago," he said with a laugh.

There it was again: Chin-Chin. My big chin. My self-will. My father's teasing, which now came from Eisen's mouth as fellow feeling.

Arm in arm we walked through the Great Gate, over the bridge, and up the zigzag path on Primping Hill. Our four feet clattered together, companionable. It was something new. Always I walked alone, or behind my father. Eisen coddled my elbow, and my thoughts drifted to Tomei, my ex-husband. They drifted to the woman, whoever she was, who was married to Eisen.

We came to the docks. A boatman stood by. His small, roofed wooden craft nudged the pier.

"Here," said Eisen, pulling coins from his purse. "We'll take her out for a paddle."

I sat under the canopy and drew my cloak around me while Eisen pushed us out with the oar. We glided. The water was still and reflected the low, snow-filled clouds. He pushed us beyond the noisy restaurant boats with their gaudy lamps and past the scattered working boats that came and went all night long. We reached the centre of the river, where a wide swath of water moved quickly and smelled of the deep. Wet snow drifted in thin lines and then sank.

It was colder there. Eisen put down the oar with the exaggerated care of a man who knew he was impaired. He stood and the boat rocked. I giggled. He made his way back, tucked his kimono under himself, sat beside me and pulled me into the warmth of his body.

What happened next I will not describe to you. Modesty strikes. Modesty! Me? You might laugh. But I was not in charge. It was as if a spirit—slow, earthy, and amused—took hold of my blood and my bones from within. This was new. I was cold, but I was melting, deep red. Eisen braced himself to balance me, but not soon enough. We fell to the floor of the boat.

This in itself was ridiculous, not to mention painful. We coughed a little and spoke to each other in broken, courteous phrases, like strangers who had been riding in this conveyance and were forced on top of each other by an earthquake. We were restrained. We tested each other. Then we both gave up the act.

We became rapacious—grasping and utterly selfish. I had known nothing like it. It went on—for how long I have no idea—and then it was over. I was dazed and very cold with melted snow and splash. Eisen too seemed shaken by the violent sequence. We both came back to ourselves slowly. The boat was rocking. The lamp at the prow was flickering. For anyone watching, it was a clear announcement. We laughed.

Eisen got to his feet, retying his kimono with dignity. I sat up and retied my obi. Another boat had drifted near. I could just make out two dark, urgent figures.

Eisen sat looking away from me at the water with the oar in his hand. The clouds had moved off. I could see stars buried deep in the river. We had drifted away from our boatman on shore. Eisen cursed. It would take a bit of rowing to get us back to the dock. I didn't mind. I shook out my clothes and tied the warmest, driest parts to me. Then I sat and waited as he pulled against the current to get us back to dry land.

WITH MY FATHER ABSENT I controlled our money. I counted it out carefully when I paid the vendors, unlike Hokusai, who tossed money at people's feet because he felt it was beneath him to deal in it. Then, no fan of consistency, he would do the opposite and beg for it. I saved what we were paid and hid it with his seal in the tangerine box behind the statue of St. Nichiren. I kept us alive; I did the commissions he found dull. Yet Hokusai hated me to manage us: he changed everything when he returned after months of absence.

It was two days before the new year. He came in steaming from Uraga, full of fresh, cold air. I was cramped from sitting so long. I jumped up to greet him. One leg was all pins and needles and buckled under me. I stumbled.

He laughed. "Oh, clumsy one! Oh, daughter mine, you don't change!" he said.

Perhaps Eisen had spoiled me. He always said it was a pleasure to set eyes on me.

"I am sorry," I said, in a not-so-sorry voice.

"Now don't be sad! I've come to be with you for New Year's. We will all be one year older. I will be seventy!"

And I would be thirty.

"We have our visits to make. And the monies to collect."

"And bills to pay."

"We must have money from the publisher. *Thirty-six Views* is so popular!"

He was very pleased with himself. And he looked healthy. A second youth was on him. I wished to be happy, but I simmered with resentment. Was he to have two lives and I none? He sat and called for tea, for sweets. He loved sweets. I didn't keep them in the house when I was alone. I preferred salty things. I sent a student out to get some.

A feeling of festivity came over the studio. I lit a pipe. I drank sake. I watched Hokusai, full of stories, wagging his head, putting on a show.

"It's all that *beru*," I said. "It's made you into a boy again."

"Nonsense. I am the Old Man. I am the oldest man in the town."

He showed me his latest drawings for the Fuji prints. He was expanding the series to forty-six; after that, he said, he would do one hundred more.

"But will you be able to think of so many? And each one different?"

"I will, I will. I am young again, didn't you say it?"

It's true he seemed his old self. His speech never slurred. His eyes were bright, and though I was beginning to think of sleep, he bounced with energy. I had something to tell him. I had told no one yet, and it pleased me very much.

"See what I will be working on in the coming year?" I said. I held out the note. It was from the publisher Suzanbo. "He is asking me to do the illustrations for a new edition of *100 Famous Poems by 100 Poets*."

My father snatched the note from my hand and scanned it. "He has written asking that Oei do these illustrations?" he said. "And not her father?"

I cast my eyes down and set my head on an angle.

"There must be some mistake."

Maybe his eyes were not so good after all. He had to read the note again and again. He looked up at me in quite comical confusion.

"Are you sure that is what it says? I don't think so. I think they are asking you to arrange for me to do it."

I had no need to look again. I had looked many times. "He commissions me."

"But why? There must be some mistake. Why are they asking you and not me?" He seemed bewildered.

"Because they like my painting style, do you think?" I said dryly.

"Your style? What do they know of your style? I know your style. I am your father. Your style is the style I give you. No one else knows your style."

Now he was getting angry. He flung the note to the cats. He puffed out his chest and blew.

"Suzanbo knows my style," I said, as mildly as I could. "People know, after all. I have my students here. I am busy while you are out of Edo. Where is that note?" I retrieved it from my friends the cats, who had been pawing it. "He's asking me because he wants to me to do it!"

"Oh, no. That's not a good idea. I would do a much better job," said my father.

"Different . . ." I allowed. "More expensive, for sure."

"No. *Better*. Certainly better. For the *waka* poems? There is no question."

I was angry. But I was not permitted anger. Anger belonged to him. I allowed my eyes to go dead.

Hokusai saw my feelings. He puffed a little more, and then turned with the pivot of his heel from child to stern patriarch. "You know, Daughter, that I appreciate your style. I have said so. But trust me in this. I'll take this commission. Give me the note. I'll write back to Suzanbo and do these myself."

29

LAUGHING PICTURES

MY FATHER APPEARED ONE NIGHT. *Atanda, atanda-bate.* I heard him just outside the door. He came in but didn't greet me. He circled the room, tossing up my cloak where it hung, looking for something.

"So it's Eisen now, is it?" he said heavily.

How did he know?

"Don't worry, Old Man. He's not here," I said, as Hokusai continued his restless search. I wanted our easy banter. But my father acted like a jealous lover.

He sat down finally and I got him tea. As he took it from my hands I saw that I was forgiven but still to be chastised. "Married, married. He's married. You don't learn," he said.

They said Eisen and I made a strange pair. He was ten years older, a debaucher, a man of the town. I was the gloomy spinster and my father's drudge. But how we laughed! When we could, we met at the theatre. He wanted to be a playwright. But his work was too full of explanations. I told him that. "There's nothing to say. The actors just want to strike a spectacular pose, and to have many complications in the action. They don't need your thoughts!"

I remembered too late that men don't need my advice. I put my hand over my mouth. It was a gesture all women made to stop their tongues. Was I becoming coy as well?

"But, please, don't listen to instructions from me," I said. "My husband wouldn't."

"More fool he," said Eisen, who knew Tomei's work. "Please continue. I can't divorce you, because I have not had the pleasure of marrying you. I would beg you to be my wife, but you would refuse me," he said, gallantly. "I am a dissolute and a poor artist. And anyway"—I had wondered if he would mention it—"I'm married."

"A minor detail," I said.

With Eisen, I returned to the teahouses. We drank and shouted and made rude jokes. The courtesans came and went, their soft hands wafting like smoke. The censors were dogging our tracks, making every kind of legitimate picture a crime. The men painted *shunga* for private customers. Eisen said, "Why don't you do it too? Hokusai used to be one of the best."

The sake drinkers laughed. "How could she paint them? She is a woman like a man. What she knows about love and sex would only fill a walnut shell."

I smiled in what I hoped was a mysterious way.

"She has an imagination, doesn't she?" said Eisen, pushed to defend me.

"That's more than you could ever expect from any woman."

I inclined my head to the side, on that sharp angle that could mean anything. But on the way home I was dejected.

It was Eisen who encouraged me. "They think you're a manly woman? Who better to illustrate a book of laughing pictures? You know both sides."

THE NEXT DAY HE CAME TO GET ME as soon as night began to fall. We went to the market that had sprung up on the grounds of the Asakusa temple. We sat under a wooden awning at a little restaurant that sold Nara tea. This was tea poured over rice, a proper meal. The sake was not good, but it was cheap. Eisen seemed nervous. The serving girl knelt beside him with another serving of sake.

"Should you wish to undertake the *shunga,* I believe I can help you with your research," he said.

It was a proposition. When we rose Eisen rocked back on his heels and reached for my elbow.

"Come," he said. "We'll go to my room."

We hastened, wordlessly, down through the covered stalls, barely nodding to the other artists we passed along the way. What could we say if they asked us where we were going?

"You are so serious," I said.

He was poking his hearth to get a flame up. His rooms were more elegant than mine. I stood, still wrapped in my cloak, which I had also put over my head and ears.

"Ei!" he said. "What do you do to me? You are not beautiful. You are not what a woman should be. You are not helping just now to stoke my fires . . . But I want you nonetheless."

"I've heard it all before," I said. "Until you get to the part about wanting me."

He gave up with the hearth and turned away. Behind his back, a small orange flame jumped.

"It is the triumph of the intelligence over the merely carnal," he said. "Was your husband your first? Or do I have some early deflowerer to match?"

"You do."

He guessed. "Sanba? He was the age of your father, wasn't he? Well, I am much younger." He laughed at himself then.

The room was growing warmer.

He came to me and opened my kimono with his hands. He found my undergarment and loosened it. His fingers went down my belly. It was round and solid.

I put one hand behind his neck. He began to bow, his spine curling under my fingers. His mouth, his eyes, and then the top of his head brushed my lips. I pulled the kimono loose from my shoulders and pressed his head to one side. My nipple was standing.

"Where did you learn to do that?" he said.

"I didn't learn it. It came with desire."

His head moved over to the other one. "Same thing?"

My kimono settled halfway down my arms and chest, as it was tied around my waist. I had been initiated when I was barely older than a child. But that girl had died with Sanba. Now I was a woman.

"A woman with mass has a certain appeal," mused Eisen.

He turned me to the back. His hands moved over my shoulders and down my spine, feeling each protruding knob of my backbone. My skin rose to his touch.

I wondered if it was possible to faint from desire. In a play it would be. "Perhaps we are in a play," I suggested.

"I am," he said. "I always am."

He parted my kimono further, over my belly. I reached back to touch his. The belly was coiled as if a hairless beast slept just under the skin. I arched my back and pressed my neck into his chest. He put his lips on my nape and moaned.

"I will lose myself," he said.

I parted my legs.

That was the beginning of our two-brush production.

Eisen was a tall man. While standing erect, I could rest my head on his chest. With my father gone, he sometimes stayed all night. In the evening after work, he would drink. I had a little sake too. Then he liked to make love. I studied him: his feet, curled with muscle tension as he loomed over me; his face, that fixated stare men get as they approach their climax. He kept his eyes shut. I kept mine open. I examined his member, which I had not had occasion to study before. It was like a salamander, moving blindly with its smooth, wet head.

His thighs were lean and straight, much straighter than the average man's, or than my father's, which were bowed. His buttocks were not hard or round, but tucked under, a little wide and smooth. His chest too was smooth, his nipples dark, large, and flat. You had to wonder why he had them. His kimono remained on at all times, as did mine: my room was cold, and the erotic potential of our dress enormous. The soft material sliding away from your skin, opening, letting hot body parts meet.

I was full figured; he was thin. I liked his boniness. I liked his hard shins, his hipbones, and his elbows as they pressed against me, navigating my softness by feel, inching towards where he needed to be. He did not rush once he was there, which made me happy. I liked the pushing, and finally his arched flop; he looked like a fish that has been pulled from the shallows.

He was funny and he was available; we fell into the habit of each other. I was not in love, as I had been with Sanba—as I half thought, sometimes, I had been with the Dutch doctor, whom I had met for only an hour three times, five years earlier. Being in love was a foolish idea, as my father said—a fashion, a swoon courtesans used to distract themselves from the awfulness of their lives.

We shared no dreams or longing. With Eisen it was a coupling of needs with requirements. Freed from the urgency to please the man because I "loved" him, I did what I wanted. This was very different from giving myself, or submitting, or becoming limp and docile in the belief that it fuelled male desire. It was by accident that I found I could enter into a roll upon the mats with a cool head and all my curiosity intact.

"Why don't you try pressing from the front?" I said when he pursued me at the back door. "Not inside, just outside, like that."

"You have the tricks of a courtesan," he grumbled, complying and laughing as he did.

"I know nothing! Nothing! I'm just trying to feel good."

He told me about women who sat unmoved by men's attentions, reading books while they were being made love to. But I was the very opposite. It was not disinterest but close attention that he saw in me. I was having ideas for pictures while we were making "love."

I tried being on top, and he found that entertaining too. "I must make a note," he mumbled as I let the breast of my kimono open towards his lips. "This is really rather good."

The kimono with their happy, graphic possibilities heightened the pleasure. It was fun to feel as if I were in the pictures I had designed for so long.

Together, Eisen and I took on a *shunga* commission. The private buyer could afford the fifteen pages of large canvas in four colours. He wanted a silly story under the title *Images of a Couple*. I remembered what I had seen as a small girl. With Shino in the brothel, I'd witnessed people rolling together, men mounting girls, girls' feet in the air.

We were paid well, and for a time I had plenty to eat. I sent money by messenger to Uraga. We got more commissions then. I found my father's designs for couples in love positions and began to use them. But my own way of seeing began to appear on the pages. My figures were rounder than Hokusai's. The world was a fishbowl, and the man—whichever man—was on the outside, looking in. The woman was on the inside, swimming in it, knocking against the glass. Perhaps drowning in it. Their robes ballooned around them.

We made up a story about a courtesan and her client who went out on a date on the Sumida in a small boat with a roof. The man paid a tip to the boatman so he would let them take the boat by themselves while he waited on the pier. Eisen wrote the dialogue. I had to remind him to keep it short.

COURTESAN: *It's such a nice prow. Give me one more, one more time of nice harpooning.*
MAN: *Port the helm! Port the helm!*
COURTESAN: *Like this? Like this?*

Shortly thereafter, the *bakufu* outlawed the little covered boats, permitting them only on rainy or snowy days for the purpose of transportation.

We were in the midst of yet more hard times.

WE SIGNED A BOOK OF SHUNGA TOGETHER. We wrote in large characters on the cover "*In-yo wago gyoku mon ei*," meaning, "joint work by man and woman." *Gyoku-mon* means "jewellery." A woman was a possession, a jewel of our *mon*, our gate, or name. On one page the man and woman were having sex under the heating table. I drew a book on the quilt, half-falling off the table. On the top right corner of this painted book, we wrote: "Written by Shishiki Gankou and Josei Insui."

Shishiki Gankou was one of my father's names, which he had sold to Eisen when we needed money. Josei Insui meant that the painter was a woman, Ei.

It was Eisen who convinced me to sign that little book within the book with my own name.

Before too long Eisen and I had a contract to do another work. It was to be called *The Sexual Joy of Women*. We were sitting around thinking up ideas.

"What would make a woman happy in congress?" he asked.

"To have a lover who was all fingers coax her to conclusion without entering her."

This was how we thought of the octopus.

Our story was based on a folktale. The heroine was an *ama* diver who was abducted and was being escorted to the palace of the King of the Undersea. The octopus was her escort. He had his young son with him. He asked the *ama* what she would like. She asked him to make love to her. It was originally a tale of female self-sacrifice: she was pleasing her escort. But in our version, the *ama* was adventurous. They paused in the lee of some rocks, and the octopus served her there with his great wide mouth and his eight tentacles.

Eisen wrote his usual ludicrous dialogue: he tucked it in all around the great reclining forms of the woman and her bulb-headed amorous friend, which I drew.

> SQUID MAXIMUS: *My wish comes true at last, this day of days; finally I have you in my grasp! Your "bobo" is ripe and full. How wonderful! Superior to all others! . . . All eight tentacles intertwine without and within! How do you like it this way?*
> MAIDEN: *There! Good, good. Aaaah! Yes, it tingles now; soon there will be no sensation at all left in my hips. Ooooooh! Boundaries and borders gone! I've vanished!*
> SQUID MINIMUM: *After Daddy finishes, I too want to rub and rub my suckers at the ridge of your furry place until you disappear . . .*

I took the design to the publishing house. The publisher assumed my father had done it. He said, "That Hokusai! He has the most grotesque imagination! He will think of such horrors!" He shook his head over the design, but he took it. "Has he gone too far this time?" murmured the publisher. His cheeks had become frozen. "This poor *ama* diver is paralyzed with fear."

"No, no," I offered. "I can assure you, she is in raptures."

30

THE SIGN OF THE NIGHTHAWK

I DIDN'T SLEEP, with my father snuffling and kicking on the other side of the room. In the morning he was down on his knees as usual, chuckling over his brush sketch of the God of Good Fortune—jovial and busy, his Hotei looked quite a lot like Hokusai himself.

In the alley I put my hands on the small of my back and arched my neck to the sky. Then I curled my spine over and swung my head down around my ankles. I did some dipping and turning, squatting and reaching, in an imitation of the training I'd sampled with Shino years ago. I was coaxing my good spirits to return.

Another spring was surely on the way. I felt the sun on my skin and there was warmth in it, not the mere, cold imitation of sun of only a week ago. In the alley the usual preparations for New Year's went on. Women were pounding rice for *mochi* balls. My neighbour was putting up the pine and bamboo over his entrance.

"So the Old Man has returned!" he cried out.

"How did you know? He came at night under his cloak of invisibility." With his stick and his stride and his incessant chanting, he was recognizable from blocks away.

"Ha, ha. He brought his purse with inexhaustible supplies of money, then, too?"

"I wish!"

I didn't often speak to these people when I was alone. I'm sure they saw me as gloomy and withdrawn. But when my father returned—though at first I was resentful—my stiffness began to melt. At least he had the effect of joining me to the world.

"Will you be starting the cleaning today?" the woman asked me shyly. It was tradition to clean house from top to bottom, and pay and collect all bills so one entered the new year fresh. Just thinking of it made me tired. Today and tomorrow we should air out the house, wash the bedding, sweep away the cobwebs, and dig out the crumbling wrappers the cats left in the corners. That and the bills. I went in to face the Old Man.

"Father, we need to talk about money."

"Chin-Chin," he said jubilantly, "I have made a pretty God of Fortune here. He will provide."

"He has provided, but not to us. And we owe a great deal."

"Troublesome," he said absently, with one eye on his drawing. "And not unheard of."

"The bill collectors will come today. And I cannot think of one place that we could go to collect money." I went to the orange crate with the statue of St. Nichiren in it and pulled out the papers that blocked the back of it. There was all the money we had. Only two hundred *mon*. I showed him.

"Then it's a good day for us to move house."

I groaned. To move again? But it was less work than cleaning. When you were gone from the quarter the merchants tended to forget your little debts. "Do you think so?"

"Oh, I do, I do. A new vantage point on the world. Do you know, I have always wanted to live in Fukagawa." The area he named was downtown, near the Mannen temple and the Eternal Bridge.

I thought it over. It was a pretty, arched bridge. And moving solved a number of problems. Beyond our debt and our dirt, there was Monster Boy. His father had died the year before. This made my father, as the surviving male relative, officially responsible for Monster Boy's debts. And he had located me when I moved back to Asakusa. If we left, it would take the young man a little while to find us again.

"We'll go, then."

We both sat down to write letters. Hokusai gave instructions to various publishers, and I sent word to Eisen and my students.

We packed and were on our way in a few hours. The neighbours looked knowingly at our retreating backs.

In Fukagawa we found a clean-swept set of rooms that had been vacated that same day, probably by others wishing to avoid the year-end debt collection.

We set out our mattresses and our painting bowls. I had gone to the well to get water when I saw Eisen walking my way. "You can't hide from me!" he boomed. I found myself smiling for the first time that day.

"I never wished to." I brought him inside to greet my father, who was already hunched over his work happily.

"I just happen to know some artists around here. Come with me. We'll have an 'old year forgetting party.'"

In a teahouse several streets away vats of sake were helping men brush off the old and welcome the new. I joined them, but my father had only a few cups of weak tea. He left us there and went to the temple. He would chant until midnight, waiting to hear the bell toll. It would toll 108 times, once for each human vice.

"Did you tell him you wanted to sign?" Eisen prodded.

"No." I could not.

I have to admit that Eisen's questions led to daydreams. I began to wonder how it would be if I were, as Hokusai had been—and might be again, with the success of his Mt. Fuji prints—the most famous artist in Edo.

I was quiet that evening.

I watched the other artists, famous too, each for one thing or another. They took the corner position in the room, sitting back with arms out along the walls on either side. They proclaimed with mouths open, faces alight with expression. Not loudly. They had no need to be loud: people went quiet when they started to talk. Smiles of satisfaction melted down these men's faces. They set forth opinions, jokes, commands, questions, and stretched out their arms to beckon the serving girls: bring it to me, bring the rice bowls, bring the sake, bring me the accolades.

How could I be one of those men? Women sat small and correct and silent. Their mouths were red and tiny, pinched around the lips. Morsels of food were carried there and almost invisibly sucked in.

I thought of Mune and her friends. They had more confidence, being in the merchant class. But their accomplishments were under wraps, as were their bodies. If I complimented a female student, she denied that what I said was true. She made way for a man; she gave in to a man's opinion; she flattered a man. "Man is superior, woman inferior." That was doctrine.

I thought about my signature. Was that what was needed? Instead of his? But publishers knew that "Iitsu" meant Oei. Everywhere my work was mixed and confused with his. Even in Hokusai's head. Even in my head. My wanting to be known was only a sign of vanity, one of those vices we were about to hear about.

At midnight we went to the temple to hear the bell toll. It did indeed toll 108 times, each one of which went to my heart.

THE NEXT MORNING Hokusai did not feel well; his extreme good spirits were fading. He lay on his mattress. He watched my stabbing brush. He saw the deep pigments I mixed. "Too much paint," he murmured.

I grunted. What was there to say?

"I have an idea," he said. "Why don't you do one of the *One Hundred Views of Mt. Fuji*?"

"That series is yours."

"It's mine, but I am your father! I want to share it with you. Why don't you do the New Year's view?"

"Because I want to do my own commissions; I wanted to do the *waka* poems, which you stole from me." I could hardly believe I had spoken those words.

"You bring up that old question?"

He lived in a constant present, while I was getting old. "Yes, I do." He tried to make amends. "Here, do one. Do it."

It is considered good fortune, at New Year's, to see an eggplant, Mt. Fuji, and a falcon. (You might ask why the eggplant. Because they were phallic? Because the Shogun Ieyasu loved them, or because their name sounded like the words meaning "to achieve something great"?)

I sketched a black falcon, in close-up with a faint Fuji behind. The falcon was killing a pheasant; both predator and prey were perched on an eggplant. It was meant to be my little black joke. The two birds were entwined so you couldn't distinguish one from the other. The predator was at the neck of the pheasant, whose head was snapped sideways, on a sharp angle, with his eyes wide open.

My picture was out of place in his series. "What has happened to the humorous and optimistic Hokusai?" they would say. "Why this dreadful vision to see in the New Year?"

THAT NEW YEAR CAME IN and went out, and another and another after that. I was not counting, exactly, except to say that my father's behaviour grew more preposterous with his age. He made the forty-six Fuji. He began to work on the next hundred views. He assumed that the public's appetite for these was insatiable. And maybe it would have proven to be. But the publisher ran out of money and the blocks sat without being printed.

A SPRING MORNING. I loved to be up early, when the wandering monks were just coming to the streets to beg. When the tofu vendors set up their carts. And the bathhouse master was lighting the fire under his cauldron. I loved the smell and crackle of the wood. I loved the *clunk, clunk* as money started to change hands. I watched the teashop girls as they were just getting to work. They ordered a huge breakfast from the carts, although they couldn't spare the money.

I set out, walking. I was alone again. Hokusai was gone, an old man on the road. I had the day to myself and spent it crossing the canals of Edo, stopping at markets and bookstalls and teashops. As the afternoon stretched on, I turned my steps towards the Yoshiwara. My heart kicked in my chest just to take the few uphill steps on the bridge: I had grown up walking those streets. I liked its tilting, off-kilter position—against, but part of, the shogunate. I liked their spirited, doomed resistance. I loved its blatant commerce, the festivals and frantic lures, the courtesans parading under castles of hair, and the doubleness—beauty and cruelty.

I was drawn back down to the poorer streets, to the brothels alongside the moat where, as the sun set, women arranged themselves behind the lattice. There was such heaviness in their movements despite their youth, despite their thinness. They tended one another nervously, a flock of birds. I shuddered at the strange animation that came over one of them when a client came close to the slats and beckoned. In the low lamplight, the dark pickets of the fence laid black lines across the women's bodies. Their faces were heavily whitened, their cheeks slack with boredom, and from their piled-up hair the clutch of pins, the *bin-sashi*, stuck out like spokes on a crazy wheel. Shino—lost Shino—had taught us to ward off attacks with these hairpins. I could still remember the steps to that "dance."

Mune, who not only patronized my studio but also introduced her friends for lessons, had begun to bring me commissions for scroll paintings of women of the Yoshiwara. She and her elderly mother, Hokumei, acted as go-betweens; I did not know who the art lovers were who bought these pieces. It was mysterious and entirely anonymous, but when a commission came it was with ample money for paint and gold, and I delighted in the work. I came here to watch, but I drew nothing until I was at home alone. Courtesans reading by starlight, courtesans behind the lattice—these were my favourite subjects. I used no subtlety in colour: the black was black and the lit area was glaring white, nowhere to hide. I painted the onlookers from the back, with their dark wraps concealing their faces, and beyond them the watched women melting under high, bright lanterns.

What sort of people were we to invent this class of woman solely formed to please a man? I had asked the Dutch doctor that. Now I asked the question again, to anyone who would see, in my paintings. Who were we to force them to be supplicant? To sit on display rolled in bales of fabric and skin caked white like parched earth. To sleep until noon and work all night, tending men. To speak and move and even think like children, like the possessions they were. Who were we to distort lives this way?

I could not watch without thinking of the brave and fragile Shino, who had been my sister and my mother, as my blood sisters and mother had failed to be. Her spirit had carried her through even this ritual of the lattice and into marriage—and away from me. No doubt the blind man took good care of her. Could she bear his ham hands on her? His fat, stuffed fingers probing? And what did she make of his sightless intensity, so different from my father and his laughing, all-seeing eyes?

Mitsu, font of all gossip, had reported that the blind man had succeeded as a moneylender.

"He has an excellent clientele, you wone *beleeve*," she had said to me, winking at Eisen. "That woman's living high up on the hill now. Climbing back to where she came from—but this time ther'z no noble fami*lee*, only money, keeping her there. *Izn it?*"

It had been many years now. Twenty years, when I counted. I had lived an entire lifetime. I supposed I was nothing to her. The child of her secret lover, a lover whom she was forced to abandon, and who had abandoned her. My father remembered her, I knew: he had no other woman. She had forgotten us, doubtless. We moved so often, nearly every year. We kept the wanted as well as the unwanted off our trail.

But one day, as if I had conjured her, I saw her.

I was strolling a narrow canal behind Yoshida Street, a moody backwater near Nihonbashi. There was a deserted washhouse on a platform where local people came to wash vegetables and do laundry. Beside it was a noodle house where I sometimes bought soba from a dogged husband and wife who kept their business going despite a dearth of customers. But this day I found they had gone out of business.

I walked slowly by their premises. A blue-uniformed policeman waved his baton—get along—and then saluted. It was in an empty house like this that the last big fire in the Yoshiwara had begun, only a few years ago. That explained his presence.

I stopped at the tiny bridge that crossed the still canal. It was evening, and the moon was high. It slipped between the rooftops and lay on the still water, giving a little light to this dark place.

I saw a woman come out of the doorway and begin to walk along the path, close to the wall. She was wrapped in a cloak and quick as a cat, but her long, straight back caught my eye. Before I thought about it, my lips were speaking.

"Shino!"

She did not turn around. She did not stop, but slowed just perceptibly.

"Shino! It's me, Ei."

"I know," she said. "One does not forget that voice."

I understood then that she had been avoiding us.

"Don't you want to look at me?" I said softly. I was so much older now, thirty-seven. That meant she would be forty-seven. She walked like a girl. "Have I angered you?"

She looked away, towards the lighted, busy streets. She reached into her sleeve as if looking for something. "Don't stop here," she said. "You'll give us away."

Give who away to whom? I did not understand. She was free, and probably wealthy.

"Walk past," she commanded.

I walked past, a few feet from her body.

"My husband doesn't know I'm here."

I felt a surge of my old hatred of this blind man.

"But can we meet?"

"Not tonight. Come tomorrow. I'll take precautions. Go to the house you saw me leave, at twilight. Cover your head. There will be candles. Follow them."

As I approached the narrow canal, I noticed that the little noodle house I had thought abandoned had a shingle. It read, "The Sign of the Nighthawk." The window papers glowed: there was candlelight within. I put my face near the door and scratched, and said a soft "Good evening."

The door opened. Eight female heads turned in shock.

"It's all right," said Shino.

She stood amongst a clutch of haggard women. They were seated on old sake barrels. They held mirrors, and the tongues of candle flame reflected off the surfaces around the room, like yellow birds. She wore an apron. She hardly looked at me. With a paintbrush and a pot of rice powder she was buffing the cheeks of a woman much the worse for wear.

"Pardon me for the secrecy," she said pleasantly. "But as the prostitutes are illegal, helping them is illegal too. My husband does not approve."

I saw faces scarred, toothless, and pockmarked—blemishes that were indeed the sign of the nighthawks. But they were laughing and flushed; there was heat in the room from a charcoal burner. Shino's helper was making rosebud lips out of narrow, lined mouths. One woman took softened wax from a candle, shaped it between her thumb and fingers, and set it on her nose, the end of which had been eaten away, I supposed by syphilis. She patted away with her wax, adding bits, squeezing with her thumb. I wondered how it would stay on.

"So this is your vice," I said, taking refuge in the rough irony that was my father's. "Good works. I knew you'd still be misbehaving."

"Nor have you lost your edge," she said.

I wanted to take her in my arms and embrace her. But eight women with half-made faces listened.

Shino's long face was fuller and she had stopped hiding her strength: her gaze was frank and humorous and to the point. Her married status still surprised me, the shaved eyebrows and blackened teeth. Her hair had gone from its deep, rich black to grey—grey at the top of her head and over her ears, black in the large, loose knot.

"It suits you, married life," I admitted. "Though I still feel, after all this time, unfairly cut out of it."

"It was not my wish," she said. "But necessary."

To cut my father out, yes. But me? Why me? Was the blind man so vindictive? I didn't ask.

"Are you happy?" We both said it at the same time. Our audience of haggard and half-made faces laughed. It was strange speaking in front of them, but I could see Shino would not be moved from her task.

"I am very happy," she said.

"I too. And your esteemed husband?" I said without a trace of irony.

"He remains well, the gods willing. And your father?"

"The Old Man is often on the road. He has had success with his *Thirty-six Views of Mt. Fuji* and is in excellent health despite his years."

"Astonishing," murmured Shino, "and I would love to hear more about you. But the women must get ready. They need to be out for the evening soon."

The woman who was trying to fill the hole in her nose called out for help. But Shino was doing hair, rolling tangled lanks of it and pinning it up. I stepped in, and that was how I found myself rolling tiny bits of warm wax and plugging them into an eroded nose. When I was finished, both the nighthawk and I were pleased.

"You're good with a brush. Draw some lips—make them tiny and red."

I supposed the women had once been beautiful, at least beautiful enough to sell themselves. Now they could not practise in a brothel. Shino helped make them presentable enough to catch a client on the street for a few small coins. When they left, cheerfully enough, for their evening's work, I sat on a rice caddy and took the tea she offered.

"They'll eat tomorrow," she said.

"You keep them working," I observed.

"If they had any choice, they wouldn't be doing it. And every day brings hope—the makeup brings hope."

I listened. Shino's eyes were glowing. She had plans: she was trying to convince a brothel owner to let her open a hospital.

"Please excuse the drama of our little subterfuge. But my husband sometimes has me watched."

I supposed that he was ashamed she had been a courtesan.

"No," she said, "it's because he gets his licence from the Shogun. I endanger him with the work. My friendship with you would be even worse. The North Star Studio is always under suspicion. Hokusai paints in the Western way. He sold to foreigners."

"You're not afraid to help the nighthawks, but you are afraid to see us?" I was wounded, and tears came to my eyes.

"I haven't forgotten you," she said. "I buy every little piece of work you do—a print or a handbook, even the *shunga*."

"Under my father's signature?" I said.

"I know the difference."

I REFUSED TO ACCEPT SHINO'S BAN. I went past the little house now and then. I drew rosebud mouths in crimson, and with a tiny razor I cleaned up the napes of women who needed hair to grow in the two points that marked a virgin. She always pushed me out of there as quickly as she could. The last time she was truly angry with me.

"I said you must not come!"

I stayed away for a long time. When, months later, I walked along the narrow canal, I saw that the house was dark. The Sign of the Nighthawk was gone.

And there were no more commissions for paintings of Yoshiwara Beauties. The fashion then was for Chinese legends—safe subjects, nothing to do with the regime. I was lucky to find a rich patron who wanted one.

31

APOLOGY

I WAS ALONE IN THE NORTH STAR STUDIO when Matsudaira Sadanobu came to visit. He was old and fat. His retainers filled the doorway and frightened my neighbours. He bowed in humble fashion and asked for my father.

"I never know where the Old Man is. He is on his travels," I said shortly.

"Your father was beloved by Shogun and commoner alike," began Sadanobu.

"Ah, but apparently not by those in between," said I, "the administrators, the councillors, the censors?"

"Yes, by all. We all loved him."

I took note of the past tense. Did this man know something that I didn't? I called for the neighbour's boy to get us tea.

"I am a writer," said Sadanobu, warming a little. "I understand the difficult life of the artist."

"Oh, yes. I recall your written works," I said as we waited. "There was that famous line you wrote in the edict announcing the Kansei Reforms: 'There have been books since times long past and no more are necessary.'"

He flushed. "That was long ago. Force was needed to save the people. The city had become decadent. History will judge us. I did not want to leave such art as you people created on the record."

"You were afraid of history."

"But I understand that my actions created harsh times for writers and artists. I have come to offer my apologies."

Apologies? We were not ready for them.

"I understand that Hokusai is not well. I myself am near to death. I would like to see him before I die."

Hokusai was going to die? Was that the rumour?

I retorted: "Hokusai will outlive you. He has already outlived two wives and all my sisters. They died in their twenties, but that is the life of the poor, is it not? He may even outlive me."

Sadanobu endured my cold words.

"If you seek forgiveness," I told him, "better to go to your temple. You will not find it here."

"I want to undo the wrongs I have done in this world before I leave it."

"Only a man of exceptional arrogance could even imagine that was possible," I said.

His voice rose alarmingly. "You hold on to the past. That's not what your Buddha preaches. I loved your father, as I loved the other artists and writers."

"And that was why you handcuffed us?"

"Yes," said Sadanobu, "that was why. To prevent harm. You expressed the evil and the corruption within us. We had to stamp it out. But it was not personal."

"Our hunger was personal. Our hiding was personal. Unfortunately for us, it is all personal. Who is senior councillor now?" I said. "Not Sadanobu. Who is Shogun now? The corrupt Ienari. But who is Hokusai? Hokusai is still Hokusai."

Beads of sweat formed where the fat man's hairline would have been had he not shaved it. I saw he did not look well. He may have been near death, But I had no sympathy. My heart was a stone.

"I thought he had changed his name to Iitsu," he muttered.

"No," I said, to further confound him, "Iitsu is me."

Despite my brave words, the censors were breaking us down. I wondered, sometimes, if the age of the *ukiyo-e* was coming to an end.

Hokusai was writing an introduction to his book *One Hundred Views of Mt. Fuji.* I smoked my pipe.

"I believe there is nothing of great note in the things I drew before my seventieth birthday," he said. "In my seventy-third year, I finally apprehended something of the true quality of birds, animals, insects, and fishes, and of the vital nature of grasses and trees.

"I expect that in my eightieth year, I'll have made some progress. In my ninetieth, I will have penetrated even further into the deeper meaning of things. In my hundredth year I shall have become truly marvellous, and at 110 every dot and every line I make will have a life of its own."

How he tempted the gods!

The first two volumes of the book were finally published. The third volume was advertised and the blocks cut, but there was no money to print it.

There was another crackdown, an earthquake. And then the rain came. It rained out the crop. The harvest was only one-quarter what it should have been. Summer abandoned us the next year, and the next. The *bakufu* told us the gods were punishing us for our corruption. The price of rice multiplied three times. Peasants were dying in the countryside; people said bodies were stacked at the sides of the roads, to clear the way for others to walk.

Hungry people do not buy pictures. What hungry people do is borrow from moneylenders.

EISEN AND I HAD SPENT THE EVENING drinking and were walking home through the temple grounds. A storyteller had propped himself up at the foot of a tree and was beckoning all passers to gather in front of him. I seemed to recognize the man. He had thick hair and a stocky body and he could throw his voice.

"Listen to me! I have a story of true events. It has happened in our city. It is a story of the blind moneylender."

It was pouring rain, as usual. Our umbrellas were drums. The peonies were soapy ruins on the path. I took Eisen's elbow. "I want to hear this." The storyteller had hooked me with his eye. He began,

> The blind moneylender was a large and canny man with an acute sense of smell. He would have known that the pack of thieves had targeted him that night. He would have heard them following him at a distance, laughing about how they would torture him with knives.
>
> He was a brave man too. And he loved his wife, who had been a courtesan. He had bought out her contract, and the two lived happily together.
>
> The blind man led the thugs away from his home. He went slowly along the Dike of Japan until it narrowed and took a hard right-hand turn. He knew the space by the smell of the lacquer

trees and the sound of the carts, the horses, and the feet going by. He stayed near to the sound, knowing that if he was alone, they would attack.

He came to a small bridge over the canal. He became confused. One way was the cooler, moist air towards the edge of town. The other side was better, he thought. So he crossed. But he had forgotten. On that side of the water, there was a theatre. But it had burnt down, leaving an open space.

It was as he crossed this space that they closed in and danced around him with whips. He swayed like a bear, sensing, keeping his balance. He was strong. He caught the first two who jumped him and threw them in the canal. The rest of the thugs laughed to see their chums in trouble. Then they lost patience and caught him with ropes, like a bull, and pulled until his skin rubbed raw.

He shook off these punishments. He seemed to feel no pain. But this maddened his attackers. Someone got a torch and lit the ropes. He could smell the oil and the smoke. He made a run for it and burst the ties, but they threw fire at him, and then the oil. After he was charred black, they pushed him into the water.

Some people said it was the bakufu who did it. He had become too rich.

Eisen hissed in my ear.

But my head was roaring; I could not hear. "What about the moneylender's wife, who had once been a courtesan?" I shouted.

The storyteller just stared at me. "No more story." He collected the coins people had thrown on his mat.

I turned to Eisen. He was stricken, not with fear, as I was, but with glee.

"It's my moneylender, don't you see?" He began to shout with laughter. He let his umbrella drop and turned around in a circle, looking at the sky, his face washed with rain. "Don't you see? If he's gone, he's taken my debt with him."

Eisen had built his brothel by borrowing from a moneylender who specialized in brothels. When it burned to the ground and his courtesans fled, he never rebuilt and never repaid, and he feared the moneylender's thugs. "The man was bald with huge hands; he hung his rosary on his ear," he said. "Is that the one?"

"That is the one," I said.

I SEARCHED FOR SHINO on the slope behind the Shogun's castle. Dead only a matter of days, her husband had entered legend. I only had to ask, "Where is the house where the blind moneylender lived?" And the way was pointed out.

Suspicious women opened the screen to me with reluctance. I found my friend kneeling in a room with gold-leaf walls. She saw me but would not speak. I went away and came back the next day, again to be grudgingly admitted. Still she would not speak.

I came back a few days later, and this time an apparition came to slide the screen open. She had shaved her head. She was perfectly bald, as bald as her husband had been. But his head had been a tuber, and hers was a tulip bulb. Her eyes were huge. Her cheekbones jutted. Her pale scalp was blue like the moon.

"Your hair!"

"I only wish my husband had been here to shave it. He'd have done a much better job." She rubbed the back of her head with its uneven bristles. "You have an eye for detail—please." She handed me the blade.

As I bent over her nape she whispered that she would be allowed to stay in the marriage house only if she married her husband's sighted brother. The family and the tax officials were already fighting over the money.

"I have refused," she said. "No more. I had a husband when I was a child. Then I had a lover, and after that another husband. Surely I can't be asked to do more for mankind."

That buried gleam was in her eyes. She might have been grieving him, or she might have been relieved: I could not tell. Whatever it was, it seemed to bring her back to herself.

"Did you love him?"

"You have asked impertinent questions all your life. I'll answer this much. I was used to my blind man," she said, "and that, after all, is very much better. He could hear a butterfly land. I liked knowing that he couldn't see, that he followed me with his ears. I liked him such that I will not have his brother, no matter what the penalty. I am old! I will not submit to marriage again."

I knew what she would do. The head I was shaving told me. "Taking up with the gods won't leave you free from the ways of men," I said.

"I've made up my mind," said Shino.

"Don't be so quick." I wanted her to stay with me. We could live together and perhaps tame the Old Man when he came in from the road. "You exchange one captivity for another."

She gave me a half smile and shook her head. "You are right. We are never free. We exchange cages. But we are released from time to time. Now is such a time."

"That's not what I meant!"

She would go to a temple, but only for a short time. She planned to be a pilgrim on the roads.

She took my face in her cool hands for one minute, and then asked me to leave. She had to pack her belongings. Her in-laws would at least let her store them in the house.

And so the blind man who had stolen her first stole her again in death. And then he stole from me yet again. This time he took Eisen. My friend was free of debt. He no longer had to stay in Edo. With his freedom, he committed the unpardonable: he went off with Hiroshige, the young rival, as we still called him, to paint the scenes of his *Fifty-three Stages of the Tokaido*. He always said he had a penchant for betrayal.

IN EDO, EVERYONE SPOKE OF THE OLD DAYS. The censors had won. You could not make a living making prints anymore. The business was finished. At least the best artists in it were finished.

In 1841 the Shogun Ienari died—he of the falcon hunt who had laughed at the chicken with its red dyed feet. He was as dissolute as his councillors thought we were. His death was celebrated. Seven days later, eighty prisoners were let out of the jailhouse; they marched in a parade, toothless, gaunt, clothes half-eaten by rats—that is, unless a family member had sent them something new to wear. It was if they'd been asked to stand up and exit their graves.

The new regime rapidly clamped down on whatever was left of our life. Which was nothing. Hokusai was making a book that would not be printed. The private commissions for my painted scrolls came no more. I happened to visit the studio of a potter. I had an idea when I saw that the smallest drops of clay from his fingers lay on his floor. I asked permission to collect them. I brought the clay home—enough to fill the palms of my two hands. From it I made a set of tiny ceramic dolls, forming the procession of the freed prisoners. I painted the dolls in bright, unrealistic colours.

"Make something happier," grumbled Hokusai.

"What could be happier than escaping death?" I said. But I then made models of the Niwaka Festival dancer procession and the Korean ambassadors on their visit to Edo. Each figure had an elaborate ritual costume. I worked the clay with my thumb and forefinger. Each figure no bigger than a thimble. Then I painted them exactly as they were. These figures kept me busy all day, and I found the work absorbing. It was a way of recording our times. I was not, like Sadanobu, afraid of history. I believed it would vindicate us.

I got a carpenter to make me a little wooden box to keep the figures in. Strangely, these dolls were a big success. We sold as many as I could produce, and although the male artists scoffed a little, I could see they would have loved to be earning as we were.

The next year, terrible news: another writer was investigated. This time it was Tanehiko Ryutei, the samurai novelist whose satire, *The Rustic Genji*, had been published in instalments for over ten years. I suppose the *bakufu* wanted to know how it ended before they called up the author on the White Sands.

After his investigation, Tanehiko committed suicide.

We were frightened. Tanehiko's work, like ours, was in the cache that von Siebold had bought and packed for export. They had gone out of Japan and into the wide world. It was a mixed blessing: we were known to outsiders but suspected of treason within. It had been quiet for more than a decade. But perhaps in the new regime, our transgressions would be dug up again. Worn down, we anticipated disaster.

BECAUSE MY FATHER WAS BLESSED with such age, I rarely thought of my own years adding up. To observe that his declining years were occupying the best of mine would have been disloyal. He was afflicted more now by the palsy that had come to him years ago, and which he thought he had conquered. But he was an improbable eighty-two, and though I was a child of his advanced age, I was now a startling forty-two.

I noticed changes, although he tried to hide them from me. His hand shook. He had to concentrate with a fury to keep the shakes from blurring his line. He had a new recipe for long life: dragon-eye evergreen fruit, white sugar, and a gallon of strong potato whiskey, *shochu*, left standing in a sealed jug for sixty days. He took two cups morning and evening, without fail.

He spent the time in between praying for long life and relief from the bullying of Monster Boy. He began to paint lions he called demon-quellers. He returned to the brush technique he had learned from the nobles early in his life, and he completed each sketch in sixty seconds of concentration, without lifting his brush. Sometimes the beast flew through the air. Sometimes it lay low and snarled. Often when he finished one of these sketches, which he called "exorcisms," he would ball it up and throw it out the door.

Then suddenly Hokusai announced that he was taking to the road again. He was going to walk across Japan to the sea on the other side. He believed he could find work outside Edo. He took his long *bo* and left.

I was alone. I made my dolls. I did the odd bit of work for a temple. I took to praying at the women's temple, though I drew the line at sticking pins into cubes of tofu. For months I heard little of him, only that he had walked all the way to the distant mountains of Nagano. There, he had chanced upon the estate of an art patron and samurai called Takai Kozan, and he had been given shelter, and even work.

Then he reappeared. He stayed part of the year and then left again. I was alone.

32

THE EIGHTEEN

TODAY A LONG LETTER ARRIVED. The plea from Hokusai was clear: "Come to me. I need you, Chin-Chin. Kozan has made us a little house by a stream."

"My father is asking for me," I told the vendor of the best noodles in our quarter. I sucked in the soba. The next stall had silvery broiled fish on skewers, very salty. Farther along was eggplant smeared with sweet miso paste.

The fish man grunted and gave me two skewers. The vegetable man was not keen to part with anything from his wooden trays, but he did. The sake vendor's blazing placards and rude spouts tempted me, but I went past. I was heading to the storyteller at Senso-ji temple. I had become friendly with this man. He was grizzled and dishevelled. I sat beside him on his mat.

"My father asks for me in Obuse. He cannot do the work without me. I'm not surprised. He is in his eighty-sixth year. Decent men, respectable men, are dead in their fiftieth."

"Hmmph. So, so," hiccuped Yasayuke, waving away his tobacco smoke. That combined with the incense from the burner almost, but not quite, covered the odour of his kimono. It was stiff with earth and sweat. "You are an old woman yourself."

"Don't be ridiculous. When you have an old father, you cannot be old; you must be young."

He accepted my offer of a skewer of fish.

"He wants me to go to him."

I pulled a thin, rectangular box out of my basket. It was the size of my forearm. I unpacked the tiny figures made of clay, painted with the deep colours anyone could recognize as my own—deep tea, crimson, the orangey red called *beni*, dark green, and several shades of blue. I stood them in order on the lid of their box. It was a procession of the castle guards. Rounded and armed, they represented flag bearers, officials, samurai, and even the Shogun himself, although no doubt there was a law against it. But he was so small, only the size of the last joint of my little finger. This is what I was reduced to.

"These are the original *keshi ningyo* dolls! Accept no substitute!" I called out to the passersby.

"No one will buy that one," said the storyteller. "It's gruesome. Make a nice marriage procession."

As I sunk my teeth into one blackened bit of fish and tore it off, a woman came to stare at my dolls.

"How much do they cost?"

"Five *mon*."

She looked with longing. The procession was not beautiful, but it was true. I had seen it. She had seen it too—men with placards naming their crimes, guards with wooden staffs, the ruler wide on his sedan chair. I watched her idly as she wavered. Could she afford it? I kept chewing. I made no attempt to persuade her. And she moved on.

I passed the letter over to Yasayuke.

There was more writing after my father's, by the rice merchant himself, inviting me to share the mountain refuge with my father. I was to travel with the merchant caravan Juhachi-ya, the Eighteen. Kozan had got me a transit visa to pass through the *sekisho*, the checkpoints on the route. It said I was the daughter of Koyama-san, owner of Juhachi-ya. The final line of the letter was this: a warm travelling cloak would be waiting for me at his shop in Edo.

"He has provided for me, and I am to drop everything to get there."

"What is there to drop?"

"Everything! The North Star Studio, our commissions, my students, *keshi ningyo* dolls . . ."

There was something else. I had a new and very young friend. Her name was Tachi, and she was my niece, the daughter of my brother Sakujiro. Sakujiro had gone up in the world as we had gone down. He now worked in the counting houses of the Shogun. His wife disapproved of me, but the little girl came to visit when she could.

"If you are robbed and killed," my friend said, his misbehaving eye smiling, "I will tell the story. You will enter legend this way." The storyteller had been all around Japan. That was one reason he was so popular. He could describe the wild valleys and the splashing waterfalls, and he could whistle like the birds that hid in the tops of ancient cedars.

I laughed with him. "I have already entered legend. I am the devoted daughter of the Old Man Mad about Painting. I am Iitsu, the secret brush. I am 'She who paints but does not sew.' And now I am to be disguised as a merchant's daughter."

"You'll talk like this." He put on his female voice; he drew a cloak over his head, pulled in his chin. He simpered in high tones. "I must travel from Edo to our home in the mountains because my old father is ill. I am not harmful to anyone."

Then he jumped to his feet and leered down at me, a *bakufu* guard at the post station. "Where is your husband?"

Again the cloak transformed his face.

"I have no husband. What man would marry me? I am strange." He allowed a little drool to escape the side of his mouth and crossed his eyes.

He puffed himself up. "The woman is simple. Let her pass."

But it was just a game. I knew how to speak like a merchant's daughter: I taught such women every day. I was not afraid. But I resolved to ask my brother if I could take Tachi with me. She could speak for me. I knew the girl was curious about the outside world. He would say yes, not because he wanted to please me or even her, but because he was a snob, and we would be visiting a respectable samurai family, a rich man.

I PULLED TAKAI KOZAN'S LETTER out of my kimono. The head carter read it, looked me over, and gave one short, sharp nod. Kozan was the boss, and this was the cargo he wanted.

He cast a scant look at little Tachi, wrapped and still beside me.

"My daughter," I said.

The oxen were bellowing and thick-skinned and black with road dirt. The men who drove them were no different. One of them lifted me and plopped me in the cart. I would ride with the brass temple bell and the bales of silk and the farm implements. Tachi was lifted beside me. She sat on a pile of books and prints with a wrapper from Ichibee, the *rangaku* bookseller.

My plain indigo kimono was hidden under a thick cloak. My head was wrapped in the scarf Kozan supplied. We approached the checkpoint. When I was a child I passed here disguised as a boy; now I passed as a samurai woman.

We travelled beside the coast. I gazed at the waves, remembering my father jumping in the foam. I told stories to Tachi. At night we came to a post station and pulled up at an inn. We two went off to a room of our own, our bodies cramped and sore.

We began to follow a river upstream. Fuji, the Peerless Cone, was on my left hand. Then it was gone and the black, jagged rows of rock stood up, sawtoothed and vehement. Through the gaps we saw white peaks. The men sang oxen songs. I learned to arrange the bales so my bones remained intact despite the jogging.

This was the world beyond Edo. This was what the people longed to see.

Even now, in late March, there were patches of snow. The sky was *beru*, and the wind was a melody from the samisen of a sad courtesan. Down and up the old trail went, full of stones that had been turned by hooves. We came to Magome, a staging town. Shops stuttered up beside the steep road, selling straw sandals and wooden kitchen tools. I bought a pair of sandals. At a bookshop I saw a fake Hokusai print with thick lines, bad colour, and blocks that were not aligned. Years before, we had an apprentice we called Dog Hokusai. Apparently he was still at work: his forgeries sold in the country, while my father and I could not get work in Edo.

We passed a wheel with a thick tongue of water turning it. The men pointed: "Snow is melting on the mountaintops." We stopped to eat tofu broiled in brown sugar and noodle soup with mountain vegetables. House-boys from the inns offered prostitutes. Juhachi-ya didn't stop. Priests and pilgrims gathered at crossroads. The Eighteen shouted for them to make way for our wide and implacable beasts.

After this town we would come to the steepest part, the pass.

"Strange Daughter," the carters called, "you can get down from the cart now."

Tachi jumped down too. The sandals were good and my feet flattened out to meet the stones. The men sang and we marked time by hitting the side of the cart. Bearers passed, going the other way. Far away, farmers worked in their fields, which were narrow, snake-like, between ridges. A *sashiba*, a grey eagle, flapped in a tree above my head. It chased a smaller bird and seized it. Up and up and up.

My chest began to heave.

"Nearly at the top," one of the men grunted.

We sat on a stone bench, four men and Ei and a child. A waitress came out of a tiny hut to serve us tea. It was familiar to me, and then I knew. My father had drawn this scene: the delicate waitress, the teashop verandah perched over the edge of the steep cliff, the blue hills far off and green ones nearby, and the road beaten flat as a silk ribbon heading through the trees. He had come before us. We were in his footsteps.

Now the path curved along the edge of a hill. Beside us was empty space.

"Ooooh!" Tachi and I held on to each other.

There was a wall of trees growing far down the hill on one side; the sun pushed through the high branches and scattered rays at our feet. The curve was long and spectacular; I felt as if I were walking around the balcony of a giant theatre. The treetops swayed like heads in a crowd of thousands. Plumes of bamboo leaned and sighed in the wind. What was to come? What was to come? The path sloped a little and then a little more. My sandals slapped and slapped harder as my weight pushed me downhill.

I steadied myself against the cart. This was the world and I had only had reports of it before. I had only mixed its colours before. I saw the fat groom brushing the fatter samurai horse beside the inn; the carpenter dropping his tool in the water as he tried to fix the narrow wooden bridge. I imagined my father sleeping in the pine needles. I saw Hiroshige with his sketch pad, remote and serene, sketching the distant views.

We reached the top of the pass. The road went down from here, in both directions. I listened to the wind. The men untied the oxen. They put their headscarves in the stream and tied them on again.

"Going down is the hard part. Keep out of the way."

They tightened their belts. They got in front of the cart, shoulders pressed to the boards.

The goods slid forward. The bushels strained against their straps and the barrels rumbled on the wood. The load had been heavy to bring up, and now it wanted down in a hurry. The hindquarters of the oxen snapped from side to side. The carters hopped behind the cart, using their weight to pull it backwards so it didn't break its traces and crash into the oxen. When the path curved, the cart veered to one edge or the other. The carters swore and leapt and hung from the covered wagon.

Tachi and I ran behind.

The oxen plodded on, seeming not to notice the mad dance, the loud protests from the wooden wheels, the dragging and hopping of the men to keep the cart in the track. The men stopped and wet their foreheads. They swore and drank water and started again.

We came to the Spirit Trees. This was a famous place. There were two trees here that were inhabited by spirits. One was the vengeful ghost of a woman who was murdered. The other was her husband, who was the guilty party. For all the caravans, it was the place of resting. There was a small inn and an *onsen*, a hot spring.

The sun was slashing horizontally through the bare tree trunks by this time. The carters took off their harnesses, and the oxen were sent to the stable. The Eighteen were known here. The lead carter explained that I was "an item due to Koyama. His daughter, they say." Large wink.

"More like his mother."

The innkeepers exclaimed with delight over Tachi and took her off to the kitchen for food. I heard them singing and laughing. The carters began to drink and the prostitutes arrived, bringing mountain soba with mushrooms. I ate my noodles alone, sucking them up loudly. The innkeeper watched over me. The sun disappeared behind the hills, and the trees were now in darkness.

There was a strange welling in my chest, as if I had been struck on the breastbone. This feeling had come several times since I got my father's letter. I never wept. At home, in the dark studio with my father, tears were like jewels; they glittered, out of place, a luxury from another sort of life. But this huge, black place welcomed them. I wiped my face with my sleeves. I smelled the cool damp of the earth.

Half a dozen carters went to the bath. I half-saw them scrub themselves over hot stones with little cloths. In the velvet darkness they climbed into the water. They lay with their heads back and their feet stretched out in the pool. They let out gusty cries of exhaustion.

"Come and join us, Katsushika Oei," they said.

They knew my painting name?

"You are the daughter of the famous Old Man. Come and join us. We will greet the gods in the middle of the night."

No one was there. Only the murdered woman-spirit in the trees and her murderous lover, now reconciled in petrifaction. And I was old, after all; they were no sexual threat to me, or I to them.

I took off my kimono, so I wore only my underskirt. I walked with a small cloth for cleaning myself to the water's edge. I squatted, a shadow in the darkness. I pulled off my undergarment. I could see only the outline of my legs and my arms, but not the flesh of my body. I could feel the steam coming from the hot water and it beckoned me. The air was cold and intimate on my skin.

There were pine torches by the doors of the inn. But none shone any light here. The carters' dark faces tilted side by side amongst the rocks. I slid in; the water was so hot it felt like ice.

With my hand I brushed something bobbing on the surface, and I almost screamed. I thought it was a male organ, and from the way the men guffawed, they meant me to. But it was a small wooden cup filled with sake floating on the surface of the water.

I downed it and reached for a refill. The men's voices rose into the canopy. I lay my head against the stone rim of the bath. My body bobbed like that wooden sake cup; my body and the cup and the water were the same.

The moon appeared. Everything was silver and had a shadow. The trees were shedding their bark in long strips, and these hung like hair down the long, straight, thin necks. Oh, oh, it was astounding. They were like my father's ghosts. I looked straight up into the nets the treetops spread. The stars winked through steam and leaves, sly and quiet.

This was the world and I was out in it.

"Here is the freedom, Strange Daughter, that you have longed for," the world said to me.

"Thank you," I replied.

The men filled my cup. I became a firefly, lighting in and out of the conversation, there and not there. I smiled into the darkness. My father would not live forever, even though he wanted to, even though he prayed every day that he be allowed to. Why should he be? I did not wish for his death. But I wished for a life that would stretch beyond his. Was that so wrong? I wished for my own life. That night, I saw it winking, almost within reach.

JUHACHI-YA SLEPT ONLY A FEW HOURS and packed up at dawn. A soft rain was soaking the bamboo. Its golden tassels leaned out from secret centres. We moved down through the narrow river valley, reaching a one-street village lit by red lanterns at dusk. A mist hung over Tsumago, caught on the top of the hill. But the sky was lifting: it would clear. I went to a roadside shrine and purified myself. I prayed thankfulness for this beauty. I prayed forgiveness for thinking of my father's death. He would be impatient to put me to work.

When we arrived at last in a dusty cloud at Obuse, Juhachi-ya put me down first and then unloaded the rest of the bundles in front of Takai Kozan's storehouse. The women took Tachi off, making a fuss over her. My father came to greet me. He looked older, bent and wizened. "Oei, Oei," he called, as if I were a long way away.

I took his hands. They were cold.

"Hey, hey, Old Man. How about it?" I said.

"I ya' ya' yaaam g-g-goood," he said. "Bu-bu-but I fell off th' la-aa-aader." It was what I had feared. His palsy was back.

33

OBUSE

I SQUATTED BY THE LITTLE GUTTER of running water. I dished up several cups of it and then rocked back on my heels. The town was on a flat plain with an orchard. White mountain peaks stood up all around—an orange glow came off them as the sun rose. Steam rose from the little stream, and there was a thin edge of white on the grasses. Yet the afternoon would be hot. There was a rumble of wooden barrels from the direction of the sake factory.

Hokusai had perhaps died and gone to heaven and arranged for me to join him. Tachi had been met with kindness and had full days flying kites with other children. We had a little house a short distance from Kozan's studio with this running gutter beside it. He had taken on a big job, painting the ceilings for two carts for O-bon, the Festival of the Dead. He had made a fine design of waves. But his eyes were not sharp, he was too weak, and now he was stumbling with the palsy. Grinding up the pigments was hard work, and he was not used to it.

The waves were choked up in wooden frames.

"Those are different to the waves at Uraga," I said to him. "They will be very difficult to run through," I joked, teasing him. "If you lie down at the edge of the sea, you will be tossed in amongst them."

He grunted. "A-a-angry wa-waves," he admitted. "Crowd of them."

In one of the panels the waves went around in circles. In another they were heading straight up, as if to swallow the viewer.

We named those Masculine Waves. We named Feminine Waves the ones that tended inward. We worked and we laughed together. Or I laughed and he gave his bizarre, twisted barks. I was happy that he recognized two energies, the female and the male. I felt that he was telling me he knew me, deeply, as an artist.

Kozan himself painted the frames. He put angels in them in the Western style.

Sometimes in the evening we visited Kozan in his studio. He played the three-string koto looking out the second-floor window. From here we could see the estate, the neat, narrow passageways between warehouses, the tousled fields, and the road. We could see the pine trees tied up with their triangles of rope so the branches would not bend. If anyone came along that road, we would see them before they saw us.

The room also had a secret door. The door was hidden inside a cabinet and led to a secret staircase to the outside. He could escape unseen, if necessary.

I looked into the faraway mountains, marvelling that I had come through them. Like the glass prisms in Western books, they shattered the light, becoming transparent against the bright slabs of sky.

When it got dark, Kozan lit the small lantern and showed us his books. They were written in Dutch, but there were pictures. Some were of guns—long and short, large and small. For sure we would be punished for seeing these things. I was more interested in the box that made pictures, called a camera. Kozan took pleasure in my amazement.

I had the quiet, those days up in the mountains, to consider myself. I was content in myself. I had no longing. And strangely, men had changed in their attitude towards me. They saw something they liked in my face, my figure. They respected me. There was something tentative, even careful, in their treatment of me. Maybe I had changed. I had aged well. My strong bones gave me the look, now, of a woman who had once been, if not beautiful at least of interest. Little did they know!

Another wealthy patron by the name of Sakai came from Matsumoto. This man's home was here in the mountains, but he had a shop in Edo near the bridge to the Shogun's castle. He had many prints by Hokusai, including all forty-six views of Mt. Fuji. But meeting Hokusai was not the purpose of his visit, I could see. It was a pretext. A certain nervous excitement was in the air, and I knew the men spoke about politics. Sakai was a sympathizer with the forces that wanted to open Japan to the world.

WE FINISHED THE WAVES. I began to make the deep red we needed for our new project, the ceiling of a temple outside of town. We were also writing a manual about colour, which my father wished to have published, perhaps to lay a claim to these techniques in the face of any imitator who might follow.

A shy boy approached. This was Iwajiro, second son of Koyama, the rice merchant and miso-maker, owner of Juhachi-ya, a well-off citizen of the town. He wished to learn painting.

I agreed to teach him, and we met often. One day I went as usual to his house. The young man showed some talent. I corrected his grip and the pressure of his fingers on the brush, and set the number of repetitions he was to make of a bamboo branch. As he worked I looked through the openings in the screens towards the centre of the town.

Two samurai rode in the gates. They dismounted and handed off their horses and, passing very near to where I stood watching, disappeared into Kozan's studio. One was Sakai, the collector from Matsumoto. The other seemed to know his way in the little town.

"Who is that man?" I said to Iwajiro.

He looked up.

"That's Kozan's teacher, Shozan Sakuma."

I was impressed, and frightened. I knew about Shozan Sakuma. He was a learned man, a *rangaku-sha*. But he was dangerous. He had a school in Edo and spoke against the isolationist policies of the *bakufu*. He wanted a state where our spiritual knowledge combined with Western practical knowledge.

They left a lookout who scanned every direction, turning and turning like a windmill. Hours later they emerged, with Kozan, who saw them off, clapping their backs and wearing a pleased and secretive look.

"Old Man," I chided my father when I got home, "you are a sneaky old thing. Here I thought you had a peaceful mountain refuge. Now I discover that this little town is a nest of enemies of the Shogun."

He smirked and kept on drawing his demon-quelling lions.

"You side with the rebels. And you never admit it. You are afraid it will limit you as an artist. I know you."

He only laughed. He had no sense of danger, and he felt no responsibility to tell me when he led me into it. When he was playing around, he made a stamp with the sign meaning "one hundred"—the age he wished to be, but not the highest age he wished ever to be. He hadn't even begun to use that yet.

"Old Man, you think you are so powerful. You think that by saying a thing is true, you can make it become true."

But there were other times when, in the abrupt darkness that came as the sun disappeared behind the mountains, he admitted the day would come when he was gone.

"Chin-Chin, wha' w' you do wh-when the Ol' Man's gone?"

"I'll do just fine. Just as I have been."

He drew little receipts for our payment. He put his face in profile at the top, a cartoon, himself bald and wrinkled with some straight hairs sticking out the back of his head. His ear was a huge upside-down snail. His eye socket was deeply set, his nose straight, and his chin a wobble sinking into his neck.

Underneath he drew me. My face was like a mask. I had a great, wide forehead from which my hair sprang back in waves. I had a dot of paint between my eyebrows; my mouth was a firm, straight line, tending neither up nor down. Strong-jawed woman.

"You ma' a paper li' this e'eryti-me. Ma-mak-ke sure get pay."

He put his stamp on it. "Hokusai, age 88."

The Ganshoin temple was a small, pretty Buddhist temple, which was very old and had been rebuilt a few years before. It sat beside a small pond that was noisy with frogs in the spring. Kozan hired Hokusai to make a Ho-o bird for its ceiling.

The phoenix is an auspicious bird that lives so long that plants begin to grow on its body. We put three kinds of plants in the design. We put leaves of the *goyo no matsu* (the five-needle pine). These looked like scales, or feathers of the bird laid closely one on the next. We also added fine green laurel leaves and then, finally, two big brown leaves of a plantain plant. One of the plantain leaves overlapped the other. This left a space the shape of a large triangle between them. We looked at this space and noticed that it looked like Fuji-san, the symbol of our country.

We drew the pattern in black ink. This ceiling painting was to be enormous, the size of twenty-one tatami mats. Takai Kozan liked our design very much and asked us to mark in the colours.

When it was time to begin, our helpers laid twelve large cypress panels on the floor, four across and three along. We made a copy of our original design in *sumi* ink on the twelve boards. I mixed the paints—first the white layer to cover the whole surface. Then, one board at a time, I applied the reds, yellows, greens, and blues—*beru,* of course and another, very bright. Finally we decorated the Ho-o bird with small bits of gold leaf.

The bird was fierce and tightly coiled, his beak up against his back, his eye powerful and black. He seemed to stare at me no matter where I stood in the room. We called it *Ho-o Staring in Eight Directions.* My father rested a great deal; he directed me, pointing this way and that, and pretending to be scandalized if I took a shortcut, scolding me lavishly, occasionally offering a single word of praise. At times he knew he was growing weaker, and accepted it. Some days he was confused and could not find his outer garment, or was unable to get up off his knees. Then my heart broke.

On other days he turned on me with a face of stone. "Now what are you arranging for me?" he would say in a poisonous voice. He made me so angry I said to myself, Fine! Let him grow old and foolish. It is time he went! This is too difficult.

Always after one of his angers he would laugh like a baby, his shoulders going up and down, his face crinkling up between mouth and eyes, and I melted and feared the day he must go.

THE HEAT BROKE WITH A WILD STORM that heralded autumn.

It started with a column of grey cloud in the distance. I was walking by the river when the wind hit my back, pushing me home. In our little house I found my father asleep. The wind played around the outside, rustling and pushing, banging a loose gate, making the branches of the pine sway. I placed our painting goods under the mattress. I feared that the roof would fly off.

The bombardment began, a chorus of clattering. I couldn't imagine what was hitting us. It sounded like little wooden balls. They struck the metal pots outside the door; they struck the roof and made a different, more deadly sound. And now they struck the rocks, which began to chime. Were these bullets from the Western muskets?

I looked out and saw round white ice balls falling and leaping back up from the ground, demented. I began to moan. Hokusai pushed himself erect and rubbed his fists in his eyes, and began to chant his sutras loudly in time with the battering.

It was like a rain of arrows. I covered Hokusai's old bald head with my arm; I was hiding, but I wanted to see. The noise was astonishing, high pings of metal, low pings of wood and straw and lead tile, hard cracks of rock being struck. My father cited punishment from the gods and thought they were trying to kill him.

"Th-thun-thun-der gods are c-c-coming for me!" he cried. A long time ago he was walking along the Tokaido and lightning hit him, throwing him into a rice paddy. I knew this story. For years he had boasted: heavenly fire had touched him once and left him shaken but alive, and now he was safe from it. "They cannot kill me," he had said. He was Raijin the Thunder God.

But now the story changed.

"I was too proud! The Thunder Gods are coming to punish me!" He was frantic with fear, and he made Tachi cry. She hid under the desk while the storm went on and the Old Man gibbered on the futon.

In the face of this I had no option but to be practical. "It's weather, Old Man," I said. "Only weather. It came from the mountains," I kept saying. "It will go back there." But I too believed in omens. I was afraid that the politics of our host angered the gods.

At last the town was completely still. I looked through the paper windows, some of which were torn, and saw piles of the dangerous white shot everywhere. "Stay inside! Come away from the window!" Tachi cried.

More thunder rolled in. The lightning followed—forked, ragged shoots that crossed the open sky in one flash and were gone. The rain began after that. "This is too much!" We held each other under the onslaught.

Finally the storm passed. Hokusai fell asleep, but I stayed awake. Later the storm returned. This time there were no strings of white fire. After the rage and growl of thunder, the sky itself went an all-over daylight white, throwing all the trees and buildings and even their tile roofs into instant visibility, as if day had flashed on and then gone out. The whole sky was white now, and then black, and then white again. Shadows burst up and then dissolved.

I paced our little hut. I looked out the paper windows. I wished I could paint what I saw: the village frozen, the Kozan house, the houses of the elders, the simple farmers; every one was silent. Where had the people gone? How had this storm disconnected the threads of our living together so no one even looked out?

I waited for the flashes that made shadows appear and gave trees and houses a dark presence in precise outline. Each time, I tried to remember how it had looked before the light went out. The storm went on all night, and rain fell, melting the hail. In the morning I was exhausted from lack of sleep, and so were all the people in the town.

In the morning my father was unable to get out of bed.

I knew it was time. We would have to go back to Edo.

34

Exorcisms

WHEN JUHACHI-YA DEPOSITED US in Edo I put my father into our tenement. If he did not lie down or stay propped against a wall, he fell down. The *yoi-yoi* palsy or the touch of the Thunder God, something was getting him in small, stealthy attacks.

We went back to the daily exorcisms. He would concentrate fiercely, make a lion image in only sixty seconds, then struggle to his feet and go straight out into the alley. He crumpled the page and threw it down on the ground. Sometimes his hand was so shaky that the brush picture was illegible.

People would walk by and pick up these pieces of paper, uncrumple them, and knowing the great master lived within, hurry away gloating over their prize. After seeing this, I began myself to slip outside when Hokusai's eyes were closed, pick up the balls of paper, smooth them, and hide them.

NOW BEGAN THE MOST DIFFICULT TIME. We moved three times in that next-to-the-last year, from Honjo across the Sumida back to Asakusa, first to Tamachi, then to Umamichi, and finally to a tenement on the grounds of the Henjoin temple. There we remained, finished with running. We had accepted our fate. We were strangely calm.

The kabuki theatres near Nihonbashi had burned, and they were moved to the Asakusa temple, right near us. We were on the margin of respectability, surrounded by entertainment and by water—canals, the river, and marshes.

In the city it was said that Hokusai was able to work without glasses and walk long distances every day with back unbent. But that was a dream. In darker moments we faced the truth. He could not leave home again. We declined an invitation to return to Obuse. He lay or knelt in our tenement, and I sat beside him. I was nearly fifty years old. "Lucky me, I still have a father to make me feel young," I joked, although in truth he was killing me.

I saved my thoughts for Eisen, again my friend. He had given up printmaking with Hiroshige and now wrote novels. The occupation suited him. As he grew older he took younger and younger women as his bedmates. I saw him walking with one of them. He shooed her: "Go! Be gone! Here is a real woman I want to see!"

We gave each other small, broken hugs and parted again—the prostitute, I could see, darting out to join him from some shopfront where she had waited. It didn't matter. I had the sense that I had disappointed Eisen by not becoming famous enough. Perhaps I had disappointed Sanba too, wherever he was: "You have an important life to lead!" he had said.

Was this my important life? Or was there another that had eluded me? My days had all come down to this: ghost brush, muse, and nursemaid to the great man. As he faded, my love grew stronger. If I ever wondered what it was for, this endless labour, this ill-paid work, I had only to look at his beloved face and know I would do anything to disguise the helplessness there. My work did not matter. To quote Sadanobu, "There have been books since times long past and no more are necessary!"

I saw it now. Making pictures resulted in nothing more than making pictures. There was no reward. If we were lucky the earnings helped us survive as long as the work demanded. There was no virtue in it. Only a few knew my work, but they respected me. A soft life, fame? Grand ambitions had never been mine. They had been my father's, but he was wiser now, and thought only of improving his art.

But then work, strangely, came my way.

I illustrated a tea dictionary that was much admired. Then came the *Illustrated Manual for Women*.

I was happy with my new commission. I made elaborate small figures in the intense colours that were my trademark. I put my heart into it. It was better, more concentrated, more original than it needed to be.

For the opening spread I created a crowd, an array of dark-clad women. One was a courtesan with fourteen hairpins and a hemline recognizable as the Hokusai/Oei look of controlled frenzy, kicked up on the side so she could do her figure-eight step. One was a nun with a black hood over her hair. One had a toothpick held coquettishly to her mouth and two black dots on her forehead. Another was a woman from the countryside in plain cotton; another wore a kerchief, while one had very long, black straight hair tied in one bunch, coming together below her waist.

I showed all the tasks and ways of women in my town. Bridal processions, the debut of a courtesan. ("What's the difference?" Eisen laughed.) Table settings. (How would I know?) The right way to apply makeup.

Outside, autumn deepened. In rare moments a shaft of sun would strike the earth, exposing the rubble of our lives. The treetops were frail crowns of black against the sky, but their lower halves held on to browning leaves. They seemed to be captive, while their leaves skipped away, free at last.

I got up early, went out to get tea, and came back. I worked until twilight, then dried my brush and saw my father off to sleep. Small white flakes whirled in the air, landing on my cheek and turning to water. I worked quietly beside Hokusai's mattress on the *Illustrated Manual for Women*.

Disciples dropped in. Katsushika Isai had taken over our work in Obuse, having travelled there with Juhachi-ya. That made me jealous. The young man Tsuyuki Kosho had also been to Obuse and had dealings with Koyama the rice merchant. Isai said that my father had given him his seal of Hyaku, one hundred years. It made me uneasy. I did not believe this was so.

I drew a rectangular tray. I put nine round bowls on it, in three rows of three. I made another rectangular tray: six round bowls on that one, in one row of three, with one on its own, and a row of two. Perhaps these represented different meals. I drew a large bowl with a fish lying on it, the head and tail drooping off the edge, and a tray with a hen, small thing, beak off one side and tail feathers off the other.

This was the way not to do it: clumsy housekeeping, a classic sketch that should have the X drawn through it.

Here was a woman serving from a bowl of noodles. Would she eat those noodles herself? No. She was holding them high over the bowl with her chopsticks up around her eyes, the bowl at her chest, a baby on her lap. The people sat at small, individual black tables with a tray top on which were plates of fish and bowls of rice waiting to be served.

The seal of Hyaku had been for the future. The future was in my hands. I would speak to my father about it. But my father was difficult to make sense of these days.

I made pictures of shells and spiny creatures, a picture of a schoolroom—children working on figures on the floor, learning to write the characters. A large standing abacus to one side. And in front, with his back turned, a sleeping bald man—ah, the teacher!

I drew the steps in making *sakura* cookies: four women picking cherry blossoms off a branch and saving them on a cloth. Another leaning with both hands on a big rolling pin that has a lump of dough wrapped around it. It was a beautiful scene, more beautiful than such a handbook deserved.

In small frames, usually at the top of the page, I made icons for trees, mountains, ferns, scrolls. Lanterns, butterflies, hills, holly, birds in flight, a flute, wooden clappers, a kitten with a ball of wool, pine needles. Grasses, tree trunks, a thatched pavilion.

Along the frame I drew crowds in little shops, bolts of fabric piled one on top of another, men displaying the fabrics, women choosing. Diagrams: how to fold paper, the latest way to tie the obi. I had never had the slightest interest in these feminine accomplishments. But I was good at "small," and they were fun to draw.

I drew a temple. I put candlesticks on tall stands and, along the roof beams, bits of folded paper, hanging. Women with long hair, a thick wall of it hanging past their knees, tied only once, at the waist, in the nobles' style. Another sunk into a deep bow with her fan to her face. The deities were at the top of the frame, floating in clouds.

I drew the game of incense identification. A woman poured a bit of scent on each of several handkerchiefs. She came before her lover, who was relaxing on his futon, knelt with the handkerchiefs and wafted them past his face. She let her sleeve fall open so part of the fragrance he caught was her own. Lily or rose petals or pine boughs in the snow or almond blossom.

I thought of other scents: behind the brothels in the Hour of the Snake; in mid-morning the stench of vomit and night waste; the remains of a feast fought over by dogs.

Or the smell of age, the smell of my father wasting on his cot. The smell of his clothing, the smell of our room, of cat piss and confinement, of stale food wrappers.

Gusts of wind knocked the dry leaves off their perches and sent them protesting against the thin wooden walls and screens. I felt closed and heavy and motionless, like a stone in the bottom of a river.

Yet I found a kind of peace illustrating that manual. Nostalgia filled me and rose like a net billowing overhead. Women's lives: wonderful and terrible. And mostly strange to me. Yes, at one time I had a husband. I remembered the dull workings of his brush. "You're beautiful," he had said to me once. "You could just relax for a while and be beautiful."

My father thought me ugly. But I wondered why I had taken his opinion and not the opinion of my husband, who may have been a fool but loved me.

Other women had children: I was barren. Unlike Shino, who had earned her barrenness in the Yoshiwara, I came to this state naturally. The gods had seen to that, and I was grateful.

I drew the life cycle of an egg. First a sphere with two circles within, then an egg shape, then that egg shape with separations as head and two legs began to sever their shapes from the egg. Then there were five: head, arm, arm, leg, leg. A curious leaf-shaped or star-shaped figure. Then this figure stretched out more, head, arm arm, leg leg, and trunk. On the next page I would at last show that it was a boy with a full head of black hair, standing on two legs.

Babies became children. Those could be nice. Or not. I had painted them for the Dutch doctor. I had Tachi; she came to me. Mothers, sisters, another joy of women. I had no one left. Even Shino was gone. I drew a mendicant nun with her bowl.

In one final sketch nearly at the end of the book, I had some fun.

Two gardeners, one leaning over his shovel, the other pouring water from his wooden ladle out of his wooden bucket, were planting cherry trees on Nakanocho Boulevard. Their legs were knotted and their buttocks bare with a strip of cloth between them. A young woman leaned out a window-sill above, flirting. Not recommended behaviour.

I completed the commission. The book was printed in large quantities. It was a success. Everyone spoke of its beauty. My name was on it, and my signature. I was almost famous, and we ate well for a time.

35

NEW YEAR'S, 1849

SOMETIMES THE OLD MAN was almost as he had been.

Hokusai got up off his mattress, his blanket in his fist, his eyes big with wonder at yet another day given.

"Greetings on the last day of the year," he said. "Where is my *shochu*?"

"You know where your *shochu* is."

Not wanting to stop my brush, I jerked my hand towards the jug. He gave me a sidelong, low-lidded look, sticking out his scrawny neck like a turtle, and went to get the ladle. Dipped it, filled it, drank two ladles one after another. His eyes watered, and I could practically see fumes coming up his throat.

"Is there breakfast?"

"I went to the stall and got a pork dumpling," I said, somewhat grudgingly. "He boiled one just for me."

"What is that you are doing?"

"Twilight at the green houses," I said. "The women on display in the latticed verandah. The men looking in."

He looked at my paper. "Affecting."

He burped up more fumes, went to the door, slid it open, and looked out. With his bandy legs apart he held on to a buttock cheek with each hand and squeezed. He forced air between his buttocks so that it rattled. And he laughed.

"Perhaps in this new year, I may die."

This dying talk was an idle threat. Hokusai did not wish to die.

"Death will cut into your drawing time. How is your leg?" I said. He was rubbing the side of his hip. When I asked, he stopped.

"I think I will go up to the mountains again and see Kozan."

"There you go, making promises you won't keep," I joked. But as I said it, I felt sad. He would never go there again. He attributed his weakness to the storm in Obuse, the return of the lightning. "I was paralyzed," he often said. But this time he could not walk it off. His Chinese herbs and exorcisms, in the form of paintings, had no more effect.

"I tell you, King Emma of Hades has built himself a little house in the country. He wants me to do a little scroll painting for him. Remember, Daughter, when they carry me away, to put my drawing materials with me!"

He looked at me so sharply I knew he was serious.

"I won't."

The fierceness left his face and he was immediately joking again.

"I expect I'll have a nice little place on Inferno Road. Happy to see you if you pass that way!"

"You may go to hell, Old Man," I said, "but you won't stay there long. You've never stayed anywhere long."

He came back in and folded himself on the tatami beside me. I braced for the inevitable end-of-year discussion.

"Dear Father, today is the day we dread. The day we try not to imagine. But it has come. It's time to pay our bills."

"Why do you bother me about money, Ei?" He gave me a look that said it was all beneath him.

He shifted over onto his knees and elbows. His bottom end was now up in the air. He picked up a brush and pulled a roll of rice paper out from under my stack. I noted with irritation that he was now painting while my brush was idle.

"Unfortunately, those who must pay us are not so numerous."

"That is likely true," he mused, almost in spite of himself.

"Perhaps the publisher has money for me from the sales of the *Illustrated Manual for Women*."

"When did I make that?"

"You didn't. I made it."

"Ah, yes. I recall it. The one that shows the correct way for women to behave on every occasion in life. As if you would know!" He cackled into his chest.

"I didn't say I made the rules. I only drew the pictures," I said testily.

"Ah."

All of a sudden his brush, which had been poised—perfectly, ominously poised—woke up and darted back and forth, circling, spitting, on the surface of his paper in a burst of furious energy.

"And of daily exorcisms? What are we owed for them?"

"But you threw them in the street, don't you remember?"

THINGS WORSENED IN OUR COUNTRY. Foreigners were circling without, and within the battle between Western-leaning samurai and those who wished to keep us closed accelerated. One of the porters from Juhachi-ya came to our home. He bowed to the floor in the doorway. I had become careless of my appearance; I must have appeared mad. My father's battle to live or to die had left signs of scuffle in me.

"He speaks only rarely," I said. I didn't want other people to hear how badly he slurred and stuttered.

"It's you I've come to see. We're going back to the mountains. The business is bankrupt. This is our last trip. We will take you if you wish. The gods are against us. Edo will burn again, burn to the ground. There will be robbings and killings. It will not be safe, miss."

I rolled up eighty-six sketches that I had rescued and hidden after Hokusai threw them out. I had to be secretive because it made him angry. He believed it to be part of the efficacy of the charm to throw them away. Now he believed them sold.

"Take these to Kozan. It is all we have."

The porter left.

Silence. The brush again: furious, jabbing, delicate, twisting, splayed—then still. I hated to be cross with him. I hated to remind him he was not powerful anymore. We love the arrogance of the strong and hold it dear no matter how it crushes us. I could not bear to see him humbled; I would rather humble myself. I would rather live under his mad regime.

"No more for the festival cart ceilings, then?"

"Last year."

He lifted a bony buttock cheek and farted again.

"There was the St. Nichiren . . ." he began.

He was right. There was one. He had painted it for the temple. And a strange painting it was. St. Nichiren sat on a cloud and beneath him in rows cringed a hundred balding believers. A dragon's scaly tail circled under the saint, but he was too busy reading his scroll to notice.

I was excited for a minute. "You're right. We never saw any pay for that picture."

"I could not ask. The temple."

"No."

"But someone may come."

"Yes, someone may be sent. Is there any more?"

"Did you sell dolls?"

"When I did I took the money and we spent it on food."

And that was it: our tally.

"What do we owe?"

"The largest amount to the temple for the rent of this room. The second-largest to the vendor for our food. The third—"

"The third to the drinking house," he said. "I never go there. You do."

"I buy your *shochu*."

"And are we ahead or behind?"

"We are behind, Father. You must know that."

He brightened. "We could move on."

I knew he would say that. I had tried at the time of the last move to make a list of our living places, got to the number ninety-three, and stopped.

"What is this? One hundred views of Edo?" I asked. "One hundred filthy lodgings? No, Old Man, I won't move again. It is enough. Three times last year! The paintings to pack. Our bedding. The pot and teacups."

"I don't know why we have that pot. We never use it."

True again. I fell silent.

"We like our rented houses, do we not?"

"I don't."

He looked mortally wounded.

"You don't? But it is our way."

"I'm tired of our way."

"Then you would stay behind?"

Was he really suggesting he move off by himself? "No, Old Man, of course I wouldn't."

"Then good. Let's go."

It was an obsession with him. Our houses, like so many sketches for a final work, like so many lotus-leaf food wrappers, used and discarded. Such restlessness! Running from the censors. Running from Monster Boy. Running from the *bakufu* because we were labelled as lovers of the West. Running from time and age. No more running for me.

I pretended to be lazy. I yawned. "It all seems like such a bother. Why not just stay here?"

A picture was beginning to grow under his brush. He was painting the tiger again. All last year he painted tigers, in rain, in snow. Their paws were soft, their bodies powerful but muted somehow, turned upon themselves, as if they did not know which way to go with all that energy. But his hand shook and his brush fell to the mat.

"If we just owned our little house," I began. I don't know why I bothered.

"Chin-Chin!" he cried in frustration. "There are none but rented houses in this world. Why should we try to keep one? Our true home is north, at the North Star. If we kept a home on earth, we would only have to give it back. We rent the house of this body, do we not?"

This was Hokusai in his pious mood.

"If we rent our bodies," I grumbled, "I have a complaint for the one who gave the lease on this one."

He laughed. This was the type of joke I was supposed to make, and he was supposed to laugh at it. Yet I really had no complaints of my body. I patted my stomach: rounded. My legs: strong and wiry. I did not sicken. I did not tire. I painted all day and caroused in the teahouses until the small hours of the morning.

"I agree that any home we have on earth is temporary."

He nodded approvingly.

"But that is not a reason for us to make it more so."

My father subsided—and this sent a tiny splinter into the wall of my chest. He cocked his head, half-listening, now trying to pick up his brush again. His tiger was prowling in the most wonderful shape, head to the right, tail swooping from right to left, mottled torso forming a diagonal mound between.

"You do it," he said, reaching out towards me with his brush.

The tiger got a white yap in perfect profile and an open mouth. Hokusai eyed it and jerked his finger. To the brush, then the ink pot, then the centre of its face. I added a black dot for the tiger's nose.

I had never seen a tiger. We had no tigers in Japan. The creature was one of myth to us. But I knew cats. This tiger was like one of the cats that had followed me since I was a little girl. I made the tiger pace, as a cat would, switching his tail dangerously, roaring in silent, stilled anger as the rain poured on him and softened every hair on his body so it appeared to be velvet.

Hokusai sat up and slurped his tea. His lips were sharp and stretched over the edge of the cup. Such old lips, lined and dry. They could live forever.

"Today," I said, "instead of moving to a new set of rooms, we will clean these ones."

"Huh," he said. "You will. I have the palsy."

My father grinned, his toothless, wrinkled face lighting with some kind of gladness: he was giving me what I wanted. He swiped his fist out towards me and took the brush from my hand. Conversation closed.

It was my turn to resist. "I don't know how to sweep."

"I'll show you," said Hokusai.

"Will you? Have you known all this time? You could have taught me."

"That was for your mother to do."

"She tried. In the same way she tried to teach me to sew."

We laughed over that one.

He took a piece of the paper that had wrapped the rice balls I bought for last night's dinner, dipped his brush in my ink, and began.

First he drew hands on the broomstick. He had never been any good with fingers, and I couldn't help noticing the thumb was inside out. Then he made a quick set of footsteps, like the instructions for the latest dance. First the feet, then the whole body. A figure appeared with a few strokes. The figure was me, short and spry, knobby of knee and elbow. I turned this way and that, the broom ahead of me, the broom flying, circling, possessed. The dust flew out of invisible corners.

"This is not sweeping," I protested. "This is drawing."

"Ah," said Hokusai, eyes twinkling in the old way, "always the confusion."

And just by the way, he had done a better—funnier, more lively—illustration of a woman's activities than I could do. And just by the way, since the moment he yawned his first words, I had not made a single brush stroke on a work of my own. I had only finished his tiger.

There is room for only one brush in a household.

Admittedly, it was late in life for me to discover this.

And then Hokusai doubled over, softly, because his body had almost no weight to it now—it was all light and fire—and fell to the mat. His eyes closed and he was breathing heavily.

"Hokusai?"

He did not answer, but a small smile played on his lips.

"Are you playing a game?"

He did not answer.

I looked at his wiry, curled body on the mat and chose to think that he was resting. I sat beside him, and time passed. Now the little argument we had about moving on seemed remote. It had become impossible, without our noticing. Here was an old man gasping on the floor.

I rose, resolved to do what every housewife in Japan did on the last day of the old year—sweep the place clean.

But we didn't have a broom.

I went out to the unagi seller who lived next door and borrowed one.

I followed the instructions. One hand over the other on the broom handle. One foot ahead of the other. Reach the arms forward. Pull back and scoop under. Flip up the grass ends of the broom to push the dirt away. Do this around in a circle, collecting the dirt in one place. And then—

Sweep, sweep, sweep. I was raising a storm. The dust was whirling around. It was in the air, creating a lovely haze in the daylight that streamed through our little door. But soon it would fall. Where did dust go? He would be dust. And I would be dust, one day.

His gums parted. He grunted, wanting *shochu*. I held it for him.

"I came into the world with nothing and I will leave it with nothing," he said.

I had heard that before. But I did not like to hear any more about him leaving.

Two of the disciples made an appearance. They greeted my father, who struggled to sit up.

"Is the unagi grilled yet? Go get me some, Chin-Chin. I am hungry."

"I'm going."

The old eat like horses.

36

FRIENDS

WHUMP, WHUMP, WHUMP. The unagi woman was pounding the eels with her wooden mallet. I hurried past. It was icy in the temple square. I tucked my hands around my ribs, into the sleeves of padded coat. Tomorrow would be the beginning of warmer days; surely it had to be. Moving across the windswept open centre, beyond the protection of the trees, a man was bent low behind his barrow, using it to shield himself. He stopped and stepped out from behind his load, bowing.

"How is your honoured father?"

It was the kindness that unnerved me. My voice came out a wail. "Hokusai is on his mat. Hokusai will rise no more," I said.

I was immediately sorry, as the man looked terrified. He muttered his apologies and went behind his barrow.

I bought some bonito and then begged two very special eggs to tempt the Old Man's appetite. The fishmonger wrapped it for me.

"He is well today?"

He asked this every day, and he knew the answer. But I had had enough of scaring the neighbourhood.

"He is well, thank you. Telling me stories. Already has his brushes out."

Eating took all his energy. Watching him I lost my appetite. I took my usual seat beside him and picked up my brush.

I drank too much sake last night. I smoked my pipe too much last night. I stayed up too late. I cried to think of the new year and how we would live. Now my mouth tasted like ashes and my head was tight as the skin of a *taiko* drum. Meanwhile, the Old Man industriously crawled on the tatami with his bottom up in the air.

I went back to my painting of courtesans and lattice. Over the women's heads I wanted stars like the ones I had seen in the countryside. Little sparks, like moth holes eaten in the fabric of a dense wrapper. I wanted light to come through them, light from another place. I didn't know how to make stars on a night sky. I was trying when a scratch came at the door. Another New Year's visitor.

I slid the screen away. She had a white cloth wound over her forehead and tight under her chin. It fell over her shoulders and her chest. Under it she wore an ordinary short coat, a padded skirt, white *tabi,* and thonged sandals. But nothing could disguise her, not the nun's hood or the wet mud of the roads. She carried a bamboo flute.

She bowed low. I bowed lower. Hokusai remained on his elbows on the floor and did not look up. I was filled with emotion. I signalled the nun to enter the room.

"Hey, hey, Old Man," I said. "You have a guest."

He looked up. He could not stand.

Shino bowed low and congratulated him on his health, his home, his good fortune.

I noticed suddenly that it was too cold in our room, and that it was bare. We had nothing—only the orange crate nailed to the wall with the statue of Nichiren in it—and my hair was unkempt.

I stirred the fire. I called the neighbouring boy to bring tea.

"We can only burn the charcoal dust because anything else makes him cough," I said.

Hokusai squatted, never letting go of his brush, moving it. He was silent.

"I was in my fifteenth year," said Shino, "when I was sent to the teahouse to get a special tea for Fumi of the Corner Tamaya. When I was there I met an artist."

"I was in my forty-fifth year," said Hokusai. "I carried the child Chin-Chin on my shoulder. My new wife had given her to me. I was selling my pictures in the Yoshiwara."

"I had been sentenced to the Yoshiwara to serve as a courtesan for raising my hand to my husband. In fact, I had sliced his ear. I had been a lady-in-waiting at the Shogun's castle."

"I never knew that!"

"There was a time I was to be a polisher of mirrors in the Shogun's court," he said.

He looked up, into her face. He made circles with his hand in front of his chest, then he stopped and peered into the circle that he had just rubbed clear, and he frowned and began to rub it again. He spit and rubbed, peered and rubbed, and pursed his lips.

"In the Shogun's palace there were many idle women. The young ones were beautiful. And lonely." He grabbed at his crotch and pulled and laughed. "There were many secret places in the Shogun's court—rooms and rooms, corridors going on forever. You could slide into a cabinet."

Shino was quiet, getting used to the way he was.

"Lots of laughing going on in the Shogun's court," he said, again gesturing obscenely.

"I know it," I said.

"You don't know it," he accused. "What do you know about men? You are Oei of the strong jaw, who does not like men."

"How can you say I don't like men? I devote myself to you."

He gave his gummy grin. We were trapped in our madness and showing it to our guest.

"Shino has come to see us," I said.

"I am pleased."

But his mind, on seeing her, had begun to speed backwards. "It was discourteous of me to turn down Nakajima after he adopted me," said Hokusai.

"Why did you do it, then?" I asked.

"I didn't want to polish mirrors." He looked at me as if I were stupid. "Never again would I be responsible for the cleanliness of a thing, an object, or a place. Never again have to turn my back on people because they were powerful. So I got freedom." He laughed. "Freedom to look, without hiding my face."

We were silent.

"But the Shogun's ladies, they were good. They bought the *shunga*. Without them we would have lost it all. Everything killed off by the censors." He looked at Shino and came back to today. "Ei is my sun, and my moon. And you are Shino, my star."

I left them together and went out to the *ageya*.

I passed the kitchen and, greeting the owner, left my outer jacket and went to the "fishing net room," where, as usual, men sat at the low tables smoking and roaring with drink. I slid to a seat against the wall.

"There she is, the most famous woman artist in Edo. Of course, the field is not large," came the voice. "How many women artists can there be?"

Hiroshige moved sideways to make room for me.

"As many as can be spared from the beds of the men of Edo," I replied. "Beds where most of them toil in obscurity."

He gave me a pained smile. He hated anyone to best him, even with a line.

"There are many women, you are right. But only Oei was chosen for the *Illustrated Manual*. I wonder why?"

"Could it be because of her parentage?"

The men's foreheads gleamed in the lamplight, their eyes shone. But their mouths were lost in the dark. I drew smoke into my chest.

"No, it cannot. And anyway, who cares about old Hokusai? He has lived long, but he is no source of inspiration today."

Hiroshige was my senior but only by a few years. Now he fancied himself the king of *ukiyo-e*, the famous printmaker of famous places. Of course, he was only copying what my father had done fifteen years before.

"Oei was chosen as a novelty: a woman to do the drawings, that's a good idea," he continued. "And it worked. But it can't be repeated."

"Yet I would welcome the chance to try," I said.

"It is a beautiful book. Oei-san did a good job," came another voice. Eisen. Always my defender.

I watched the samisen player, her white and downcast face intent on the strings. The sad words from a very old song.

> *Gallantry and love affairs*
> *Are only while we live.*
> *We will die at last, will die.*
> *Come let us drink our fill, carouse,*
> *We know no tomorrow.*

I made my way out to the wooden walk above the sunken garden. A giant metal lamp, saved from the fire, cast its light down into the gnarled tree roots. A cat sprang up and brushed my legs; I picked it up and stroked it. Raindrops, half frozen, glittered on the ends of the pine needles. Fallen needles gave a copper sheen to the earth. Some were carried in the trickle of water that snaked between the great bulging roots.

A movement disturbed the dark at the far side. Two figures parted, men in bulky costumes. Lovers? Or samurai conspirators? One and the same, these days. Both were doomed.

I recognized one. It was Sakuma, Kozan's teacher from Obuse. The conspirators had such bold plots: they would break the Tokugawa. More and more one heard of Western ships touching down on the eastern shores of Japan, of their sails trembling beyond the reach of our guns. Von Siebold had told me, twenty years before, that our system could not hold back time. But I had lived so long this way, it was hard to imagine it could ever end.

A *taiko* drummer burst laughing out of the *ageya* hall onto the walkway. He had removed his shirt in the heat inside. His skin shone, rich and bronze. The party followed him outside.

"Give us a verse, Oei!"

The men pulled me back inside. "I will," I said. "I will."

"Will it be lewd?"

"For lewd, you won't beat the Old Man."

In front of me appeared a small water dish, rice paper, some black ink. I pulled a brush from my folder of brushes inside my kimono.

"Try this," said Eisen. He showed me a strange device. It had the hairs of a brush. But it had a thicker stem, not the usual lacquered wood. It had a hole and a tube you squeezed. He showed me how to fill it with ink.

"I got it from Hiroshige. He invented it so he could sketch on the road."

Two boys dressed up as girls got up to do a song. It was very sweet. One played a little tinkling flute while the other minced.

> You are divine.
> You are perfect for marriage.
> You have class.
> I have only one thing to ask.
> Do you take it in the ass?

Their faces were all angles, the lines of nose and eyes like warriors'. My fingers itched to draw them. But who would buy a drawing of these faces?

Eisen and I took a rickshaw to the Ryogoku Bridge to see the New Year's fireworks. Bundled onlookers filled the long arc of the bridge, which stood on its many thick wooden legs high over the wintry Sumida. The surface of the river was placid and boats large and small were anchored, waiting for the show. We stood at the high point—the boat with the fireworks discharger was beneath us. At the signal balls of gold and red flew high over our heads, curved, and began to fall, shedding coloured fire.

Eisen brought his drinking flask up to his mouth. "I loved you once," he said. "But you were spoken for." The river flowed silently in the darkness, a black lacquer base for the flowers of light and fire that plumed above. Who had spoken for me? Hokusai, of course. My father.

"My father says he will not die. But death is approaching. And so we wait and pretend it isn't."

"It is the pretense that exhausts you," said my good friend.

I looked farther over the railing into the black. "You're insane!" my father shouted at me. But he was the crazy one. How could I say this without betrayal?

"He is not himself," I could say. "The Old Man is not available." That would be polite. Eisen was my old friend. Yet there would be no confiding. I tried it this way: "The repose of old age, he doesn't experience. He forgets. He insists. He changes his mind. He tries to run. He cannot walk. I obey his every word; I don't expect him to be wrong. He is mad. So I am mad too."

More fireworks arced over our heads, bursting with the accompaniment of the roars of the crowd. Below, on the moving water, the boats rocked in their straight lines as people stood to watch.

"He is angry because he is dying. And you are not."

It began to snow, the flakes spiralling down from a great height, past our faces, falling to the water. I patted my friend's arm, grateful for his presence.

We said goodnight. I would walk and walk as the night gave way to the dawn. At first the snow melted away into blackness when it hit the road. But it kept falling. When I reached the temple at Asakusa, snow was catching on the branches of the pines and there was glittering ice underfoot.

37

Un-daughter Me

BUT IT WAS NOT MY FATHER who died first. It was Eisen.

So he too was gone, my great friend.

The year did not improve.

My father became more frail, and more insistent. He lay all day on the thin mattress we had unrolled on the tatami mats and now never rolled up.

One day was worse than the others.

I called the boy to get the doctor. Shino had given me money, which I had hidden from Hokusai so he would not spend it on sweets or throw it at a vendor who came to collect. The doctor came.

"There is nothing to be done," he said. "It is old age. It cannot be escaped."

Later Hokusai woke up. He began to beg. He could do so much, if the gods would only give him ten more years. He could become a great artist. He begged for ten, then eight, then, wheedling, even one. One more year, and he would become great.

It broke my heart to hear. He could get everything he ever wanted from me, but the gods were not at his beck and call. Immortality was not to be granted, not in this case.

I sat beside him and listened to him bargaining with the gods.

"If I can't go on as Hokusai, I agree to become an elephant or a blind man, a turtle or a fox."

"A fox is good." I said this to ease him, but he was angry. He turned on me.

"Hereafter my failures will all belong to you, Ei. And your success will belong to me."

What could he mean? But I knew. That his bad works would be understood to have been from my brush, and my best would be assumed to be his. And it was probably true. I dared a sardonic laugh while I admitted as much. That set him off.

"In my next life there is one thing I will not be: a father. This link of me to you will not survive death. This tie will die. I will be free of you!"

He wounded me. "Die, then!" I said. "I shall have no father. Die and thereby un-father me," I sobbed.

"I shall, and un-daughter myself."

We were silent for a few minutes. Then he thought better of this plan and tried to win me back.

"But what am I without Ei, my daughter? She brings my tea. She knows my stories. Every picture I draw is carved not in wood but in her mind. She came from me . . ." But he couldn't stay on this positive line. "From all the wasteful seed. The sons and daughters. Of all of them, why this one?" he raged. "This aberration, this woman-not-woman."

I hid my face so he could not see my grief. He spoke to his god.

"Of all my deeds, the one to engender *her* outlives me."

Eisen's words helped me. My father was angry that I would live, to paint, while he would not. I steeled myself against him.

But then, he would weep. "I ask forgiveness. I regret what I have done. My greatness took away hers."

He went silent and I thought he was asleep. But not.

"Ei," he said, "you have time. When you are un-fathered, break loose and go on your own path."

"What is my path?" I said. "How will I know it?" In not letting me sign my name he wrote me out of history, which he liked to keep for himself.

I had sworn to Eisen: "He will take me to the grave with him. He makes me old before my time." Is the grave my path? No, it will not be.

"Do it. Go ahead. Die and un-daughter me, then." I whispered that. But what would I be? What would the world be without my father?

The disciples came to watch over him, dry-eyed. They bowed, and waited, and watched the breath rise and fall in his chest. Then one by one they left. I saw the ones whose veiled eyes confirmed that they disliked the fact that his greatest disciple and his closest relative were one and the same, and a woman.

"Chin-Chin! Come to me. Write it down!"

He had composed his *jisei*, his farewell verse.

Though doubtless only as a ghost
Yet evenings sprightly will I tread
The summer moor.

In Obuse he had worked on this simple verse too. There, it had another line to it, which now he forgot. It was:

And frequent visits to Japan of foreign ships.

A strange line, and one that ruined the poem, but I knew why it was there. It was the release he waited for. Now he knew he would not survive long enough to see it.

I dreamed that Eisen came. His whorish old face with eyes puffed from drink gazed on me like an old nurse. "I loved you," he said. "At least I think I did. But you were spoken for."

"Love!" I said. "I would like to take up again this subject of love. I think it is nothing but a rat's fart in a windstorm. And you can quote me on that."

I ASKED THE BOY NEXT DOOR to bring tea. When it came Hokusai was someplace else in his mind.

"Die, then, Old Man, and un-daughter me," I told him again while he lay and seemed not to hear.

In an hour, I thought better of that. Un-daughtered, what was I then? What was the world without my father swaggering ahead along the road?

"Old Man, you went ahead of the crowd. They didn't forgive you that. Not the censors, not the Shoguns, and especially not your fellow artists. By the time they caught up, you had moved on."

He smiled at that.

And me—I came along forty years after, myself. And these trappings of the world became my story. Trappings! Who called them that? An excellent word. I was trapped! The daughter in the service of her father. His dominance, his sensuality had overrun the boundaries. There was the faint echo now, of his animal presence, and of the three of us daughters in the studio. Father.

The judgmental thing I feared in him, I saw in myself. He had to exact perfection from himself and others. He did not accept that perfection was out of reach. He hurt people. Shino. My mother. He hated any deviation from his precious path—he showed no compassion for others. I stood over him with my head cocked to one side, as if listening to a voice from elsewhere. He neglected me, fought me, but never discarded me. I was all he had.

I loved him.

IT WAS DAY. I heard the voice of the fish vendor. "Eel to sell! Fresh from the market. Swimming in the marsh one hour ago!"

All night I had watched him grow more beautiful. The face so thin that the skin clung to his skull, translucent like hot wax around a lit candle. The thinking part of him was moving out, vacating its space, ceasing to know. I took his hand. He begged forgiveness for his failings, and then he asked me to carry on making pictures.

He had spoken of wanting every line to be true. He had begged for just ten more years. He would continue striving to paint the truth.

But I knew the truth he sought was nothing. It was a phantom. An idea of perfection. Phantoms appear in different guises to us all, and that was his.

I told him he would be reborn as a tiger, a tiger in the snow.

I held his right hand. It was unchanged: large, square, wrinkled, firm, so infinitely, invisibly capable that I was in awe. Could all that skill die in an instant? Surely not. It had taken so long, so very long, for every inch and cord to learn its canny powers. I was calm; he was calm. We had not had many such moments. This is the tragedy of death. It was bringing the peace we had ruined with our restless lives.

He squeezed my hand, my finer hand, and gave one more tremendous "Hah!" The hand went still and he was gone. Like that.

I kept the hand in mine a long time. Then I grew tired and lay beside him.

And now it was day. People began to arrive. Although I had told nobody, they knew. "He's gone," they said, peeking in. They had felt his spirit travel on. Bounding, they said, across the fields.

It was the eighteenth day of the fourth month—10 May 1849 in the Western calendar. The plum had been and gone, and the cherry blossoms too. It was a beautiful day to be dead.

I am writing to tell you that my father went to his rest today, in the morning. He was peaceful and willing to go. [Lie.] He is in our lodgings as we prepare for the funeral procession tomorrow. I hope you can be with us.

The visitors left their coins folded in beautifully painted paper. I sent the boy to buy a plain box for his ashes. Neighbour women came from the tenements. They sat beside me sewing his death clothes of bleached cotton. I smiled with them at my clumsiness. "She who paints but does not sew" was sewing. I washed his body myself. We dressed him, and the apprentices put him in the coffin. Katsushika Isai was there and Kosho. They jostled for position around his corpse.

I found brushes, ink pots, and rolls of paper. I took the powder of some of my deepest pigments and tucked them in small cups. These cups I wrapped in fine paper. I wrapped all of this in a cloth and tied it at the top. I tucked the package beside his body.

The priest came from the temple and chanted the Pillow Sutra by his side.

That night people kept arriving. They brought soba noodles in broth, his favourite dish. It was important to be merry, and I was. I heard my voice, echoing in the silence where his had been.

When they left, and before the dawn, I began to paint. I wanted to paint a beautiful lantern for the procession, and that is what I did. As my brush moved of its own accord, I mourned. There had been no luxury, no ease in our life, and none in his death. I had not objected to this, as my mother had done. To have done so would have been to break faith with my father. But now, for this day, I wished for one formal kimono to wear, just once in my life.

In the morning a temple messenger came with a large box: a kimono and all the attendant belts and ties. "The nun left it with us for you. It belonged to her when she was a married woman." It was lavender with purple iris and red-headed cranes.

The women dressed me, tying the wide obi in place. Outside the procession formed. I had made many models of funeral processions with the *keshi ningyo* dolls. I knew the order by heart: first lanterns, then paper flowers and fresh flowers, and finally caged birds which would be released later, to bring merit to him. Then came the incense burners and the memorial tablet covered with thin silk, and finally the coffin.

"This shabby quarter has never seen so fine a funeral," said the unagi seller.

We fell in line. The disciples one by one—Katsushika Isai; Tsuyuki Kosho; Hokuba; Sori III; Suzuki Hokusai II; Taito II, who had travelled from Osaka when he knew my father was failing. Takai Kozan sent his representatives. And simpler folk: those in the quarter from whom we bought the skewered fish and the charcoal for the *kotatsu* and the sandals. Tosaki-san, who made the famous sweet that Hokusai loved, was weeping. My friend Yasayuke the storyteller. Shino, of course. Samurai and priests and scholars, and yes, court ladies. Even the *bakufu* were present.

There were the publishers and artist friends in their suspicious droves, eyeing one another. They had buried Hokusai ten years ago. But now, finally, he was stilled. Death had caught him. It had caught his friends first, and his wives and most of his children too. Only I was left.

But no, there was family: Sakujiro and Tachi; even the dreadful Monster Boy, crying crocodile tears.

We were one hundred in all when we walked the short distance through the tenements on the temple grounds to the old quarter of Umamichi, one mile away. They said that only male relatives should carry objects, but I insisted. I carried the lantern I had painted. At the temple we set our items on an altar. We offered incense and the priest chanted. We handed out sweet bean jelly in shape of lotus flowers and leaves; that was our obligation. Certain people who were not members of the funeral party pushed in amongst the crowd and got sweets, which they took away outside to sell.

My father would have put it in a picture.

After the funeral we carried the coffin to the cremation spot outside the city. I walked behind, carrying the certificate from the temple, a permit to burn. We arrived: the coffin was put in the oven, and the door was sealed and my paper stamped. We waited until dark. Firewood made a weak fire and cremation a bad smell, so it was always done at night.

Into the fire he went. I gaped. It seemed too soon. The flames leapt on his small offering. I hated it. It was his very life, not even one day ago. Who could be sure he had truly departed? Never would I allow my own bones to be burnt.

Whatever lived inside those ferocious bones snaked up to the stars leaving a dragon's tail of white smoke.

Part 5

38

THE CHIMING BELLS

AT FIRST THEY LEFT ME ALONE, which was what I wanted. I slept,
I woke up, I missed him. His groans, which had been frequent; his crazy
laugh; his ghastly visions. No one came around, not even Monster Boy.
Maybe he had got himself killed by his gangster friends because of his gambling debts.

Yet I heard over me the nasal, rhythmic series of syllables that I knew
from my father: "*Myoho renge kyo. Ho ben pon dai ni. Ni ji se son. Ju san mai
an. Jo ni ki.*"

Sometimes I joined in.

"The wisdom of the Buddhas is profound and cannot be measured. Its
gate is hard to understand. And difficult to enter."

I woke up. Had I got out of bed that day? I wasn't sure. I forced myself
awake, drank stale water, stumbled outside to the toilet, splashed my face at
the well, and stumbled inside again. My eyes were bleary, but I thought I saw
a nun in a white headdress sitting beside the mattress.

"You must not fight it; you must allow yourself to be sad," she said.

"I'm not sad," I said. I lay down and pulled my blanket up to my eyes.

"You always say that. But you often are."

That made me cry.

"Stop trying to hold on to time that has gone by. You must let things go."

"I have let everything go!" I protested. "What are you talking about?"

I slept, and woke up, and drank tea, and she was there.

"Come with me," urged Shino, "to the monastery in Kyoto. The old capital. You can live by the chiming clocks and paint."

"I can't leave. I have to lie here. I have art under the mattress."

She laughed. "That's the worst excuse I've ever heard."

But I was afraid it would be stolen. I told people that I saved my father's filthy mattress out of respect, but really it was my safe place.

"I can't leave it."

"We'll take it, then."

Shino helped me to roll the papers and silks and place them in a long cloth bag for travelling.

"I can't leave my cats," I said as a last-ditch attempt to escape this journey.

"They will be fine. They're too fat anyway, on her garbage," she said, pointing to the unagi seller.

I roused myself to do the courtesies. I made a gift of Hokusai drawings to Tosaki, the man who made the sweets my father had loved. I thanked everyone for their gifts. Someone had been sending chestnuts. What did I do with those chestnuts? I didn't remember eating them. I wrote to Iwajiro, my student in Obuse, giving him instructions so he could continue his work.

There was work to finish, work that would be signed and stamped "Hokusai, age 88." I had the seal in a small bag tucked in my kimono sleeve. When I undressed for the night, I hid it in the tangerine box that still graced our wall, with the little statue of St. Nichiren. The other seals, fancifully saying "Hokusai 100," I did not have. Isai maintained that my father had given it to him.

I went to find Yasayuke the storyteller. He was at the foot of the bridge, half-buried in a crowd and dishing out futures with abandon. I pushed my way between the people and shook his arm. "I've come to make you an offer: stay in my tenement for a few months. I'm going on a pilgrimage."

He did not like a roof over his head; he was not used to it. He shook his head and whined. There was crusting under his eyes.

"You know it. Beside the well," I said. "Next to the unagi seller. She'll feed you. There's charcoal to burn in the kotatsu. It's already autumn; in winter you'll be glad of it. Let the cats sleep inside when there's frost"—I spoiled them—"but not the apprentices. Tell them I've gone travelling."

SO WE WENT BEGGING, SHINO AND I. We stood by the side of the road and Shino played her flute. At the sekisho she explained that she was going to her mountain monastery; I was her sister who had suffered the loss of her ancient father and must pray for him. The guardsmen were not interested, and we passed.

"Do you see?" Shino was exuberant. "How easy life is because we are no one?"

Shino begged so graciously that our bowls were never empty. By the end of a day we had enough coins to stay in a pilgrim's inn.

It took us seven days to reach the pass. As we climbed up the hill, water ran down beside us. We passed the grey milestones with characters carved in them. The sun whitened the tile roofs in the post town. We begged two backpacks with woven cloth straps to go over our shoulders. A gutter led the water over a wheel from which it fell, silver onto stone, making a gentle chucking sound. "It's a steep hill for old ladies," said a man as he dropped a coin in Shino's bowl. *Pching!*

I heard clear sound for the first time in months. Until that moment I had heard only through the din of my pain.

That evening we sat on the stone benches beside the road. Shino's music warbled. I stared into the fugitive blue hills. I could see far into the distance, where peaks were misted and whitened. The world was coming back to me.

In the moonlight Shino swivelled and darted in her white hood, glowing like a ghost, and it made me laugh. She practised her *kata* on me. She pinned me to the ground in about three seconds. Two old ladies. I was fifty, and she was nearly sixty. She still looked fierce.

"I hope you never use those fighting manoeuvres on me," I said.

In the daylight Shino bowed her head modestly and talked to me of religion. "We must be honest and gentle. We must be merciful. We must be respectful to our fathers and husbands. We must be patient."

"Are these not rules designed by men to turn women into perfect helpers, wives, and mothers?" I said. In Buddhism, women had to follow all the same rules as monks, but also an additional set for "feminine morality."

"You may not like it, but it is a way to freedom," said Shino. "You must learn to dissemble. And not with that sulky look. You must let them think you are entirely in their hands. And you will have freedom. Don't you see? I have only myself—and the spirits, who pay little attention to me."

Autumn deepened every day. In the post towns, the houses ran in unbroken dark lines on either side of the road, their red tile roofs wet with rain. Horses whinnied in the stables, and daimyo retainers pulled their reins.

Shino's feet were blistered, but still she played her flute, and in the darkness she moved in her strange patterns using the sticks as weapons. Together we performed the demon-queller *kata* with long feathery grasses, slashing forwards and backwards and swirling.

We took the turning away from Obuse towards Kyoto. I had never walked here before. I came out of my stupor enough to realize that she too had lost him. I examined the smooth face for the sadness that must be there but found none.

IN KYOTO A MONK IN DARK BLUE ROBES roped tightly around his waist and a sedge hat that hid his face seemed to be calling my name. "O-eh, O-eh." His hands were folded across his chest over a prayer script. He and his roaming partners repeated this as they walked in circles. They gathered, then disappeared down an alley. When they'd gone I could hear the birds.

Shino told the abbess that I was a famous artist in Edo and the daughter of the great departed master. I was given a room.

I became a visitor to temples.

Alone in the gardens of the Zen temple at Ginkaku-ji, I walked. I had been walking for weeks, and now it had become a necessity. The sky was thick with threatened snow. The trees lay thin shadows on the gravel. These were the gardens of a long-ago Emperor, built for his rest when he had finished his rule. I heard the chanting of the monks, like the grumbling of a low, many-footed, many-throated beast. It was soothing, if you were in agreement. Like everything in my world.

How had the Emperor walked? Hands clasped, head down. He didn't need to watch his feet: nothing was allowed to be in his way. Why should he look? He had seen it all: moss beds, rocks like sundials, still ponds where carp sip the air, in and out of shadow. Rocks dappled with lichen in green and grey. The red blossoms that fell overnight and the gardener hastened to remove, bowling himself flat before the great footsteps, nearly face down in the walled-in transparent stream.

What did the Emperor think about?

The people. Surely the Emperor thought about the people.

But did he know who we were? That there were many of us, and that we were restless? Did he think about how to keep out the foreign barbarians?

I went to Eikando Zenrin-ji temple. This was the temple of the Shogun. I saw the gate by which he entered. I looked beyond the wall to see the path where the Shogun walked when he visited this, the Emperor's city. I wondered, How did the Shogun walk? What did he think about?

I supposed he thought up new rules. How to keep us spending so he could collect taxes. How to keep us afraid. How to stop the rumours. And of course, how to keep the world away from our shores. These things must have been on his mind. We artists, the actors, half-people that we were, dumb animals that we were, used all our ingenuity to outwit him. And often we succeeded. But he! He had to always invent more ways to keep us in line. How difficult for him.

I went to the temple famous for the Eternal View. It was chock full of monks chanting. The lead monk kept time with his mallet, striking a wooden tablet. They too were saying my name: "do o do eu do ei ei ei."

What were they praying for? And what was my father praying for all that time, chanting the Sanskrit words he never understood, but for whose sake he turned his back on friends and would not greet them?

His immortality, I supposed.

But the man had turned to ash: I was the witness.

I went to Nanzen-ji Garden. This was for the abbots. It was my favourite, with the sand cone tickled by its broom in the morning. And perfect, perfect, with the moss carefully groomed, picked clean of every single stray blade of grass that got into it. Under the moonlight it had a mystic gleam, as if it were inhabited by light.

This was how the world was meant to be—for them: Emperor, Shogun, Abbot. Towering. Awe-inspiring. Calmed. Unchanging. But for us, the lowly people, change was all around. Here in the imperial city samurai wishing to restore the Emperor clashed with those wanting to open the country to the West. Sometimes a body was displayed, a crackdown overnight, a nest of rebels found.

I found a rosary soothing. Day after day, I shirred the beads between my thumb and fingertips. Shino took me to her own hidden temple in a mountain gorge a little way above the city. Unable to act as priests in Kyoto, the nuns practised their devotions there. They believed that animals, rocks, and plants had understanding. I smirked to see them bowing to a goat, but then thought better of it. There seemed no reason not to respect a goat. Certainly I respected cats.

There was an old slippery monkey tree that had cracked open; its trunk gaped. In the cavity a pine tree had taken root. The pine grew straight, but old, dead branches of the slippery monkey entrapped it. The young branches pushed through the holes where branches once had been. It was protected: lucky. But misshapen, disguised: unlucky. I saw that this pine tree was me. I had been inside the monkey tree, trying to push past the dead arms of the father.

There was a poem in that temple. I memorized it, and on my homeward journey I chanted it too, along with the Lotus Sutra.

> The evening bell, solemn and bronze
> In the grandfather temple down the hill
> Sounds dimly here.
> Slow beat of the mountain's heart, perhaps,
> Or determined pulse of pine tree (gift of the birds)
> Growing out of a crotch of the slippery monkey tree.
> All one, perhaps—bell, mountain, tree,
> And steady cicada vibrato
> And little white dog
> And quiet artist-priest, carver of Noh masks
> Fashioning a bamboo crutch for the ancient peach tree,
> Symbol of strength, symbol of concern.

WHEN SPRING CAME I WRAPPED THE PAINTINGS of my father's last years in the travelling bag and tied it on my back. The new paintings I had made, exorcisms in their own way—of cats, goats, trees, potatoes, anything that was alive—I wrapped in red cloth and presented to Shino.

"You will return to the world," she said.

"I will."

We said our farewells. I did not know if I would ever see her again. She was old, and I . . . I had nothing. But I wanted out of my monkey tree. I wanted to be an artist in my own right. To live by one brush.

39

BATTLES

I ENTERED THE ALLEY walking with long strides, assisted by the walking stick that my father had used. There was Yasayuke, enthroned on the stoop outside my house. He had gathered the neighbours to greet me.

"We've known for days that you were coming."

"How did you know?"

He gave his round-shouldered, eloquent shrug. "It was the gossip of the Nakasendo. 'The master's daughter is returning home. She is cured of the madness that took them both in the last few years.'"

The unagi seller with her brown and wrinkled walnut face put her fillets of eel on the charcoal grill and offered me a homecoming gift. The cats wound around my ankles. Now, because of my time in the temple, I could see into their eyes and know their thoughts.

I sat down to eat and to listen as Yasayuke spun tales of his time in my alley. When he was gone, I stowed my very few precious things—the seal of age eighty-eight, the silk on which I was working, my new finished work— under the rotten old mattress. There was no other place.

THE APPRENTICES CLUSTERED in my doorway. So many of them, more now than ever, it seemed. Dozens, three dozens, with their bits and pieces of my father's names: Hokuba; Hokuju; Taito II, who was old and ill; Katsushika Isai himself, about whom I had been thinking. He had been a good friend to us and had even lived in our home for some years. But I did not know what to think about him, since the days when he'd visited us in Obuse. He brought good wishes from Iwajiro, my student, for which I thanked him.

Pre-eminent was Fukawa, to whom I had written when my father died. I had given him certain works to complete. Yet I was not sure I trusted him. Nor did I like Tsuyuki Kosho, the young man. To my great irritation, he had appropriated the name Iitsu.

"That name is not available," I said. "Everyone knows the works signed Iitsu are by me."

"He promised it to me," Tsuyuki said.

He lied. I knew Hokusai would not have done that. But the master was not there to speak for himself. There were so many battles that this was one I chose to step away from, something I came to regret. At the time I simply thought, If this man wishes to be dishonourable, there is nothing I can do.

The apprentices were like an unruly family. They loved my father, but the Old Man had lasted so long. They were glad I had cared for him when he was ill. Yet they resented my nearness to him in death. And they all needed work. For years I had made decisions about the work we did. But then my father was alive, and I had clearly acted with his blessing. Now they questioned me. Could Hokusai's daughter inherit the seal? Did the Old Man wish it? Would his memory not be lessened when his mantle passed to a woman?

They muscled through the door with a great show of reverence for the dead. But amongst them they said, in voices loud enough for me to hear, "She is just a daughter. She cannot inherit the seal. She is not the first amongst us."

The seal was two things: it was the practical way of stamping a painting or print as being by Hokusai, and it was also the symbol of the artist's power. I had the seal of eighty-eight, but to the disciples that did not mean I was to inherit the mantle of greatness. And with Hokusai nothing was simple: there was this other seal, of one hundred.

I explained that Hokusai had left nothing, that they should be content with the bits and pieces of his names. That they must find their own way.

"The Old Man was crazy in the end," they said. "Otherwise you would not be the one to inherit the seal. Before he went mad he said I could have the—"

It tried my patience past its limit. I had spent every minute for five years with the Old Man as he declined. I suppose you could call him crazy. But it was the same habit of mind he had displayed all his life, only more extreme.

I had ruled, in secret and by tricks. I had spared us all the bald truth, and it was now held against me.

"The master alone was in charge of this studio," the Hoku-boys said. "You were only ever his helper."

"He was palsied!" I said. "He was dying! Who do you think did the fine work?"

"Oh, the details, maybe," said someone offhandedly.

Fukawa, a smooth man of about my age and a fair painter, raised his arm to still the rising voices. "Listen to the master's daughter!"

They grudgingly fell silent.

I opened my mouth to speak, but Fukawa continued.

"We know you are responsible for much that has been produced. But you cannot do this work without him here to tell you how."

It had been a very long time since Hokusai had told me how to paint or design. In the last decade it had been the reverse, if he had ever been working. And they knew it; they had seen him. I was insulted. I stood up and gestured that they should leave my home. It was another decision I came to regret. They muttered and moved off resentfully, and no doubt congregated elsewhere to complain about me.

To calm myself I went for a drink in the old teahouse. I smoked my pipe and wished for the counsel of Eisen or even the long-lost Sanba—someone who believed in me. There was no one left I could trust. In my heart I knew I could continue to lead the studio forward. How could I make the world listen?

I made my way home. It was dark. The moon had wandered off, and dawn was nowhere near. I saw a geisha sliding in her high clogs. She came to a standstill waving her long-fingered hands. "Oh, help me. P-please, I am sli-ding!" Useless creature. In a few hours the street would come alive: the outside men with their shovels and weather-darkened skin would come down the centre of the road.

Dirty old world—how I loved it.

My room was empty. I lit the lamp. It was in those small hours, one day after the next, that I completed the paintings I had promised my father I would finish. This one was a tiger bounding through a snowstorm. It was a portrait of the Old Man. The summer moors of his death poem had become winter fields. I made his claws. I made the needles of the pine branches to mimic them. I made the fine hairs of fur on his hindquarters. I made the soft pads of his feet, under his toes, modelling them on the toes of my cats. I gave him a beatific smile. Bending close to the silk, I made Hokusai's signature, as I had so often done. I pulled out the stone seal from its hiding place, behind the statue of St. Nichiren in the orange crate, and with a little red ink stamped it on the fabric. "Hokusai, age 88." I blew out the lamp and went to bed. The sun was rising.

It was noontime before I woke up. The neighbours, those who did not see my lamplight, called me a lay-abed and scolded—affectionately, I add, but scolded nonetheless—that I was a drunken woman.

In broad daylight, I checked to see that the paint was dry. I rolled the silk and tucked it under my arm. Genial to all my detractors, I walked into the sunlight and straight to the shop of Sakai-san, outside the gates of the castle. He was the son of the wealthy merchant I had met in Obuse, a slim and elegant man, like a Noh dancer. He did not look like he could withstand a strong wind. But he had excellent taste. He held his hands in front of his chest to take the scroll from me. Then we unrolled *Tiger in Snow*. Sakai's intake of breath made me proud and happy.

"I have other works from my father's last years," I said. "I'll bring them one at a time." We arranged that he would give me money when I needed it.

And in that way time passed.

"WHAT WILL YOU DO?" asked my brother Sakujiro.

He appeared in the doorway, surprising me. I was sitting in the *kotatsu*, tucked under the quilt, drinking tea, just waking. Feeling it necessary to achieve equality, I scrambled to my feet.

"What will I do?" I repeated.

As Hokusai's oldest living son, he had inherited responsibility for me. It was a strange question all the same. What I had always done. What I *was* doing. "Work as an artist, live here."

"But how can you, without the Old Man?" he said.

He was a good brother. He was not stupid or coarse. He was even a little cultured: he wrote haiku; he had a pen name. I put on my downward and sideways glance.

"I see that is my answer," he said. "You can't."

"Of course I can. I am. I have been and I will be working as an artist."

It was as if I hadn't spoken. "Come to live with us," he said. "We have taken over the house in Uraga. I have been promoted to accounting manager," he said. He was paid eighty rice barrels every year.

"You could have helped us." It came out of my mouth.

"He had you," my brother said. "That was all he wanted."

I looked into his face, astonished.

And he went away, scowling at my door as he went. "I will be back."

So much had been hidden by the hugeness of Hokusai. Here were my brother and I, both in need—I to be freed of my father's grip, and he to feel his father's love.

He came again.

"Sakujiro!" I said, bending over my work and barely lifting my head. Would we ever recover from the imbalance created because I had too much father and he had too little? I was painting a miniature of flowers. So many petals, each one gold or orange. Each one like a slim tongue curling upward, red on top, yellow underneath.

"Ei, my sister"—he came straight to his point—"you cannot continue to live on your own. The studio has broken up and you cannot make a living as one brush."

"What have I been doing? You can see that it is quite possible." And I was not always on my own. I visited my students; I went to stay with patrons for whom I did commissions.

"I gave you time: I supposed you would have work of the Old Man's to clear away . . . You are not getting younger."

"A few years is no time at all."

He threw up his hands in frustration. "You can't afford to be choosing. I am offering to look after you."

He paced in my small rooms. Three steps to the back wall, three steps to the front; three steps to the far wall, three back. His toes were at the edge of my fabric. I daintily moved it an inch away.

"What are you doing? Still trying to make a go of it as an artist in your own right?"

"I'm not *trying*," I said mildly. "I am doing it. As I have done for a long time. Even while Hokusai was living."

I begged him to sit, and he did. I called the boy next door to bring us tea. We sat with the bowls in the palms of our hands, warming them but not our hearts. I tried reason. I explained to him carefully that for the past many years, while Hokusai was alive, my work had kept us going. *My* work, not his.

It was the last time I tried to tell anyone this. Sakujiro simply did not believe it. He told me I was crazy. He put down his tea and leapt to his feet. He shook his fists at me. My words hung in the air. He batted them away. He stood over me. This meant he had to look down on the top of my head, which was inclined to my silk. I could feel him studying me. Crazy old woman, he was thinking; she suffers delusions.

I felt the blaze of humiliation. I was furious. I hated him then. I hated everyone for the way they saw me. My anger came bubbling up my throat. I opened my mouth.

But just in time I remembered Shino's advice: dissemble. "Let them think you are entirely in their hands." I sensed a way out, sniffed it out like a dog. My father had said I was the next best thing to a soothsayer. You should go to Uraga, a voice told me. Uraga is a nice place. Take up his offer. Satisfy his vanity. Just for a little, go along with this idea. Then he'll leave you alone.

I angled my head to the right. As a gesture it might resemble submission; it could be taken for assent. I lifted my chin, to see into his eyes. They were opaque. I gave a little smile.

"I won't lie to you," I said softly. "The work is harder to find."

"You see? Of course it is. Changing style never stops for anyone."

"I can still rely on Takai Kozan. He is paying me 2 *ryo* of gold and 2 *bu* for the silk scrolls of chrysanthemum. It is more than he paid us when my father was alive."

But he heard only the name and nothing else.

"Kozan? You see! That's just the problem. You'll stumble into trouble. Those pro-Western samurai are very dangerous. They are fomenting revolution. And that art dealer you see, the one with the shop near the Shogun's castle, he is also marked as suspicious."

"Sakai-san? Dangerous?"

How did he know I went there?

My brother paced in his bare feet on the tatami as if he were a judge taking evidence. "We are agreed, then. You will not go on living here," he said. "You will come and live with my family. On the seashore. It is cleaner. You will be healthier."

Why did he care? Was this love? Did he mean to repair our broken family? I was not able to judge.

I simpered. Difficult for me, but I managed it. "You would take a helpless old lady into your household?"

He smiled, victorious. "You are my sister, after all."

"All right, I will come, just for a short visit. We'll see if this act of kindness is one that we can all live with."

To myself I thought how good it would be to see the ocean waves again.

40

BLACK SHIPS

AND THAT IS HOW I CAME to be present on that night.

I had walked out of Sakujiro's garden and then beyond. I climbed the hill. I stood overlooking the sea. The wind was at my back, blowing away from the land. It tore my hair out of its knot, throwing it over my face. A feeling of freedom came to me, from such a simple thing. The town was below me, homes lit by small lanterns. It was July 8, 1853, by the Western calendar. Night had fallen. White rows of foam turned themselves over on the beach, but farther out, hard crests like little mountain ranges of water hared off. The water was moving away from us. Beyond the visible crest, the ocean became one with the misty grey sky. There was no horizon.

Promising Yasayuke and the apprentices that I would return, I had closed the doors of the North Star Studio. I was a defenceless old woman being sent to live with relatives in Uraga. For Hokusai this place had been a safe hideaway from the searching eyes of the *bakufu*, a simple fishing village. We had played in the waves here.

But this had been only the surface. Now Uraga was the tip of our outstretched fingers. Since Western ships had appeared in the bay, Western-leaning samurai had made it a meeting place. Perhaps they always had. Conspiracies were hatched here. The *bakufu* were wary: cannons were mounted on these very hills, the hills of Miura, above the town.

How much of this had the Old Man known? Had he met Kozan here? Why did he keep this from me? To protect me? Or just to protect his secrets, which were numerous.

The moon came through a cloud and I saw something coming in on the waves. What was it?

More moon, and I saw it was a man struggling with an oar. He was light; his skin shone in the moonlight. I could see no boat or waves. Then the moonlight was gone and he was too.

The moon came out again. I saw him, farther in. I saw that he was the first, a small pilot boat. Something much larger was coming behind.

It was a black ship. The white foam tossed and obscured it. The background swallowed it. But that's what it was: a dark, edgeless boat. It looked like a visitor from the spirit world.

Gradually, the mist cleared; the moonlight came through. I saw another and then another black ship. They were sailing against the wind. And they were breathing white smoke. They came dancing into Edo Bay from the open sea.

Oh, I was dumbstruck to see that magic: the ships moving forward when the wind pushed them back.

The foreign ships had arrived.

The Old Man would have said my witchery brought me here, for this moment. And he would have been laughing if he were here. He would have been running and jumping if he could. I stood still, awestruck. It was happening. Hokusai had missed this moment, and by only four years. "And frequent visits to Japan of foreign ships." In Obuse he had written this line as the ending of his death poem. Later, in Edo, when he was near to death, he had taken it out. Hedging his bets, as always.

"Hey, hey, Old Man," I shouted so he could hear me from hell. "How about it?"

I was so lonely, suddenly, standing there. I missed my father, and I missed Eisen, and I even—reaching back, into the moments when the idea of the West had first entered me—missed von Siebold. He had foreseen this too: we had spoken of it. It was inevitable as death, as life. My old life and its people were becoming relics. A new world was advancing on us. I was here, and alive, against many odds. Why had I, almost alone amongst those I loved, been chosen to survive to see it? I wanted to shout to Shino, but she was far away from here. Tucked up in her old temple above Kyoto, she was, I hoped, safe from the strife that took us all.

Standing on the Miura hill, with the inevitable presence of the enemy, the conqueror, the liberator beneath me, I imagined the Dutch doctor tracing these inlets and bays that led into the heart of Japan. Some people said that the foreigners were using the maps von Siebold had obtained by treachery to find their way to our ports. Was it true? I could still see his hands, strong and long, with flat-ended fingers, wily and intelligent. I could still see his beautiful wide brow and his long thin lips that seemed to be smiling on me from far away, reassuring me.

Now I alone was present as the black ships came. I felt the wind and threw back my hair, which was blinding me. I knew by their huge white breath, by their pushing forward in the night against the wind, against nature itself, that the ships were not to be stopped. The Shogun's efforts would be for nothing. The foreigners were coming, and they would break open this little world.

I wailed into the wind, truly a witch. Longing and fear filled me. Longing to be let loose, and fear of the red-headed barbarians, of soldiers with guns, of samurai at war. Fear of the red-headed barbarians and longing to see someone I had loved. My men! They had all deserted me. Why me? Why had I alone lived to see this?

If these ships could sail upwind, then anything could happen. Perhaps I could see those lost men again—von Siebold, my father.

The black ships, three of them, were there, and then the mist rose and the moon was hidden and they were gone into darkness. There was nothing but a blank page of grey and black from sand to sky.

The wind dropped suddenly.

I could hear voices, horns, the bellows of animals. On my hilltop I paced in their invisible presence. I spoke urgently to my father: "Old Man, Old trickster! Exile in sleepy Uraga? I doubt it. No. You knew this was coming. You and those samurai, plotting. You were looking over the waves. You always yearned for the Western world. You wanted to be famous there too. Now look: the barbarians are coming! You hoaxed me, you hoaxster."

I saw in my mind the secret staircase from Takai Kozan's studio in Obuse. His retainers scanning the roads. I remembered sitting in the company of Shozan Sakuma and looking at the book with drawings of how to make the new thing called a camera. Sakuma was now sentenced to house arrest for nine years for preaching treason. Kozan would be happy. He and my father. Why did they choose a phoenix to be painted on the ceiling? Did it conceal a message? Japan was burning and would be destroyed, but it would be reborn, like the phoenix. Uraga was the place where this fire had been sputtering for years. Now it was about to burst into flames.

And my brother had urged me to return to Uraga for safety!

It was a wonderful, terrifying joke.

Buddha teaches that there are phases of everything imaginable. All that appears to be solid is in flux and might even be imaginary. Waves are driven by some energy from the deep, and also by wind. They become foam and fog.

Then something more solid moved. The ship was alongside the hills! The pitch of the waves rocked it. It was like a clumsy brush, like the reed broom that Hokusai had used to make that giant Buddha, writing history.

At the narrowest part of the channel now there were gun batteries on the hills on both sides. The Shogun had ordered that any Western ships reaching the narrows be fired on. But no guns fired. The black ships moved invincibly, up the wind in the middle of the channel, out of range of either side. One, two, three. There were rocks in that narrow passage, visible when the air was clear but hidden in the fog on a night like this. These ships did not come up on the rocks. They continued, right into the heart of the bay.

They were demon ships.

Beneath the hills there was nothing but silence and darkness. I was truly, thoroughly, frightened. They had entered. I remembered my father telling me the world was round; it was a fishbowl. He had walked all over its outside, looking across the surface. I felt that night that I was on the inside, swirling in the water, knocking against the glass. Drowning in it. I went home to my brother's house. I stood over Tachi with tender fears for her. I lay in bed and stared at the night. These foreigners had such powers. What would they do to us?

At first, nothing.

By dawn the guns had been moved nearer. The *bakufu* had commandeered a hundred of the small fishing boats and put a cannon in the front of each, to be sent out to fire on the ships. But this was futile.

We gathered on the cliffs to watch. After the guns, the first things out were artists in little boats, sketching. But I returned to my vantage point under a tree on top of the hill. Here is what I drew: A great, heavy-bodied black ship with its three masts and many strips of netting. Its sails furled horizontally along poles. The flags tearing out the back as the mysterious power moved the ships against the wind. An unfurling banner of black smoke above, the breath of the dragon. A box in the centre of the ship sitting low in the water, with wheels that turned like the waterwheels. A man, a tiny figure dwarfed by the striped flag above his head.

41

HOUSEHOLD CHORES

TACHI AND I SAT IN THE GARDEN. The family of my brother lived in comfort. There was a small pond with carp; there were trees that fringed the edges, and black rocks that shone when it rained. From a certain corner you could just catch a glimpse of the sea. I told her the ghost story of the Tokaido. I had seen it on the kabuki stage.

"The beautiful young woman Oiwa lived by the water's edge, where the marshes run alongside the Tokaido Road. She had an evil suitor. Her father refused to give her in marriage to the man, who was called Iemon. So Iemon murdered him. But it seemed the refusal was too late in any case. Oiwa and Iemon were already living together, and she was already pregnant by him. She bore the child, but then the villain Iemon turned against her, saying she was ugly."

"Why would he call her ugly? She was beautiful," protested Tachi.

"The reason for Iemon's treachery was that he had visited a nearby lord and caught sight of his granddaughter. The lord allowed the two to meet, and then he allowed Iemon to marry his granddaughter. Oiwa, who had borne his child, was only a poor woman, and she was not truly married. The lord was evil as well, and he thought that she and her child were of no account. To erase all trace of the lovely Oiwa, the lord sent her poison disguised as a healing potion for after childbirth. She drank it and became a hideous ogress."

I pulled faces, stretching my mouth and ears and puckering my chin. We laughed until we could not speak, but Tachi was caught up with the injustice of it all, so I had to catch my breath and continue.

"Iemon then killed both Oiwa, the mother of his child, and her servant, and he tied their bodies on either side of a plank and pushed it into the river. The plank floated sometimes with one body up and sometimes with the other. Old women gathered at the river's edge and saw this."

I remembered this as one of the most terrifying scenes. Tachi was twitching with horror and delight as I told it. I created the scene: bodies merging and submerging in the water, dead hair and dead limbs floating, turning blue.

"The two murdered people became ghosts and haunted the lord and Iemon. In his sleep Iemon saw the hideous ogress who was once his beautiful young lover, and attempting to slay her, he murdered his new wife by accident. Oiwa, who was born in the Year of the Rat, then made her ghostly presence known in the form of rats. As the play ends, Iemon is swarmed and will be eaten by rats."

I gave a large, satisfied sigh at the end of this: the evildoer had been punished, and in such a fitting way.

"That's good," said Tachi in a high but firm voice. I could see her imagining the hideous death and deciding that it was right. "But—the new wife—why did she have to die? Was she evil too?"

"I don't know," I said. "It seems she was punished for the evil of her father. Let's ask . . ."

Then we both looked into the night sky. It was where my father and I had looked for answers when I was her age, and I told Tachi that. She looked solemn, and we quested in silence. She was an excellent partner in such activities. Tachi and I would go into the pine woods after rain to find the special pine mushrooms. When we brought them home, Tachi cooked them for me. I ate them because they granted immortality.

"If I am to live to be very, very old," I told her, "I want you here too. You must eat these too."

Sakujiro's wife interrupted: Katsushika Isai had come to visit.

"This is suspicious," said the other women of the household. "Why would he want to see this old woman? What is his game?"

Their narrowed eyes followed Isai and me as we found the low stone table in the garden. Tachi followed us and sat quietly nearby. Her back was turned, but I knew her ears were alert.

Isai was a tall, hawk-featured man who stepped as if he were walking on lily pads and whose narrow mouth worked nervously in pouchy cheeks. He glanced in amusement at my sister-in-law and her mother, whose shadows were clearly visible moving behind the screens.

"How is it for you here?" he said.

"I am asked to clean the kitchen," I said. "To cook the rice." I made a loud guffaw for the benefit of the women, whose shadows scattered, and he smiled thinly.

"Not your field of expertise. Now if they wanted you to go to the market, that might be better."

"They save that task for themselves. They don't like to let me out."

Isai had opened a printshop in Yokohama. It was where the foreigners were contained by the Shogun. I had been in that town. There were two streets of ramshackle buildings, a few storehouses called by the foreign name of "godowns," and some lodging houses on swampland. The whole town smelled like the sewage that collected nearby.

The muddy streets jostled with sailors and Chinamen and whalers and ladies with great big balls of fabric sitting on top of their bottoms. There were brothels, of course, where dull-eyed girls languished on porches. There was a butcher, always surrounded by a crowd of Japanese curious about beef, which was suddenly the fashion for eating. There was also a shed with a printing press in it. The foreigners used lead instead of wood for printing.

Isai had learned a little English to communicate with the foreigners.

"There is a market for our work," he told me. He was to be known as one of the last *ukiyo-e* artists. Inside Japan, we were dying. But outside the country, we had been discovered.

"More than a few of those foreigners are looking for Hokusais," he said.

"I am not surprised," I said. The Old Man was famous. It was what he had wanted. I said I hoped my father received this news in his new home in Hades. "The Old Man wanted life after one hundred years, and it seems he may even have it," I said.

"But it is not a joke," said my visitor. Isai had a problem. His customers did not like to hear that Hokusai had been dead for six years, and that there were no new works by him.

"There must be prints around," I said.

And then, in the garden, where Tachi's little ears were pinned back to hear us, Isai wondered aloud if I could design Beauty prints like my father's.

"You mean like the ones I have been designing for years?"

A smile played on his lips. "We know you had a hand. That is why I am asking you. But of course, they were his work. They bore the seal of Hokusai."

"My father stopped making Beauty prints thirty years ago," I said curtly.

He said nothing. He would profess not to know that now?

"I wonder if you would come to work with us."

I allowed my head to droop. He had asked me the wrong way. In any case, refusal is the first step in a negotiation.

"I cannot move to Yokohama. I have moved too many times."

"Live here if you prefer. No need for you to travel to Yokohama to see the designs carved and printed. I can come here."

Isai was not a bad man. I even liked him. He told me he had old Egawa, my father's favourite woodcarver, working with him.

Again I demurred.

"There are two reasons I will not leave this house," I told him. "One is the girl, Tachi. The other is that the stars here in Uraga are brilliant. When I am allowed out at night"—here I gave him a wry smile—"I search for Myoken."

He knew what I meant—I was speaking to my father.

"The Seven Stars are very bright in Yokohama," he said.

The truth was, I did not want to live anywhere. I wanted the road. I now wished to adopt the ways of the Old Man, which I had hated when it was his time to ramble. I hoped it was not too late. These were amongst the things I said to his star on my nightly walks. I still got commissions, though no more from Obuse. But Mune and others found their way to me for the odd scroll painting. Life was tolerable. I liked the old ways, where I could go for a time to live with a student and teach. Sometimes too I could go back to the tenement at Asakusa in Edo. I did not wish to stay still, that was the fact. Now that movement was permitted, I could not stop indulging.

"Yokohama is very dangerous, with all the strangers in the port," I said, though I was not frightened at all. I knew from my own soothsaying that I would not die at the hands of a foreigner.

"I would assure your safety," he said.

They needed me badly. No matter how they tried, all the disciples with all their Hoku-names could not do the master's work as well as I could. But they would not admit it.

I told him I was not ready to make a decision, and he left.

———————

THE STARS WERE NOT AN EXCUSE I offered to Isai. My attachment to Uraga's night sky was real. If I managed to escape the house, when the family feared I was drinking sake with men, I climbed my hill, looking out to sea and up into the sky. Stars shivered. They beckoned. They were flirtatious.

"The *rangaku-sha* tell us that stars are burning balls of gas."

"Oh! How sad!" said Tachi.

My father had not questioned the stars. But so much new knowledge had flooded into Japan that it was hard to hold to the old beliefs. It was painful to admit that he was following a ball of stone and smoke moving without purpose in a vast emptiness.

The country was under siege. It wasn't just the barbarians. It was the struggle within. Assassins roamed the roads; a foreign diplomat was struck down by a swordsman, and the politician who had led us to the Treaty of Friendship with the United States of America was murdered as a traitor. The Emperor was being called on to expel the foreigners, but he had no money. The *bakufu* made sure the Emperor was poor. Samurai who wanted the Emperor to seize control were flooding to Kyoto, the imperial city. The *bakufu* arrested those they could find, but others went into hiding. And brigands took advantage of the confusion.

I was neither a believer in the old nor a follower of the new. I was like the fortune tellers who sat at the feet of the great bridges in Edo. Knowledge leapt into my head from an unknown place. This place was none other than my own intuitions, an inner garden I had developed in our lean years that had remained alive, though it was largely reviled by my family. Little seeds were planted there, and in my solitude I cared for them, examined and fed them, and from these notions came larger visions.

Tachi, my little niece, was not little anymore. She was fifteen years old. They would be trying to make an advantageous marriage for her, but it would not be easy. She was a different girl, stolid and sensible. She asked many questions, which was why I liked her.

"Do you want to hear a ghost story?" I said.

"Yes, please!"

"Once there was a serving maid who was employed by a man and a woman, his wife. They were both very, very mean. When the serving maid did not clean the dishes properly they beat her. Then, because her eyes had been blackened in the beating, she could not see. She was drying a dish when she dropped it and it broke. The man and woman were so angry that they beat her again. And she died."

"Ooooh," said Tachi. She was listening in total delight. Perhaps her life was dull. Certainly it was circumscribed: she had to help at home, and although she had been to school, she was considered to have enough education.

"After she died she came back as a ghost."

"What does a ghost look like?"

"What does it look like? Have you never seen a ghost?"

"I see strange things at night," said the young woman in her forthright way. "But how do I know if they are ghosts if I don't know what ghosts look like?" She had stocky legs and her stomach protruded. Her eyes did not blink and she was not shy.

"Good point!" I said. "But your question is hard to answer. Every ghost is different. I saw one that looked like a cabbage floating in a pond. You know, the leaves were all wavy around its head, and there were no eyes, only a round—"

"Ugh," said Tachi.

"Or . . ." I reached for brush and paper. "What a gap in your education, my dear! Let me show you the ghost of the servant girl."

"Did you see her?"

"Do you think that we can see everything there is? The world is full of things we can't see at all."

"That's funny for you to say because you're a painter," said Tachi.

"It's true," I told her. "But painters don't paint only what we can see. We paint invisible things too. I did not see this particular ghost, but I think my father saw her. He drew her picture in a book."

I got out my ink stone and poured myself a little water from the bucket that sat on the floor. I sketched the gaunt face and the long neck and the long, wet hair of the serving maid. "She fell in the wash water when she died," I explained. "Her neck was two feet long. Inside it were saucers, spaced apart, giving it the look of a paper lantern or a paper dragon."

Tachi was suitably horrified.

42

Champagne

AN OFFICIAL CAME, a messenger from the local government. At the door, the messenger had knocked his head on the ground with elaborate courtesy. Inside, he bowed continually and wished to present me with an invitation to a formal dinner in honour of the visiting foreign ambassadors.

The invitation was addressed to the Great Master Katsushika Hokusai's Daughter, the painter Katsushika Oei. It read, "The Governor of Yokohama District would be most pleased to enjoy your presence at a dinner to meet his Excellency, the British Ambassador."

It was fantastical, like something out of a kabuki story. I thought at first it might be a trap. But I knew how to respond. I had learned in the long ago past, when the Shogun's messengers came to the studio and Hokusai went on picking fleas out of his cloak.

"But it is not possible," I murmured, turning my head away. The more I demurred, the more exquisite the messenger thought my manners. But I meant it. Unfortunately, under the code of etiquette that required every assent to be framed as dissent, there was no way of truly saying no.

"I have no means of transportation," I said.

"The governor has already assured us that you will be picked up and delivered," he said.

"I have no one to accompany me," I said.

"If it pleases you, Katsushika Oei, you will invite a member of your family to accompany you."

I asked my brother Sakujiro. He could not quite accept that the invitation was for me either: in his mind it was for his father, and therefore should be for him. I almost felt sorry for him. The poor man was torn between pride and disdain: pride in his father, disdain for the "commoner" art.

His wife viewed my invitation as part of the seditious influence of the barbarians. "Hokusai represented by his daughter!" she murmured. "Our traditions are truly being tested."

Sakujiro said that times were changing.

"Changing so much that we should have women at formal dinners?"

"Yes," said my brother. "Carpenters have learned to make chairs and tables. Temples are partitioned to accommodate the emissaries. Ladies go to dinners."

In the garden, his wife complained to her mother. "From the time of their first arrival onshore, the American officers have raised toasts to 'the absent ladies'—and not only to their own, but to the absent Japanese ladies."

"A gross impertinence!" The mother had phlegm in her throat and constantly cleared it into a dish. Spit, spit, spit.

I wore my one good kimono, lavender with the red-headed cranes; this had been Shino's—I had worn it to Hokusai's funeral, long ago now. My sister-in-law was at pains to explain that it was no longer in fashion. She offered me others, more muted, more suitable, she said, for an old person.

But I was not deterred. I even painted some red on my lips the way I had learned to at the Sign of the Nighthawk.

THEY SAID I WOULD NOT LIKE CHAMPAGNE, but I did. Two foreign ladies looked at me askance as I downed glass after glass. I didn't get red-faced or sloppy the way their husbands did either. Sakujiro stayed at my side.

After the meal a juggler made an iron top climb straight up a stiffened rope and spin on a knot at its high end. Then a conjuror came out on a raised platform, like a geisha's stage. His hands were beautiful, thin and veined: I twitched to draw those hands. He folded a piece of white paper, opened the folds, inverted them, and refolded, until he had a pretty white butterfly.

Then he put his hand in his opposite sleeve, pulling out a fan and opening it in the same instant with a flick of his narrow wrist. The paper butterfly sat in the palm of his left hand. He fanned, creating a breath and then a breeze; the butterfly began to gently flutter its wings. The movement was so sensual; I felt the tickle on my own palm. The butterfly rose slowly, and then suddenly, as if it was startled, it leapt up several feet.

The foreigners nodded to one another with widening smiles. How clever these little Japanese fellows were.

But it was magic. They forgot—we all forgot—that the butterfly was only paper. It zigzagged across the tables. A foreign officer tried to catch it. It darted up and escaped. Two other men in uniforms jumped up to chase it, but the butterfly sank and spun—never too far away from its creator's fluttering fan—still out of reach. People shouted and pointed. After a few minutes they became convinced the conjuror had a live butterfly up his sleeve, which he had substituted for the paper one.

I heard a translator ask how he trained the butterfly.

The butterfly bobbed, as if thinking to land again, but there was nowhere—the magician had hidden his left hand—and so it rose, flew high, and then dropped down again on the edge of the fan.

But in a few seconds it was off again, investigating nearby dishes as if it might find nectar there, even—making us gasp—coming close to the burning tapers on the tables. It sped, it whirled, it rose, and it plunged; it never faltered, never fell, always found the air that was pushed its way by the fan.

I was moved: the craft of it, the sham, the painstaking practice the conjuror must have endured, the dedication to his illusion of fan and paper and air and wrist. The unearthly intelligence of the conjuror's beautiful hand, with the veins running up and down in it. Fragility danced to the tune of impossibility—buoyant and dauntless.

The barbarians were silenced, awed. But I could see their regret: this was not an item that could be bought, shipped, replicated. This is why they are barbarians, I thought. Paper butterflies—and everything like them—will be lost when we dance to their tune.

People pushed back their chairs, making a sound like a room full of irate hens. At that point a translator behind me stepped forward. "You are Madame Hokusai?"

"I am," I said. My brother bowed. I did not. I had taken on Hokusai's habits.

"The evening has run away with us," he said. "I had intended to present you . . . There was someone who wished to pay his respects to you. But it is impossible. Everyone is leaving." He gave me a helpless look. "Did you enjoy yourself?"

"I did," I said, and I meant it. The bubbles of the champagne kept rising in me, and the butterflies flew in my head as we jolted in the dark by palanquin to an inn. Then, later, the champagne let me down badly, and the world seemed suddenly empty and without purpose. Who could possibly have wished to be presented to me?

TWO NIGHTS LATER my brother joined me in the garden. Behind us the pine tree tossed at the top of the hill. The sound of waves reached us on windy nights like these. I took the horn-shaped pastry he offered. I pulled a tiny bit off one end and put it gently inside my lips.

"You eat like a woman tonight," said Sakujiro kindly. "But it is rare that you behave like one."

Perhaps in his mind it was a simple observation, without injury intended. I decided to take no offence.

"I am trying to make concessions to your household," I said. "It is not necessary to smack my lips. But it is necessary to paint."

He nodded.

I reached for another sweet. "Are these from Tosaki?"

"Yes, he sent them. For you, actually."

He handed me this little lifeline—I was not forgotten by those who had loved my father—as he tossed a crumb to a waiting bird. My heart hardened.

"Tell me," he said, "does it trouble you that you receive no recognition for this work?" He gestured vaguely at my little row of brushes, always beside me, especially when, like now, the light was nearly gone from the sky.

It was a question with a hidden blade. Sympathetic in appearance, and yet cutting.

"I am recognized by the people who matter to me," I said. A blade in return.

"I know you've done the painting," he said quietly. "*I* know it."

I said nothing. What was there to say?

Dissemble, came Shino's instructions. You will get your way in the end.

"You do me a great honour, Sakujiro, to acknowledge the work I continue, to assure that Hokusai's fame lives on."

"Of course, times are changing," he said. "Japan will become modern. We will all be forgotten, and our small, old-fashioned ways."

"Perhaps," I said. A bitter thought escaped me. "And I shall be accused of forging my father's work when what is taken for his work has been my work for a long time. That is funny, don't you think?"

He did not laugh.

"I sometimes wonder . . . Our father wanted immortality. Did he mean that he wished to live this life forever? Or did he mean that he wished to live on forever in his work, outside of our country?"

That question had occurred to me too. "Perhaps both."

"The matter of recognition puzzles me. It seems natural that an artist wants it. And why shouldn't you? I have wondered how you stand it. How did you tolerate all those years with the Old Man?"

I threw him a hostile look.

He paused and then went on. "Of course, you are a woman. I suppose that makes it different. But, Oei, I have learned this much in my life"—he puffed himself a little—"women are not so very different from the rest of us." How proud he was to make this observation. "I say to myself that perhaps you learned to distrust the desire for recognition. After all, your father spent his lifetime behaving badly in order to get it."

His statements were simple, and accurate.

"You mean *our* father."

"He turned himself into a clown. Remember the giant Buddha and the blood-red chicken feet in front of the Shogun? Remember his perverse pride, pulling fleas out of his kimono while the purchaser rested on his heels? All so he would be known as an eccentric. All to get attention. And you were dragged along with it. This act, this way of behaving . . ."

Sakujiro's wife slid out the screen and stood listening. He went on.

"Perhaps you made a pact with yourself? To say, 'I don't care if people see me as a fool. If my work is ignored'? Or perhaps you thought, This is for him, because he cares so much?"

I didn't know the answer to his question. Would I have told him if I did? He was good to me, but I sensed that he would do his best to insure that whatever I wanted, I would not get. "Yes," I said. "It is as you say."

Sakujiro stepped closer to me.

"Yes or no? You don't care? I don't believe it. You want to survive as one brush. You want it known that you were the great Iitsu. Now you seek immortality too. You want it, Ei. You want it as badly as he wanted it."

I inclined my head. I was perfectly in control. I spoke mildly.

"You misunderstand me, Brother. I care nothing for great fame. But you are right. All people wish to be admired. To be given credit. As I will never be admired for my beauty or my grace, I would like to be acknowledged for my work: Oei made this."

I knew he'd buy it. As long as I was humble.

But my humility was an act. I lived as my father did, by caustic humour. This was beyond Sakujiro's understanding. The Old Man's behaviour—imperious, rude, self-centred—amused me. It injured Sakujiro. And Hokusai was extraordinary. I knew that. So much better than the others. To be in the shadow of one so large was close to being in the sunshine.

"But there is one thing, Brother. One thing you perhaps do not appreciate. One person knew: our father did. Knew that I was great, and sometimes greater than he."

The smile was wiped off Sakujiro's face as if with a wet rag.

"There were days when he allowed it. 'She paints Beauties better than I do,' he told his friends. Eisen knew. The disciples knew: Fukawa, the smooth one; Isai. They knew. That was the trouble. That *is* the trouble."

"Is that what goes on now?" he said, as cold as cold.

"There is turmoil. Who is to be Hokusai's heir? Who will inherit the seal?" I bent my head again over my painting. A fleeting look of fear crossed Sakujiro's face. Could it be that I had power now? It was a strange notion but one that grew in me. He too wished to be our father's heir; but I knew the art, not he. This practice he had despised became daily more valuable through the surprise agency of strangers to our shores.

It might have been this notion that made me speak again after a few quiet minutes. "I am not happy here," I said.

"Why?"

"Your wife believes I should do housework." She was still there, stuck against the screen, hoping to be invisible.

"But you have nowhere else to go," he said.

"On the contrary; I have many places. I can go back to our tenement at Asakusa. Or to Yokohama. Or I can travel and live with students."

This made him angry. I was not to travel! He spouted all his reasons. It was a dangerous time. Politics! Highwaymen were slashing foreigners on the Tokaido! Only the other day a foreigner was cut down by rebel samurai while riding through a village near Yokohama. There were thugs and barbarians everywhere.

I made no answer, and he went into the house.

IT WAS NOT TOO MANY DAYS LATER when Sakujiro's wife imposed more rules for me. She laid them, in her indirect way, on my brother first. "She can't walk by the sea. She's an old woman. The neighbours criticize. If she insists on drinking and smoking, it must be out of sight!"

I heard every word while I was sitting under the stars with my pipe.

Sakujiro came out to see me. His hands rose a little from his sides and fell. Poor man—he was tortured. I could see that although he agreed with her, he understood me too.

"She didn't like our father either!" he whispered. "You're too much alike."

We giggled. I had a good feeling. Perhaps after our frank words, brother and sister had come to an understanding. He knew that I could not wash dishes and prepare meals for the rest of my life.

The next morning, over our tea, his wife called me a masculine woman.

"You are unnatural. You are not a woman!"

She was a sexless creature herself—shapeless, her face pasty, her body constantly wrapped. How such a woman could have given birth to the bright button that was Tachi I could not imagine. She stood in her little kitchen hissing.

"Is that so?" I said.

I really think I frightened her. I had half a mind to tell her there was more woman in my left buttock than there was in her entire female line. But instead I did the unpardonable: I laughed.

"How do you know what a woman is? You think she's a household drudge? It appears that you do."

She began putting coal in the stove.

"A woman has a mind. A spirit. A woman also has a body and knows how to have pleasure in it," I said.

"What a thing to say! At your age!"

I had made up my mind to leave, but I had not told her yet. I was not anxious to give her the pleasure.

THAT NIGHT after dinner I lit my pipe.

"Perhaps you would clear up the dinner food and dishes," Sakujiro said.

"I'm sure I am so incompetent you would not wish me in your kitchen," I said.

His wife huffed and banged her pots.

"Why must you be so difficult?" he said sadly.

"I can make a living as one brush," I told him. "Why would I bother with these old household chores?"

Tachi and I retreated to the garden, from which remove we could hear Sakujiro and his wife fighting. They tore into each other just as my mother and father had done. Unlike our father, Sakujiro did not win.

The next day I tucked my brushes in my sleeve and set out.

I felt pain to say goodbye to Tachi. But we had agreed on a secret code. Whenever I needed to get away and didn't want to explain, I would say I was going to paint the inn at Totsuka. It meant I was on the road, but she was not to worry. I would see her again soon.

That is what I told them, careful that Tachi heard: a man named Bunzo had invited me to paint the inn at Totsuka.

I went back to Edo.

43

CATFISH

THE RUMOUR RAN UP AND DOWN THE MARKET. You could see it travelling, like a small wind-borne demon: people bent and heard it, then it whirled and ran to the next ready ear. In its wake the vendors began to pull down their awnings. Women scooped vegetables off the grills and piled them in barrels. Those who hadn't heard shouted to know. When they heard, they clutched their babies. Older brothers yanked little girls by the hands.

"Why do we have to go home?"

"The foreigners have broken through from the sea all the way to Edo."

"Invasion!" people cried.

The word was repeated and echoed all down through the arcade.

Beside me, Yasayuke the storyteller was concluding a rousing tale of how the hairy barbarians fornicated with foxes, and how the half-fox offspring— men with long, furry tails and sharp teeth—came to kidnap innocent maidens from their beds. The audience was caught between the desire to flee and the delicious terror of remaining to hear.

In Edo the gossip was all of danger, of newcomers, of politics, of events from far away that were casting shadows on our little alley. I had wanted the doors open. But I had not anticipated what the coming of the barbarians would unleash. I felt danger even in the temple grounds, rustling in the branches of old pine trees above our heads. The crows talked of nothing else.

"Look at them run!" Yasayuke's crowd was gone. Mothers collared their children and dragged them like dogs. They doused their cooking fires, which hissed and smoked. Rolled-up mats were disappearing into barrows.

"This panic is the fault of people like you," I told him. "Spreading rumours. You should be ashamed."

The temple bells began to toll. Carts were pulling out of the market, and there was a din as the drivers tried to manoeuvre into line to get over the bridge. The barricade was shut in any case.

"Oei-san, you too should be afraid. It is always the one who is not afraid who is murdered. Did you hear about the five Russian sailors who were hacked to death in Yokohama? They didn't believe the warnings either."

The panic was infectious. The market was emptying. Firemen set their ladders against the top floor of the temple. With their barbed poles they crawled over the curved tiles, shouting orders to sleeping guards below. I picked up my blanket and began to wrap the clay dolls. "No point in staying here. I won't sell anything."

I picked up *Kawara-ban,* now a printed broadsheet. It said this was not an invasion. One American and his Dutch translator had entered Edo. That was all. I joined those brave enough to have a look: we stood ten deep at the sides of the streets. The foreigners were on horseback. They were guarded before and behind by soldiers. They seemed very high above us. The horses' hoofs made the only sound. The people were silent.

On the way home I passed a barracks. It was full of soldiers. It had a terrible smell. I knew that smell.

Cholera.

It often started when a great number of soldiers filled the barracks of a poor area. Some people got a watery diarrhea and soon got better. Others got the diarrhea very badly and all the water came out of them. They got cramping in the legs, and they died in a very short time.

I reached my alley. I went to the well. The walnut-faced unagi seller was there ahead of me.

"That smell." I scrubbed my hands as if the smell would come off. But it was here too.

"It is the sickness caused by the barbarians," she whispered. "The barbarians kill men and allow foxes to possess the corpses. That is what spreads it."

"That is nonsense," I said. "Cholera has been around for a very long time. The barbarians have not."

The woman stared at me with hostility.

"It has nothing to do with foxes," I said. "Although I do admit—and it has been observed—that the foreigners at Yokohama are very strange about what they do with foxes."

There was no point making a joke. "You see?" challenged the unagi seller, returning to her grill to light it.

"They like to dress up in pink jackets, get on horses, and ride wildly through the marshes, chasing them." I'd seen prints of this in the bookshop. "But they don't do unnatural things with them!" I was considered something of an expert on foreigners, due to my father's business with them. "And if they did, why would the cholera strike us, in the backstreet tenements of Edo?"

Hokusai and I had never got cholera. We had attributed this to the prayers and charms we recited. There was a dance that people did to avoid infection: I saw children being coached by their mothers to skip and hop with one foot high and arms straight overhead, then turn and repeat it on the other leg.

I took precautions. I returned to the bookshop and bought a little book, *Cholera: Before the Doctor Comes*. It advised me to take Chinese herbs. I walked to the herb seller with the list in my hand and spent a significant amount of my precious earnings.

Coming home again, I saw a dead body in the lane. The stench was awful. Shame made it worse. Trying to hide their symptoms, people went secretly to wash their clothes by the river, or hid behind the houses to relieve themselves. The traces were building up around us. I covered my mouth with the end of my sleeve.

I did not get cholera this time either.

But the old unagi seller got it: one day she was a little weak, and the next she was taken away to a hospital. The *bakufu* had tried to help the poor, giving us soup, and then this help had turned hostile. The woman's son came to cook the unagi, but he was no good at it. He said he had tried to visit his mother but was told she was very sick and had died.

"But she was not so sick when she went in to that place," he said bitterly. "They take old people there to get rid of them, because they think they will give other people the cholera." This grown man was a good son but a bad cook, and his eel was made bitter by his rage.

"They blame the foreigners, but the military itself is trying to kill us," he said. "The world is out of balance, and we are all going to have more misfortunes; this is only the beginning."

The tenements were less crowded when the epidemic at last eased off. But still I stayed on, for the comfort the place recalled, for the past.

I chanted and chanted. I smoked my pipe. I drank sake. I fed the wild cats. It was an odd and backward way to mark the passing of our era. But that's what I was doing. The masters were gone. Greatness was gone. Utamaro had died in my childhood. Hokusai had died. Eisen had died even before my father. Now Hiroshige.

But I was lucky. Remember what I said: lucky and unlucky. I was alive. I was here to make the journey from the old world to the new one. I was ready to play in the affairs of this new time. The wave had picked me up and carried me past. It was my father's last gift.

I still had certain paintings in my possession. From time to time I finished one and signed it "Hokusai, age 88." I put the seal on it. Taking care that no one knew, I went to see Sakai in front of the Shogun's castle. Sakai was always glad to see me and paid me what my painting was worth.

Then the catfish came.

I was inside and had slid the door shut. The cats were restless and crying as they paced the rim of the room. I had a handful of coal and was about to light the *kotatsu* when I felt the ground slip away under my feet. Perhaps I was sick. I had eaten only apricot-filled sweets for dinner, but I'd had many of them. I thought when the fire caught I'd put on the kettle for tea—I usually sent out for it, but I didn't want to go outside again.

When the ground dropped out, I found myself on my knees. I let go of the coals and grabbed the heating table, but it too slid away from my hand. The earth was shifting, breaking; it did not stop but continued to fall, and the walls of my house fell too and the wood partition between the next house and mine began to crack and to fall.

Women screamed in the alley and men called other men to help. I said not one word, but grimly held on to my *kotatsu*, which was at least a firm weight. It fell and rolled, taking me with it. I cracked my head on a beam; something splintered—the beam and not my skull, I presumed. I grimly gripped the iron coal burner. It was lucky I hadn't lit the stove yet or I would have burned my hands. Then I wondered where the roll of oiled paper that I had planned to use to light it was.

It didn't take long to discover it, in the corner where small flames were crackling happily amongst the wrappers from my takeout meal. Before I could stand—the ground still treacherous and, as far as I could tell, on a sharp angle—these flames had danced right onto the pile of drawings there.

"Hey!" I shouted, as if the flame were a cat and I could shoo it. I let go of the stove, waving my hands, and fell on the papers, somehow finding the kettle and pouring the water out. And by the way, where were the cats? Fled, the cowards, with no thoughts of me. Now the papers were ashy black and wet, but they were not burning. My own fire was out, but I could hear and smell that others' were not. Up and down the alley, even while the timbers were crashing and the houses sagged, women ran with wooden buckets to the well. The cry went up for the firefighters, but where were they? Our neighbourhood heroes. Were they stuck on the other side of the barricades? Were they drinking somewhere, or hiding in the brothels?

I finally decided it was safe to let go of my anchor and set the stove on its feet. I went out my door, which was not a door anymore but a hole under a dropped beam, and found a panicked crowd at the well. The women passed their buckets to one strong boy, who dipped and filled each one and passed it to other boys, who ran back to fires along the alley. By now I knew it was an earthquake.

"We knew this would happen," the people were saying. "It is because of the barbarians. The catfish that supports all of Japan is moving under the earth."

"It won't be the houses falling that will kill us," they said, "but the fire."

The children were sent to kick and smother the small flames that tried to connect our little houses. Men were lifting the beams and looking for anyone lost, while boys ran back and forth with their buckets. The earth was still rumbling and shaking.

"The catfish!" they said to one another. "There, it rolled and flipped its tail. Oh, when will it stop?"

"Only when it has put right the balance," said some. And still the earth shook, and now there was thunder too and lightning.

"Katsushika Oi! Oo-Oei! Yoo-hoo!"

Down the centre of the alley and covered in ash waded Yasayuke, seemingly unperturbed, waving to me amongst the panicked residents who were pulling their blankets and their pots out of their little collapsing tenements.

"My friend," I said lightly, "do you want a place to sleep?"

"No," he said. "I am not at all concerned for me. But you are a woman and need protection."

He said that knowing it would annoy me.

"Come to the temple. It's the only safe place." He took me by the hand and pulled.

"I can't."

"Why?"

"The cats."

"What nonsense! They sold you out at the first flash of lightning."

"I can't leave my things."

"What things?"

"My paintings."

The beam of the next-door house was lying across the doorway. But the house was not burning, not yet. With their water buckets the residents of the little alley would keep it from burning.

The orange crate with the statue of St. Nichiren in it was still on the back wall. I took the statue out and removed the seal of Hokusai and put it into my sleeve. I collected my paints and brushes, rolling them in a cloth and tucking them inside my kimono. I sorted through the ash and charred remains of the drawings that had been in the corner. Then I pulled up the mattress. The precious pile of "Hokusai" works and silk paintings, letters and receipts was safe there. I rolled them and put them in a travelling bag.

44

AFTERSHOCK

IN THE MORNING the firefighters arrived, waving their banners and their long metal hooks and pole vaulting and singing at the top of their lungs, with minions running behind with bamboo ladders. Yasayuke and I were still alive. Everyone was at the temple, under its heavy overhang, holding on to their children and their barrows. I did not like it there.

"What if the temple falls down? Under those heavy beams is the worst place to be," I complained, my fingertips on the seals in my sleeve.

"How could the catfish bring the temple down? He is not that powerful."

The shaking began again, and I threw myself to the ground. When the wind began to blow ash I went with him to the big tree. I knew it had old deep roots that clawed into that earth, and it seemed to me safer than even the giant-beamed temple.

He joined me, and as we sat together, others followed—some who were injured and others who were shaking with cold and fear. Runners came by shouting the news: the quake was worst in the central area, where the government offices were. It was bad too along the river lower down and closer to Edo Bay. There, many houses were in flames and the fire was spreading. People were buried under collapsed stones.

"Do you hear that? It is divine recompense for allowing the foreigners to come to our country. The catfish knows the *bakufu* is weak and must be replaced."

"That is foolish superstition. Don't you see?"

The ground shook again and again. Feet ran past in the dark and lanterns waved, and men called out in unison as they hoisted a water barrel or a wall that had come down.

The barricades were up on all the bridges. We could not get out of the district. "They're containing us instead of fighting the fires. They'll see us burned to death!"

I wondered, for the first time, if I would have as long a life as my father. I had not imagined that I might be cut short; I'd intended to be rewarded with thirty years of freedom, or forty, after his death. I was strong and as agile as he had been, and could renew myself when thwarted: I had done it forever.

But that was before. Although the years of my father's life had been dangerous, their cycles of crackdowns and famines were predictable. Now I faced an unknown world. A telegraph in Yokohama sent messages along the Tokaido by wires. Also in that port city, sumo wrestlers moved in a constant belt, carrying huge sacks of rice and silk up the ramps of foreign ships. Peasant farmers sold silk to foreigners and became wealthy if they survived their neighbouring clans' impulse to murder them as traitors.

And now the catfish, on top of it all.

Sheltering under the tree with us was a diviner, that figure from old pictures, with his long pole with paper fortunes tied on it. He reached out. "Oei," he said, "you will not have the auspicious life your father had. You will have only a dozen years from the time of the arrival of the barbarians—and that is all."

The next day dawn came without light. The smoke of thousands of fires curdled the sun. At noon there were more movements of the catfish under Edo, and the news of thousands of dead, all along the river as it ran down to Edo Bay.

I WAS SITTING ON THE STEP outside my crumpled dwelling, stroking the cats and watching the babies play in the rubble, when Sakujiro appeared.

"Ah, Sakujiro. How does it go with you?"

I was genuinely happy to see him. I had heard nothing since I had left his home. The earthquake was two weeks ago. I was worried about Tachi. "Is everyone well?"

He told me his wife and family were well but his house was badly damaged. His garden bench had broken in two pieces, just where I had sat on it. No doubt the wife saw meaning in that.

"First the cholera kills so many," he said, "then the earthquake. There are seven thousand dead. All the carpenters are building coffins. It will be a long time before we can rebuild."

"I am sorry," I said. I truly was. But the satirical mood was too strong to resist. "But I am sure the deaths from sickness and disaster were not intended as a personal inconvenience to you."

Sakujiro curled his lip.

"In the tenements we can rebuild by ourselves. But your magnificent structures cost a great deal more to replace, and you have to pay the poor to do the labour. Your accounts must tell you that."

He shook his finger in my face. "You speak without caution. Your words are like acid!"

But their truthfulness shot me full of energy. My words gave me back just a little of that which had been denied me. I know I should have dissembled. Could he understand why I spoke as I did? I did not even try to explain. Perhaps I should have. Instead I held out my arms to him. "Do you dislike your sister, or only disapprove of her?" I said.

"I disapprove of artists who disrespect our regime!"

"It was your father's way," I snapped. "He would have disapproved of you for being too respectable!"

"That is a filthy lie! My father was not political. He knew how to stay alive, even if you don't."

"And who, then, should speak for the afflicted ones?"

"Why, no one, of course." He stared at me. "The Shogun is their father. He speaks for them. Or are you one of those who favour the return of the Emperor?"

He walked around me, turned his back, and walked away, crossing the narrow back street. Then he turned back towards me and narrowed his eyes, as if removing my surroundings from the picture helped him see me. I was shocked at the next words.

"You are bitter," he announced, "because we have money and you do not."

We had been making progress as friends. I didn't want to fight. I tried to mollify him.

"Let us be agreed. Money is not the cause of this dispute," I said. "There is cause to celebrate. The earthquakes are over. They were terrible, but they signalled the change our father waited for his entire life. I don't normally believe in signs, but to peasants like Hokusai—"

This incensed Sakujiro. "Peasant! His mother was a descendant of Lord Kira."

I pointed to the door sign still hanging on the collapsed beam. "A peasant of Honjo," it said.

His face turned red. "Hokusai was not above laying claim to his noble ancestry either, when it suited him. You are the peasant, you . . ."

I rocked back on my stoop and blew the tobacco smoke out of the side of my mouth. If I was to be an old hag in an alley, then I would play the part.

He went on. "You say you have no money, but I wonder. Everyone knows that Hokusai commanded enormous sums for his work."

"Oh, that old story! I am surprised that the son of Hokusai cannot be more original."

I reached for Sakujiro as if to embrace him, though I would never. "I wish my father had been more prudent with his cash, but as you know yourself, it was not possible to teach him good habits. Please, Brother, may I give you some tea? Let me call the boy—"

But Sakujiro was too far gone in his anger to respond.

"And why don't you make tea like any normal woman?"

I was stung.

"Why must we fight about our father?" I knew the answer. It was not who he was, but whom he loved. "Brother," I said, "you came first for him. You were the son. He was not able to show it. But that is how he felt." It was a lie, but an easy one.

Sakujiro drew breath. "I have not come to fight with you. I have come once again to warn you. You must leave this place. It is dangerous. You are old."

What was this word they bludgeoned me with? "Old"? Old was not me, not yet, not by twenty years. I was not even sixty. At sixty my father had worn red and called himself "one again," Iitsu. At sixty he had his best work yet to come.

"This is a safe place," I protested. "Alcock"—I said the English word slowly and carefully and watched to see that it impressed him—"the British ambassador walks out from his house and around the market, buying pictures and toys. I sold him a set of *keshi ningyo* dolls . . . And you are wrong that I am old. I rise every morning and chant. I am quick and ready. I am less old today than I was when Hokusai died," I said.

"This place," he said very slowly, "has fallen down around your feet. There has been disaster after disaster. And you are without defence."

It angered me greatly to hear him say it. But this time I dissembled.

"Of course I must listen to you, as the oldest male," I murmured. "But I don't understand. If I do not stay here, where will I go?"

"You know where. To Uraga."

"We tried that already."

He looked miserable. "I cannot leave you here. My conscience will not allow it."

"And you cannot take me with you. Your wife will not allow it."

Finally there was a tiny smile on his face.

And I saw that he did love me, my brother. He loved me as duty would have him love me, although he hated me for what I was.

"Give up your feeble-minded revolutionary glee at this misfortune! It is not a sign! There are no signs. There are no portents. There is no grand story where the downtrodden city-dwellers come out the victors. Our time is a string of accidents, and only the Shogun can protect us."

He spoke as if he alone knew what was to come.

"There will be accidents, disease, and corruption. There will be chaos. Do not be buried in it. If the next cholera epidemic doesn't kill you, the censors will root you out. Or the anti-foreigner forces will find you."

"I want to live as long as Hokusai. A diviner told me that I had at least twelve years of life left." Suddenly it seemed like quite a few.

He struck his forehead with the heel of his hand. "Stubborn, stubborn, primitive. It's true our father lived a long time. But these are terrible times. And how did Hokusai survive anyway? Everyone knows. He had you to look after him."

Tears came to my eyes. No one before, other than Shino, had acknowledged that my care of Hokusai had propelled him to his great age, that this "miracle" had been made at least in part because of my labour. Why, then, should I have only one dozen years more? Unfair! Unfair!

Sakujiro too was shaking with emotion. He touched my hand.

"The world is topsy-turvy. The world is going mad. Uraga was a refuge for our father. It can be one for you," he said.

I went to the temple and prayed. Was Sakujiro right? Must I leave Edo? What did the deities think? Was Sakujiro simply jealous of my freedom? No, at heart he was decent. I knew that my brother was right: I could not stay any longer in the tenement.

I had the idea, kneeling there, that I could please him and myself too. I remembered Katsushika Isai's offer. The disciples were gathering in Yokohama. His shop was selling prints to foreigners, and not only that, the newspapers so favoured by foreigners needed pictures. Should I try Yoko-hama, heart of the foreign invasion? The heart of the new export enter-prise of the Hokusai disciples?

Then a strange thing happened. As I was backing away from the little shrine, a nun approached. I would have passed her by, but she stopped me.

"You are Katsushika Oei, the painter of birds and flowers and cats?"

I could see that she referred to my peaceful respite in the old temple in the hills above Kyoto.

"I am." I bowed and we both raised our heads to look in each other's eyes. I recognized her then as one of the nuns who had practised her devotions in that place. I grasped her hands. Tears welled in my eyes at the memory of that time of retreat.

"Did you know that our little old temple by the monkey tree was broken up?" she said. "We have all been moved to different cities."

I had comforted myself with the idea of Shino there. I was startled, and heavy-hearted.

"Where has Shino been sent, then?"

The nun gripped my hands tighter, lifted and lowered them in happiness. "But of course you haven't heard."

I hadn't. If anyone had wished to reach me, they couldn't; since my father's death I had moved from place to place and left no traces.

"I pray it is not bad news."

"Oh, no. Something wonderful. It seems"—here the nun pulled us closer together (even nuns are prone to gossip, but when they do they try their utmost to disguise the fact)—"it seems she is the daughter of an exalted family."

"Ah." I knew that.

"The imperial women came to find her. She has been made the abbess at the Temple of Refuge."

I stammered my thanks and left the temple quickly. I was in a rush to be gone. I sat a long time by the bridgeposts with Yasayuke. I thought of the diviner's words, a prediction that meant I had only a handful of years left. It had been weeks since the earthquake, and now as we watched the guards removed the barrier.

It was another sign. It was time to leave Edo.

45

POULTRY LANE

YOKOHAMA WAS A SCRAMBLING, low place with dirty water running between the streets, and sailors from all nations drinking, and sad little brothels. Katsushika Isai gave me a room in an inn a few doors up from his printshop in Poultry Lane. He was the last of the ukiyo-e artists. A bout of cholera had taken my old friend and rival Hiroshige away. He was in his sixty-second year. He was buried in the inner garden of the Togaku-ji temple, Asakusa, beside a little pond, and his grave marked by a stone flanked by palm trees. I knew the place. He was three years older than me. Isai had a workroom in his shop. There I drew designs for woodcut prints, while old Egawa sat behind with his tools and carved the blocks. We made prints with bright colours featuring Western men and women, and showing all the changes in Japan. I did not sign them. We made our own seal for the shop.

I was pleased. I had found a way to go on. Isai was not my only customer either. I sometimes made pictures for the English newspapers, when the editor came to ask. And occasionally one of our old patrons gave me a commission. It was not the way it had been, however, when we could go and live there for months, taking our time. All that was over.

I bought food now to eat at the little table in my room: squares of tofu and bamboo shoots and cuttlefish and sweetened duck with taro. I bought my favourite miso-smeared cucumbers and white radish with its black-green wilted top leaves, the tiny fish grilled golden brown on skewers, and sour plums from the market. I spent hours window-shopping, like the careless girl I never was. The foreigners walked the wooden sidewalks with their heavy square-toed shoes. They brought their women too. They shouted and hailed one another across the mud-filled streets. They haggled for prices and carted off barrels and barrels of anything that could be bought.

In the bookshops there were dictionaries for barbarians with pictures of what our words meant, and other dictionaries so we could learn English. It was there I made a strange discovery. I picked up a little book—*An Open Letter to the Japanese,* it was called—by Doctor Phillip von Siebold.

The sight of his name shocked my body, drying my throat, striking a hammer in my chest. You would think that I was a silly young courtesan. As my father had so cruelly teased. It had been thirty years. I remembered the intimacy of our talks. And how I longed for my window on the world when he, collector of flowers and insights on the female of the Japanese species, was gone.

The book had been published in Japanese in Nagasaki. It appeared that the exiled traitor von Siebold had been allowed back in the country.

I skimmed his words. Von Siebold said that he had been looking out for the good people of Japan all along, even while he had not been allowed to come here. I could hear his voice in the words. He said he had foreseen our being overtaken by foreign powers. He said it was all happening as he had known it would. China had lost the Opium Wars to Britain and was now forced to trade the drug with the English. We were next. He had tried to warn the Shogun. In a royal letter from the King of Holland he had advised Japan to open itself, rather than be opened by American gunships. But the Shogun did nothing and kept his letter secret. Therefore the *bakufu* were not prepared and could only capitulate when the Americans arrived.

I read on, amazed that he was allowed to put all this in a book.

Von Siebold explained that the treaties giving Americans free access to our ports were not fair to the Japanese. The price of Japanese silver was too low, and the traders, who were making 200 and 300 percent profits on the goods they bought in Japan and sold in the West, were cheating us.

I bought the book.

At home I examined it thoroughly. There was no picture of Phillip. I wondered if I would recognize the Miracle Doctor. Or he me. I had been young then. Strong-jawed woman. I had grown into that chin, somehow. They said I was old, but I was not ugly, not anymore. I even thought I gave a pleasant impression to those I met. I had not a single wrinkle in my face, but there were streaks of steely grey in my hair where I pulled it back from my forehead. And I had learned to laugh.

One day when I was washing out my paint dish at the gutter, a cluster of foreigners entered at the far end of the alley. This was not unusual. But this group had some very tall men, and something in the posture of one of them caught my eye.

I had known he would come. I had known since the banquet that the Dutch doctor had not forgotten me. But I had left my brother's home and did not know if he could find me. But the printshop of Katsushika Isai would interest him, perhaps because it advertised the works of Hokusai.

He was walking quickly and scanning both sides of the alley, where the wooden houses stood on short stilts a little above the muddy ground. I crouched and kept my eyes cast down. As he came closer I realized it was not von Siebold I recognized, but a much younger man. The young man was just the way the father had been when we met thirty years before.

At the sight of this young man tears sprang from my eyes.

Oh, terror. I had gone soft. I kept my head down and prayed they would stride past. I did not want to be seen. So much for my many dreams of this man, or rather of his father.

They passed me without a glance and entered the shop.

Isai came with his soft voice to touch my back. "Oei-san, the Dutchman is looking for you."

"He cannot be."

"He wants to speak to the daughter of Hokusai."

The residents of our alley stuck their heads out their doors. I saw my home in this young man's eyes: low, ramshackle structures; people who were unkempt; children who were dirty; gutters that smelled. He had never seen me on my terrain.

"You must tell him I am not here." I was panicked. What had I been thinking of, dreaming of such a man? My pride in myself collapsed. Probably I was ugly after all. I never looked in mirrors. What was to see? Every day I wrapped my long hair around a comb and stuck it in place with one long hairpin. I used no cosmetics, and jewellery would have been in the way. I wore a simple robe with a black obi. Over it I wore my working smock with its splashes of paint here and there—very few, as I was careful.

"Oei, go to greet him! He can make you rich."

It shamed me that money was all my people thought about. I took the small bowl in which I had been mixing red with both hands. I sank it in the water and lifted it up. I swirled the water so it made circles. The dried red came off the sides and began to sweeten the clear water so it became thin, transparent crimson, thickening as I continued.

I was acting like my father. I had considered his balking very unfair when I was a child, when I had to do the social easing. But the indignity of my poverty and my pride in my work were too much in conflict for me to speak.

The young man came walking. He looked across me, scanning right, scanning left. His eyes met mine.

"It is a pleasure to meet the daughter of the great master, Hokusai," he said in poor Japanese.

I found some lost graces. "I knew your father." I smiled. "You are his double."

Von Siebold the younger extended both his hands to me, and I gave him mine. I stood awkwardly, my arms and hands sticking straight out in front of me from the waist like handles on a cart. I had adopted my father's strange habit of refusing to bow. Or rather, I had given up the strange habit of bowing.

"He will be very pleased to know that I have found you," he said.

I looked into his stark blue eyes, which were only the second pair of blue eyes I had ever seen. And they were not the same as his father's. They were cold.

"Extend him my best wishes," I said.

The Dutchmen left soon after.

Only a few days later the little troop of tall men appeared again. There were two von Siebolds amongst them. And the people of that quarter who were standing alongside, watching this encounter between the yellow-haired barbarian and the daughter of the famous painter who was herself as famous a painter as a woman could be, murmured and called one another closer to watch.

His hair was now white. It was even more beautiful.

They led us to a teahouse and made us sit. I was grateful that this did not have to happen in my poor room. Nonetheless, the son would not sit, nor would he take tea.

I did not ask von Siebold about his Japanese wife. I asked about his Japanese daughter, Ine. Von Siebold told me she had become a midwife. He was proud of her. But I could see her existence troubled his fully European son.

The talk flowed. How did it flow? Why did it flow? There were few people in this life with whom I could talk. There was Sanba. There was Eisen. Strangely, too, there was von Siebold. All that time ago I had been able to speak my thoughts to him, and he understood. We had looked kindly on each other. We had disagreed; we had warmed to each other.

But that had been in the old world, under the nose of the *bakufu*. He was then one of the only foreigners in the country. His words had been my first messages from the outside. You are not like other Japanese woman, he had said. He did not understand why they settled for so little. I had clung to that idea. Instead of being a man, as my relatives accused me, I might resemble some woman of a larger world. Some woman who was not willing to settle for only a little.

Now we met again—not in a new world or in the old, but someplace ugly in between, where a new world was being born. I was almost nostalgic for the dangers of those days, so much simpler than the dangers now.

"I love them both very much," he had said that about his Japanese family. And I had asked him if he had a European wife too, and he had laughed and said no. Only one wife. But I supposed he did take a European wife afterwards; this white-skinned son was proof.

As we spoke I could see him puzzling: Why is this daughter of the great master working down this mud alley? Why is she in poverty?

"Your father, Hokusai," he said, "lived to a very great age. He had tremendous energy and a stubborn nature."

He grew animated to speak of the man. But he had never met Hokusai! It was always me who came to the Nagasaki-ya.

Isai and the disciples stood around nodding. Now that my father had become a national hero, it was impossible to say anything negative about him.

"How were his last years?" von Siebold asked.

I listened, my head cocked to one side.

"What was it like at the end?"

"Difficult," I said.

"Ah, but you were with him," he said.

To my great alarm, the tears were welling again. And why? My brother had made me feel this way when he said he recognized that my attentions had kept our father alive. Was this what I needed? To be acknowledged? But that was a Western need, was it not?

This was the frightening thing about foreigners. In their presence one began to feel foreign emotions.

What could I say about my father?

Could I say that in his youth, his sensuality overcame me? That in his age, my father had abused me, taking umbrage at each little error and each little deviation from his precious art. Even though I was his daughter it was not right. I knew that now.

I could say now of my father that in aid of "making pictures," he hurt people, especially those who loved and served him.

"Vast ambitions. And yet, I must suppose that by the great age of ninety, he was ready to pass away?" said von Siebold.

"No," I said. "With his dying words he begged for ten more years."

I would have liked to say he asked for my forgiveness and asked me to continue to make pictures. That too had happened—but by the time he died, he had recanted.

There was silence between us then, as if my father had just entered the room. After a moment von Siebold spoke.

"And, Oei-san, how is your husband?"

"He is no longer living," I said. "But before that, we were divorced for many years."

I could see him making a note in that way he had of observing my race. "Unusual." His face furrowed.

"It was not so unusual," I protested with a laugh. "My sister divorced too. I lived with my father from the time I last saw you. Together we painted and taught at the North Star Studio."

"And now? Where do you live?" he said.

"I have many homes. I make my living with one brush."

He did not ask to see my work.

"Do you have children?"

"I have none," I acknowledged. "But I have students. The disciples of Hokusai are also concerned with my welfare." I nodded to Isai. This was true. I did not have to say in exactly what way they were concerned.

"Hokusai is the most famous Japanese artist in Europe now," he said.

I let my head sink to its customary angle above my right shoulder. "I have heard the works are popular."

"More than popular. They have taken Europe by storm!" Now he waxed his old enthusiasm and sprang from his seat. "They are influential. Many artists, especially in Paris, praise him and look at the *manga*."

Isai and Tsuyuki Kosho—the one who called himself Iitsu II, to my great annoyance—were taking careful note. I did not feel their presence was friendly.

"A designer named Félix Bracquemond found the *manga* sketchbooks in Paris and soon copied motifs from it. He praised Japanese design to the sky amongst his group of artist friends. He showed the sketches to all his friends, who were all great artists, and he began to make work based on them."

I said I hoped my father was listening from the next world.

Von Siebold walked around in a circle on his long legs. "Of course I knew this long ago. Hokusai was a genius. I knew it before the great artists of Europe got on to the fact. That's why I bought those paintings from you. I am collecting, still," he said. "I would be interested in anything you have of your father's work."

Here came my dilemma.

If I said, "There is nothing; all is gone," he would have gone away without buying. And there would have been no sale for the disciples. Tsuyuki and Isai were watching me carefully. I might as well call them what they were: forgers.

"He has been dead now many years," I said, stalling for time.

Right there, I could have told him.

I could have said, "Dr. von Siebold—Phillip—my father's work is my work. It has been so for a long time. In fact, as long ago as when you bought your *Promenading Courtesan*, I was the painter."

But would he believe me?

"Those pictures weren't signed," I could say. "And you never asked. *A Fisherman's Family* and the *Two Women and a Boy*—the picture of the nursing mother. My father was ill those years; he wasn't working. I drew the straight lines with your pencils and I used Dutch paper. Those are the works you call Hokusai's. They are my works. I made them for you. Especially *Promenading Courtesan*. My whole heart went into that."

I could have said that.

But I did not. I was under the eyes of Isai. I was under the nose of Tsuyuki. And something more—another reason—stopped me from speaking the truth.

Was I afraid of them? I think not. They needed me. I was the only one who could imitate the master so the imitation could not be detected. Naturally, because in most cases, I was imitating myself. Furthermore, I had the seal.

Why, then?

I was afraid of myself.

Why did I pass up this chance to save myself? From simple embarrassment? From long habit of being a ghost? Had I developed a preference for being a ghost? Become disgusted, as my brother Sakujiro suggested, with the whole idea of fame? With the celebrity that drove men to distraction and devilry? Yet I had wanted so much for Phillip to know me and know who I was, truly. Now that I had the chance, I ducked.

Somehow I didn't want all that noise in my life. It sounds strange. I do not understand it. I only know I did it.

I said, "You must be careful. There are many forgeries. Especially since his death. The picture must be signed. And it must have the seal on it. And his signature."

I said, "It is very difficult to find something by Hokusai. But I can look in the private homes where I have stored the work. I hope that for you, I might find something. Because of your long relationship with us, yes, I will try."

He ran the tip of his tongue along his lips in a gesture I remembered. His eyes widened and smiled at me.

"But I will need a little time. Please, may we meet in another month?"

"Of course," he said. "Of course."

Von Siebold took the bait so easily. And then I felt sad. Had I nurtured the belief all these years that this golden-haired god would be my champion? Surely not.

He was pleased and bowed to everyone around the circle. I walked him to the end of the street. On parting, he kissed my ink-stained hand.

"My dear Oei, you should know that the whole world is excited by things

Japanese: your fans, your kites, your umbrellas. People love your porcelain. And especially your kimono. Oh, the exquisite patterns in the fabric! Of all these, the *ukiyo-e* are first in line of magic-making."

"How beguiling we are," I said brightly. "We had no idea."

It seemed so ordinary that we would walk side by side down a street. The strictures that had governed my life were collapsing, and the oddest part was that once they had collapsed, it was as if they had never been there at all.

46

WHITE BUTTERFLIES

I STOPPED WITH MUNE at her home on the way out of Edo. After two nights, I left.

I set off very early in the morning. As always, I put the Hokusai seal in my sleeve, along with my brushes. I took my case of pigments. I rolled my paintings that I had stored there into a cloth bag. I had my long *bo* for a walking stick.

Totsuka was the sixth stop on the Tokaido. With luck I could be there by nightfall. The inn was a big one—rustic, unprepossessing. Hiroshige had made a print of it in his Tokaido series. I might indeed, to amuse myself, stay there; although I had invented Bunzo's commission.

In the print, the inn was a friendly place, its thatch roof overhanging the wooden verandah just steps off the road. A carved grey milepost marking the Tokaido was beside it. A stone lantern marked the foot of a small humped bridge. A waitress stood in front, welcoming. It was obvious that Eisen drew her, when he was working with Hiroshige. She was short even on her raised clogs, with the large head that was his style.

In the centre of the print was the back end of the horse (a steal from Hokusai); the horse's tail blew sideways in the wind. The arriving travellers were hunched as the wind struck their backs, an inshore wind off the sea.

Totsuka was a flat, marshy place, but just beyond it a steep hill rose straight up from the water. Over the bridge, the road wandered into dark woods. Despite the friendly inn with its beckoning waitress, the place was forlorn; the ocean beyond was fine on a sunny day but harsh in winter.

I took a ride in a cart. Then I walked. I had made good time; it was still afternoon when I saw the inn ahead. Bunzo would welcome me with a room and a meal.

But as I approached I felt the cold, clammy air of the tomb. I saw horses being led around the back. I thought I spied Tsuyuki. But why would he be there? Suddenly the scene—the open door, the bright banners, the beckoning waitress with the head of an Eisen courtesan—made me cold.

It is not for nothing I am called a witch.

It was the twelfth year after the earthquake of 1855. In the Western calendar, 1867. I was sixty-seven years old. My hand went into my sleeve pocket and curled around the Hokusai seal. I hesitated. I had a little more daylight.

I made a sudden change of plan.

I turned back. Ugly clouds arose, and in minutes there was a rainstorm. It was a bombardment, as if the world were angry that I had escaped. The drops clattered on my umbrella and smacked on the path. As I walked the clouds blew off. It was clear and cold.

I took the steep path to Kamakura. I began to climb before noon. I had not seen Shino for fifteen years. My life had not been easy during these times. I was rougher, I knew. But I did not doubt her loyalty.

Here, in the high land above the seafront, weather moved across the earth like lightning. The day had begun with rain, but now the sun shone. I entered the clean brightness of an alpine meadow. My winding path led across it. It was like a pathway in a dream. After the storm it felt fresh, yet ancient.

I came to a field of white butterflies.

There was some brambly bush that they liked. They lifted up and settled again, like soft feathers above open mouths. The bushes were breathing.

The white butterflies were everywhere; they opened to circles and folded to thin lines. Against the mountains, stopped and stoic and ragged, they looked so frail, so light.

The beauty of it made me long to live.

I saw an old man, silhouetted, his childlike dark form with all its concentrated energy on a log bench in that wide upland meadow.

It was Hokusai.

My *bo* hit the path with each alternate step—*click, click*. My backpack jingled. The Old Man did not hear me. He was engaged. He was waving his arms, and his face was fierce with concentration. He was conducting a butterfly symphony. They fluttered from all parts of his amphitheatre. Around him in the green hummocks and hollows of the meadow were flowers— wild asters and anemones and alpine forget-me-nots.

The meadow spread around us—open, spongy, a little salty from the sea below. A golden eagle looped above, dove for a squirrel but was defeated by the cloud of butterflies.

They were under the baton of the Old Man.

I paused at the edge of this frame. It was worthy of his best.

He waved this side in, then he signalled that side out. He had them rising, dispersing. He closed off this section with a tight circle of his hands. Then he closed off the other. He leaned back with his stick between his legs and closed his eyes and smiled. His butterflies subsided, but not entirely. They mustered for a second act.

"Old Man!" I called. "How about it?"

He roused himself, lifted his right hand, and broke into uproarious laughter. The squirrel squeaked and ran in sequences from one hideout to another, and the eagle's shadow drew figures only he could have created.

He did not turn his head. "Chin-Chin, I do not see you. But I know your voice."

"Have you lost your sight, Old Man? Come back as a blind man?"

"I have not lost my sight. I have used it up. I used up enough sight for five lives. But I am happy. For sure I got no rest until it was gone. I was so tired of seeing!"

"Are you quite well? Do you need me? I will come to be with you," I said.

"So you will, Chin-Chin. But not yet. It isn't time! Go on, go on."

And then I couldn't see him anymore.

The path ran above and alongside the ocean. Below me seawater, thick with roiled sand, pushed against the cliff. Trees shot straight up from their precarious holds on the side of the bank.

I passed an inn. I had tea and rice cakes. I kept on walking, across a causeway.

The weed was mica yellow. The water was aqua blue, the sky pale and flecked with cloud. Now I could see Fuji. The face of the mountain was stolid and unmoving.

It was a long walk and I had time to think. Things I wished to tell him: about tigers, which to my father had been imaginary. I had painted him as a tiger in the snow and then a tiger in the rain, without ever having seen one. Now that Japan was trading with the world, two tigers had been imported and sold. This was in the Yokohama newspaper. They sat in cages. Not nearly so exciting as ours had been. Our fantasies were being pulled in like kites that had lost their wind.

I would bring this and other news to Shino. She would greet me with palpable joy. I would present my work, which I trusted her to keep. We would go to the hot springs together. The Temple of Refuge would be my refuge again; it would be my Obuse—safe and still—where I could prepare for the end.

Assassins roamed the country these days. But no one was on this stretch of road. I shrugged off the dark feeling that had come over me at Totsuka. I was not in danger; I was no one, with only a little money and my brushes. The stone seal was a weight deep in my kimono sleeve.

I came to the gate. No one greeted me. The hill was steep. I thought of the time years ago when I had run here to get my divorce. I had gone all the way in deep snow and not felt the hill. Now I felt it. At last I saw nuns.

"Old woman!" they said. "Come and rest."

"I will be most glad to do so," I said, instantly adopting the cultured sound that Shino had tried to give me. "I am an old friend of the abbess. Could you tell her that Oei is here?"

Shino walked with a cane and did not seem surprised to see me. She was ancient. Her beloved face was long and full of light.

"You have come," she said. "What a perfect afternoon."

"Yes, it is," I said, "now that I have found you." I had the impulse to bow at her feet, a rare one for me, and I did it. She touched my head.

"You've walked a long way. You look like that turtle again, the way you did when you were a child on his shoulder."

"I was going to another place, but I turned back."

"Why?"

"Because I need to prepare."

We had a meal and then she said she would show me some treasures. "We have many things of value here in the temple," she said. "They are here for safekeeping."

She took me to a series of rooms. It was dark, so she raised a lantern.

Once, when I was young and we briefly had a little prosperity, my father gave a painting party. He collected his works and pinned them to the walls, where they beamed their grace and light.

Now here were *my* works, deep with colour and longing. Never before had I seen them together: the Chinese legends, the boy viewing Mt. Fuji from the arm of the willow tree, the prints and paintings on scrolls, and the picture books—my *Book of Tea* and my *Illustrated Manual for Women*—even the *shunga*.

"You?" I said. "You were the patron?"

"Not always."

We walked around together, looking, and Shino asking, remarking on this and that.

There was *Girl Composing a Poem under the Cherry Blossoms at Night*. It had been a commission that came through Mune. It was a courtesan with a brush in her hand. The stars were twinkling in the dark sky.

"I can see why you loved to paint the prostitutes, like this one. Men have taken some broken pleasure in her helplessness. But still she will never be conquered."

I said. "I understood a little of what it was to be a slave."

Shino sighed. "All humans are slaves. I grant you that women have no freedom, except those freedoms men allow them. But men themselves are the playthings of gods. They may run the world. But in the end, the world is an illusion and their power is smoke."

"I suppose," I said doubtfully.

She drew her finger along the plume of smoke that rose behind Mt. Fuji in the painting where the dragon is disappearing.

"You know that already," she said.

I took out my pipe case. It was my favourite possession, black lacquer, decorated with leaves of grass. I withdrew the narrow wooden pipe with its small silver bowl, its iron stem, its gold band. I undid the metal closing in the shape of a snail and opened my tobacco case. I took up a taper to light it; it flared sweetly in the dark room.

This was a conversation we had had before.

"New ways are coming," I told her. "I have seen over the horizon. There is another way for women."

"You have seen this?"

"I have."

A puff on my pipe made me brave.

"Here's something else I have begun to think: Hokusai was a good painter, but he was no great master. That was a fantasy we all subscribed to. Just someone we needed to believe in."

"He was ordinary and he loved the ordinary, and that was his rare, rare gift. His goodness came in spite of himself."

We argued as we always had. We debated celebrity, which had been the obsession of our age, the ideal we promoted with our prints, and the way we little people of Japan had asserted our rights. We all wanted a little bit of it, and so we strove to improve. Vanity—had it not been a force for the good?

No, no, said the abbess. How sickening was the idea of worldly greatness, in the truest sense, Shino told me. She said it led to corruption of the soul and of all the gifts. It was the root of all noise and distraction, all vanity. It did not bring peace. It looked good only from the distance. All this I listened to and nodded my head and drew in tobacco and pondered.

But beauty, I protested. Was that different? The goal of every painting I made. What was that for? What was its power? Was it simply for pleasure? Or was it something deeper, something spiritual? It had been my grail. I had followed it because it was within my grasp, at least on the page.

She didn't have answers. They don't, these nuns.

I slept in a small room near my paintings. They were such company! The work of my years. I thought about my father and the butterflies. I thought about his simplicity, his joy, and envied it. Bullies do end up being joyful more often than the bullied. It's not fair.

In the morning I told Shino that I would die soon. I had seen the heads of many men pressed together, moved by one emotion, watching one spot. I was the object of their attention, and it was frightening.

"One must be ready to die at any time," said Shino.

Sometimes it's frustrating to have a nun as a friend.

"Teach me to believe," I said. "I want to live forever. You know the idea: after a series of dialogues with a virtuous nun, I will become enlightened and never die."

"You too?" Shino laughed. She thought she had caught me out. But I was ready for her.

"Not like my father. He may keep his immortality. He had no peace. I heard him die, and with the last rattle he was begging for just one more year, one more so his art could become perfect. My desire is different," I told her. "I want stillness. I want cats."

"Cats?"

"I want permanence of colour. No fading. And no putrefaction! Promise me." The decomposition of the body appalled me. They studied it so assiduously, those nuns—all nine stages of it, in gruesome detail. They seemed to take pleasure in that. "Do you remember? In the little temple in the woods above Kyoto?" They had to memorize the nine stages of decay. They went from "newly deceased" to "distension" to "rupture." There were pictures and details of each. There was "exudation of blood" and after that, with a poem, "discolouration and desiccation." So muddying! Later came "putrefaction" and "consumption by birds and animals." I didn't mind that so much. But what about "suppuration"? There was consumption by worms and "shrinkage into a bundle of firewood."

"You remember them very well," said Shino dryly.

"Parched to dust, wasn't that the last?"

"These are the great doctrines. This is the great wisdom of the Lotus Sutra."

"I don't care. I don't want it."

"I understand," said Shino. "What can we do?"

"I want brightness. I want my body, old friend that it is."

Shino was thoughtful. And then she said, "We have a way."

It had been practised by certain monks and nuns for centuries.

At night we went to the hot springs. We talked and laughed and stretched our feet so that they rose in the foam as we had done years before when I was a child. I told her my fears. That they wanted me gone. That my existence had become inconvenient, because how could the disciples forge Hokusai when his original "forger" could do it better? How could they forge Hokusai when the ghost brush was still painting and the works with the Hokusai 88 seal kept showing up?

"I want it to stop," I said. I pulled the seal from my sleeve. "I would like to leave it with you in the Temple of Refuge, where no man would ever take it."

THE ANCIENT CHINESE HAD SOUGHT IMMORTALITY TOO. They believed that by combining yin and yang, dark and light—specifically, mercury and lead, or yellow and the very dark colours—they might get an elixir to preserve the body forever. Shino had some ingredients. There were others that she had obtained from the Dutch scholars. We worked often to improve our pigment, and while she herself did not desire to be preserved, she began to hope that I would be successful at least for myself.

The flowers I needed for the final pigment grew in the fields above Kamakura. I collected the seeds of *beni* and ground them to a deep, deep red. I sometimes ventured down the mountain to the field of white butterflies, where my father had said, "It isn't time. Go on, go on."

I wanted him to recognize that my time was coming. But I never saw him again. Shino walked with me at first. But she was frail. Her porters ran behind and insisted that she ride.

Autumn came. The darkness fell earlier and earlier. It was the Hour of the Monkey, around five in the afternoon—in the old days, the time the parade of courtesans would begin—when we took our last walk. The leaves of the giant trees lay, coppery, pinkish, and wet, underfoot in the lamplight. The damp air pressed down on us. We could see in the west the sky shot with pink from the disappeared sun. Then we saw the moon rising in the east, enormous, glowing, round.

Both moon and sun at once! We knew it was a sign, although we assured each other that we did not believe in signs.

I went to sleep peacefully.

When I woke up there was a crowd in front of my little house. They wore the names and faces of my father; they were his disciples of old and of late—Isai, Tsuyuki Kosho, even Iwajiro was there. Iwajiro, the boy who had been my shadow. My enemies and even my friends were there, a rolling thunder of round heads.

"Give us the seal, Katsushika Oei," one of them said. I couldn't see in the dark. "We are the true heirs of Hokusai. We will carry on the name. No woman inherits the seal."

"You are deluded," I said. "The seal alone does not make one his heir."

"If you don't give us the seal we will make sure that you never work again," they said.

"I cannot give it to you. It would be wrong. My father left it to me."

I would have told them that my father was a fiction, that they had named themselves for and followed and set their lives upon a fabrication, and that they too were fabrications as a result.

"We will take it from you, then," they said regretfully.

I was about to tell them that I did not have it. But I was cut down—a short sword in my ribs to immobilize me and a *katana* strike to the neck. It was not well done. My head was half lopped, right at the place my neck always bent, like a flower head snapped on its stem.

Blood beat out of me. I lay on the ground. I heard shouting and the guards' feet pounding. The white gown of the abbess appearing, and her thin, weak body spinning this way and that, performing her ridiculous *kata*. The men disappeared. I wish I could say it was her prowess with her *naginata*. But alas, I think she just frightened them off. She looked like a vengeful spirit.

How did they know I was there? Who had followed me? Who had dared to enter the compound of the Temple of Refuge? Maybe they hadn't intended to kill me, but my defiance, my usual defiance, inflamed them. Too late I recalled Shino's advice to dissemble.

Shino leaned over me. Her sorrow was contained. This was her gift, the gift of containment. A feeling of ease came.

"Remember," I said, "no fading. No putrefaction."

I was heavy, heavy.

The blood that was in me ran and ran; it ran all over the stone in front of the door to the Treasure House and around to the back, where the guards were shouting and mounting their horses for the chase. This river of blood should have left my body empty, but it did not. I was as heavy as ten people when they tried to drag me off the doorstep.

"You cannot move her," said Shino. "There is only one way for this corpse to be moved, and that is for her killer to return. If the killer returns and takes one hand I will take the other, and she will be light as a leaf and we will bear her away."

The guards brought back the killer. I could not see his face. He was one of the forgers. It didn't matter which. They were all the same—all manifestations of the father I had helped to create.

He took my left hand and Shino took my right. I stood and together we walked. That disciple's face was not clear, but I could hear him. The guards took him away.

Shino and I retreated farther into the temple precinct.

THEY HAD THEIR POTIONS, their pastes, and their medicaments. The chanting nuns laid my body out and washed me.

And they prepared me for paint with the heavy white coating we always used. Every bit of skin—my legs and my arms and the round ends of my fingers, the cracks between my toes, and the pale blue hollow behind my ears. They painted the lips of my labia, those private places that painters had seen before, and in the hollows between my thigh muscles. They painted the ridge of my spine and the bristling hair and slack skin under my armpits; the worn soles of my feet, with their many horizontal lines; my wrinkled, dry heels; my lips and the lids of my eyes. I felt the soft bristles of their brushes run over the stretched and plump stomach skin and the sensitive white place under my jutting chin. I swooned to their chanting.

They had a basin of my red pigment, which was intended to preserve the body. They took me up by my feet and my head, with two others at my hips, and laid me in the water. If a part of me floated above the surface, they gently pushed it under. When I was done, I was red as a berry all over and sealed to fight off decay. They dressed me in my white death clothes and stretched me in my coffin.

They made no record of this body. The nuns from the Temple of Refuge were powerful. I was gone from my country and my time. From my family and my friends. From art and from history, almost.

47

VAULT

I AM LEFT TO MY OWN DEVICES. I hear the drip of water from the roof in winter and see fireflies on summer nights. There are cats too, their bony spines rubbing against my coffin. For a time certain of my paintings surrounded me, but after Shino's death the doors were cracked open and the works carried off. I wanted to see them again, see where they'd got to—one reason I interrupted this red-skinned repose. In that, I am satisfied. Partly. There are others, spread around that fractious world, in vaults or down in forgotten chests, that I will not see again. And here I lie.

Rebecca wandered by in the temple grounds not long ago. She examined the gravestones and tried to find the view over to the sea. She took her camera and snapped pictures of a tiny shrine where a flower had been left. Looking for me, I suppose. I didn't call out.

I am the unbeautiful, the untended, the unintended, the unofficial painter.

At the age of fifty-seven, I felt a surge of tremendous power. At sixty-seven, I had disappeared and was presumed dead.

I am the brush. I am the line. I am the colour.

There are facts I would like to talk over with my father. The world is round. What does that mean for waves? Do they shoot off the edge? Or curl around and come back, licking the surface, like your tongue would a rice ball or an ice ball?

He was a scattered man, always pulling a geographical escape, always adopting a new name. His money he pissed up a wall—yes, I liked that expression. His talent he flashed and then grew bored of, flashed again so it burst out of the rock like some gusher—and then drought. He squandered.

He wasted. His pride was immense. He tossed gold coins on the floor for us to count; he was above such things. He exploited us all, but mainly me.

He was my father.

"Go with him," my mother said. "I have no more patience for it. You be the one. You love him."

A life sentence, that one.

On this subject of love. Shino says it is the greatest of mysteries. I said once and I say it again: it is nothing but a rat's fart in a windstorm.

You can quote me. I am Oei. Katsushika Oei. Katsushika I take from the place where Hokusai was born. Oei is what he called me. Some people say my father was difficult. I can't agree. He was not difficult. He was impossible.

I am she, Hokusai's daughter. Painter of deep pools of colour and perfect, fine lines. A woman who loved food and drink and tobacco. Soothsayer. Consumer of the mushroom that has, as promised, given me immortality. My body dyed red and wrapped in a winding sheet, I lie preserved, a great painter in my own right. A fine woman loved by more than one man. And who loved several in return. But none, I promise you, more than the Old Man.

It could be my epitaph. Perhaps it is. But you would have to find my grave to know.

And that you cannot do.

ACKNOWLEDGEMENTS

FROM THE START, the historians of Japanese art whom I approached have welcomed the entrance of a novelist into their field. They have been generous with their knowledge, their connections, and their time. Part of the joy of writing this book has been making their acquaintance and learning about the world of *ukiyo-e* prints and paintings. To the following I owe a debt of gratitude.

John T. Carpenter, Donald Keene Lecturer in the History of Japanese Art at the School of Oriental and African Studies, University of London, and Head of the London Office of the Sainsbury Institute for the Study of Japanese Arts and Cultures. His open mind and subtle interpretations of prints and calligraphy guided me.

Dr. Ellis Tinios, Honorary Lecturer in the School of History, University of Leeds, and special assistant to the Japanese Section of the Department of Asia, British Museum. His encyclopedic knowledge of the field of Edo-period illustrated books and prints is mixed with great enthusiasm.

Dr. Patricia Fister, Professor, International Research Center for Japanese Studies, Kyoto, Japan, introduced me to Oei in the first place, and Professor Kobayashi Tadashi, Professor of Japanese Art History, Gakushuin University, Tokyo, and Director, Chiba City Museum of Art, Japan, discussed her disappearance and influence with me.

I am indebted to Mr. Kubota Kazuhiro, formerly Chief Research Curator for the Cultural Affairs Division in Obuse, Nagano Prefecture, Japan, and currently Research Associate at the Japan Ukiyo-e Museum, Matsumoto. He offered me unlimited use of the results of his labours in archives and collections across Japan. His passion to discover the truth about Oei and her work inspired me.

I would also like to thank Sakai Nobuo, CEO of the Japan Ukiyo-e Museum in Matsumoto, and Curator Koike Makiko at Isago no Sato Museum in Kawasaki, Japan. The London art dealer David Newman gave me hours of his time and was highly entertaining.

Librarians Jack Howard at the Royal Ontario Museum Far Eastern Library and Mariko Liliefeldt at the Japan Foundation in Toronto have been invaluable.

Twice I took Ellis Tinios' course at the Rare Books School of the University of Virginia and loved it. The Freer Gallery was very generous in allowing us to see its collection and use its facilities. Barbara Nettleton read the manuscript in an earlier draft and provided many helpful comments.

And the Toronto translator, journalist, and storyteller Yusuke Tanaka has worked with me at every stage, providing insight and humour along with scrupulous translation of letters and documents.

Emily Honderich made the companion website *theghostbrush.com* and Robin Honderich made the video *The Finer Hand*.

My agent, Helen Heller, has been involved with the novel at every stage, and my thanks to Iris Tupholme of HarperCollins for her exceptional efforts on behalf of the novel. I also thank Janice Weaver and Sarah Wight for the complex copy edit, managing editor Noelle Zitzer, and the whole team at HarperCollins Canada.

My faithful and tolerant partner, Nick Rundall, has lived with this novel for years; my grown-up children, Robin and Emily, my sisters, Trudy and Sue, and my amazing parents, Doris and George Govier, are never far from my mind.

I have read many books about Hokusai and the *ukiyo-e* of the Edo period, too many to mention here. I encourage readers to go to the companion website to the novel, theghostbrush.com, to view source material and images.

GLOSSARY

ageya: inn, banquet hall

bakufu: feudal government of the Edo period

beru: blue pigment imported from Europe

bijin-ga: pictures of beautiful women

bin-sashi: hair ornaments

bo: long staff

daimyo: lord

gyoji: government officials working as censors

Juhachi-ya: the number eighteen, here the name of a merchant caravan

kago: sedan chair carried by porters

kata: pattern; in martial arts, a sequence of movements

keshi ningyo: very small ceramic dolls made in sets

kosode: outer garment

kotatsu: table heater

koto: stringed instrument, like a wooden harp

manga: quick sketch

mochi: rice paste

momme: small unit of currency

mon: unit of currency; also gate

moxa: A dried herb substance burned on or above the skin to stimulate an acupuncture point or serve as a counterirritant

naginata: long pole tipped with a blade

netsuke: small, carved wooden charm

opperhoofd: commander of the Dutch at Deshima

rangaku-sha: scholars of Dutch learning

ryo: large unit of currency

saiken: guidebook to pleasure quarter

sakura: cherry tree or blossom

samisen: bowed instrument

sekisho: security gates at entrance and exits to the major cities

shinzo: apprentice prostitute under the age of sixteen

shochu: distilled spirits made from potato, buckwheat, etc.

shoki: demon

shunga: erotic pictures; "laughing" or "spring" pictures

surimono: picture with poem written on the page

tabi: socks

tatami: woven straw floor mat

tayu: grand, highest-ranking prostitute

Tokaido: one of the great roads of old Japan, leading from Edo to
    Kyoto

ukiyo-e: woodcut print, literally "pictures of the floating world"

unagi: barbecued eel

yakko: a noblewoman sentenced to a term as a prostitute as a punishment

yarite: housekeeper of a brothel, often a former prostitute

Yoshiwara: licensed pleasure quarter in the city of Edo